For Nick

who made this book possible

THE
frat boy

A NASHVILLE NEIGHBORHOOD BOOK

NIKKI SLOANE

PROLOGUE

Madison

My heart beat erratically, too fast one moment and too slow the next. Sweat trickled down my back. The boy I loved was leaving, and there was nothing I could do to stop him.

I'd had plenty of chances over the summer to ask him to stay . . . but instead I'd *encouraged* him to go. It was a tremendous opportunity, I'd told him. Jack had been accepted into the international business program at Davidson University, which only took a handful of students each year. This would open doors and set him up with a job once he graduated.

And it included a semester abroad.

When his passport arrived last month, God, he'd been so excited. Jack had always yearned to travel, to see the world, but he'd have to do it without me. There was no way I could take a semester off when I only had three semesters of college left, and I certainly couldn't afford to go to Germany with him.

So, even though it killed me, I pretended to be thrilled. I wasn't going to let him give this up, and I loved him too much to hold him back. Plus, if I made him stay, eventually he'd resent me.

He *had* to go.

My gaze followed Jack as he wove through the line for security, his passport and plane ticket in hand. There was a curved neck pillow clipped to his backpack, and I watched it bounce with each step he took, rather than look directly at him.

Because that was too hard. Too painful.

Just the shape of him moving toward the TSA agent made my eyes blurry and my chin quiver. I'd held it together when we'd said goodbye, but my insides were made of glass—and now they were breaking.

We'll talk every day, he'd assured me. *It's one semester. I'll be back before you know it.*

There was no way that was true.

But I'd nodded and attempted to squeeze out a smile. I didn't want to be sad and ruin this day for him, plus I didn't want his last memory of me to be a crumbling face, streaked with tears.

It felt like the end when he kissed me goodbye. He could swear up and down we'd be fine with five thousand miles between us, and I desperately wanted to believe . . . but I just couldn't.

There were too many people who'd let me down in my past for me to stay optimistic. I'd learned the only promises I could count on were the ones I made to myself.

Jack handed his passport over to the agent, who waved him through after a quick evaluation. I sucked in a breath and held it as he followed the roped off section that briefly turned him back toward me.

He slowed, and alarm washed through his handsome face as he saw how stricken I must have looked.

"Madison," he said, lifting his voice over the noise of people waiting for security. "It's okay. Don't cry." He delivered a comforting smile as he began moving again. "I promise, we'll be fine. I love you."

I pressed my lips together, swallowed the stone in my throat, and nodded.

I wasn't able to speak, wasn't able to tell him I loved him, too. But at least it meant I wasn't able to tell him not to make promises he might not be able to keep.

He held my gaze all the way until he reached the corner, lingered for a final moment, and then disappeared around it.

I stood utterly still, holding the crushed pieces of myself together. I didn't know what else to do. How was I going to walk out of this Nashville airport, go back to the car I'd borrowed from a friend, and carry on like a small part of me hadn't just died?

I was so in love with him.

Oblivious people moved around the busy ticketing area, hurrying to get where they were going. They were starting a journey, not ending one, and God, how I envied them. I wanted to have that excitement about what came next, instead of this crushing fear.

Jack was going to come back a changed man; that much I was sure of.

And I dreaded I wouldn't fit into his new life when he returned.

ONE

Madison

Dark clouds loomed on the horizon, and Jenn—my sorority little sister—looked worried.

"They said it wasn't supposed to rain today," she muttered as she glanced down at her pristine sneakers.

I kept my tone light. "We tried to warn you."

It was April, which meant spring showers, and it had rained every day this week. My gaze shifted from her to the obstacle course in front of us, where brown puddles dotted the field. Had there ever been grass on it? It was all dirt and mud now.

Every time Lambda Theta Chi had made it to the finals and competed for the Fidelity Cup, the race had been a slog. If anything, the muck had made the final race more fun. In our house, there were pictures in the front hall from previous years where the sisters were cover head-to-toe in mud.

This year, the base of the course was worse than I'd ever seen. The rope nets, climbing walls, and beams rose over a giant mud pit. It wouldn't surprise me if someone had run a hose to the course to increase the slop.

"It'll wash out," I offered Jenn, trying to be helpful. Worry abruptly sliced through me. "You're not thinking of backing out, are you?"

She looked at me like I was talking nonsense. "Of course

not." Her focus swung to the group of guys across the way, and her expression solidified. "We're going to crush them."

Atta girl. She was only a sophomore, but she understood what was at stake.

I peered across the field to the boys of Sigma Phi Alpha, who wore matching blue t-shirts with their letters printed in gold across their chests. I straightened my shoulders and narrowed my gaze.

During Greek Week, there was a week-long tournament between the sororities and fraternities, which might have been friendly back when it began fifty years ago, but it was entirely serious now.

In addition to the Greek-wide blood drive, every house battled for the chance to win the Fidelity Cup. There were different events each day, where only the winning houses advanced, all the way until the head-to-head finals.

We'd survived. After the dance-off, the tug of war, trivia, and chariot races, we Lambdas were still standing. We'd made the finals a few times before . . . but hadn't ever won the cup.

Not in fifty years.

It was what our competitors, the Sigs, had been throwing in our faces ever since we'd arrived at the obstacle course this afternoon. Plus, they were the returning champs, which— yeah. This was another thing they fucking *loved* to point out.

"This is the year," I said, "Lambda Theta Chi gets its name etched on the cup." Winning it on its fiftieth-year anniversary would be all the sweeter.

Jenn nodded in total agreement and began to stretch, warming up for her leg of the relay race. The rest of the Lambdas who were competing today stood nearby, and

Yasmin jerked her head toward the group of guys who looked like they were either half asleep or nursing a raging hangover.

Maybe both.

Her smile was downright evil. "Just look at them. They have no idea what's coming."

"I know. I almost feel bad for them," I said, even though it was a complete lie.

Some of the obstacles in the course favored strength, historically giving the men an advantage, but we'd planned for this.

The monkey bars? Carrie was a pole dance instructor. She had the upper body and grip strength to easily stay competitive.

The log jump section? Luciana had been a track star in high school, and her best event was hurdles.

Zoe spent last summer in Utah and was big into freeclimbing. The wall climb should be a piece of cake for her.

There were other legs that weren't physical. There was a puzzle to solve and cups to be flipped and something gross to be eaten. It felt like the challenges where scripted from some low-budget reality show competition, and although we were battling for a trophy and a cash prize, there were no cameras here.

The only people watching the competition today were those from the other Greek houses who hadn't advanced. A few of them had even volunteered to be impartial judges.

There was a table near the start and finish line of the obstacle course, covered in a black tablecloth that flapped in the wind, and the large, elegant cup was perched on top. The Fidelity Cup was silver, with delicate, elaborate handles on each side, and was beautifully engraved with all the previous winners.

After their win last year, the Sigs took turns carrying the cup around all day, drinking something from it that I assumed had a dangerously high alcohol content, because they were the notorious party house.

It was a miracle the thing had survived unscathed, but the trophy looked great. Not a dent or a scratch marring its shiny surface.

As much as we Lambdas desired the cup and its bragging rights, we wanted the money that went along with it even more. To compete in the Greek Week tournament, each house had to pay an entry fee. A small amount went to offset running the competition, but the rest was prize money. It meant if we won, we'd get five grand, and then we could replace the water heater we so desperately needed.

Our house was older, and unless you got up early, you could forget about getting anything other than a lukewarm shower.

I hadn't realized how much therapy a good hot shower could deliver until they were gone. God, I was so tired of cold showers. My gaze traced over the Fidelity Cup with longing.

Jenn's voice turned frosty. "Is that who I think it is?"

Without looking, I knew exactly who she was talking about, but like a fool, I followed her gaze anyway. When my focus settled on Jack, a sharp pain tore at my heart.

"Who's that?" Yasmin asked.

"Madison's ex," Jenn said quickly.

"He's a Sig?"

"Yeah." My voice was flat. I told myself that seeing him

again didn't bother me because I had expected it. He'd been home since January, and it was just dumb luck we'd competed in different events during the week.

I'd run into him once on campus, maybe a month ago. I'd been so caught by surprise, it had sent me running—like, *legit* running. I'd bolted from the quad, not stopping until there'd been no air left in my lungs and campus was far behind.

He'd wanted to see the world.

But what he hadn't planned on was that he'd get so homesick. Ten days after he'd arrived in Germany, he was already considering coming home. I didn't know what the right answer was. I selfishly wanted him back, but it was likely his homesickness would pass, and I didn't want him to be filled with regret.

So, I told him to just give it a few more days. There was another girl at the international dorm who was struggling too, he'd told me the next night when we'd Zoomed. A nice girl from Georgia who reminded him of home. They became fast friends, and she was there when the time difference kept me out of reach, when I was in class or asleep.

Three and a half weeks was all it took.

He'd been gone less than a month before climbing into bed with someone else. He'd had the decency to confess it to me, his eyes brimming with tears and his voice full of shame as he asked for forgiveness.

"I love you," he'd cried.

I retreated into myself, numb from the pain. "People in love don't sleep with other people."

I'd hung up, turned off my phone, and crawled into bed. I was a wreck, but the worst of it didn't come until the following morning. When I turned my phone back on—there were no calls or messages from him.

He'd made no effort to try again or fight for us.

We hadn't spoken since that day, which meant there'd been no closure, and that . . .

Fuck, it was devastating.

He didn't look like he had a care in the world right now as he laughed with his frat brothers, all of them acting like they'd already won the cup. My insides bubbled with turmoil as I ripped my gaze away and shoved the sensation down. Jack was unconcerned I was here.

I could do the same.

"I thought we weren't allowed to date Sigs," came from Kayleigh, a freshman.

Tiffany let out a short, humorless laugh. "Don't be silly. You can date whoever you want. I wouldn't recommend the Sigs, though." She turned to throw a pointed look my way, and her tone was patronizing. "Right, Madison?"

I got along with Tiffany all three years we'd been Lambda Theta Chi sisters, but we weren't exactly what I'd call friends. I got the strange feeling she didn't like me, although I had no idea why. As far as I knew, I'd never done anything to her, and chalked it up to our personalities just being too different.

She was all Type and much too serious. It made her a good president of our sorority, though. She was super organized, direct, and great at shutting things down before stupid drama could develop, which invariably happened whenever a large group of people lived together.

It was clear she was waiting on a response from me about dating the Sigs.

"No." I sighed. "I don't recommend it either. There's a reason they have the reputation they do."

"That they'll fuck anything that moves?" Kayleigh asked.

"Yeah." I fought to keep the pain from my voice. "Because it's true."

The exchange seemed to satisfy Tiffany because she went back to her stretching.

"Lambda Theta Chi," a voice boomed from a bullhorn, "and Sigma Phi Alpha, please move to your stations."

I'd limbered up, but everything inside me went tight anyway. It was the moment of truth. I knew what leg of the race I was running, but I didn't know who I'd be competing against.

Please don't let it be Jack.

I wished good luck to the rest of my sisters and trudged toward the end of the course, avoiding the mud even though it would be inevitable. I had purposefully worn shoes and clothes I didn't care about because the final dash I'd have to make was through the worst of the muddy field.

My heart climbed into my throat as the Sigs dispersed and Jack, along with a few of his brothers, began to head the same direction I was going. If I could put my emotions to the side, I might have been able to see how good this matchup could be. Jack had a terrible sense of balance.

But I couldn't put my emotions away. They clouded my head and robbed me of my focus.

Every step he took toward the platform at the end of the course made my nerves jangle, and my breath went short—only to completely stop when he abruptly turned.

He picked his way through the muddy puddles and

moved to take his spot at the front of the tire run section. Relief washed through me in a wave so strong, I felt lightheaded.

Oh, thank God.

I passed the large climbing wall and strode to the base of the steps behind it where a guy waited. I recognized him from earlier in the tournament, but I didn't know his name or which house he was with. There was a silver whistle hung around his neck, so I flashed a warm smile.

Couldn't hurt to be friendly with the referee.

He smiled back, but then his gaze moved past me to the Sig approaching, and the guy's smile grew wider.

"Hey, man," he said in greeting to my competitor.

I turned, and my mouth went dry.

There were about forty guys at the Sigma Phi Alpha house, and although I didn't remember his name, I knew him. The Sigs were fuck-boys, and the guy in front of me? He was the single biggest contributor to their house's reputation.

He couldn't have looked more stereotypical frat boy if he tried. He was tall and muscle-bound, with dark hair and a deceptively wholesome smile. He could be classified as either handsome, cute, or hot, depending on the situation and how he wanted to operate.

Every Sig party I'd been to last year, I'd seen him go upstairs with a different girl. At the time, I'd judged him and thought it was gross.

But now?

Well, fuck. I was sort of jealous of him.

College was supposed to be my window for experimentation, my sexual Rumspringa. Instead, I'd spent my best years at Davidson University being faithful to Jack, who wasn't nearly as interested in sex as I was. All it had gotten me was a broken, bitter heart, and a feeling like I was behind. That I needed to make up for lost time and have as many wild experiences as possible before graduation.

The obnoxiously hot frat boy stuck his hand out toward me. "Hey. Colin Novak."

I took his offered handshake and squeezed tighter than I normally would in an effort to dominate. "Madison Perry." My smile tasted overly sweet. "I'm going to enjoy beating you."

Pleasant surprise glinted through Colin's eyes. Then, his laugh was deep, full-throated, and I wished I hadn't liked the sound.

"I hope you're good at dealing with disappointment, then." The handshake was over, but he didn't release my hand. "What am I saying? Of course you are. You're a Lambda."

My mouth dropped open, and he stared at my parted lips for a long moment. There was something lewd about it, like he was considering what his dick might look like if he put it in the empty space I'd created.

I snapped my jaw shut, jerked my hand back, and swung my attention to the referee, giving him an expectant look.

"Oh, right. The rules." He wrapped a hand around the cord his whistle dangled from and gestured to the set of weathered, wooden stairs that led up to a platform.

It was a few feet off the ground, and two long beams jutted out to another platform across the way. The planks were narrow—but wider than the balance beams I practiced on during my many years of gymnastics. They were also twice as long and, rather than being perched over mats, these were suspended over a muddy pit.

"No touching the ladder on the climbing wall," the ref continued, "and you can't set foot on the steps until you have the baton in your hand. If you drop it or fall off, you have to come back to the steps and start over. No climbing back up on the beam. Got it?"

"Got it," Colin and I answered at the same time.

The ref nodded. "Once you get to the other side, it's a foot race back to the start. First one to cross the finish line wins." He backed up until he could see around the tall climbing wall and peered toward the start line. "Okay, I think they're getting ready to start. Good luck to you both."

"Thanks," I said, but the ref didn't seem to notice. He was too busy watching Colin, which was weird. Were they bros?

Competing last meant all the pressure was on me to bring this thing home. If we were behind when Zoe came over the wall, hopefully I could make up some of that time. But I'd fucking love to have a head start on Colin and visualized myself sailing across the finish line while he was way behind, still trying to cross the beam.

The wooden climbing wall was maybe twelve feet tall, so it blocked our view of the course. We'd have no way of knowing how our teammates were doing, but there was a big crowd at the start line, and I expected we'd hear their encouraging shouts.

No one else was allowed on the course once the bullhorn siren went off, which was the starting pistol. Everyone had to stick to their events until it was over, so no one accidentally got in the way of the competitors.

The announcer's voice boomed from across the field. "Lambdas and Sigs, are you ready?" He paused as we let out our battle cries. "Then may the best house win. On your marks. Get set . . ."

The siren wailed, and the crowd erupted in cheers.

TWO

Madison

My pulse leapt into double-time, and I swallowed thickly, stealing a glance at Colin. He stood a few feet back from the pair of ladders that descended the backside of the climbing wall. His stance was ready, and his determined gaze was fixed on the top of the wall. Everything about his posture screamed it was 'go time.'

So, I did the same.

The waiting was tense, and since I couldn't see what was happening, I listened for any clues as to how my team was doing. My heartrate climbed as the voices of my sisters swelled abruptly, overpowering everyone else. Their encouraging words were strained and desperate. Some of them uttered phrases like, *"that's okay"* and *"shake it off."*

Something bad had happened, and it sounded like we'd fallen behind.

My suspicions were confirmed when I heard the thud of feet on the other side of the wall, scrambling upward. They were too heavy to be Zoe's, not to mention, they were paired with male grunts of effort that came from the other side of the ladder Colin faced.

When the guy appeared at the top of the wall, my heart sank, and panic rose in its place. It didn't sound like Zoe had even started her climb yet.

Fuck, how far behind were we?

"You got this, Zoe!" I yelled, having no idea if she was even close enough to hear me.

I recognized the guy coming over the wall because I remembered Jack bitching about him. Riley was known for asking his brothers to get him stuff at the liquor store and then never paying them back. It had gotten so bad, they'd come up with a code word so he never knew when anyone was doing a liquor run.

But he was an heir to an energy drink company, and his parents had donated so much money to the school, the field house was named after them. It meant no matter how annoying he was, he'd never get kicked out of Sigma Phi Alpha. He gave them clout.

Riley must have had the baton stashed in his pocket or the waistband of his shorts, because he held on to the wall with one hand and then produced the shiny red baton in the other. He dropped it down to Colin, who took off the second he had it. His feet pounded up the steps behind me at the same time I heard Zoe begin to scale the wall.

Shit, she was fast.

"Yes, girl," I shouted. "You're almost there!"

Riley slung himself over the top of the wall and came down the ladder express-style, with his feet outside the side rails, bypassing the rungs like he was on a submarine and needed to get to the bridge.

I tried to ignore him. My attention was zeroed in on my teammate, but I couldn't help but notice his approach in my peripheral vision.

What's this guy's deal?

Zoe crested the wall with our blue baton tucked under her chin. She leaned over and lifted her head, releasing the baton to drop right into my waiting hands.

Except—

That didn't happen.

Riley moved in, pushing me out of the way and snatched the baton out of the air. As soon as he had it, he turned and chucked it away. The baton glinted as it went, sailing away from me and landing right in a muddy puddle at the far side of the wall.

He glanced back at me and flashed the smile of an absolute asshole. "Oops."

"What the *fuck*?" I demanded, but I didn't have time to wait for his response. I needed that baton—plus a miracle—if we had any chance of winning now.

I dashed into the sticky mud, expecting to hear the trill of a whistle from the ref. I mean, I'd clearly been impeded, making my face heat to a million degrees. I was a diehard rule-follower, and they'd just cheated.

But when I snatched up the hollow blue rod from the puddle . . . I heard nothing.

Nothing, that was, except Riley's shitty laugh.

"Hello, ref?" I yelled angrily, trudging as fast as my mud-caked feet would allow.

The referee's stunned gaze was locked on to me, his hand holding the whistle frozen halfway to his lips. It was like he wasn't sure if he wanted to blow the whistle or not. Maybe he was too scared to, or maybe he just wanted his boy Colin to have a healthy lead.

He wasn't going to do the one thing required of him. As

usual, I couldn't fucking depend on anyone else. If I wanted to win this thing, well, I had to do it myself.

My feet were slippery on the wooden steps as I bolted up them, and I clutched the baton so tightly it made my hand ache, but I wasn't about to let it slip from my grasp. When I reached the top of the platform, I saw just how far of a head start Colin had on me, and I clenched my jaw. He was nearly across, walking slowly with his arms extended out from his sides.

The tide could turn if he fell.

Years of practice had taught me how important it was that your hips and shoulders stayed centered over the beam. If you got misaligned and didn't fix it quickly—or if you went too far outside the cone of stability—you were doomed.

Colin's shoulders abruptly wobbled, and he stopped moving.

Had I wanted it so badly, I'd willed it into existence? It was comical the way his arms flailed as he listed dangerously to one side. He tried to correct how off center he'd become, but he overcompensated and pitched his hips the opposite direction, sealing his fate.

"Shit, no," he groaned as he bailed off the plank, landing on his feet in the mud below with a satisfying *splat*.

I sprinted across my beam, going as fast as my slick shoes would allow without jeopardizing my balance. Meanwhile, he turned and darted back toward the platform's stairs, running so fast he slung mud everywhere, kicking up a rooster's tail behind him.

Even though it was risky, I couldn't help how my gaze found his for a nanosecond. I wordlessly told him that his team had cheated, and it *still* wouldn't matter.

Because I was going to win.

Blood rushed loudly in my ears as I reached the platform on the other side, ran down the steps, and made the turn. My adrenaline surged, propelling me forward to the finish line off in the distance. I could see people jumping up and down and hear the ecstatic screams of my sisters as I dashed toward them.

The mud, though.

It was thick as cement, and every step I took, it felt like it was hugging me, trying to trap me in place. My ankles protested as I fought against its vicious grip. Was I running in clay?

I was halfway to the white ribbon stretched across the finish line when the mud refused to release my shoe, yanking it completely off. I stumbled, but managed not to go down, and kept on pushing.

You have to win. Just a few more steps.

My sock came off next, and I grimaced as the cold, wet mud squished through my toes. I was tender footed, and prayed I didn't step on anything too painful, forcing my legs to keep churning. I wasn't tall and didn't have a long stride, so I had to make up for it by moving my feet as fast as I could.

Forty yards out, I was sure I was going to win. The rest of the Lambdas were clapping with joy, hugging each other. I pumped my arms, trying to carry myself through the finish.

But the last twenty yards, something changed. I heard the slog of fast footsteps behind me, and saw the excitement freeze on my sisters' expressions. It was replaced with dread, and their focus shifted to the boy behind me, the one who'd somehow conquered the beam on his second attempt and was now threatening to outrun me.

"No," I gasped as he pulled alongside and began to inch ahead.

The muscles in my legs burned. My lungs ached. But no matter how hard I dug inside myself for those last five yards...it wasn't enough. Colin was too tall, too fast, too good.

He vaulted across the line a fraction of a second before me, and the white ribbon stretched across his chest before breaking.

We hadn't finished slowing down before we were swallowed by the crowd. The Sigs body slammed their boy in victory as the Lambdas circled around me, perhaps acting as a shield of protection while I bent forward, put my hands on my knees, and hung my head, struggling to catch my breath.

There was a roar of voices around me, but I couldn't hear them. All I could focus on was how they'd cheated. Riley had illegally touched our baton and thrown it aside, costing us valuable seconds. If he hadn't, I would have beaten Colin to the finish with several seconds to spare.

Their victory was stolen from us, and I was going to get it back.

"They," I panted, "cheated."

Only Jenn seemed to hear me. "What?"

I sucked in a breath, straightened, and fixed a glare on the guys huddled around Colin. "The Sigs *cheated*."

My voice was raised enough that it pierced through their celebration, and several of them turned their attention toward me.

"What's she talking about?" one of the guys asked another, who shrugged.

"I'm talking about how I would have won," I hobbled toward the Sigs, ignoring that I was half barefoot, "if your guy Riley hadn't intentionally slowed me down."

Colin materialized from behind his brothers, wearing a skeptical expression and muddy handprints across his shirt from where people had grabbed him in celebration. He stepped up and looked down his long nose at me. "What, now?"

"Riley took my baton and threw it away. I had to go chasing after it."

He glanced over my head toward the end of the obstacle course where Riley, Zoe, and the referee were slowly making their way to join everyone else at the finish line. Colin considered my statement for a single moment, and then shook his head.

"I didn't hear a whistle."

My hands hung at my sides, and I balled them into fists. "No, and I would love to know why the ref didn't use it. All this happened right in front of him."

Riley marched through the mud, and as he approached, he had the balls to look confused. "Did we win? What's going on?"

Colin jerked his head my direction. "This one says you cheated."

Riley slapped a hand to his chest in a gesture that screamed, *who, me?* His gaze found mine and zeroed in. "How exactly did I cheat?"

"You took my baton and threw it across the—"

He waved a hand like he didn't want to listen to any nonsense. "No, sweetheart. You *dropped* your baton. Don't go blaming me for your mistake."

Sweetheart?

Anger swelled like a tornado of bees in my head, and it was so intense, my vision blurred for a moment. I had to draw in a slow, measured breath to collect myself before speaking, because I worried my outrage might make me spiral out of control.

Thankfully, this gave time for Zoe to make her way over to us. She'd stopped at one point during her walk and pulled something from the muck, and as she came closer, I realized she'd retrieved my shoe for me.

"Tell them," I pleaded, "how you saw Riley steal our baton."

She pulled up short when every pair of eyes on the field turned to her, and her mouth opened, readying to speak. But nothing came, and when her gaze landed on mine, I saw the truth. She wasn't sure what to say.

Her voice was hesitant. "My foot slipped right after I let go of the baton, and I nearly fell. By the time I got back over the wall, all I saw was it on the ground and you running after it."

"See?" Riley put his hands on his hips and sounded vindicated. "She dropped it."

It was a fucking miracle flames didn't come out of the sides of my face. "*I didn't.*"

"Yeah?" His tone was calm and matter-of-fact, like a lawyer arguing a case they already knew they were going to win. "Let's see what Elijah has to say." His focus swung toward the referee. "You saw her drop the baton, didn't you?"

Elijah's expression went blank, concealing whatever thoughts he had about going along with the lie, or if he should do the right thing and strip the win away from the Sigs. His eyeline fell subtly, just enough so he couldn't see me as he nodded. His voice was small. "That's right."

It sounded terribly unconvincing to me, but that didn't matter to the Sigs. This was more than enough proof for them, and some went immediately back to celebrating.

"No," I said. *"No."* I flung a finger toward the Fidelity Cup. "Lambda Theta Chi is the legitimate winner. That cup is ours."

The guy who had the bullhorn clasped at his side was on the Greek council, which oversaw the tournament. It meant he was essentially the head judge, the final say. He gave a long sigh. "Look, the referee didn't blow the whistle."

My frustration was reaching critical mass. "Because he's in on it with the Sigs!"

A few of the Sigs scoffed and had the nerve to look offended, but none more so than Colin. He rolled his eyes. "Jesus, you're a sore loser."

"No, I'm not," I hissed. "Because I didn't lose."

Maybe she wanted to distract and diffuse the situation, or perhaps it was meant as a peace offering since she wasn't able to back me up, because Zoe came over, bent, and set my mud-filled shoe on the ground beside my bare foot.

It was a nice gesture, but it didn't help with the isolating feeling that crawled up my spine. No one believed me, maybe not even my own sisters. Some of them were looking at me with skepticism, and a few with outright side-eye. Definitely Tiffany, whose gaze was critical.

It felt like a hole opened in my chest, but it wasn't in my nature to give up. As I bent down to shake the mud out of my shoe, I tried to think of a way I could prove I was telling the truth.

No one believed you last time either.

I couldn't focus on that. It was hard to think about anything except how muddy I was. I could really use a shower—

Shit.

All of us would want one when we got back to the house,
which meant the hot water would likely run out long before I
got my chance. Without that prize money . . . how many cold
showers were in my future?

The injustice of it all brought fresh outrage into my veins.
I jammed my foot into the shoe, not caring how gross it was,
and glared up at Colin while I tied my shoelaces. "This isn't
fair. You cheated."

His face contorted, and suddenly he was no longer the
stereotypically hot frat boy—he became the asshole kind. "I
hear cheating's a recurring theme for you. At least, that's
what Jack said."

Something inside me broke.

I sucked in a sharp breath, and then I was no longer
in control of my body. It meant I was powerless to stop my
hands as they reached out and clenched fistfuls of the mud
in front of me. I was merely a passenger as it was scooped up
and compacted into a loose ball.

This was done so it would be easier to throw. More accurate at hitting my intended target.

Maybe he sensed it coming, but disbelief had him locked
into a statue, because Colin didn't move an inch as I hurled
the mud at him. My target had been center-mass, and even
though the ball had broken up a little as it traveled through
the air, my aim was spot-on.

Mud splattered across his chest, and he stumbled back a half-step—not because of the force I'd used, but merely surprise.

As I stared at his wide eyes, I felt mine mirror his.

Oh, my God. What the fuck had I just done?

The crowd around us had gone silent, frozen in place. No one moved, other than the wind ruffling some people's clothes or hair. I glanced down at my dirty hands and couldn't believe what I was looking at.

I'd never lost my temper like that.

I opened my mouth to apologize, but I didn't get the chance. Colin snapped back to life, bent down, and loaded ammunition into his hands. There were flames in his eyes as he stood and prepared to return fire.

Once again, my body took control from my mind. It was what got me to dart out of the way just as he slung a huge glob my direction.

While I had avoided it, whoever had been standing behind me hadn't, judging by the girl's horrified gasp. I turned to see his victim, who had so much mud covering her face, it took me a moment to realize he'd hit Jenn.

She stood awkwardly, like she didn't know what to do, before clawing the mud away from her eyes and slinging it to the ground.

"Oh, my God," I cried. "You hit her in the face!"

He'd been aiming for yours, a voice in my head whispered.

Colin looked stricken. Perhaps he wanted to apologize or say he hadn't meant to hit her, but the damage was done.

The outrage flaring inside me was shared by all my

sisters, and some of them were quicker to act than I was. The first volley of mud came from the Lambdas, striking not just Colin, but several of the Sigs in the vicinity. And with that, one of them let out a battle cry, and mud was hurled our direction.

It vaguely reminded me of that scene from the movie *300* where so many arrows were fired, it darkened the sky. Mud rained down, splattering everywhere. It was in my hair. In my eyes. And worst of all, in my mouth.

I had fired the first shot, but once Colin retaliated, we were engaged in all-out war. The field was carnage, and no one was safe, not even the other houses who'd come to watch. The bullhorn guy tried to duck out of the way, only to get pelted across the back.

It was stunning how quickly we all descended into chaos.

People ran, some using others as human shields to hide behind as they gathered mud to sling. It was the great equalizer, painting everyone brown and obscuring which house they were from. There was friendly fire, and anarchy reigned.

I squatted and shoveled as much mud as possible into my filthy hands, readying to unleash hell on the next Sig I could identify.

Was it dumb luck that the first one I recognized was Jack?

He was twenty feet away from me, but somehow sensed the target on him, because he turned in place and stared at me. His gaze dropped to my loaded hands, and then snapped back to me with worry flooding his expression.

This is your chance. Get him.

I reared back, readying to throw, but my strength faltered. As much as I hated what he'd done . . . it was surprisingly hard to hate him, and so I hesitated. I was stuck like that, locked in place by indecision. On one hand, he was a Sig and deserved it. But on the other, he'd been my first love. It was harder to sling mud at someone I'd had such a strong connection with, and I—

A chunk hit me in the side of the head, clogging my ear and knocking me sideways. I glared at where the mud had come from.

This Sig? Well, he was easier to hate.

There wasn't a clean spot on Colin Novak, other than a few parts of his face, and those were what I aimed for when I unloaded on him. One was a direct hit, and he sputtered, wiping the grime from his nose and mouth.

There was a playful scream beside me, followed by laughter. Some of the people were enjoying the mud fight, just having fun. But for Colin and me? This was deadly serious.

I was just about to grab more mud when something shiny caught my attention out of the corner of my eye.

While everyone was too busy fighting or jokingly wrestling in the mud, the Fidelity Cup sat unnoticed on the table. Somehow, the tablecloth had made it this far with minimal mud splotches decorating it. It was like everyone knew to treat the trophy with the respect it deserved, and especially on its fiftieth anniversary.

I'd told Colin the cup belonged to the Lambdas, and now I wanted to show him.

Even under all the mud, I could see his expression change. He knew what I was planning, and he didn't like it one bit.

"Don't even think about it," he yelled over the frenzy

surrounding us. "That's the Sigs'."

I bolted toward the table, which forced him to do the same.

It was even harder sloshing through the mud this time, and although I had a head start, just like last time, he caught up to me. We reached the table at the same moment, both reaching out to get a hand on a handle.

"It's ours," Colin said, taking the cup off the table and trying to jerk it free from my hold.

"No," I growled. "It's ours." I yanked on my handle, desperate to wrest it away from him.

Some part of me understood how utterly ridiculous this all was. Two adults fighting over a trophy like a Little League game gone horribly wrong. But in the moment, I wasn't able to process it. Everything had been a disaster today, starting with seeing Jack again, and then Riley's cheating which no one believed me about, and finally Colin's cruel comment.

It was more than I could take, just like the force we were exerting on the old, delicate trophy was more than it could take.

I tugged with all my strength, only for a section of the handle to break off in my hand.

When all that force was suddenly gone, Colin wasn't prepared. He tipped backward, slipped in the mud, and began to fall. He landed hard with a painful sounding crunch, flattening the bell of the cup beneath his big, stupid body.

THREE

Colin

On Monday, things went from a mild clusterfuck to a total fucking disaster.

I was in between classes, chilling in the lounge of the student union when my friend Jorge appeared beside the chair I was using to try to take a nap. His voice was unnecessarily loud, causing other people to look over at us.

"Hey, man. Have you seen this?"

I hadn't a clue what he was talking about. "Seen what?"

A folded newspaper was dropped in my lap. The campus paper, according to the masthead. I blinked my tired eyes as I unfolded it.

Well, now I was wide awake.

I sat upright and leaned over, scanning the large, bold text before moving on to the huge, full-color picture below.

Greek Week Ends In A Mess, the headline announced.

And there I was, covered in mud, with both hands wrapped around the handle of the Fidelity Cup. Opposite me was that Madison girl from Lambda Theta Chi, who was also dripping with mud and had the other handle in her grip.

Because of the angle of the photo, you couldn't see my face as well as hers, but there was no mistaking her pissed-off expression, or how we were engaged in a tug-of-war like a couple of goddamn toddlers. The picture had to have been taken seconds before the handle broke and I fell.

I was sporting a nasty bruise on my side—but hadn't mentioned it to anyone. Last thing I needed was to remind people of what went down.

But there was no getting around it. A few people had posted clips to TikTok that were racking up views, and with this front-page story, the whole school would know.

I didn't bother reading the article right now. There were two smaller pictures beneath the fold. One was mid-action during the mud fight, and the other was of the flattened Fidelity Cup. Parts of it had crumbled like aluminum foil, and others had bent and warped, creating jagged, pokey edges.

It'd hurt like a bitch.

Jorge sat on the end of the fat armrest of the chair beside mine. "Greek council called a mandatory meeting tonight," he pointed to a spot of text in the second paragraph, "to discuss that."

As I skimmed the line, anxiety crystalized inside me. "They want to retire the tournament?"

Oh, man. I couldn't be the one responsible for ending fifty years of tradition. Every Greek student would hate me because each house looked forward to the competition.

Plus, each time we'd won, we'd used the money for something awesome. This year's winnings? They would be put to *even better* use.

Grady Coleman and I were in the same pledge class, but he'd fit in the house far better than I had. It was a fact he was a cool guy, easy to hang with. This was proven every day by the way he could share a room with obnoxious Riley when none of the rest of us could.

A few months ago, Grady's mom was diagnosed with breast cancer. He didn't talk about it much, but Riley mentioned he'd overheard them talking on FaceTime. Grady's mom was struggling with taking so much unpaid time off from work, sick from the chemo.

I couldn't remember who pitched the idea, but all of us upperclassmen had decided if we won, we'd give the money to him to help her.

Our victory party on Friday night had been postponed. Our president thought it'd be in poor taste after I'd fucked up the trophy and started the mud fight, but on Saturday, we let Grady in on the plan. As soon as we had the check from the council, we'd hand it over to him.

He got worked up, and maybe a few of the other guys did too, but if that happened, I didn't see anything.

It was a nice thing. Made us all feel good after a shitty ending to the week.

But it wouldn't have happened if Madison Perry had gotten her way.

I'd never gotten why she'd been with Jack. Well, I understood it for him. She was hot as fuck. But Jack? He was an okay guy, but he was a nerd and, for lack of a better word, forgettable.

That had to be why she'd cheated on him. I assumed she'd forgotten all about her boyfriend as soon as he was out of the country.

"What happened with Madison?" someone had asked him he'd gotten back from Germany.

He'd been embarrassed to say, but finally revealed she'd cheated on him.

The guys had called her things she might have deserved, but I didn't join in. She could do better than Jack, and she'd obviously figured that out. The only thing I could blame her for was not ending it sooner.

It was weird to me that Jack had moved on so quickly. He'd come back from his semester abroad with a new girlfriend, some girl from Georgia Tech. He wasn't even with her anymore. Now he was dating some sophomore Tri-Delt.

He couldn't stand to be single, apparently.

Me? I was the complete opposite. I fucking loved being free, plus I hadn't come close to meeting anyone I wanted to be with long-term.

For some bizarre reason, my focus returned to the picture of mad Madison in the newspaper. Even with mud on her face and glopped in her honey brown hair, her looks were undeniable.

Shame about that personality, though.

Jorge probably figured I was reading the article, rather than staring at the girl's picture. He tucked his hands under his arms, making him look even broader than he already was.

"You better be at the meeting, man," he said. "People will be looking for someone to blame."

I got what he meant. I needed to go to defend myself. Maybe I did deserve a small amount of the blame—everyone knew it was the guy who retaliated who usually drew the penalty. But as far as I was concerned, Madison owned ninety-five percent of it.

I hoped she wouldn't be there, and she'd get all of it.

The Greek council meeting was held in one of the lecture halls of a communications building, and . . . I'd gone to the wrong one.

"It's in Franklin," I said to the girl wandering down the hall, who looked as surprised as I had been that the place was deserted. I recognized her from one of the mixers last semester but hadn't a clue what her name was.

She turned around and fell in step beside me. "I could have sworn they said Jackson."

"Yeah . . ." I quickened my step, not just because I was going to be late, but because I wanted to put some space between us.

But she matched my stride, easily keeping up. "Did you ever get your Titans hat back?"

"What?"

"Last time we talked. You said you let your friend borrow it and you were sure he'd never give it back."

My brain jostled inside my head, scrambling to recall the conversation, but the girl looked unfamiliar. Unless—

"Shit," I said. "Did you and me . . ." I made finger guns, pointing them to her and then back at myself.

The girl dug in her heels, coming to a hard stop. "Oh, wow."

I wasn't sure what to do with that because it wasn't an answer.

Her face twisted with disgust. "Don't worry. It was as forgettable for me as it was for you."

There was no way that was true, but I wasn't going to say that out loud. My chest tightened with embarrassment. "I'm sorry."

My apology was genuine. I hadn't meant to be a dick— sometimes I was stupid and just said things without thinking. But she didn't care and couldn't get away from me fast enough.

I put my head down and hustled out of the set of glass doors. All the communications buildings were grouped together, so I jogged across the pavement to the large brick building next door.

Fuck me, the meeting had already started when I arrived, and I had to find my house among the crowd. The lecture hall was huge, with stadium seating and large projector screens up front. On the floor, the council sat facing the audience, a long table spread out in front of them.

Finally, I spotted the Sigs in the left section of seats, halfway up, and I moved as fast and silently as possible to get into my saved seat beside Jorge.

"Nice of you to join us," he muttered under his breath.

"I thought it was in Jackson Hall," I whispered back.

"Let's make sure everyone understands where we are," one of the women on the council up front said into her microphone. "The administration has always tolerated the tournament, but they'd like it better if it didn't exist. This debacle not only makes all of us look bad, it's just the opportunity they need to make us stop running it."

Several in the audience got vocal, voicing disapproval.

"No one got hurt," someone in the crowd muttered.

A guy on the council grabbed the microphone in front of him and leaned forward in his seat. "That's not true. I know at least one person went to urgent care after the fight."

The councilwoman leaned her elbows on the table. "Some of you might think it's no big deal. It was all in good fun, but—come on. We know better. That mud fight was ugly. It was immature and a freaking embarrassment. What's worse is the story's picking up national interest. The university is ashamed of what happened, and we all should be, too."

It was clear it was the councilman at the end of the table's turn to speak. "If we want to run the tournament again, the school has conditions. Some of them are things that won't go into effect until next year, but one needs to happen right away. As in, tonight."

Immediately, I didn't like where this was going. His voice was too heavy, too serious.

"Sanctions," the councilwoman concluded. "We've discussed some options, and we need to act so we send a message that we don't condone what happened, and also to ensure it won't happen again."

All the house presidents sat in the front row, and one from another fraternity spoke up. "What kind of sanctions?"

"No prize money will be awarded this year," the councilwoman answered, her gaze flicking up to where us Sigs were seated.

Our president, Charlie, was instantly up from his chair. "Wait a minute. Sigma Phi Alpha won the tournament, fair and square."

"Did you, though?" someone asked from across the room. The hall was packed with students, and yet it was easy to find where the voice had come from. So much for Madison skipping the meeting.

She sat back in her chair with her arms crossed and an angry expression, and I couldn't tell what pissed me off more. That she was still going on about us cheating, or that she looked just as hot tonight as she'd been when we'd competed against each other.

The councilwoman either didn't hear Madison or decided to ignore her. "What's not fair is that the Fidelity Cup got destroyed as a direct result of the fight your house helped start. Instead of giving the award money to the Sigs, it'll be used to fix the cup."

"If that's even possible," one of the other councilmembers added.

I couldn't stop myself from looking over at Grady and seeing the crushing disappointment. We'd promised him the money for his mom, and now it was being taken away. That wasn't fair to him, and since I'd played a part in causing it, I'd do my best to fix it.

"That's putting the blame disproportionately on us," I said, rising from my seat. "We didn't start the mud fight, and I wasn't the only one who messed up the cup. Why are the Sigs the ones who have to pay to fix it?"

While the rest of my frat brothers murmured their agreement, Charlie turned and threw a look at me that told me to shut up and sit my ass down. I slid back into my seat, and satisfied, Charlie turned back to the council.

"Colin has a point. Lambda Theta Chi is just as responsible, if not more."

"That's why the Lambdas will be fined half of the repair costs."

Charlie had given me a threatening look to be quiet, but I couldn't help myself. "What if I cover the Sigs' part of the repair?" I still had some money saved up from my summer job at the gym. "Will you award the prize money then?"

The councilman at the end of the table looked at me like I'd just offered to buy him a drink at an open bar. "No. There's no way we're going to give an award to a house that started the fight. Any award money left over after the cup is fixed will be donated to the Greek scholarship fund."

My pulse thudded. Fuck. Why the hell had I retaliated? If I'd just let Madison throw that mud at me and not fought back, I'd have come away a hero. I slunk farther down in my seat, stewing. This was so much more her fault than mine.

"The council has also decided to place both Lambda Theta Chi and Sigma Phi Alpha on probation for a year," the councilwoman said, taking a dramatic pause, "and suspend them from competing in the tournament for the next five years."

The crowd had been quiet up until now. There were gasps and instant chatter as people voiced their opinions to their friends. Some spoke directly to the council, either telling them this was too harsh, or it didn't go far enough.

I sat motionless as I processed it, but a girl in the front was on her feet and put her hands out, trying to get people to be quiet so the council could hear her. Was she the Lambdas' president?

"There's got to be a better option," she said. "Don't punish the entire house because of one," she searched for the right phrase, "bad apple."

"Tiffany's right," Charlie said. "Five years because of one person's mistake? And it's not like the Lambdas and Sigs were the only ones involved. Half this council was there, throwing mud just like everyone else."

I nodded, but then froze. Was he considering *me* as the bad apple?

Tiffany said it like Charlie was missing the point. "I don't even care about the tournament."

"Of course not," Jorge whispered to me. "The Lambdas have never won."

She put a hand on her hip. "It's the probation I'm objecting to. We can't afford not to participate in rush week in the fall."

Charlie's posture stiffened, and although I couldn't see his face, I imagined he had an expression that screamed, '*oh, shit*.' Because without rush week, it meant it'd kill our chances of attracting pledges next year.

Tiffany's tone was direct. "Like I said, there has to be another option that doesn't potentially kill my sorority's future all because one girl made a bad choice."

The councilwoman eyed her critically. "You want to make a suggestion?"

It was surprising how quickly the answer came from her. "Remove the bad apple."

"Tiffany," Madison bolted up to her feet, "what are you doing?"

"It's the best solution." Tiffany kept her eyes on the council and her back turned on Madison. "Hold the individual responsible, not the entire house."

I had to hand it to her. She was ruthless, selling out her sister to save the organization. The place had gone quiet again, and even though she was across the room, I'd swear I could hear Madison's pulse thundering all the way over here. Her chest rose and fell rapidly, like she couldn't find any air to breathe.

"But," she said in a powerless voice, "that's where I live.

Please don't do this."

"If we go that route," one of the councilmen said, "remember there were two individuals responsible for starting the fight."

His gaze landed on Charlie, and my mouth went dry.

My heart stopped.

They weren't just considering kicking Madison out, but me too. In fact, they looked at my house president now to sign off on my eviction notice.

"So," he spoke slowly, like he was trying to delay the inevitable, "our option is probation and tournament suspension, or . . . eject Colin from Sigma Phi Alpha? No other sanctions will get imposed if we do that?"

The council members glanced at each other to see if they were all in agreement, which they seemed to be.

The councilman on the end leaned closer to his microphone. "The school would have to approve our ruling, but yes."

"All right."

He didn't even think about it, or how Sigma Phi Alpha was my literal home. I glared down at him and climbed out of my chair, which was extra difficult because of the knife he'd stuck in my back.

I was a legacy.

My father, grandfather, and two of my uncles had been Sigs. It was one of the only things my dad and I had in common. If I told my parents I'd gotten kicked out, that was it. The final straw for them, and I could kiss college goodbye.

"Please have your students cease all chapter activities immediately," the councilwoman said to Tiffany and Charlie. "And I'd suggest they start looking for alternate housing right away."

Everything was moving too fast. My legs felt weak and unreliable. Even if Davidson University wasn't experiencing a housing shortage—which it was—it was also fucking April. Where the hell was I going to live?

My gaze drifted across the sea of people staring up at me as I searched for answers I wouldn't find. Instead, my focus landed on the other person who looked just as fucked as I felt.

I'd never hated someone before.

But as I stared at the girl who'd gotten me kicked out of my frat—the one who was responsible for the fact I was about to be homeless—an acidic taste filled my mouth. That was the moment I knew I hated Madison Perry with every cell in my body.

FOUR

Madison

I had to be moved out of the house by five p.m. on Friday because on Tuesday the school had approved the sanctions. I was no longer a Lambda, but Tiffany had graciously given me until the end of the week to figure out where to go.

I'd come back to my room after the meeting on Monday night and cried myself to sleep. It wasn't the first time my whole life had changed in an instant, so maybe having one experience under my belt would help me through this one, I told myself. But it was still hard and overwhelming, and I allowed myself one night to wallow in self-pity.

The next two days, I spent every spare minute looking at options, of which there were few.

There would be no refund on what I'd paid for board through the end of the semester. I had absolutely no money for housing, so there was no way I could put down a deposit, plus first and last month's rent on a place—even if I found one available. No one was looking for roommates in April, not when there was only a month left in the spring semester.

It wasn't like I could move back in with my parents. They lived five hours away in St. Louis.

And I certainly couldn't ask them for money.

By Thursday morning, I was in a total panic. I had twenty-nine hours to find a place or end up sitting with my stuff on the front curb of the sorority. I had enough money in my bank account I could stay at a hotel for a few days, but it'd be tough to afford to eat too, and what was I going to do after the money was gone?

Some of the girls tried to help. Danielle's aunt and uncle lived close to campus and had a spare bedroom. She'd said she was going to talk to them about letting me stay there, and at this point, all my eggs were in the Danielle basket.

Jenn stood by my closet, pulling sweaters down off hangers and packing them neatly in a box. She'd offered to help me get ready for the move because she could tell I was struggling to do it, plus I didn't really have the time if I was going to keep searching.

I was seated at my desk in front of my laptop, scouring the internet for any new postings about people looking for roommates. I was forcing myself to reconsider some listings I'd ruled out earlier for being too sketchy.

Today I was too desperate to have standards or worry about getting murdered.

"What's this?" Jenn asked.

I turned to watch as she pulled out a hanger that was covered in a plastic garment bag.

A pang of sadness ricocheted through me. "It's a dress I bought for our formal, back when I was with Jack."

I'd found it by accident during the summer on a clearance rack and had been thrilled it was in my size. I'd fallen in love with the rose gold dress. It had a plunging neckline and was embellished with tiny lines of sequins that trailed down onto the skirt, which was layers of sheer fabric. I loved the dress so much, I'd hung on to it after the breakup, thinking I'd find someone to go to the dance with. But now? I wasn't going to Lambda Theta Chi's formal . . . because I wasn't a Lambda.

"Do you think I can sell it?" I asked. "It still has the tags."

Jenn lifted the plastic and looked at the dress, issuing a soft, wistful sound. "Pretty. Is it designer?" She went to check the label, and when she saw it wasn't, she shimmied the plastic back down around it. "Maybe."

I appreciated her attempt to sound upbeat when I knew the answer was no.

She resumed her packing, and I was struck with guilt. "You don't have to help me if you don't want to," I said softly. "I'm not your big sister anymore."

She tilted her head and gave me a pointed look. "I'm helping because you're my friend, Madison."

"Well, I really appreciate it, friend."

"Of course. Hey, I know this sucks," she said, "but I can think of at least one silver lining."

She was always so freaking positive. "Yeah? What's that?"

"I bet your new place will have a hot shower. I told Yasmin this morning I'm about ready to suggest we do shower shows on OnlyFans to fundraise for that water heater." Her tone had an edge of sarcasm, just enough for me to wonder if she was being serious or not.

My pulse quickened as the idea struck me. "Would you?"

"Do a sex show? Please. Nobody would pay to see," she swept a hand down the length of her body, "this." Which was silly. She was cute, with a nice curvy body, but she seemed entirely unaware of her attractiveness. "What about you?"

I leaned against the back of my chair and thought about

how to respond to her question. She'd probably expect me to answer quickly, to make a snap decision. It wasn't something that was supposed to require careful consideration, and yet . . .

"I don't know," I lied. "Maybe." Because my answer was yes, but I wasn't sure if she'd judge me for it.

Her movements slowed and her expression changed, but it wasn't to criticize. She looked curious. "Really?" When I nodded, the corner of her mouth quirked up into a slight smile. "My cousin is a cam girl. She says the hours aren't great, but she makes good money."

"I'll keep that in mind," I said in a joking tone, although I was completely serious.

As she returned to face the closet, my mind raced. I was sexually inexperienced, but I wasn't a prude—nor was I shy. What if the answer to all my problems was a simple, yet unconventional solution?

I sat on the edge of the bench and swallowed dryly, struggling to keep my nerves at bay. The lobby of the hotel was fancy and busy, and it seemed like no one noticed me waiting there.

My gaze was hyper-focused on the entrance. I had no idea what to expect about this meeting, other than it would be with a person named Nina. She'd been the one to respond to the email I'd sent, and after we'd chatted through text messages, she'd asked me to meet her here.

I'd been people watching when an elegant blonde

woman appeared and pushed her way through the revolving door. She wore sky-high heels, an expensive dress, and I was pretty sure her Louis Vuitton handbag was not a knock-off. My breath caught as she spotted me on the bench and began to approach.

This was Nina?

She seemed to be in her mid-thirties, with flawless skin and a killer body. I was struck by how she looked more like she was the talent, rather than the owner of an adult film company.

"Madison?" Her voice was deep and smoky, and kind of sexy. "Hi, I'm Nina." She thrust out a manicured hand for a handshake, which I took.

"Nice to meet you." I hoped she couldn't see how intimidated I was. Everything about her screamed money, plus she was so beautiful, it was disorienting.

She smiled and motioned toward the hotel bar. "What should we drink?"

When she started toward the mostly empty bar, she didn't watch to see if I was following her—she just assumed I would.

So, I did. But my brain went empty as I tried to come up with a sophisticated drink. "Uh . . ."

"They do a great pomegranate martini here. You want to try that?"

"Sure."

She leaned over the bar and placed our order, but she didn't take a seat while we watched the bartender mix our drinks. The hotel was swanky and upscale, and when I glanced at the prices on the drink menu nearby, I saw how proud they were of their cocktails. Nina rested a hand on the polished counter and looked at ease in her nice clothes, whereas I felt out of place.

I'd done my best to dress the part. Tight jeans, heeled booties, and a black sweater that was cut low to show off some cleavage. Now I was wondering if I'd tried too hard.

"You're a student at Davidson, right?" she asked as we watched the bartender strain our ruby red drinks into martini glasses.

"Yeah. I graduate at the end of the fall semester."

"Your major?"

"Forensic accounting."

She reacted how people usually did when I told them. Surprise, followed by interest. "Big fan of math, are you?"

"I like numbers," I said. "They don't lie."

She seemed to find that answer fascinating, but then our drinks were ready. The bartender set them down, and she handed him a credit card. "Let's keep it open." He nodded, and she picked up one of the drinks before turning to me. "There's a table over in the corner. We can talk there."

I was careful not to slosh my drink as we made our way to the small high-top table with two tall chairs. Once we were settled into our seats and she'd taken a sip of her martini, Nina focused in on me.

"You're really pretty." She said it more like an observation than a compliment.

"Thank you."

"Why don't you tell me about yourself? I'd like to get a feel for you, and after that, I'll tell you about me, and we can talk about the house."

I took a sip of my drink, both to work up the courage and

to stall so I could prepare what to say. But the fruity drink distracted my thoughts. "Wow, you're right. This drink could be dangerous."

"Right?" She smiled.

I gently set the glass down and let my fingers rest on the base of the stem. "What do you want to know? Like, my experience? How many guys I've been with?"

She blinked. "I was thinking more about you as a person. If everything works out, you'd come live at my house."

"Oh." My face got hot. She wanted to interview me as a potential roommate. "Right. Well, I think I'm easy to live with. I'm the kind of girl who makes her bed every morning and doesn't leave dishes in the sink. I wear headphones when I'm watching something in my room, so I'm quiet. I mind my business and respect other people's stuff."

"That's good." But it was obvious this wasn't what she was looking for. She cocked her head to the side. "What made you respond to my ad? You can be honest. I promise you won't get any judgement from me."

"I need money—or a place to live." I dropped my gaze down to my fingers on my martini glass. "Or both, ideally."

"Hey, I get it. Ten years ago, that was my story, too. I was broke, and living in Hammond, Indiana. Have you heard of it?"

"No."

"It's the armpit of the Midwest, to give you an idea of what it's like there." She pushed away her sour expression and returned to normal. "I was desperate and willing to do anything to get free, so I answered a casting call for an adult film. That led me to a career in sex work, and most people don't believe it, because they don't *want* it to be true, but it changed my life in amazing ways."

I tried not to scrunch my face or look dubious. "Really?"

"Yes," she said. "Absolutely no regrets. I love what I do, and if it wasn't for that audition, I wouldn't have met my husband." She smiled to herself, as if recalling the memory, before her eyes refocused on me. "He usually comes with me to these meet-and-greets, but he had another appointment tonight."

"He's in the porn business, too?"

This question amused her. "He's Scott Westwood."

"Oh." She'd said it like I should recognize the name, but I didn't, and my blank expression thrilled her even more.

"I guess you don't watch a lot of porn. He's pretty famous." She took a sip of her drink. "If things work out, we'll change that. You'll want to see what kind of content other companies are putting out, what makes a great performance. But I'm getting ahead of myself. I still need to know about you. Where are you from?"

"St. Louis."

"What brought you here? School?"

"Yeah. Davidson has a top tier business program, and they have an in-state exchange program with Missouri." Otherwise, I never would have been able to afford it. It also helped that it put some space between me and my parents, which was needed after everything that had happened.

"Can I ask what happened with your housing?"

Her question was casual, and I parted my lips to speak, but wasn't sure what to say. If I told her I'd gotten kicked out of my sorority, she'd ask why, and then I'd have to admit one of the most embarrassing days of my life. Plus, she'd think I had anger issues and I'd lose out on the only housing lead I had now—Danielle's aunt had said no.

Nina must have seen the fear in my eyes because her expression filled with concern. "Hey, it's all right. Everyone at the house respects boundaries and your personal life. You only share what you're comfortable with. If it was a break-up with your partner, or a problem with your roommate, that's all I need to know."

"Yes," I said quickly. "A break-up. That's what it was."

I felt awful lying to her, but this was too important to get wrong. *I just need to make it through the summer.* With hard work and luck, I'd find an affordable apartment to rent, or a place looking for a roommate, for the fall semester.

And if I wanted to twist logic, I could argue my relationship with Lambda Theta Chi had ended—they'd dumped me like a bad girlfriend.

"I'm sorry to hear that," she said. "You doing okay?"

I sucked in a breath. "It was sudden, but yeah. I need to focus on moving forward."

She gave a reassuring nod. "That's the way to do it." Her smile turned devious. "And I'm sure we can help take your mind off them."

I forced out a smile.

"Speaking of that," she said, "have you done anything like this before?"

"No. I mean, I've sent some nudes to my boyfriend, but nothing more than that."

"But you think you'd be comfortable with performing? It's not like I want to talk you out of it, but you need to consider the impact this will have, especially long term. You might be okay with showing everything today, but five or ten years down the road that could change. The internet is a big place—much bigger than when I started—but it's still *forever*." Her tone was serious. "Once you ring that bell, you can't un-ring it."

I took in a deep breath. "I understand."

"Okay." She seemed satisfied. "Have you done any acting before?"

My head bobbed in a nod. "I was the lead in the school play my senior year."

"Oh, that's great." She looked pleasantly surprised. "Did you take the pictures I asked for?"

My chest tightened. "Yeah."

I pulled out my phone, scrolled to the hidden album of photos I'd snapped earlier, and passed my phone to her. She studied the pictures thoughtfully, like they weren't images where I was buck-ass naked.

I'd done my best to look sexy and pose how she'd asked, and I was grateful when she'd said I'd only have to show her my pictures when we were in person. She seemed to be exactly who she said she was, but still. I wasn't about to email nudes, especially ones that showed my face, to a complete stranger.

"No issues here. You've got a great body." She handed my phone back to me. "So, besides the money, why are you interested in doing this?"

Once again, my brain went blank. I should have prepared for this like a job interview, but our meeting had come together so quickly, I hadn't had time.

Nina took pity on me. "I guess what I'm getting at is,

when our performers enjoy themselves, so do our viewers. Does the thought of doing this . . . turn you on at all? I get that you're nervous, but is part of you excited too?"

Under the table, I pinched my knees together, but I could have sworn she still noticed. My voice dropped to a whisper. "Yes."

Her eyebrow lifted in perfect time with the corner of her mouth. "Yeah? Anything particular you're interested in?"

All the moisture in my body began to migrate south. She was a gorgeous woman, and the way she stared at me was provocative, like she was thinking about having me for dessert. And if she wanted to, well . . . maybe I'd let her.

She'd asked what I was interested in, and so I gave her an honest answer.

"Um, is it weird if I say all of it?" I took a quick gulp of my martini, giving me courage to say the rest. "When I got to college, I thought that was the time I was going to try all these new things. New experiences. I was supposed have sex in wild places, with guys, or girls, or guys *and* girls. But instead, I spent two years with him, and . . . none of that happened. My window is closing."

Nina gazed at me like she'd found a diamond in the rough. "Oh, girl. It's not closing. There's no expiration date on experimenting, and you don't need permission to find who you want to be."

I pressed my lips together. On some level, I knew what she was saying was true, but I struggled anyway. My college life had been nothing but pressure. Pressure to pick the one job I'd be happy to do for the rest of my life. To have wild, life-changing experiences. And maybe to find my soulmate.

It was a lot to pack into four years. How the fuck did anyone do all that?

"Here's my thought for the rest of the evening," Nina said. "We'll finish our drinks, and then we'll go to the studio. If you feel like auditioning, I'll find you a partner. And if that goes well, which I bet it will," she winked, "and you're interested in doing more, I'll give you the full rundown of how we operate and the house rules. If you decide it's not for you, no problem. We'll pay you a thousand dollars for the content and that's it."

She let me digest that as she took a sip of her drink, and her eyes studied me, gauging my response. Maybe she worried I'd need more convincing.

"I think you'd have a lot of fun," she continued, "and I'd love to get a chance to help you explore all the things you want to. What do you say?"

My voice was tight, but my pulse thrummed with excitement. "I say it sounds like a plan."

During the drive to Nina's place, we chatted about mundane things. The movies we liked. The songs we didn't. But still, I struggled to keep up with the conversation. I was nervous. How could I not be? When we got there, if I was willing, I'd sign a contract, take off my clothes, and fuck a stranger while she filmed.

It was ridiculously wild.

And *exhilarating.*

I felt like I was going to vibrate out of my skin.

As advertised in the online posting, the house wasn't far from campus, but I hadn't expected it to be in such a nice neighborhood. When she turned in to the subdivision with an elegant brick sign, I peered up at the houses with wide eyes.

Each seemed to have a garage big enough for three or more cars. Elaborate swimming pools in the backyards peeked out behind wrought-iron fences. The lawns were impeccably landscaped and maintained.

And a few of the houses were so large, I could have used the terms *sprawling* or *mansion*.

She turned in to a driveway that curved and sloped upward, and my gaze followed the path to the home nestled between mature trees. It seemed to be the biggest of the houses, looming over the rest of the neighborhood.

When one of the garage doors rolled back and Nina eased her luxury SUV into the spot, my heartbeat quickened. It wasn't because she was still somewhat of a stranger—I felt safe. Plus, I'd told Jenn about my plans and shared my phone's location with her.

No, my heart raced because it was settling in what was going to happen, and I was eager for it. The money, the opportunity, the experience . . .

All of it.

I climbed out of the passenger side and took in my surroundings. Since the house was built on the side of a hill, the garage had tall ceilings, and there was a wooden staircase the led up to what I assumed was the main floor. But we didn't take the stairs. There was a door on the far wall, and Nina headed that direction.

Once we were through it, she flipped on a bank of light switches and set her purse down on one of the U-shaped desks tucked in the front corners. The room was small and L-shaped with a hallway running along the left wall, and I got the feeling it hadn't been planned this way. Perhaps once it had been one large space, but now it was partitioned off to fit the homeowners' needs.

"Welcome to the editing bay," she said. "You can put your stuff here."

There were several monitors arranged on the desk, and she wiggled the mouse, waking up the computer. I bit down on my bottom lip as multiple images appeared on one of the screens. It seemed to be different camera angles of the same empty bedroom.

There was camera and lighting equipment neatly stacked beside the desk, and a bank of batteries glowed green, having finished charging.

The phone vibrated in Nina's purse. She retrieved it and glanced at the text message. "Awesome. Scott's on his way back." She opened one of the drawers of the desk and rifled through the papers until she found what she was looking for. "This is our standard contract for one-off shoots."

She'd pulled multiple pages, but only handed half of them to me. The other half she set on the desk on the other side of the room, then tossed a hand toward the weird hallway.

"Let me show you the studio, and then you can look over the form. There's more space in there."

The "studio" was bigger than the editing area, and it was the same bedroom I'd seen on the monitors, which I found disorienting. You'd never know it was night outside or that we were in a basement. The room was bright and airy, with faux windows on either side of the bed, and diffused light streamed through the frosted glass.

The queen-sized bed was fitted with crisp white sheets,

and the tables on either side were decorated with fake plants and muted artwork. It was the perfect background, interesting enough to look at without distracting from what the real show was supposed to be.

The wall opposite the bed had a large ring light on a tripod, and a camera mounted just in front of its center. And behind that, a flatscreen TV was perched high on the wall. All the same camera angles were visible in different boxes on-screen, and I saw myself and Nina in them at various angles.

She noticed my gaze on the TV and gave a soft laugh. "You don't have to worry about that. When your guy gets here, I'll explain to you both where your marks are, but it doesn't matter that much. Everything in front of the lights has coverage. We mostly use the monitor for staging and practice."

"Oh." My word was breathless.

When your guy gets here, she'd said.

My grip on the contract tightened, making the paper wrinkle, reminding me of its existence. I glanced down and zeroed in on the Petal Productions logo at the top of the page, which was modern and slightly feminine. It was much prettier than I would have expected for an adult film company.

"Why don't you have a seat and read that over?" she said. "I'll go grab a pen."

The only place to sit was on the bed, and so when she disappeared through the open doorway, I took a seat on the edge of the mattress. The contract wasn't complicated. It spelled out what I'd be paid for the scene, and that Petal Productions would distribute it digitally via their subscription platform only.

I was still working my way through the second page

when she returned with a pen and a bottle of water, offering them both to me, which I took.

"Do you have questions?"

She meant about the contract, but I couldn't help it. My curiosity was getting the best of me. "What can you tell me about the guy I'm doing this with?"

"Not much, but only because that's Scott's department. He's bringing in someone new tonight as well."

"Someone new?" My anxiety spiked. I'd been banking on my partner having experience. Wouldn't it be better if he knew what he was doing? That way he could help guide me.

My concern must have been visible because Nina straightened. "If that makes you uncomfortable, it doesn't have to be this new guy. I'm sure Scott will do it if you'd rather partner with him."

I just barely stopped myself from screeching it. "You mean, your husband?"

Was something wrong with me? Because her expression made it seem like *I* was the one being weird. A thought hit her then, and a grin stretched across her lips. "Ah. You're worried about fucking my husband."

I had no idea what kind of face I was making and tried to keep it blank.

"Okay." Her tone filled with amusement. "First—it's acting. We don't get jealous because this is just work for us. Second—there are a shit-ton of people who'd pay to get to fuck Scott, and keep in mind, in this arrangement, I'd be paying *you*."

Did it look like I needed more convincing?

"Third," she added, "do I think it's hot when he fucks

other people?" Her eyes glinted with lust. "Yes. Yes, I do."

I couldn't wrap my head around that.

People in love don't sleep with other people.

But she was so matter-of-fact. So confident. And that was . . . kind of amazing.

Still, as much as I believed her, there wasn't a snow-ball's chance in hell I was going to fuck this woman's hus-band while she watched. I was all for new experiences, and the idea of strangers watching turned me on, but—good God.

Baby steps.

Nina threaded her fingers through her blonde hair and pushed it back over her shoulder. "This other guy? I've seen his headshot, and I think he's fucking hot, but Scott's a pro. So, it's up to you on who to partner with. I don't think you can make a bad choice."

Was it really a choice, though? I cleared my throat, try-ing to shake free the sticky sensation caught there. "Uh, I'll try the new guy."

With that settled, I refocused on completing the contract. There was a large section about risk and the production com-pany's mandatory condom policy in audition scenes. When I finished reading and truly digesting the information, I stood and carried everything to the bedside table and began to fill in the blank places with my personal details.

It was surprising that my hand was so steady, given how static electricity surged through my system. I was buzzing with both trepidation and impatience as I scribbled my name and the date across the bottom line.

It'd been two months since I'd last had sex, and that ran-dom hookup had been so underwhelming, it was easier to pretend it had never happened. But that meant it felt like it had been decades since anyone else's touch had lit me up.

Hopefully, that changed tonight.

I handed the contract and pen to Nina, and as she signed her part, I unscrewed the cap on the water bottle and drank down an enormous gulp. I was screwing the cap back on when we heard the office door creak open, and footsteps came into the other room.

". . . there was a puddle of coolant under her car," one of the voices said. The footsteps stopped abruptly, as if the person was confused. "Nina?"

"We're in here." She peered at me like a parent waiting for their kid to open a present on Christmas morning. My heart vaulted up into my throat as the two pairs of footsteps grew louder and the men made their way toward us.

The first one through the doorway had to be Scott. He was in his mid-thirties, with dark blond hair that was long on the top and short on the sides. He threw a friendly smile my way, and then a look to his wife that seemed to say, *I approve*. My mouth was bone dry as he moved aside, and my scene partner stepped into the room.

I sucked in a sharp breath, and everything went utterly still.

No, a panicked voice screamed inside my head. *Not him*.

He jolted to a stop when our gazes locked, and something dark flared in his eyes. It was as if shock, outrage, and heat all rolled into one and created a brand-new, unnamed emotion.

As I stared at the irritatingly hot frat boy, it took every ounce of strength in me not to explode.

What the *fuck* was Colin doing here?

FIVE

Colin

If it was embarrassing to get starstruck, did that mean it was extra embarrassing to be starstruck over meeting Scott Westwood? The guy was a fucking legend—like, literally. He'd been in the business a long time and must have performed with over two hundred people.

"Married," I repeated in disbelief.

"Yeah, man," he said. "Two years now."

My gaze went to his hand on the steering wheel of his BMW M3 to confirm, and sure enough. There was a black wedding ring.

"She doesn't get jealous?" I asked. "Like, she knows what you do, right?"

He laughed. "I met Nina at a casting call nine years ago, so yeah. She knows what I do." The turn signal clicked quietly as we waited to turn left, and he lobbed a smile in my direction. "You never know with these auditions. Same thing could happen to you tonight."

Because he'd told me over drinks that the girl I'd be auditioning with was just as fresh as I was.

"I better not meet my future wife at a casting call," I said.

The smile evaporated from his face and his tone turned dark. "Yeah? Because it's okay for you to shoot porn but not her?"

"No, no, it's not that at all." I rubbed my fingertips against my forehead. "I meant the wife part. I'll sound like a dick, but I'm not really into the long-term stuff."

Or commitment in general, but I kept the comment to myself.

He said it in a patronizing way, like he didn't believe a word of it. "Oh. I gotcha."

The car made the turn and prowled down the street, and as our conversation lapsed, I started to feel the pressure again.

Earlier, I'd walked into my meeting with him full of confidence. I was good-looking, with a good-looking dick to match, and I'd had sex in public places a few times before, so I felt comfortable I'd be able perform when the camera started rolling.

Shit, I'd never been shy.

But as Scott and I talked, the gravity of the situation hit me like a sledgehammer. If tonight didn't go well, I'd have no choice but to tell my parents I'd been kicked out, which meant I'd have to beg them to let me come home.

And it was likely they wouldn't.

They already knew about the mud fight, thanks to the media, but thankfully they didn't know the whole story. Just my participation in the fight was enough to earn me a threatening phone call from my father.

Fuck, I could not blow this audition.

When Scott turned right at the familiar brick sign, I sat up straighter in my seat. "You live in this neighborhood?"

"Yeah." Suspicion crept into his voice. "Why?"

"I have a friend who lives here, too." Was that true? "Not all the time," I revised. "Just when he's home for the summer from Vanderbilt." I pointed to the road as we passed by it. "His dad's house is down that street."

"Small world."

It both was and wasn't. This was the wealthiest neighborhood in our Nashville suburb, so it wasn't that surprising. But it kind of blew my mind that Preston lived so close to Scott Westwood's home, and we had no idea. Although in our defense, my friend wasn't home much during the school year, and we hung out at his place even less these days. Plus, Scott's real last name was Woodson.

I wanted to keep the conversation going so Scott would think I was easy to hang with. "So, you met your wife at a casting call. How'd that go? You did the scene and then asked for her number?"

He turned, driving the car up the steep driveway that led toward an enormous house up ahead. "Not exactly. I wanted to ask her out after we finished filming, but I also didn't want to come off as a creep, and I was so busy thinking how I was going to do it, I almost missed my opportunity."

Once we were parked in the garage beside a Porsche Cayenne, I followed his lead and got out of the car, all while he continued his story.

"I offered to walk her out, and that's when I knew she was coming home with me." We went through a door into a strange office-like area. "There was a puddle of coolant under her car." He pulled to a stop and glanced around the empty space. "Nina?"

"We're in here," came a voice from down the hall.

Scott moved toward it, so I did the same, not getting much of a chance to look at the computers set up in the awkward space. He turned a corner, stepping into a room that was staged as a bedroom, even though legally it couldn't be. The windows were fake.

My brain slowed as I saw the woman who had to be Scott's wife. Shit, she was hot. A tall, lanky blonde with a body built for fucking and—

The blood in my veins stopped, solidifying.

My brain disconnected and shut down.

All I could do was stare at the girl who'd fucked up my life.

"This is Colin," Scott said, oblivious to the anger swirling around me like a dark cloud. Was this some kind of joke? Because there was no way stick-up-her-ass, mad Madison Perry was supposed to be my audition partner.

"And this is Madison." Then Nina pointed at me and turned to the girl. "See? I told you he was hot."

Madison's voice was flat. "We've met."

My heart began working again, and as I pulled in a short breath, my hands clenched into fists. Not because I wanted to fight, but because there was so much tension coursing through me, I needed something to hold it back.

I wanted to tell her to get the fuck out of here. This audition was too important to me for her to screw it up. But, shit. If she was supposed to be my partner, didn't I need her?

Scott's gaze bounced between me and Madison. "So . . . I guess you two have already—"

"No," came from us in horrified unison.

Was it possible she'd decline to do the scene?

I glared at the girl across from me, who had the nerve to look the best I'd seen her yet, and my blood burned hot.

My head was opposed to the idea of fucking her, but

my dick? That was another story. *Think about it*, a persuasive voice argued. *Don't you want to fuck the girl who'd fucked you over? Wouldn't it be hot to have her on her knees, sucking your cock, or bent over the bed as you drilled her from behind?*

I pictured Madison naked and sweaty, gasping for breath between moans, begging me to make her come.

Well, now I wanted *that* a hell of a lot more than her bowing out of auditioning with me.

Everyone sensed the friction in the room, but Nina was the first to speak. "I'm getting the impression you two aren't exactly friends."

"We're not," I said, forcing myself to sound casual. "But it's fine. It's not a problem for me."

Madison understood the challenge I'd issued and glared back in defiance. "It's not a problem for me either."

A cruel smile tweaked my lips. She'd tried to sound strong but failed. As far as I could tell, this was win-win. If she backed out, that wasn't my fault. They'd find someone else for me to audition with. But if she went through with it, I'd get to show off how good I was. Maybe even get her addicted to my dick and then cut her off.

"Okay." I could tell Nina wasn't one hundred percent convinced this was going to work, but she shifted her focus to her husband. "I put his contract on your desk. She's already signed hers. You want to grab that and some in-ears while I go over the basics with them?"

Scott nodded and headed out through the doorway, leaving me alone with the two women. I hooked my thumbs into the pockets of my jeans, doing my best to look at ease, even though I felt awkward as hell.

"We'll start with scene direction." She picked up a set of papers from the side table, which was probably Madison's contract. "During filming, Scott and I won't be in the room. If one of us is in there, the actors tend to look at us, and we've found it's better when the viewer believes it's only the actors in the scene. They like watching something that seems unscripted, even when it's not. But you'll still receive direction from us, when you need it, from the monitors you'll be wearing. They're devices that are small enough they can be hidden inside your ear."

She strode to the doorway and showed it was a pocket door as she slid it halfway closed.

"Also, this will be closed to keep out sound while filming, but Scott and I will be watching the screens just outside the entire time. If either of you ever gets uncomfortable or wants to stop at any point, or even if you just have a question, please let us know. We can always edit it out, and it's very important to us you feel safe."

She pushed the door back open as Scott came in, carrying two boxes the size of sunglass cases, and the paperwork I'd need to complete. Then she moved to one of the bedside tables and pulled the cabinet door open, revealing the box of condoms and bottles of lube inside.

"And since we're talking about safety," she pulled a condom from of the box, "I'm letting you know that protection is mandatory in this scene, and we have a zero-tolerance policy on that."

She placed the condom on top of the end table, and her focus zeroed in on me.

"You put this on—not her—when you're ready, or if one of us tells you to. If either of you removes it before we think it's safe, the scene is over. Neither of you will be paid because we won't be able to use the footage."

"Also, keep in mind," Scott said, "I'll let anyone I've worked with know you're not a safe performer."

Meaning he'd blacklist whoever violated their policy, and given how connected he was, it'd be a career killer.

"Got it?" Nina said.

"Yes, ma'am," I answered instantly.

It seemed like Madison was struggling. Not with the rules, but with the whole concept of what she'd come here to do. She had her lips pressed together and nodded quickly, but her eyes were glued to the foil packet resting on the table. She stared at it like she expected it to sprout legs and run away at any moment.

What *was* she doing here?

I didn't know much about her. The whole time she was with Jack, she'd only stayed over at the house a few times. I'd never heard any stories about her. She seemed so straight-and-narrow. Boring.

Fuck—did she even like sex?

I wasn't excited about having a partner who'd just lie there. Not to mention, it'd make me look bad.

Nina shut the cabinet door with a quiet click. "Good. So, condoms and lube are here," she pointed to the other end table, "and toys are in there, if you're interested. We've got stuff for girls and boys."

She gave me a little wink, and I had no idea how to interpret it. Was she implying I'd need help getting hard, or help getting Madison off? *Doubtful, lady,* I wanted to say, but I clenched my jaw to hold it in.

"As I told Madison," Nina said, "we've got multiple cameras in here, so as long as you stay in front of the white lines, you'll be in the shot."

She motioned toward the thin strip of white tape that was on the carpet in front of the tripod. My gaze went from that to the TV screen on the wall. There was even a camera mounted to the ceiling, positioned directly over the bed.

"You don't even have to use the bed," Scott added. "It's up to you two and the scene. We'll help you out on positioning so nothing's blocking our shot, and make sure we get the best angles."

"So, one other thing to keep in mind." Nina took in a deep breath and smiled, and her expression filled with pride. "Petal Productions is female-owned, and our brand is pleasure for all. We don't cater to the straight male gaze, and we treat our actors equally, with equal screen-time and pay. We also have a rule for everything we produce." She paused for effect. "Every orgasm is real."

It was warm under the studio lights, and a bead of sweat rolled down my spine. As if I didn't have enough pressure on me already. I was confident I could give a girl a good time, but I'd been with enough to know orgasms weren't a sure thing for some, and there were a few where it was near impossible.

I watched the rapid rise and fall of Madison's chest, and all the anxiety she displayed, I felt inside me. Suddenly, I was grateful to have the cabinet full of toys as a backup plan.

Because who would want to watch porn where the girl didn't come?

Whatever she'd been thinking about, it was decided. Madison's throat bobbed with a swallow. She set her hand on a hip and peered over at me with a smug smile. "Sounds great."

There was fire in her eyes, lighting a challenge flame. She thought I couldn't do it.

I matched her smile and then some. "Yeah, I agree."

"It's okay to embellish, to perform," Nina said, "but fake moans are a turn-off, and the last thing we want is people turning off our videos."

"Don't worry," I said. "Her moans will be real."

Madison laughed as if I'd just embarrassed myself, and then choked it back out of politeness.

It caused Nina and Scott to exchange a look with each other. Maybe they were wondering what the fuck our deal was. The room went awkwardly silent, and I knew I had to do something before they changed their minds about auditioning us.

I nodded toward the paperwork in Scott's hands. "You need me to sign that?"

He passed the contract to me but didn't let go when I tried to take the papers, drawing my gaze up to his.

His voice was low. "You think about her and not us, and it'll all work out. You get me?"

I did, and it made my heart sink. I hated Madison. I didn't want to care about her or how she felt, but if I was going to ace this audition . . .

I'd *have* to.

SIX

Madison

When Nina pulled the door closed, it meant I was alone with Colin. He'd read and signed his contract while Nina helped me put the earpiece in. It was slightly smaller than an earbud and fit tightly inside my ear, snug enough it seemed unlikely it'd fall out.

Scott went to his desk to test the sound. His voice came through clearly, and Nina moved on to assisting Colin.

It left me standing there on wobbly legs as I considered my options. A small part of me was freaking out because there'd be no turning back. No 'un-ringing the bell,' as Nina had said. And to do this scene with Colin was a nightmare scenario.

Well . . . maybe nightmare was too strong of a word.

Even if he was the village bicycle at Davidson and every girl got a ride, there was a reason for it. He was annoyingly attractive and had a reputation of having game. One time when I'd been over at the Sig house last year, I'd heard him banging some girl who was clearly a fan of his work.

I didn't care if he was a slut. He liked sex and found lots of willing partners, so really . . . what was the big deal?

No, it was his cruelty I was struggling with.

The memory replayed in my mind. Sweaty and beaten, I'd knelt in the mud to tie my shoe, stunned that no one believed what I was saying. I'd felt so alone and vulnerable and that was the moment he'd chosen to strike. Jack's cheating was humiliating enough when it was private, but when Colin announced it in front of everyone else, that was brutal.

And now you're going to fuck this guy.

We each stood beside a corner of the large bed, our hands on our hips and our narrow gazes fixed on each other. It had to look like we were going to war with each other, and maybe we were. It definitely felt like we were in a battle.

His voice was so quiet, it was likely the microphones in the room wouldn't hear it. "Don't fuck this up for me."

My lips twisted into a half-smile, half-sneer. "*You* don't fuck this up for me."

We stared at each other, ignoring the way the friction between us created sparks, charging the air. Neither of us wanted to make the opening move. It was easier to react than to act.

It was just us in this bedroom where time ceased to exist.

But we *weren't* alone.

"Uh, we doing this, guys?" came Scott's voice through our earpieces.

My pulse climbed as Colin drew in a preparing breath. I'd expected him to approach me, but he had other ideas because he grabbed the sides of his shirt and stretched it up over his head.

I jolted as his toned chest came into view. Jesus. He was made of muscle and had honest-to-God washboard abs. I blinked back the surge of lust, not wanting it.

Screw him for looking so damn good.

He flung his shirt away and lifted his chin, looking down

at me with piercing, angry eyes. "Your turn."

I didn't care that he'd ordered me to take my top off, but my body was tense, which made it hard to follow through. But I managed. I held his gaze as I dragged the sweater up and pulled it off, tousling my long, wavy hair.

This action surprised him. Maybe he thought he'd called my bluff, or I'd be shy, but no. I didn't want him, but I wanted *this*.

Heat flared in his eyes, and a muscle along his jaw ticked as his gaze traced over my newly bare skin. The gray bra was demi cut, so my breasts threatened to spill over the cups, and I would've sworn I'd seen him fight off a wave of desire like I'd just done. He didn't want to like the way I looked either.

Wow, something in common.

The room was warm, and it was getting harder to find air to breathe the longer we stared at each other. I didn't want him to come closer or put his hands on me because I didn't know what would happen.

What if I liked it?

I needed to stay in control of myself and the situation.

It was the only thing I could think of, and so my hands were unsteady as I undid the clasp at the back of my bra. Colin took a step forward, like he'd wanted to be the one to do it, but he was too late. The band went slack, the cups fell away, and the straps slid down my arms until the bra dropped to the carpet.

He froze, and his lips parted.

Had the sight of me topless short-circuited his brain? He'd seen dozens of girls naked before, I was sure, so it was kind of flattering to draw this response from him. Blood whooshed loudly in my head as his gaze caressed every inch of my exposed skin. And when he lifted that heavy gaze to meet mine, goosebumps rose on my arms.

I hoped he had no idea he was seeing something I'd only shown to a few people before tonight. I wanted to be a sexually confident woman like Nina was.

Had she heard my thoughts?

"Tell him to touch you," she prompted in my ear.

"Put your fucking hands on my body," I blurted, and my eyes widened. It had come out so much more aggressive than I'd meant it to, and if the room was a powder keg, my order lit the match.

He charged forward, and I swallowed a breath as one of his hands grasped my waist and the other cupped my breast. An anxious sigh slipped out of me at his touch, and it was so distracting, I only turned my head at the last second to avoid his incoming kiss.

"No kissing on the lips," I said breathlessly.

Colin stilled but didn't break contact, which meant my breast was still cupped in his firm hand. He was several inches taller than I was, and as he loomed over me, confusion flooded his face. It was quickly replaced by another emotion— one that looked like irritation.

He wasn't happy about this rule.

Why was that?

"Not on the lips?" His tone was dark. "Fine by me."

Although it seemed like a lie. He dropped his head into the crook of my neck, nuzzling his face in so he could suck on the sensitive skin below my ear. And as he did that, his hand moved so he could pinch my nipple between his thumb and the side of his palm.

Electricity zipped through me and threatened to make my legs go boneless, so I had no choice but to steady myself by putting my hands on his broad shoulders. His skin was warm and soft, but the mouth attached to my neck was hot and urgent.

It was crazy, what I was doing, and who I was doing it with, and worst of all, how good it felt.

My eyes grew heavy, wanting to close so I could block him out and focus better on the sensations he caused. But he was sucking so hard, an alarm sounded in my head. If he kept doing that, this asshole was going to leave a mark.

Yeah? Two can play that game.

I coursed my nails down the perfect landscape of his chest, giving him just enough pressure to leave track marks and know I was serious. His mouth finally relented so he could issue a hiss of discomfort, and his warm breath rolled down over my breasts.

My eyebrow arched as I peered up at him. I'd won that battle, hadn't I?

Except the hand on my waist moved down to grab a handful of my ass and squeezed hard enough it forced me forward into him. My nipples had tightened into hard points, and when they brushed against his bare chest, it sent another bolt of unwanted electricity through me.

He smirked like he knew.

Competing thoughts swam in my head. I hated this guy, right? He was a cocky jerk who I intended to take down a peg or two. But why did I like how he manhandled me? He palmed my breast as if he knew exactly how rough I wanted it, and I despised that he was right.

I needed to regain some of the power, so I wedged my hand between our bodies and stroked my palm over the fly of his jeans. The grunt of satisfaction he gave was begrudging, and I nearly laughed. He was already hard, and again, I found it kind of flattering. We were only doing PG-13 stuff.

"Her pants need to come off first," Nina said.

I could tell it was just as weird for him as it was for me to have these voices in our ears, because a jarring look flitted through his expression. Then Colin turned us and gave me a soft shove backward. It caused me to take a seat on the bed, and I only got a chance to glare up at him before he was pushing me down onto my back, climbing on the bed beside me.

Oh.

I sucked in a slow breath as his damp mouth started at my collarbone and dropped a line of kisses down my chest. His lips traipsed over my skin, inching toward one of my nipples. His mouth circled endlessly, but never going where I wanted it most.

A strange thought hit me then. By denying him the chance to kiss me on the lips, he planned to make me pay for it in other ways.

His teasing kisses got the best of me, and without thought, I arched and shifted. His hot mouth finally captured my nipple and sucked, pulling a whisper-quiet moan from me.

His pleased chuckle was a victory call, and that was when I realized I'd lost this battle. But I was determined to win the war. I threaded my hands in his hair and used my grip to control him when he tried to stray.

It only worked for so long, because when his fingers

began to work the snap of my jeans, I went short of breath and the muscles in my stomach began to quiver. It was one thing to be topless, but my panties were tiny, and I was about to be essentially naked.

I sank my teeth into my bottom lip as he dropped my zipper. I'd thought he'd pull my jeans down, but instead he slipped a hand under the waistband of my panties. Down his fingers inched, burrowing deep inside my pants until—

The pads of his fingers against my clit were shocking.

So shocking, I wrapped my hands around his thick bicep in response. Not as a signal for him to stop, but to have something to hold on to. His simple, light touch sent acute pleasure rocketing through my body.

"You're so wet." Colin's tone was wicked and patronizing. "Why are you so wet?"

My face warmed. "Why are you already hard?" I fired back.

He flashed a lazy grin, and it set off another alarm inside me. His smile, especially when it was genuine, was dangerous. It disarmed and clouded my thoughts, and for a split second, I forgot why I disliked him so much.

His fingers moved inside my panties, rubbing against me, and I couldn't help but bow up off the bed.

"Fuck," I groaned under my breath.

The way his eyes studied me. As if he hadn't expected I'd like the way he touched me. He stroked again, gathering another data point, verifying the same result. And as if that wasn't enough, his mouth latched back onto my breast, so his tongue could swirl over my nipple while his fingers spun slow circles on my clit.

I tightened my hold on his arm, and in response, his muscles flexed.

"We want to see exactly what you're doing to her," Scott said.

Because my pants were in the camera's way.

Colin withdrew from me, climbed off the bed, and hooked his fingers under the sides of my undone jeans, but then he paused. My heart skipped as he glanced up at me. Was . . . was he checking to make sure I was okay with this?

Beneath him, I moved. I straightened my legs, so they were hanging off the end of the bed, and toed off one of my shoes. It landed with a loud thump, and this was the signal he needed to begin peeling the denim down my legs.

I toed off my other shoe while he worked, and when he got my jeans down to my ankles, he pulled them off one leg at a time, tugging my socks off along with them. He'd been so focused on his task, it didn't seem like he'd really looked at me while he'd done it.

Now, he stood at the foot of the bed and drank me in with bottomless eyes, and my mouth went dry. In the back of my mind, I should have been concerned about the camera. Whatever I was showing him, I was showing to Nina and Scott and eventually their viewers too, but I couldn't think about that.

Just the boy who stared down at my nearly nude body like he hated the gray scrap of fabric and lace that hid the last part of me from him. Shit, it was intoxicating. The longer I felt his eyes on me, the more lust-drunk I became.

"Put your tits in your hands, Madison. Push them together." Nina's voice was tight. Was she turned on watching us?

I swallowed thickly and slid my hands along my stomach, up until I could grab a handful of each breast and hold them together. As I did it, I kept my gaze locked with Colin's unwavering one, so I saw every ounce of desire my sexy action caused. His eyes lidded and his lips moved ever so slightly as he mouthed a single word.

Fuck.

If I divorced my mind from who he was, he looked like something out of a fantasy. His chest and arms were perfectly sculpted, and I was sure his toned muscles continued beneath the underwear peeking out the top of his jeans. His brown hair was messy from when I'd had my hands in it, but that just added to the appeal of him.

I'd thought his smile was dangerous, but maybe it was his lips specifically. They were full and expressive, and when his tongue swiped over his top one, I strangled back a noise of surprise.

His expression was hungry, and the provocative way he licked his lips announced what he was thinking about doing.

I scrambled up onto my arms, and my heart banged along at a furious tempo when he dropped to his knees. A small part of me was terrified of what he was about to do, and a much larger part verged on begging for it. Those lips were going to start another battle I was sure I was going to lose.

And you'll probably love it.

He urged my knees apart then moved into the space that created, leaning over to drop featherlight kisses across my heaving chest. As his mouth inched down, it drew a wayward path toward the juncture of my legs.

The lights were warm and the cameras' lenses on us

were hotter still, but nothing compared to his mouth working across my trembling skin. I was probably shiny with sweat and needed to touch up my makeup, but despite the heat, I shivered.

I pressed my lips together and didn't make a sound when his kiss landed on the lace covering the most intimate part of me, and he didn't like my silence. His gaze flicked to mine, and the thought was loud in his eyes. *Oh, yeah? How about this?*

He hooked a finger in the side of my panties, pulled them aside, and set his mouth on me.

I melted back onto the bed, letting out a sigh. Even this wasn't enough of a response. He didn't seem satisfied until his tongue brushed over my clit and a moan tore from my throat.

"Can you move a little to the side, Colin?" Scott said. "There's too much shadow."

The flooring creaked as he shifted on his knees, settling into a new position, and I flinched when he put a hand on the inside of my thigh. It was so he could push my leg back and open me more to both him and the camera.

"Yes, good."

This time, his tongue wasn't tentative. He slicked it across my sensitive skin, teasing my clit. Pleasure burst through my center, radiating out to my limbs. Holy fuck, it felt so good.

I balled the sheets beneath me and squirmed under the power of his skilled mouth. His tongue was relentless. It lapped at me, creating fireworks of bliss, and a tremble graduated up my legs. How was I supposed to hate him when he made me feel this way? It was impossible.

He paused only long enough to fist the front of my panties and drag them down. The straps tangled with my feet as they went, and as soon as they were gone, he shoved my legs back so he could resume going down on me.

"Try to point your toes, Madison," Nina's voice instructed.

Everything was spinning, racing.

I did what she asked, then gasped for air, tipped my head back, and slammed my eyes shut. I'd made the decision to fuck him, but I hadn't thought it all the way through. Every orgasm was supposed to be real, but wasn't letting him give me one . . . some sort of surrender?

I didn't want to give *anything* to him.

But—shit—his tongue fluttered, and it made me writhe so much, I probably looked like I was being burned up from the inside. It felt a little like that, too. Every stroke was incendiary.

He had one hand resting on the inside of my thigh, but the other glided up until he could grasp one of my breasts. My traitorous body arched into his touch, encouraging him, and he made a sound that was either satisfaction or to gloat, or possibly both.

I opened my eyes and lifted my head, which— huge mistake.

It meant I could see his deep eyes watching me as his tongue flicked across my pink skin and see how much he was enjoying himself. Was this how he would be if cameras weren't rolling? Or was he a different person, playing a part tonight?

On some level, I'd understand if that were the case. I

felt like a different person, but I wasn't acting. Maybe this was the uninhibited girl I truly was, but had always been too scared to let anyone see.

It was shocking watching him fuck me with his mouth, and so hot I couldn't look directly at him. My gaze drifted away, snagging on movement above, which was an even bigger mistake, because I saw the shape of us on the TV.

There I was at the foot of the bed, him kneeling with his head in between my legs and his hands on my naked body. My gaze bounced from one box onscreen to another, seeing us from all the different angles. Overhead. From the side. One that was focused on exactly how Colin's tongue moved and licked.

As much as I hated it, it was undeniable how good we looked together.

My pulse rushed at breakneck speed while the tip of his tongue massaged my swollen clit. The moan it wrung from me—I didn't know I was capable of making such an erotic sound.

I needed to slow him down.

It was embarrassing how quickly he'd turned me on and primed my body for an explosion. My hands dove into his hair, urging him to shift position. He'd probably think I was helping, trying to guide him to just the right spot to send me over the edge, when I was secretly doing the opposite.

I was fine with it feeling good, as long as it didn't feel *too* good.

Did he know what I was up to? No matter how firm I was with my grip on his hair, he resisted. His mouth nuzzled in, his lips closed around my clit, and he sucked.

"Shit," I groaned, both with pleasure and frustration.

Besides fighting him, I had to fight my body too. I bucked, and my hips canted, trying to make it easier for him. He dragged his hands over my skin like he couldn't get enough of touching me. Up and down they moved, stroking over my legs, my stomach, my breasts.

I was coming unhinged.

Losing ground to him every second. We'd been competitors once before, and I couldn't tolerate being defeated a second time.

So, I jerked his head back away from me, and used the most forceful voice I possessed. "I want to suck your cock."

The strange thing was it wasn't a lie. There was power in having him in my mouth, under my control. I was eager to see if I could make him moan like he'd done to me.

His expression hung with surprise. My filthy statement caught him off guard, and I needed to capitalize on that. I launched up off the bed, urging him to stand along with me, and although pleasure was still ricocheting through my body, my legs were solid enough that I barely swayed once I was upright.

Colin rose to his feet and didn't stop me when my hands hurried to the fly of his jeans, but he also seemed pissed. He'd wanted to make me orgasm, and I'd disrupted his plan.

But he was adaptable. As I struggled to get his pants undone, he stepped forward, forcing me to move backward. He moved so quickly that when my back hit the wall, the end table beside us jolted.

If I wasn't so distracted, maybe I would have been impressed at how well he'd maneuvered us to this spot. The side table was next to us, the condom perfectly in reach. But I was too focused on getting his zipper down, and then nudging both his underwear and his jeans down over his notched hips.

"Turn. Back against the wall, Colin," Scott said.

I heard the tight breath he took. The frat boy didn't love taking orders from someone else, but he complied. He spun us in place, and as I shoved at his pants, Colin's back thudded against the wall.

I'd hoped his jeans would sag down his legs, but they were hung on his erection. I bent a knee and jerked his pants down, setting his dick free.

"Nice." I could hear the smile in Nina's voice.

I stilled, blinking at his nakedness. Then my glare shot up to him.

"Oh, *fuck you*," I groaned.

SEVEN

Madison

Life was unfair, so *of course* Colin had a big dick. I should have expected it since he was auditioning for porn, but it pissed me off anyway. Wasn't he blessed enough with good looks and a trust fund?

You don't know if he comes from money.

But I assumed he did, since all the other Sigs acted like privileged little rich boys. Some I knew for a fact were wealthy. Riley definitely was. The fieldhouse on campus was branded with his family's name. And, hell, Jack's family owned not one, but two vacation homes.

When I cursed at Colin, an enormous smirk tilted on his lips and his eyes flooded with pride.

"That's all for you, baby," he teased, overly dramatic.

I wanted to wipe the smirk off his lips, so I wrapped my fingers around his dick and squeezed—hard. The playfulness drained from his face, and he visibly went through a range of emotions in a single breath. Pleasure at my touch. Confusion about the pressure. Then alarm that my grip was too tight.

I'd only done it as a warning, not to cause pain, and visible relief washed across his face as I relaxed my grip. His expression shifted once again to one of need as I slid my fist down and back up the length of him in one long, painstakingly slow stroke. It was nice the way his chest lifted with a heavy breath, and I liked how he stared down at me with a plea edging his eyes. But I wasn't sure what he was asking for.

That I be gentle? More firm? Go faster?

Or that I make good on my promise of going down on him?

I settled on my knees, getting comfortable for my task. His dick was thick and impossibly hard, and when I licked my lips to wet them, he throbbed inside my grasp. Fuck, it was hot.

Almost as hot as he was.

I ringed my fingers around his base and held him steady while I teased my indecent kiss like I was some kind of seductress. I dragged the soft tip of him across my lips, taunted him with a hint of tongue, and all the while I stared up at him with an evil smile.

He leaned against the wall for support and let out a loud sigh when I opened my mouth wider and slid down. Shit, he was big. I had to work my mouth side to side to take him deeper. When I caressed him with the flat of my tongue, I enjoyed the way the muscles in his powerful thighs tensed.

Oh, he liked this. He liked this a lot, even if he didn't like the girl who was doing it to him.

Welcome to the club.

Colin's breath went uneven when I began to move, pumping my mouth back and forth on him at a steady pace. It took no time for his dick to be coated with my saliva, or for my jaw to grow tired of being held open so wide, but I kept at it.

What would happen if I made him come? It wouldn't be my fault, and it might make him look like he didn't have good self-control. Plus, then it was likely I wouldn't have to sleep with him.

A voice inside me protested loudly at that idea.

Damn it. I could tell myself I didn't want him, but it would be a lie.

At least I didn't need to make it easy on him. I moved my fist in time with my mouth, twisting my grip over his slippery skin as I sucked. My other hand coasted up his thigh, moving up to cradle his balls and massage.

My action pulled a heavy groan of satisfaction from Colin, and my gaze snapped up to watch him. He raked a hand through his disheveled brown hair, which showed off his toned bicep, and then he closed his eyes and tipped his head back. It hit the wall with a dull thud, and I wasn't prepared for how fucking erotic he looked.

A muscle low in my belly clenched.

I squeezed against it, giving myself pleasure, and it swelled when he opened his eyes and looked down at me. At first his gaze was hazy and unfocused, but as he locked on to me, it sharpened and grew intense.

I slowed, frozen under his spell. The connection between us was suddenly so powerful, it was terrifying. It was just the two of us in that moment. No other people or cameras.

The world faded out.

So, when Scott's voice came through our earpieces, we both flinched. "Can you hold her hair back?"

I backed off Colin and held still while he leaned forward and gently brushed his fingers across my cheekbones. His touch was . . . nice. And disorienting. He gathered up the strands of my hair, using both hands to hold it back in a loose ponytail. The problem was now his hands were at the back of my head, and he had the opportunity to steal control away from me.

The moment I welcomed him back in my mouth, he took over, sawing his dick in and out at the pace he wanted. I wasn't fucking him—he was fucking me. I placed my hands on the center of his thighs to brace myself, fully expecting him to hammer away or push too deep.

But he didn't.

He moved at an even, measured pace I could handle, and . . . it was sexy. The flex of his lower body as he advanced and retreated in a sensual rhythm was seriously hot. It made me want the jeans puddling around his calves gone. He should be as naked as I was.

Did he have the same thought? I'd just begun to pull at his jeans when he shifted, bringing his feet together. It allowed him to step out of his shoes, and then the curtain of my hair fell from his grasp as I was eased back. He bent and shoved everything off his legs until he was naked. His socks, jeans, boxers, and shoes were a pile he kicked away before refocusing on me.

This time, his hands weren't as gentle when he scooped up my hair and fisted it behind my head. There was more force and urgency as he guided my face forward, urging me to fit my mouth around his hard, damp cock.

It felt wrong to like how he was kind of rough, but heat pooled inside me anyway. Lust had been a dull throb when we'd started, but now its pulsing was relentless. My need had become dire.

"I'm going to make you come on this cock." His tone was dark, a sinful growl.

I pulled back, panting for air. My mouth dripped with a saliva trail, and my eyes burned up at him, making his grip tighten in my hair.

"Yeah?" I matched his aggression. "Then fucking do it already."

His eyes widened at my challenge, and the muscle running along his jaw flexed. Whatever thought was going on behind his eyes, it looked sinister and exciting. I'd had sweet and romantic sex with people I cared about. Tonight, I craved the opposite, and he looked happy to oblige.

Abruptly, Colin jammed his hands under my arms and yanked me up. I scrambled onto my feet, dizzy with how quickly he forced me to move and how out of breath I'd become. I didn't see him swipe the condom up off the table so much as I heard it, because he turned me to face the wall. The foil wrapper crinkled in his hand before it was torn open and fluttered to the floor by my feet.

A gasp tore from my lungs when he dropped down behind me, put a hand on my ass, and used it to peel me open, burying his face between my cheeks.

His kiss was shocking.

"*Jesus,*" I cried.

No one had *ever* done that to me. His mouth was lush and wicked as his tongue probed, and wires crossed in my brain. I liked the sensation, but my mind was . . . less convinced. It was so dirty. Wrong. And it made my legs tremble from how much it turned me on. I slumped over, placing my hands up on the wall to keep myself from going face-first into it.

But before I could decide if I wanted him to keep doing it, his tongue slipped down. It slicked over my clit, giving me a different, more familiar hit of pleasure. I closed my eyes, savoring the way he fluttered back and forth over the sensitive bud of flesh, and it was so enjoyable, it barely registered that he was putting the condom on.

Before I'd arrived at the studio, this was the moment I was most nervous about. I'd only had a few partners before, and I wasn't sure that when the time came I'd be able to let a total stranger fuck me.

But even though I disliked him, Colin wasn't exactly a stranger.

And now that we were here—*shit*—I was so ready.

The fact that the cameras were rolling only made it sexier. Except I was physically struggling with overload. Tremors rattled up my legs, making my whole body shake.

As he set one hand on my hip, he used the other to rub the tip of his latex-sheathed dick against my pussy. Maybe it was to tease, or maybe it was to demonstrate he was safe and ready.

Or maybe it was a warning.

I leaned over farther, setting my forearms against the wall so I could clench my hands into fists. The hope was if I tensed every muscle in my body, it'd make the shaking less pronounced—and I'd do anything to stop it.

His chest was abruptly warm against my back as he leaned in over me, and it brought his mouth near my ear. "You okay?" he whispered.

His concern only made me tremble harder, but it was with desire and not fear. "Yes," I breathed.

He hesitated, unsure. Like he didn't believe me.

I swallowed thickly and poured everything I had into

sounding powerful. "Give it to me."

I felt him solidify and then straighten. I hoped at least part of him wanted this as badly as I did. His hand on my waist clenched tighter as he sucked in a preparing breath, lined our bodies up, and slowly began to press inside.

The uncomfortable, pleasurable stretch of him made my mouth round into a silent *oh*. It was shocking how good it felt. As he pushed himself deeper, my toes tried to curl on the carpet. My head hung, coming to rest against one of my forearms.

He shoved a hand in the hair at the back of my head and tugged, forcing my upper body to arch back toward him. It was a question, but it came like a demand. "This is what you wanted?"

"Yes," I gasped. There was no other answer.

His dick just went on and on *and on* as he continued to invade. And once it seemed like he couldn't go any deeper, he stopped moving completely. Time suspended, drawing the single moment out until it was a decade long.

He said it like he was annoyed. "Fuck, you're tight."

Was that a compliment? My internal muscles clenched in response, strangling him inside me, and his breath came out in a hiss, as if his teeth were clenched. Not that I could see. All that was in front of me was my hands splayed out on the bare white wall.

Irrational fear bubbled inside me that we'd be stuck forever like this, connected, him lodged inside me. I rocked my hips forward, all the way until only the tip of him was still inside, then pushed back down on his cock.

My vision blurred from the pleasure. He was so deep and

hard, and lust demanded I do it again. This time, I moved faster, undulating on him, and I no longer cared about stifling back my moans.

It felt too good to think about anything else.

His hand on my hip clenched down hard enough it became uncomfortable. He wanted me to stop, or at least slow down, but I was enjoying the experience too much. It wasn't just how amazing it felt physically, but that I was in charge. It was empowering, and I loved using him like—

My hair was no longer taut in his grip, and the sudden smack of his palm against my ass jolted me from my stupor. This spanking hadn't hurt. All it'd done was get my attention and force me to pause.

His tone was shockingly dark. "You'll get your turn to fuck me, but right now . . . I get to *fuck you.*"

My mouth dropped open, and an inferno of anger swelled at what he implied. Maybe I should have been grateful for the reminder he hated me, because for a second there, I'd forgotten how much I disliked him.

He mistook my silence for agreement. Both of his hands gripped my waist, and then he made good on his threat. He drove into me, quickly building to a punishing rhythm that had our bodies slapping together.

I had to brace my hands against the wall to keep from banging into it, but dear God. The way he thrust his hips, pistoning his dick inside me, made my eyes want to roll back in my head. All my nerve endings were on fire, tingling with pleasure.

"Madison," came Nina's voice, "put your hair over your right shoulder and look left so we can see your face."

I lifted a hand off the wall for a microsecond, flinging my hair over my shoulder and turned my head the opposite way. I had no idea what expression was on my face. Desire? Satisfaction?

The trembling was back. It snaked up my legs, trying to pull me down and making it hard to stand with the violent way Colin beat his hips against my ass. But somehow, I managed to stay on my feet. He always had one hand on my waist to keep us steady during his blistering tempo, but his other hand wandered. It glided up over my spine, around to my front, cupping one of my breasts that swung from the rhythmic force of what we were doing.

His pinch on my nipple was white-hot and poured more bliss into me. Blood roared in my ears, drowning out the sound of my moans and cries of pleasure. He'd found the perfect angle, hitting exactly the right spot to make me climb toward orgasm.

Panic washed through me.

I'd never come from penetration alone, and I did *not* want him to claim that victory. He didn't deserve it, or ownership of my orgasm. My eyes closed and eyebrows pulled together in concentration as I attempted to hold back the rush he was building me toward.

Don't do it. Don't let him win.

I knew it was a losing battle, but I fought anyway. My breast had only been a stop along his hand's journey, and he continued up until he could wrap that hand loosely around my throat and urge me back into him. The flat of his chest, sticky with sweat, pressed against my shoulder blades.

The exertion was taking its toll on him. His labored

breath was punctuated with groans of enjoyment, and I could feel the rapid rise and fall of his chest. He wanted me to come, and perhaps he was confused about why it hadn't happened yet.

Outlasting him wasn't a reality. I had to come up with some other plan.

So, even though I couldn't really afford to take a hand off the wall, because I was using both for support, I did it anyway. As his hot breath filled my ear, I reached down, put my fingertips right above where we were joined, and began to rub.

Touching myself bumped my trembling up another notch, but it was so fucking worth it because it felt amazing. I rubbed my clit faster, matching the pace of his body plunging into mine, and the orgasm that had drawn close was suddenly right on top of me.

Just a few more seconds, and I'd be the one to bring myself to orgasm, not him. At most, he could claim an assist.

Except Colin's hand fell away from my throat and dropped down to the hand I used to touch myself. His fingers wrapped around mine, shoved my hand away, and then he resumed what I'd been doing.

No, my head gasped. *Yes,* my body cried.

"That's my cock inside you," he said, "and my fingers touching you." His tone was loaded with seduction, but also power. "*I'm* the one getting you off."

I'd been too close to stop the orgasm, so when his fingers took over, I had no choice but to surrender.

A pleasure-soaked cry burst from my lips, and an explosion detonated inside my body. It flooded through my limbs in waves of tingling heat, leaving everything pleasurably numb in its wake.

My mind emptied, making space for me to endure the strongest orgasm of my life. It swept through me like a tornado and was just as destructive. Even after it began to recede, the strength of it left me shuddering head to toe.

Worst of all, it stole the last ounce of energy I had to combat my quivering legs.

I hadn't finished recovering, but the uncontrollable shaking was so embarrassing, and without thought, I reached a hand down to try to stop it. I grabbed the back of my spasming thigh while I panted for air, but this was a huge mistake. One hand on the wall and two boneless legs were not enough to keep me upright.

I gasped as I began to collapse. My knees buckled, and I sank toward the floor—

"Whoa," Colin whispered, locking his strong arms around my body and keeping me from falling. "I've got you."

His hold set my mind at war. One side wanted to break free from him, and the other wanted to pull his warm arms tighter around me as I continued to shake wildly. He kept me in his embrace as the last of the orgasm's grip faded, and because I was flattened against him, I could feel how fast his heart was beating inside his chest.

It mirrored my own.

Finally, the trembling began to subside, but I still couldn't stand on my own. What were we going to do now?

He had a plan, and it involved scooping me up in his arms. It was stunning how effortlessly he did it, and I sucked in a sharp breath. This was intimate and sort of romantic. He didn't look at me as he turned, took a few short steps, and leaned over the bed, setting me on top of the sheets. It gave the impression he didn't want to see me staring back at him.

My eyes were wide as he climbed onto the bed and settled on his knees between my parted legs . . . which were still shaking.

God, were they ever going to stop?

It seemed unlikely, because in this position, it allowed me to see everything. I got to watch as satisfaction rolled through his expression when he nudged his cock between my legs and inched inside me. I saw the flex of his muscles in his arms and chest as he put his hands under my hips and lifted my lower body up off the mattress so he could fuck me better.

How was it possible to be so turned on by someone I disliked?

"Arch your back, Madison," Scott instructed. "Reach back and put a hand on the headboard."

When I complied, it made my breasts point toward the ceiling, and they bounced with every demanding thrust Colin made.

"Oh, you two," Nina's voice was warm, "that looks so hot."

I closed my eyes to better picture what she was seeing. How he was on his knees, holding me up at the right angle to pound into me, and how I was arched like a bow. The force of his thrusts and my hand on the headboard made it thump rapidly against the wall.

I tried the best I could to keep up with him, but I was more along for the ride. Everything we'd done against the wall had been about me, but this? This was for him.

Was he getting close?

My hand not braced on the headboard was gripping his

thigh, and the thick muscle beneath my palm tensed. In fact, everything in him seemed to cord and grow tight. His heavy breathing swelled, and his thrusts went rough and erratic.

Abruptly, he let go of my hips and I dropped to the bed. It was so he could use one hand to yank off the condom, and the other to start jerking himself off. I watched with fascination as he pumped his fist over his cock. His chest heaved with enormous breaths, ecstasy twisted on his face, and a moan erupted from his lips.

The shudder of his shoulders as he came was the sexiest thing ever.

I'd never had a guy come on me before. It shot in thick ropes, splattering warmly on my stomach and breasts, spurt after spurt until his fist slowed to a stop. I lay utterly still as he towered over me, squeezing the last drop from the head of his cock to dribble onto my skin.

And when he pushed out a long, recovering breath, he sat back on his heels, rested his hands on my shaky knees, and finally seemed to look at me.

I didn't have a clue what he was thinking about. His eyes were guarded and probably studied me as much as I did him. Sweat beaded on his forehead, and he used the back of his wrist to wipe it away, but his gaze didn't waver from mine. It only grew more intense the longer he looked at me, until I wanted to squirm under the power of it.

He moved then.

His hand slid under my neck and hauled me up, so I was sitting in front of him. I could feel the cold trickle of his cum down my skin, but I didn't do a thing about it. It was because it was clear he was considering something, and if it was what

I feared, I needed to be prepared to stop him.

His hand behind my neck slipped up to cup my cheek, and he swallowed so hard, I saw the bob of his Adam's apple. I stopped breathing when he tilted my head up and leaned down to try to bring our mouths together.

"No," I whispered when he was so close, I could feel the warmth of his breath on my lips.

He halted, frozen in place, and for a long moment he seemed to consider disregarding what I wanted. As if he needed to kiss me so badly, it was killing him not to.

He didn't, though. Colin let out a frustrated sigh and closed his eyes and the distance between us, only he brought our foreheads together and not our lips. His skin pressed to mine, and his thumb brushed against my cheek. It was just like when he'd picked me up and carried me to the bed.

This gesture was intimate and romantic.

I sat like a statue, unsure of what to do, and unsure if I'd made the right choice in refusing to let him kiss me. Maybe he lingered here because he was giving me time to change my mind. His mouth was right there, and it'd take barely any movement at all for me to brush my lips against his.

When that didn't happen, he inhaled a deep breath and rose, planting a gentle kiss on my forehead like he would begrudgingly have to settle for that.

It flipped everything upside down. I'd come here tonight to try new things, new experiences, and he'd done that, all right.

I just hadn't expected him to fuck both my body and my mind so completely.

EIGHT

Colin

My head was a fucking mess after . . . whatever that was.

You mean, the hottest fuck of your life?

Once Scott told me about the wipes in the cabinet, I'd gotten them out and tossed the package at Madison so she could clean up. She'd snatched it off the bed and scrambled away like I was a creep.

I got rid of the condom and pulled my clothes back on, watching her out of the corner of my eye. I'd seen girls freak out before. Sometimes they were embarrassed by how quickly they'd hopped into bed with me, or they became weirdly nervous about being seen naked post-sex. But whatever was going on with her now? It wasn't that.

She struggled to get dressed because she was still rattled. I'd never had someone shake like that, and I would be lying if I said it wasn't a huge turn-on. A nice boost to my ego to know I had that kind of effect on her.

But she came with side effects too.

I was kind of irritated she wouldn't let me kiss her, and a lot annoyed with myself for letting it get under my skin. Why the fuck did I suddenly care about this? Kissing was nice and all, but it wasn't a dealbreaker. It'd never been important before.

Maybe I was only annoyed because she was the first girl

in, like, a decade who'd denied me a stupid kiss. How ridiculous was it that she'd let me stick my dick in her, but my mouth on hers was a hard limit?

Further proof the girl was crazy.

She'd pulled her sweater back in place and glared at me from the other side of the room, acting like I'd done something awful to her, which was bullshit. The sex had been anything *but* awful.

I opened my mouth to tell her so, but thankfully Scott pulled the door back and stepped into the room, saving me from speaking without thinking.

"Well, that was . . . interesting," he said.

His wife followed him, and her expression said he didn't know what he was talking about.

"It was different, but that's not a bad thing." She combed her fingers through her blonde hair. "I thought it was fucking hot."

I wasn't shy, but it was weird to stand in front of them only minutes after I'd come, knowing they'd watched the whole thing, and then get feedback. At least it was positive, which was a good sign.

"Scott and I've discussed it, and we think I should give you a tour of the house, explain how we operate, and see if you're interested in joining us." Nina's gaze swung from me to Madison. "Unless you'd like another minute?"

Madison's shoulders straightened, attempting to look unaffected, but her voice wasn't as powerful as it'd been earlier tonight. "Nope. That sounds great."

Nina's attention shifted back to me, and I lifted my chin. "Yeah. I'm ready."

Scott stayed in the office area to work on editing while his wife became our tour guide. We went back out to the garage, and our feet thudded up the wooden stairs to the door at the top of the landing.

It led us into a small hallway that was like a mudroom, and then we turned left into a fancy, high-end kitchen. Everything was modern and white, with stainless steel appliances including a gas stove with a shit-ton of burners.

"Kitchen," Nina said, even though it was obvious. She strolled to the commercial-sized fridge and pulled one of the doors open. "Everyone labels their stuff, otherwise it's fair game."

Sure enough, there were names scrawled on items and colored rubber bands stretched around the drinks inside.

"If you want a mini fridge in your room, that's no problem. Jaquan has one."

She gestured toward the doorway, signaling where we were going next, which turned out to be the living room. It was just as nice as the kitchen. Sleek furniture with oversized artwork on the walls and expensive lamps decorated the space. Even though the room was classy, it was also inviting. It'd be easy to see myself chilling on the couch in here.

And it was a long way from the common room back at the Sig house, which had duct tape holding the stuffing in on most of the furniture.

Nina's tour showed us more of the main floor, including the home office, dining room, and the door to her and Scott's bedroom, before we doubled back through the kitchen and into the hallway.

This time we went right, which took us into the space

over the garage. Which was . . . another hallway?

There were two doors on the left wall, and straight back I could see the open door to a spacious bathroom. Nina grabbed the doorknob to the first door, turned, and pushed it open. "This would be yours, Colin."

She snapped the light on, revealing a long, narrow bedroom. It had a queen-sized bed in the corner, a short dresser, and a tall one for hanging clothes. There wasn't a closet, and it was then that the awkward hallways started to make more sense. The space over the garage had probably been built as one large bonus room but then divided into two smaller bedrooms.

It was still larger and nicer than the closet-for-a-bedroom I'd been living in at Sigma Phi Alpha. Nina showed us the bathroom I'd share with Jaquan, which was also a big step up from my current living situation.

It seemed like a pretty sweet deal until Nina took us upstairs and showed us the room that could be Madison's. It was a true bedroom with a walk-in closet and a Jack-and-Jill bathroom she'd share with the other girl who lived on this floor.

I hadn't meant to make a disappointed face, but Nina saw it and gave me a knowing smile. "It seems unfair, but sometimes we use the girls' rooms for filming, and girls take better care of their space. Plus, the girls have to do hair and makeup, so they get their own bathroom."

That was fair.

There was another room on the second floor, which they used for storage. The bedroom was full of lighting equipment, spare furniture, backdrops, and props, but we didn't linger.

"This tour doesn't include the back yard, which has a pool and hot tub," she said as we came back down the stairs. "Plus, we have a small pool house that we use as our fitness center."

Then she announced the tour was complete, took us back into the dining room, and told us to have a seat.

"Can I get you something to drink?" she asked.

"I'll take some water," Madison said.

"Same for me." I put my hand on the back of one of the chairs, pulled it out, and sat.

Nina headed off into the kitchen, and for a split-second Madison looked totally abandoned. Then she focused on which chair to take since I'd already claimed mine. I watched strategy roll through her, and I wasn't the least bit surprised when she went to the other side of the long table and picked the seat directly across from me.

I wanted to tell her this was her fault.

To remind her we were both looking for new housing because of her.

But I didn't say anything. I was worried if I spoke, something completely different might fall out of my mouth, maybe about how fucking hot the sex had been with her.

Her gaze worked around the room, purposefully avoiding me as we waited in silence for Nina to return. It was tense and awkward as hell.

It's going to be like this every day.

"You can't live here," I said.

Her focus snapped to me, and her eyes narrowed. "Why's that?"

"Because I'm going to live here."

Her expression turned dark. "You can deal with it or find

somewhere else to go."

But there wasn't anywhere else. I didn't have the money to afford my own place, and I couldn't crash on a friend's couch until the end of the semester without my parents finding out. Nearly all of my friends were Sigs, too.

Nina returned from the kitchen with two glasses of water and a set of black folders tucked under her arm. She plunked Madison's glass down first, followed by one of the folders, before doing the same for me.

"Go ahead and open them." She sank down into the chair at the head of the table.

I flipped it open and pulled out the papers. It was another contract, only this one was much longer than the one I'd signed earlier tonight.

"These are your offer letters," she said. "The figure at the left is the rent amount, and the one on the right is what we pay for content. If you do four videos a month, you'll cover rent." She put her hands on the table and laced her fingers together. "There's no requirement or limit on how much work you can do. If you want to do more and earn extra money, great. If you want to do less than one video a week, you'll need to cover the difference."

"How long do they need to be?" Madison asked.

"It depends on the performance. Solo scenes are like ten minutes. Ones with a partner can be as short as twenty. It could be as quick as a handjob or maybe a blowjob, but it could also be longer than an hour. It's whatever the content calls for. We also have 'story' scenes, which have plot and staging, and usually involve multiple people." Nina shot a sexy smile toward the girl across from me. "We can check that threesome box you were interested in, Madison."

Madison's gaze dropped, and as she stared at the contract on the table in front of her, she blinked rapidly, trying to cover her embarrassment.

"Two guys and a girl?" I couldn't stop myself; I was dying to know. "Or two girls and a guy?"

She sucked in a breath, rolled her shoulders back, and leveled a defiant gaze at me. "Both."

Her expression screamed she wasn't going to be shamed by me, but that hadn't been my intent. I'd only been curious. And I needed to stop underestimating her. Her gaze was searing and impressive, making me wonder if she'd been forged by fire.

Nina motioned toward the contracts in front of us. "There's no requirement on the number of videos, but we do expect variety. You can't turn in only solos, for example. Petal Productions is less than a year old, so we're still growing our library. But we'll help you come up with ideas for different content. The house meets every Monday night at nine, where we pitch ideas and set the schedule for the week."

She paused, maybe to give us a moment to digest the information.

"If it sounds like more of a time commitment than you're looking for, keep in mind we can shoot multiple scenes in one day. You can start with a solo scene, then add in a partner or two."

My mind immediately latched on to the idea of me with Madison and another girl. I'd never found two girls willing to try a threesome before, and although I was straight, I wasn't opposed to sharing a girl with another guy, but it hadn't happened. So like Madison, I wouldn't mind checking the threesome box off my bucket list.

"Do you have any questions so far?"

Madison was going to ask something, but I beat her to it. "How many people are in the house?"

"It's me and Scott, plus Abbie and Jaquan. Occasionally, we have other people come in as guest stars, but we like to have six in the house. We had a performer leave in December and another in February, so we've been looking for a while, and we're anxious to fill those spots." She glanced at Madison. "What did you want to ask?"

She glanced toward me. "That was my question, too."

"Okay. Any other questions before we continue?" When we both shook our heads, she pushed back from the table and stood. "If you accept the offer, you'll need submit to regular STD testing, and birth control is required for all our female performers. You won't have to pay for that. All those costs will be covered by the company."

She strolled to the side table, slid open a drawer, and fished out two pens.

"Once your test results have cleared you, you can perform with anyone in the house without a condom if you both agree. But if you have sex with someone outside of the house, protection is mandatory. You'll need to inform the house, and you or your partner must use a condom until you've re-tested and are cleared."

She placed a pen down beside my open folder, then slid the other across the tabletop to Madison.

"Just so we're all on the same page," Nina's tone was friendly but firm, "everything I've just offered is not negotiable. I've done enough negotiating to last a lifetime, so I'm kind of over it." She straightened. "Questions?"

"If I sign," Madison said, "when could I move in?"

This question thrilled Nina. "Tomorrow." The screen of her smartwatch lit up, and she glanced down at the text message. "Scott needs me for a second. I'll let you look over everything, and I'll be back in a minute."

Her footsteps faded as she went into the kitchen and then the hall.

I picked up the paper and began to read, but movement on the other side of the table grabbed my attention. Madison uncapped her pen, turned to the final page, and scribbled on the signature line.

Was she fucking stupid? It wasn't a race, and this wasn't like calling 'shotgun.' Whoever signed first didn't beat out the other person on who got to move in. "You didn't even read it."

She tossed her pen down on the signed contract, sat back in her chair, and looked indifferent, but I wondered if it was just a mask. "There's no point," she said. "I've come too far, and I don't have anywhere else to go."

Her statement hit me like a slug to the chest.

It was the same for me. So, I picked up my pen, flipped to the last page, and signed.

NINE

Madison

My first night in my new place was better than I expected. The bed was comfortable, the room was quiet, and after I'd finished unpacking, I'd taken a long, *hot* shower.

Abbie, the girl who I shared half of a bathroom with, came over to introduce herself right after I'd brought my suitcase upstairs. She had long, sandy brown hair, bright blue eyes, and a gorgeous heart-shaped face. A tiny silver ring glinted from her nose.

She didn't offer to help—she just assumed I'd need it and followed me down to the front door where Yasmin had unloaded my stuff. My former sister was the only one I knew who had a car, and thankfully I hadn't needed to twist Yasmin's arm too hard to help me shuttle my stuff off campus.

Abbie carried boxes upstairs, then put sheets on my bed and sat on the edge of it, filling me in on how she came to live and work at the house. She was from a small town in Georgia, with big dreams of becoming a singer, and moved to Nashville when she turned eighteen. But that hadn't panned out, so the former beauty pageant winner turned to modeling.

"When that wasn't paying the bills, I became an escort for a while."

She'd said it the same way I would tell people I used to work at Olive Garden, and it was admirable how she'd done it without worrying about how I'd react. Of course, I was in the house now, so she probably felt safe I wasn't going to judge.

"I moved into adult film, did a scene with Scott, and I've been with Petal since the company started." She sat up and tilted a shoulder toward me, striking a provocative pose and her voice turned husky. "That's when Lexi Grey was born." She returned to normal, folding her legs beneath her. "Have you picked a stage name yet?"

I'd been putting clothes on hangers to go in the closet, and my movements slowed. I frowned. "I hadn't thought about that yet."

She gave me a sweet smile. "It's important you pick the right one to reflect your brand. Pick something short and easy to remember. Don't do any quirky spellings though. You want people to be able to search for you in Google."

She was talking like I was going to make a career out of this, but that wasn't my plan. I just wanted to finish my degree. But she was sweet and helpful, and I appreciated it.

"Anyway," she climbed off my bed and traipsed over to me, "I'm looking forward to working together." There was an electricity in her pretty eyes, and she set a hand on my arm. "You're so pretty. We're going to have a lot of fun together."

My pulse jumped at her touch. It was friendly, except there was an undercurrent of sex and the air went thin—but in a good way. She was gorgeous and touching me, and knowing our attraction was mutual was exciting.

Everything here could be exciting.

When I'd packed my things up at the Lambda house, I'd decided I'd leave a few things behind. Shame. Inhibitions. My closed mind. I'd committed to living and working at Petal

Productions, and so I was all in. I'd agreed to throw myself headfirst into the experience.

My voice was soft and uneven. "I'm looking forward to working together, too."

Her smile was wide and sexy.

Once she'd left me to get settled and I'd finished unpacking, I broke down the carboard boxes and carried them down the two sets of stairs into the garage where I assumed the recycling bin would be.

There were voices on the other side of the garage, and I clenched the flattened boxes in my arms tighter as I spied Colin up on a ladder against the wall. There was a black bike nearby, and Scott stood next to it, holding a power drill and an equipment hook in his hands. It matched the set of wall hooks other bikes hung from.

They must have been making space for him to store his bike.

Scott passed the drill to Colin, and I held my breath as I watched him work. The tendons in his forearm and his bicep flexed as he drilled into the wall and the stud behind it. The flash of the memory of him naked was unavoidable and white-hot.

"Hey, Madison." Scott must have noticed me standing there, gawking like a fool. "Can I help you with something?"

Colin's drilling ceased, and he turned to look at me over his shoulder. His eyes were critical and unwelcoming. He didn't want me here.

Yeah? Same to you.

I'd wanted to avoid him, which was naïve to think was possible. I'd already run into him, and I'd been in the house less than three hours.

I swung my gaze away, planting it on Scott, and lifted the boxes I was holding. "Recycling?"

"Yup, over there." He gestured to the back corner under the stairs and the two, tall rolling bins.

One was green and the other blue, and it was obvious which was garbage and which was recycling. Not just because of the color, but several cardboard boxes stuck out of the top of the green one. I added my boxes, shoving them in as best I could.

"Does this go out soon?" I asked. "It's kind of full."

"Yeah, pick up is tomorrow morning."

Wanting to be helpful, I grabbed the handle and pulled it toward the open garage door—

"Wait, it can't go out yet." Scott sounded resigned. "It's not dark yet. If we put the toters out too early, we'll get fined."

I stopped pulling the bin and set it upright. "Fined by who?"

"The homeowners' association." He sighed, loud and long, like this was a major issue. "When we first moved in, it wasn't so bad, but the last year the HOA has gotten out of control."

Colin handed the drill back to Scott, exchanging it for the hook. "Oh, yeah. My friend Preston said the woman running it is a huge pain in the ass, especially for his dad. What's her name?"

"Judy." Scott uttered the word like it tasted awful in his mouth. "It's not as bad for us as some of the other homeowners because we're up at the top of the subdivision. We're not on her radar, and we do everything we can to keep it that way." Abruptly, he turned serious. "Which reminds me, if she comes poking around, you tell her you're part of our mentor program."

"Uh, what?" Colin asked, voicing my thoughts out loud.

"When we did the renovations, she was all up in our business and went off on how the houses are zoned 'single-family' only. We can't list it on Airbnb, and typically we're not allowed to have renters." He unscrewed the head of the drill and pulled the bit out. "The story Judy was told was that Nina and I decided to open our house to a select few college kids who couldn't afford housing. *Good* kids," he said, acting like he was speaking directly to Judy. "Respectful kids who aren't looking to party. Who only want to get their degree."

"And that worked?" Colin asked.

Scott smiled. "We're quiet. Picture perfect neighbors, and as long as we keep the number of adults living here at six or fewer, she can't do anything." His attention swung to me and the green bin. "You can put that back for now. I'll take it out later."

I nodded, and its plastic wheels squeaked as I rolled it back to its spot.

Colin finished screwing the hook into the hole he'd drilled and climbed down off the ladder. He fixed his gaze on me, and irritation seethed in his eyes. "All unpacked in your new room?"

"Yeah." I plastered on an overly sweet smile. "And it's great. So much room in the closet, and plenty of counter space in my bathroom."

His expression soured, and it emphasized the drywall dust that had fallen on him during drilling. Normally I wasn't a bitch, but he rattled me.

I was much too proud of myself, thinking I'd won this round, until he grabbed the hem of his shirt and pulled it up, using it to wipe at his forehead. This revealed his perfectly carved abs, and I sucked in a sharp breath at the sight of them. Why did I remember the way those notched muscles felt in such vivid detail?

He'd heard my gasp and saw the way I gaped at him, and his smirk told me I'd lost this battle too. There was nothing left to do but turn on my heel and hurry up the steps away from him.

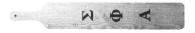

I met my other roommate and coworker Jaquan when I was eating breakfast my first morning in the house. I'd been sitting at one end of the booth in the corner of the kitchen, my attention more on my phone than my bowl of cereal, when he'd strolled in.

Shirtless and beautiful, he'd put two eggs in a skillet before he noticed me, and when he did, he flashed an easy smile. "What's up, Madison?"

"Hi, Jaquan."

He abandoned his eggs and leaned over the kitchen island, resting his strong forearms on the counter while he examined me. His eyes were dark and so expressive, they were mesmerizing. It shouldn't have been surprising that he'd be hot, but it seemed rare in the porn I'd watched that the guy's face was even shown. And if it was? It was unlikely he'd been even moderately attractive.

But Nina had said Petal didn't cater to the straight male

gaze, and this guy? He was proof.

His black hair was short, as was the perfectly maintained beard stretching across his strong jawline. There was a playfulness about him that I instantly responded to, triggering an alarm in my head.

He seemed charming and dangerously good looking, and while I'd agreed to try all sorts of new things while I was at the house—falling for someone I lived with wasn't on my list.

"Abbie was right." His voice was deep and smoky. "You're hot."

My heart skipped. "Yeah, well . . . right back at you."

He chuckled, straightened, and went back to the stove. "Want some eggs?"

"Oh, no, thank you." I motioned toward my cereal. "I'm good."

"Okay." He turned on the burner. "You want to fuck after breakfast?"

I jolted, making my spoon clatter in my bowl. "Excuse me?"

He glanced at the clock on the microwave. "I don't have anything going on for the next couple hours if you want to do a scene together and make some extra cash. We can shoot it hand-held, POV style."

Oh, my God.

I stared at him, unblinking. He was gorgeous and had just offered to have sex with me the same way he'd offered to make me eggs. Was this my life now? It was both thrilling and panic-inducing. For a half-second, I considered whether to take his offer.

When I'd come downstairs, I'd made sure I didn't look like complete garbage, but I didn't have any makeup on. I hadn't washed my hair since yesterday, and I was sure I didn't have a dry shampoo powerful enough to make me feel confident on camera.

Which meant I really needed to shower, and then I'd need to style my hair and do makeup . . .

I hadn't picked my stage name yet, either.

He'd caught me off-guard, completely unprepared for the opportunity.

"Thanks, but, uh,"—I struggled to catch my breath—"raincheck?"

My rejection was no big deal. He stirred his eggs and nodded casually. "Definitely."

When Jaquan finished cooking his breakfast, he sat across from me, and we got to know each other while we ate. He was older than I was. A grad student in his final year in business administration. He was from Atlanta and, like me, had come to Nashville because of Davidson University—their MBA program was excellent.

His face changed abruptly, like a thought had just occurred to him. "Didn't we meet once last year?"

"I don't think so." Surely, I would have remembered him. He was so handsome.

"Professor Yung had that mixer for the people who got into the international program. I swear you were there."

My heart sank. "Oh, you're right." That explained why I didn't remember him. I'd been blindly in love with Jack. "My boyfriend was one of the guys who got accepted."

"Ah. You two still together?"

Disdain flooded through me. "No."

"Good." He set his fork on his plate and sat back in his

seat. "Most guys who say they're okay with their girl doing this?" He pointed back and forth between us. "They find out they find out they have a problem with it, and especially with me."

"Is it even possible to date someone if you're doing this?" I mimicked his gesture, tossing my finger between us.

"Depends on the people." He shrugged. "Nina and Scott did it. But I think it helps when both of them are in the business. Less jealousy that way."

He picked up his plate, and as he walked it to the sink, I tried not to stare at how sculpted his body was. Everyone in the house was so beautiful—and I'd begrudgingly admit that included Colin—so it was hard not to consider myself the weakest link.

I certainly was when it came to experience.

This became painfully clear during the first house meeting Monday night when I kept having to stop the discussion and ask for clarification. Colin snickered when I resorted to raising my hand.

Nina seemed to find it endearing. A huge smile widened on her face. "Yes, Madison?"

"JOI?" I repeated.

"Jerk off instruction. It's where you tell the viewer exactly how you want them to do it. You can even include a countdown and see if the viewer can come at the same time as you."

"Aw," Abbie said in a cutesy tone, beaming at me. "She's so innocent." Her warm expression was genuine and not patronizing. Since she was sitting beside me, she put her arm around my shoulders and her voice dropped low. "Don't worry, Madison. I'll help get you up to speed."

I swallowed a breath. She was so close and smelled really

nice, and her arm lingered around me. The way she was so comfortable and friendly, it made my heart flutter. But just as soon as I began to lean back into her, her arm dropped, and she sat up straight in her seat.

"Oh! We should play that up," she announced. "The innocent thing. Let's say she's in the shower and then I come in and surprise her. She's all, '*Oh, no, I'm a good girl. I could never.*' But then I seduce her."

Everything inside me went tight at the idea of her story really happening. I pictured myself in the glass shower we shared, startled by Abbie's entrance into the room. It would be shocking, and only become more so when she took off her clothes and pulled open the door, stepping in beside me to put her hands on my body.

My mouth had gone dry, probably because all the moisture inside me had migrated down to settle between my thighs.

"I like it," Nina said. "How does that work for you, Madison?"

The room was uncomfortably hot as every pair of eyes turned toward me and I worked hard to find my voice. Not because I didn't want to do it, but because I didn't want anyone to know how turned on I was. "Uh . . . sure. I think we could try—"

"Sorry," she said, interrupting me. "I know this is still new for you, and you haven't done same-sex stuff before. I didn't mean to throw you in the deep end."

"You haven't . . .?" Abbie flattened a hand to her chest, and her lips peeled back into an enormous, bright smile. "Oh, my God. I'd love to be part of your first girl-girl scene."

"Okay," I said.

"Yeah?"

She leaned in and bumped her shoulder against mine, and the intimate gesture made heat bloom across my face.

"We could add on to it for another scene," Scott said. "One of the guys could be the stepbrother who catches his sister and her friend together. Maybe he threatens to tell their parents unless they let him join in on the fun."

My mind added to the fantasy. I imagined my hands sliding over Abbie's soapy skin as the door creaked open and my faux brother stepped inside. His eyes filled with wicked satisfaction as he plotted his blackmail.

There were two options seated at this table who could play that role . . . so why the fuck did my gaze flick to Colin first? He stared back at me, unblinking and utterly still. It was like he wasn't even breathing, and it was impossible to know if he hated the idea . . .

Or if he *loved* it.

But Jaquan spoke first. "Yeah, man. I could have some fun with that."

I felt both disappointment and relief. I hadn't done anything with Abbie or Jaquan yet, but they felt *safer*. The two of them together somehow seemed less explosive than the frat boy who was currently doing a perfect impression of a mannequin.

"Hmm." Nina set her elbow on the table and rested her chin on her palm. "This is Colin and Madison's first week. I know everyone's anxious to partner with someone new, but I don't want to overwhelm them. Plus, they haven't cleared testing yet."

Because my appointment at the clinic was scheduled for

tomorrow morning, and she'd said it'd take a few days before we'd have the results. Her focus drifted over my head and went unfocused as she considered her options.

"Let's keep it simple this week," she announced. "Colin can be the one to scene with Madison and Abbie, and you three stick to just hand stuff or oral. Hold off on the sex until we know everyone's safe and don't have to fuck around with condoms." Her attention settled on Colin. "Is that okay with you?"

His lips parted to form a word, but he hesitated, and his gaze turned my direction. Was he picturing the same thing I was? Abbie stood on one side of him and me on the other, our hands wrapped around his dick, working together to get him off. *Jesus.*

The image made me pinch my knees together.

His eyes turned so intense, I couldn't look away, and for a long moment I had the strangest feeling he was picturing only the two of us in the foggy shower. But he blinked, cleared his eyes, and tore his gaze away.

"Yeah." He nodded. "That's fine."

His plain tone was like he was taking one for the team. As if this were some kind of hardship for him.

I raised an eyebrow as my blood heated. If he thought performing with me was going to be difficult, well . . . that was *fine.* I was happy to prove him right.

TEN

Madison

My imagined scene in the shower with Abbie turned out to be very different from reality, starting with location. I'd pictured it happening in the bathroom we shared, but that wasn't practical for filming.

Instead, Wednesday afternoon after I'd finished my last class for the day, I helped Nina and Scott set up for filming in their spacious bathroom. It was bright and airy, with subtle gray streaks swirling through the floor-to-ceiling tiles in the enormous shower. It was so large, it was its own room.

Enclosed by a tall glass wall, the shower had a modern freestanding tub on one side and a long bench on the other, with the showerhead and drain in the center of the wet area.

The thing was fucking sexy, and I was envious of Nina and Scott for getting to use it whenever they wanted. Although, it currently looked like that wasn't the case. Any shampoos or shower products had been tucked away under the sinks, so the space was clean and bare.

As we set up the lights, cameras, and microphones, Nina explained how to use each one. The hope was down the road I'd be able to do this on my own and turn in high-quality videos ready for upload. She gave me tips on aiming the light, watching out for reflective surfaces, and ideas for staging.

I focused intently on what she was telling me, because if

I didn't, I'd think about Abbie and our scene, and my heart would fall out of rhythm. I was excited, but also nervous. She was so attractive and friendly, but I'd never been with another woman before, and what if I couldn't go through with it?

Nina was chill when I mentioned it. "If you change your mind, no worries. You and Abbie can each film a solo scene in here."

I looked at the large rectangular lights, draped in diffusers to mimic natural light. They weren't that hard to take down, move, and set up somewhere else, but it would still be a pain to have to start over in another location. "It's okay if they're shot in the same place?"

"Sure, but it won't look like the same location to the viewer. Like, let's say your scene is pulled back with you standing under the showerhead. Abbie's could be up close, where she's sitting on the edge of the tub. Those two videos will feel very different." She held up a light meter to test how bright the space was. "Did you pick a name yet?"

I sucked in a breath and lifted my shoulders, hoping to not look or sound foolish. "Yeah, uh," I brushed a lock of hair back behind my ear, "I was thinking Annika Adore."

She considered it thoughtfully. "That works. Any story behind it?"

"My parents almost named me Annika. It was their runner-up choice."

God, I'd struggled to find a name I didn't think was cheesy but also fit the guidelines Abbie had given me. I'd researched other successful adult actresses, and promptly fallen down a rabbit hole of the internet. If I wanted to be good at this, I had a lot to learn.

Once the equipment was all ready to go, Nina sent me upstairs to get ready. I didn't spend much time on my hair because I'd been told to wear it up in a ponytail, and even though the plan was not to get it wet, there was no point in trying to curl or straighten it. The steam of the shower would undo any effort I made.

I went light on my makeup for the same reason, and I was putting on my second coat of waterproof mascara when Abbie ducked her head around the bathroom corner. "Hey, good looking." Her smile was sultry. "You ready to get naughty with me?"

My nerves had formed a sticky lump in my throat, but I swallowed it down. I wanted this. And if I decided I didn't? No big deal, right?

Nina and Scott were waiting for us in their bathroom, and while she was busy reviewing the notes she'd made earlier today, he had the in-ear monitors ready for us.

"Just as a reminder, these are water-resistant," he said, "but not waterproof."

I took the one he offered me and fitted it inside my ear, nodding my understanding. It was then that the hairs on the back of my neck stood up with awareness. My body sensed Colin's arrival before anything else, and I turned to peer at him through the mirror hanging over one of the sinks.

He was barefoot and wore jeans and an oatmeal-colored Henley, which hung perfectly across his frame. I was instantly frustrated at how good he looked, even when he was so casual. I'd spent the last thirty minutes upstairs preparing for the scene, and yet all he'd had to do was throw on clothes.

It was such bullshit that his effortless style was so fucking appealing.

"Hey, Colin." Abbie used the same warm tone she did with everyone, but this felt like a betrayal. He was a jerk, and I didn't want her to like him. And if she had to like him, well, it was important she liked me *better*.

"Hi," he replied. His smile toward her was sexy, and I scowled.

"We didn't talk about it yet. Am I playing the part of the stepsister?" Abbie asked Nina.

The older woman laughed. "No. Trust me. Madison and Colin are born to play the roles of stepsiblings. When they act like they don't like each other, they don't have to do much acting."

Abbie's expression widened with surprise, and she looked to me for confirmation. "You don't like Colin?"

"She doesn't," he said before I could get a word in, "but don't worry. The feeling's mutual."

I sighed. "We're not friends." I repeated the same phrase he'd used the night we'd done our scene together. "But it's not a problem for me."

She looked skeptical, but then Nina began going over the script, silencing whatever questions she wanted to ask.

Thankfully, there weren't lines to memorize. We were given the setup of the scene and the direction our brief conversation would need to go to sell the story. This allowed the dialogue to sound more authentic.

When there was no more discussion and everyone was ready to start filming, Nina, Scott, and Colin exited the bathroom. The husband and wife went downstairs to the office, while Colin remained in their bedroom until it was time to make his entrance.

It meant Abbie and I were alone in the bathroom, and nervous tension began to crawl up my back. She was too busy at first to notice, checking her makeup in the mirror while we waited for a voice to come through our in-ear monitors and tell us to start. Then her gaze met mine through the reflection and she delivered a soft smile.

"Don't be nervous. I'll take good care of you."

I bet you will, a voice inside me cooed, and some of my anxiety dissipated.

The sound quality on the device in my ear wasn't perfect, but I understood Nina well enough when she spoke. "Whenever you're ready, Madison."

Like I did backstage before performing in high school, I filled my lungs with air and pushed it out at a slow, calming pace. I imagined the person I needed to become for the scene and did my best to get into character.

I was creating Annika Adore today. And she could be whoever she fucking wanted to be.

My lips widened into a smile as I looked at Abbie, wordlessly telling her I was about to begin.

"You sure you don't want to take a shower?" I asked. "That was such a hard workout." My tone was bright and upbeat as I wiped at my forehead, pretending it was sweatier than it was. "We have another shower in the guest bathroom if you want to—"

She waved a hand, brushing off my question. "No, I'm okay."

"You don't mind if I take one, right? I just need to rinse off."

The way she tilted her head and her expression changed, it was so perfect. Like her sexy plan wasn't scripted—she was really coming up with it right now, just this very second. Her gaze slid down my body, taking in my form-fitted tank top and tight leggings. "You go right ahead."

I pretended to be oblivious to her sultry voice. "There's lots of stuff in the fridge. Help yourself to whatever you want, and hopefully my asshole stepbrother stays upstairs and doesn't bother you."

Once again, she waved her hand. "He's not that bad."

"Whatever." I made a production out of rolling my eyes. "Anyway, I won't be long."

"Okay." Her voice dipped low and sexy. "See you soon."

She flashed a final smile before turning and striding to the door, which she pulled closed behind her as she left.

It was a strange sensation to be the only person in the bathroom, but knew I wasn't alone.

There was a camera perched over the sink directly across from the shower, angled just left enough so the door to the bedroom was in frame. And there were two more cameras on the other side of the glass shower door. We'd mounted one high in the corner, pointed down at the drain, and the other in the built-in alcove above the bathtub. It'd been tricky placing all the cameras where they wouldn't be in each other's shots, but Scott had figured it out.

I tugged the shower door open and cranked the handle to let the water get warm and felt the camera lenses watching me as I tugged off my tank top.

"Slower," Nina prompted.

A curse word nearly slipped out, because as far as I knew,

there was no sexy way to take off a sports bra. But I did my damnedest to make it a show and not awkward as I peeled it off, followed by my leggings.

"Make sure you toss your clothes out of the frame," Scott said, which I did.

The spacious bathroom was cold, and my nipples hardened into points as I opened the shower door and stuck a hand into the water. Satisfied it was warm enough, I stepped in and moved close to the shower stream, letting it wash over my chest and lower body.

There was a glass barrier, but the shower area was so large, it didn't help much. Cool air circulated around my wet skin, and I immediately had to turn up the temperature to avoid shivering. I had to hope the scene didn't take too long to shoot or we'd run out of hot water.

I choked back a chuckle as the thought flitted through my head. *Imagine if you had to film this at the Lambda house.* The water would have been ice cold in a matter of minutes.

There was an unlabeled bottle of body wash and gray shower poof on the tile bench, and as I'd been instructed, I lathered up and began to wash. The white, foaming suds clung to me in some places and coasted down my slick skin in others.

I hadn't been prepared for how sexy this part of the scene would be. I caressed myself, my hands chasing the bubbles down my stomach and over my thighs as I rinsed off. It was sensual and enjoyable as I performed.

"Make sure you keep your back to the door," Nina said.

I shifted my weight on my feet, turning so I faced the back wall, and continued to slide my hands over my soaked skin.

The water raining down on the tile floor was loud, masking the quiet sounds of Abbie's entrance or how she stripped down while watching me. I genuinely didn't hear any of it until the shower door opened and cold swirled around me, making me spin in place.

There was no need to pretend to be surprised. I was legitimately stunned by the gorgeous woman who stepped into the shower and began to approach me, wearing nothing but a delicious smile. There was a colorful tattoo crawling up the side of one of her thighs, but there were too many other things to look at, stealing my attention.

Her breasts were perfect teardrops, and her dark pink nipples were pierced. Her waist was slender and her hips flared, giving her a classically beautiful hourglass figure.

She was so fucking hot, I could barely stand it. The heat of her made my mind slow, and it took a full second for me to remember how I was supposed to react to her sudden arrival.

I gasped and used my hands as a feeble attempt to shield my nakedness while I backed up, moving until I was flat against the cold tile. "What are you doing in here?"

Her eyes were lidded, heavy with lust. "You told me to help myself to whatever I wanted," she closed in so there was barely any space left between us, "and I've decided I want you."

It took no time for me to lose my breath, and as I stared into her pretty blue eyes, I wondered where the scene ended and reality began. I was playing the part of an inexperienced girl, but it was the truth. She pretended to be a seductress, but I was sure that was *also* true.

If we hadn't shot this scene, would she have tried to

seduce me anyway?

Water sluiced down Abbie's flawless skin, tracing over her curves, and my pulse pounded like a drum in my neck. She was so close, and got closer still when she set one hand on the tile beside my head and the other just outside of my hip, trapping me in.

"Don't you want to play together?" Her voice was like velvet.

"We can't," I whispered.

My protest was bullshit, and a knowing smile spread across her face like wildfire. "Why not?"

"Because my parents might come home and catch us. Because you're my friend." I stared at her mouth, wondering what it would feel like pressed to mine. "And because I've never done anything like this before."

"You're such a good girl," she teased. "Don't you want to be bad?" She lifted her hand off the wall and skimmed her knuckles up and down my bicep. "I could show you how."

Her touch was featherlight, but it sent electricity surging through me. Oh, I wanted to be bad *very much.*

My thought must have been clear by the expression on my face because she looked pleasantly surprised and asked her question in a hush. "Yeah?"

I nodded quickly.

When she grasped my chin between her thumb and forefinger and leaned in, my eyes fell closed. Abbie's kiss was gentle for a single breath, like that was all the restraint she could muster before she unleashed her full power. Her lips pushed against mine, urging me to open my mouth and welcome her tongue, which I did. It slicked against mine, and a pulse throbbed deep between my legs.

I was kissing another woman.

Who was naked.

And her soft, warm body pressed to mine, stealing the last of my breath. Our wet breasts flattened together, letting me feel the silver barbells attached to her hardened nipples.

Jesus.

Her kiss was passionate, but it wasn't romantic. It was sexual and dirty, like she was fucking my mouth with hers, and it was exactly how I wanted it to be. I tried to match her intensity and clasped my hands on her face, holding on.

I was dizzy with lust as her hands began to explore my body. Her sensual touch lit me on fire as her palms coursed over my wet skin, still slippery with soap in some places. Over my arms, my stomach, my hips. She wedged one hand between my body and the wall so she could give my ass a soft squeeze. I followed her lead, trailing my hands down the sexy curve of her back.

But like she'd been with her kiss, her touch was only restrained at first. When she cupped my breasts, my noise of surprise was crushed under her dominating mouth. She gripped me tightly and slipped her leg between mine so she could push the top of her thigh against my pussy.

It was aggressive, and the pressure of it—fuck. It felt so good. I was glad to have the support of the wall at my back, especially as the pulse between my legs swelled to an ache. If that strange tremble I'd had with Colin made an appearance now, I'd need all the help I could get to stay upright.

"Mmm," she said, all throaty. "You've got such great tits."

My head thudded back against the tile as she bent down

and captured one of my nipples in her mouth. The sound of me panting for air bounced off the walls, echoing in the cavernous shower. Her lips were parted, allowing me and the camera above us to see her tongue as it swirled over my flesh.

Goosebumps pebbled across my arms when she dragged a hand down my chest and over my stomach, inching toward my newly bare pussy. Free beauty appointments were another perk of living at the Petal house . . . or maybe punishment, because getting waxed on Monday afternoon had not been an enjoyable experience.

But it was kind of worth it now, because when the pads of Abbie's fingers delved farther down, she was able to feel just how much she turned me on. Pleasure grew as she rubbed my clit, fogging my mind.

I wasn't quivering yet, but I sagged against the wall, making my skin squeal down the tile.

"Do you like that?" she asked in a low voice.

Wasn't the answer obvious? I whimpered my approval.

"Louder, Abbie," Scott said. "We need to hear you over the running water."

She didn't miss a beat as the instruction came through our earpieces. Her voice was stronger. More sinful. "And what about this?"

Two fingers pushed their way inside me, making me bow off the wall. Holy fuck. I clenched my hands on Abbie's hips, holding on to her as she thrust her fingers deeper, all the way to her first set of knuckles.

Her tone dripped with sex and power. "Do you like my fingers inside you, good girl?"

I couldn't find words. All I could do was nod.

She pumped her fingers as I moaned and writhed. Heat filled the shower, surrounding us until I was sure all I was breathing in was steam. We both looked down, watching her hand move rhythmically as she fucked me with two skilled fingers.

My mouth hung open, and she mirrored my satisfaction on her face.

"Move to the bench," Nina instructed.

I was half out of my mind, so I struggled to comprehend the order, but Abbie had us covered. She withdrew her fingers and guided me to sit on the cold tile bench. My gaze instinctively went to the camera directly across from me that was tucked in the alcove—

"Don't look at the camera," Scott said.

I dropped my gaze to the girl who knelt on the floor in front of me. Her hands glided up my parted legs and I swallowed so loudly it was audible. The outer ring of her irises was a navy blue, but the rest was a brilliant sapphire.

"Ask her what she's going to do, Madison." The way Nina sounded, I pictured her with an evil grin. Was she enjoying watching us?

My voice was shakier than I expected it to be. "What are you going to do?"

Abbie exhaled and grinned. "I'm going to kiss you," she ran her thumb through my slit, brushing it over my clit, "right here. Right on this pretty pussy."

I squirmed with excitement, but also because I was so turned on her statement caused pleasure so acute it verged on pain. I sank back in my seat and pressed my lips together, encouraging her.

Offering myself to her.

"Fuck," I breathed as her mouth made contact.

Slow, almost chaste kisses were planted on my sensitive skin just above my clit, and then just below it. She teased, drawing out my anticipation.

The slight quiver that traveled up the insides of my thighs now was so different from the scene I'd done with Colin. Those tremors had shaken my whole body, radiating out from my core, like every cell of me was connected and involved and clamoring for . . .

I wasn't sure. Definitely not him, though. Just *something*.

These little trembles were nothing in comparison. An involuntary response to the loose strands of her hair tickling my sensitized skin.

The last thing I wanted to think about when her lush tongue glanced across my clit was Colin Novak, and yet that was exactly what happened. As she used her mouth on me, I couldn't stop myself from wondering what he was doing right now on the other side of the door. Was he getting himself hard for his upcoming scene?

Was he picturing this, Abbie going down on me?

I should have been horrified at the idea he'd think about me as he jerked off, yet it didn't bother me. I wasn't willing to admit I liked the idea—even if any part of me did.

It wasn't surprising how quickly Abbie ramped up the intensity. While her tongue flicked and fluttered over my clit, she eased those same two fingers back inside me. I widened my legs, giving her more room to work with, and I traced a finger over her hairline to push a wayward strand out of her way.

The ache inside me loved what was happening, but it was also greedy. It hungered for an orgasm, and the need she created was fucking consuming. It threatened to swallow me up, to make me melt into a puddle.

I moaned and clawed at the tile beneath me. She was so good at what she was doing, and she was fulfilling a fantasy I'd had for years, and the camera was watching—

Her mouth lifted away just long enough to ask it. "Are you going to be a good girl and come for me?"

"Oh, my God," I gasped.

Her question doused me in fire, and my body was desperate to please her. My moans grew louder and more frequent as her fingers thrust faster, and faster, and *faster* . . .

The orgasm pulled me up, like floating on the surface during a huge wave. I surrendered to it, letting it carry me away into ecstasy as I shuddered through my climax. My low groan was heavy with satisfaction, and since it was unmistakable what had happened, Abbie's expert tongue ceased.

Holy shit.

Everything was tingling and warm.

She climbed to her feet and leaned over me, crushing her mouth to mine. Her kiss was blistering, and my taste lingered on her lips.

It was dirty.

And so hot.

"See?" she said as I fought to get my breathing back under control. "Wasn't that nice?"

My post-orgasm mind was too hazy to put words together. I simply stared at her and the water falling from the shower behind her, misting both of us faintly.

Finally, she slipped a hand under my elbow and gently helped me stand from the bench. "Come on," she said in a hush, but probably loud enough for the microphones to pick up. "Let's get you cleaned up."

She grabbed the bottle of body wash, squeezed a dollop of it into her palm before passing the bottle to me, and rubbed her hands together. The soap was slicked over my body, her slippery hands gliding everywhere. Her sensual touch was welcomed, and I repeated her action, using my own handfuls of the lightly scented soap to clean her skin.

As we kissed, I pictured us. Our foam-covered bodies pressed together, our hands clinging to each other while we moved under the stream of water. This was the end of the first scene, and I tried to enjoy the quiet moment before the next one would begin.

"Very nice, girls," Scott said. "We can go ahead and move on."

My heartrate had slowed after my orgasm, but it began to climb again.

The last of the soap was rinsed from our bodies, and I pulled in a deep breath when she reached for the shower door.

"Wait," I said, making her hesitate. "You made me feel so good. What if I wanted to return the favor?"

Abbie's eyes lit up, and she was such a convincing actress, I wondered how much of the thrill that shot through her expression was real. She laughed, delighted, and pulled me back toward the bench seat.

"I was hoping you'd ask," she said as she lowered herself to sit on the edge.

I peered down at the sexy woman, who spread her legs for

me, and my heart vaulted over itself. Letting another woman go down on me was only part of my fantasy, and this was the other, much larger one. I longed to try it, to hear a woman moan in pleasure and know I was the one who caused it.

My lungs were tight as I folded a leg beneath me, planting one knee on the wet floor, then the other. Her long legs were smooth under my hands as I slid my palms up them. Over her knees. Her thighs. Moving all the way until my hands were nearly together, resting at the place where her legs joined her body.

I paused.

Not because I was unsure—but because I wanted to drag it out. To build the anticipation like she'd done to me.

Abbie was too excited or impatient, or perhaps the character she was playing wanted to stay the top in the scene. Her hand moved to the back of my head, her fingers fanning out around my ponytail, and then she urged me forward. I got the impression she wasn't trying to rush me. She'd done it to show me how badly she wanted this.

I lowered into her, peeled her open with my thumbs, and dragging the tip of my tongue over the button of flesh at the center of her legs. Her moan of satisfaction was so fucking sexy, I couldn't wait to hear it again.

Her skin was soft and wet, and when I flicked my tongue, her legs flinched with pleasure. The tile floor was hard on my knees, and I was hunched over, but—dear God—I didn't want to stop. She tasted . . . different.

Good.

I closed my lips around her clit and sucked, getting her to squirm and sigh.

"That's it," she said, breathless. "Eat that pussy."

I gasped against her, my hot breath bouncing off her skin, before obeying her command. I moved my tongue in a flurry of activity. Back and forth, up and down, and—

Someone on the other side of the glass loudly cleared their throat, and my head snapped up, turning toward the noise.

Like Abbie, Colin's entrance had been silent, and my furious gaze sharpened on him. I'd been enjoying my time with her so much, I'd forgotten all about him, and so I glared at his interruption.

He stood just outside the glass with a huge shit-eating grin plastered on his face and held a phone up like he was taking video.

Abbie reacted faster than I did. She let out a sound of horrified surprise, pushed me back, and launched to her feet. And then she was pulling me up beside her, forcing us to retreat as far back in the shower as possible. Like we could run from him.

I finally got my bearings and remembered what I was supposed to do. "Oh, my God! Get out!"

"No," he said simply. "In fact, I was thinking I should join you."

"What? Are you out of your mind?" I shrieked.

"Tell us who he is," Scott encouraged.

Because the audience would need a reminder. I crossed my arms over my chest, trying to cover my breasts. "You can't join us. You're my stepbrother," I spat at him. "Get out of here!"

He had the audacity to look dubious. "You sure you want

me to leave?" He ticked his head toward the phone he was holding. "If you don't want to include me, then I guess I'll have nothing else to do but show this to our parents. I'm sure they'll be interested to know what you girls were doing in here."

I exchanged a furtive glance with Abbie, and for a long moment, the only sound was the falling rain of the shower.

He lowered the phone and shoved it in his back pocket. "Okay, then." His gaze focused in on me. "Your loss. I could have gotten her off faster."

Even though this line was part of our loose script, my pulse kicked into overdrive. "Is that so?" I swallowed a breath. "You think you can do it better?"

My voice had been unsteady, but his was not. His eyes teemed with arrogance. "I know I can."

I lifted my chin and rolled my shoulders back to stand tall. "Fine." I stepped forward and pushed open the shower door. "Prove it."

ELEVEN

Colin

Before heading downstairs to the editing bay, Scott turned on the television in his bedroom. He changed inputs and muted the sound, and it only took a half second for me to realize what we were looking at.

The camera they'd set up on the counter, the one which had the wide angle of the entire shower, was broadcasting and displayed on screen. Even though we had our in-ear monitors, the feed helped Abbie and me know what was going on and when to enter the bathroom for our parts.

Shit, when I was able to watch? I had no problem getting hard for my scene.

It was a bit easier to forget how much I hated Madison when she was wet and naked and kissing another girl. And it was weirdly hard to tell which one of them I thought was better looking—when it shouldn't have been much of a contest.

Abbie was certifiably hot.

There were her piercings, and her tattoo that made her look like a good girl gone bad. Sexy and wild, with nice tits and long legs. I'd been watching porn since the moment I'd been old enough to get around my parents' filters and find it on the internet, and Abbie was the perfect example of the girls I liked best on screen.

But . . . Madison.

She wasn't just hot, she was beautiful.

Getting to watch the very first time she was with another woman—I couldn't look away. The room I was standing in suddenly was on fire, and I began to sweat.

But I clenched my jaw as I watched Abbie bury her face in Madison's pussy, because I could hear Madison's moans float through the closed bathroom door, and it made me strangely jealous.

Like some part of me wanted to be the one who went down on Madison and got her to come, not Abbie. Which was stupid. I'd already filmed my audition and done both of those things with the girl I hated, so why did I care? Plus, I rarely hooked up with the same person more than once. The last thing I wanted was for either of us to catch feelings.

One and done was the best way to operate.

I'd have to suspend that rule here at the house, but this was work, and Scott had assured me that everyone was a professional.

Madison looked so fucking good when she came, though. Even though I wasn't the one to do it, I was glad to get to see it again, and this time without having to think about anything else. She was in side profile and the camera was a decent distance away, but I could still see how her body flinched with the waves of her orgasm.

She didn't shake the same way she had during our scene. Did I have something to do with that?

At that idea, my goddamn dick jerked in my jeans.

I was anxious to get in the room, because then I'd be in control, and the waiting was making me kind of nervous. The sex stuff I was confident I could handle, but acting was new to me, and I didn't want to suck, or fuck up the scene.

Finally, my moment came, and as soon as I pushed open the door, all my nerves evaporated. How could they not? Madison was on her knees on the shower floor with her tongue all up in Abbie's pussy, and my jeans got even tighter as my dick swelled beneath my zipper.

I held up the prop phone Nina had given me, pretending to record as I moved deeper into the room. I'd expected one of the girls to notice me, but they both seemed too into what they were doing to pay attention to anything else.

After I cleared my throat, Madison's furious gaze found mine and . . . it was fucking weird how much I liked the friction. It was almost fun going through the dialogue we needed to set the scene, ending with her pushing open the shower door and challenging me to prove I was good at eating pussy.

Her guarded eyes followed my hands as I pulled off my t-shirt and threw it away, making sure it wasn't in the frame. Next, I undid my belt and my zipper, and then jerked everything down to my ankles, so I could be naked like they were. As I stepped out of the wad of jeans, I kicked them, making them slide away quietly across the tile floor.

I wasn't showing her anything she hadn't seen before, so it would have made more sense to watch Abbie's reaction, but I kept my gaze glued on Madison. Her shoulders were tight, her eyes were big, and her breathing was shallow. It was like she still wasn't prepared to see me like this.

As I walked toward the open door, I stroked my dick, making sure I was as hard as possible, and—yep. *Check.* I stepped into the walled-off room and pulled the glass door closed behind me.

The girls stood beside each other, and only the stream of water from the shower separated us. Abbie peered at me with interest, and I liked the faint smile that lurked on her lips. I knew I looked good, but it was nice to know she thought the same.

"I didn't mean to make you stop," I drawled.

"Yeah?" Abbie asked. "You want us to go back to what we were doing?"

I grinned like it was the best idea I'd ever heard. "Where she's going down on you? Yeah."

Her eyebrow arched. "You liked watching us?"

Didn't need to think about my answer. "Fuck, yeah."

She turned to Madison and wrapped her arms around her, but kept her gaze fixed on me. She held it up until the last moment before delivering a slow, sexy kiss to Madison that seemed to stun her senseless. When she drew back, she traced a finger across Madison's forehead, pushing a loose strand of damp hair back out of her eyes.

"Let's give your stepbrother a show." Abbie's voice was full of seduction.

Madison didn't have a reply, but she let the other girl lead her to the bench. And once Abbie sat down and Madison got on her knees, I sauntered forward.

"I don't want to just watch," I clarified. "I said I wanted to join in."

Abbie's gaze was now focused on the girl whose lips were traveling up the inside of her thigh. "Then, join in." She'd said it the same way I would've expected her to say, *what are you waiting for*?

There wasn't a lot of space on the long seat, so when I sat

down, I was right beside her, our biceps touching. Madison's journey toward her destination had paused, and she hovered only an inch away from the sexy slit between the other girl's legs. Her eyes were stormy as she watched me, and something dark grew in her expression.

Oh, shit. An evil smile twitched on my lips as I recognized what it was.

She was *territorial*.

And I loved it. If she was unhappy about sharing Abbie with me, well . . . too fucking bad.

I turned, cupped Abbie's face, and crushed my mouth over hers. It muffled the moan she made, because not wanting to be outdone, Madison's mouth made contact at the same time.

Abbie didn't have any issue with me kissing her. Her tongue stroked against mine, and satisfaction coasted down my spine. As we kissed, my mind ran a hundred miles an hour. It was Madison's first time with a girl, but this was a first for me, too. I'd never been with two girls at once.

Her mouth was on Abbie, and Abbie's mouth was on mine, so we were all connected, whether Madison liked it or not.

Whatever she was doing, Abbie seemed to enjoy it, because she couldn't sit still. As she squirmed on the bench, it broke our kiss, so I moved down to suck on her neck. It was time to get my hands more involved, so I dragged one down the other side of her neck and gripped one of her tits.

The hard barbell through her nipple was sexy, but not nearly as sexy as the view when I lifted my head and peered down to see Madison's tongue moving. Her eyes flicked up to find me watching, and I expected her to look away . . . but she didn't. She stared at me like this was a challenge she refused to back down from.

The words spilled from me without thought. "You're so fucking hot."

Madison jolted like I'd verbally slapped her, and alarms sounded in my head.

"You're both so fucking hot," I amended quickly, ripping my attention away from her and putting it squarely on Abbie. "Do you like how she's fucking you with her tongue?"

Abbie nodded and moaned enthusiastically.

I held her breast steady and dipped down to lock my lips around her nipple. It pulled a deeper moan from her. Clearly, she was enjoying having all the attention on her. I swirled the tip of my tongue over the metal beads at either end of the barbell and imagined Madison's tongue was doing something similar over Abbie's clit.

Her breath came and went in bursts and was littered with soft moans, filling the shower room, and echoing off the walls.

"Someone needs to get a hand on Colin's cock," Nina commented in our earpieces, and I had to brace myself for the impending bomb of pleasure that was coming my way.

Both girls moved a hand toward me, but when Abbie's beat hers to the target, Madison looked strangely dissatisfied about being off the hook. I couldn't focus on it, though, because Abbie's fingers tightened around my dick and all thought ceased as she stroked me from tip to base.

Instinct took over.

My hand dropped from Abbie's tits, sliding down her

body until it rested on the back of Madison's head. Heat washed over me in waves from the way Abbie fucked me with her fist, and although my vision was narrowed and hazy with pleasure, I peered at Madison.

"Look at you." My voice came from deep in my throat. "Eating pussy like it's your goddamn job. How does she taste?"

Madison let out a gasp. My question had both shocked and excited her, and she paused her good girl tongue just long enough to answer me. "She tastes," she panted, "good."

Her gaze didn't waver from mine, and the steamy air in the shower thickened. The longer her intense stare drilled into me, the deeper it got, burrowing so far inside I had the bizarre idea that a part of her might get stuck in there forever.

Abbie's grip suddenly felt dangerously good, so I had to take my hand off Madison's head and use it to slow Abbie's strokes down. I grasped her hand, guiding her to the sluggish pace I needed.

It'd be helpful if Abbie was distracted. "Put your fingers inside her," I told Madison.

Her shoulders rose as she sucked in a deep breath, and then she moved. Was she nervous? Or just dragging out the moment? Because she slowly straightened, sitting back on her heels, and then dropped her gaze to Abbie's bare pussy.

When she eased two fingers inside, Abbie groaned with satisfaction and her legs opened wider, pressing against mine. Since she seemed to understand the slow tempo I wanted her to jerk me off at, I let go of her hand and grabbed the inside of her knee. I dragged her leg up over mine, holding her open for Madison.

It was an invitation, which she accepted gladly.

She leaned in so she could fuck Abbie with both her mouth and her fingers.

"Good girl," I said in a hush.

My heart stumbled when she closed her eyes. I didn't like that she'd severed the connection between us, but—

Holy shit.

The tremble was back, making her shoulders quiver. It wasn't because she was cold; it was a million degrees in this room and climbing. Was her tremor because of me? I wanted to test the theory.

"Give me your hand," I blurted. "I want to taste her, too."

Abbie pushed out a breath, maybe covering her whine over the fact I was taking Madison's fingers away from her, but that didn't stop Madison. She rose onto her knees and pressed her wet fingers into my mouth.

When I closed my lips around them and sucked, she was entirely unprepared for the fire that flared between us. Her eyes lidded with pleasure, and then went wide with surprise as her whole body shuddered.

She tried to pull her hand back, but I seized her wrist and held it still so I could suck every last bit of Abbie's taste from Madison's delicate fingers. All the while, I stared at her. Strangely, it felt like the most sexual thing Madison and I had done.

So far, my brain whispered with glee.

Did she feel the same? It looked like she wasn't even breathing. But she started back up again when I finally released her.

"She's right," I said, turning to Abbie. "You do taste good."

The faintest smile turned up the corners of her

sexy mouth.

Since she enjoyed having us both focused on her, I skated my fingertips between her cleavage and down the center of her body, not stopping until the pads of my fingers discovered her clit.

One stroke of her soft, wet skin was all it took to make her squirm. But I'd promised to make her come fast, and so I glanced at Madison. "Put those fingers back inside her. Let's make her come together."

Madison came onboard quickly with my plan. She sank back down onto her heels and pushed her two fingers inside Abbie, burying them all the way to the knuckles. Just above her hand, I rubbed circles on Abbie's clit.

It felt too good for her to keep her hand on my dick.

"Son of a bitch." She let go and latched her hand on me, grabbing whatever was closest, which ended up being my forearm. "You're going to make me come."

This scene wasn't anything like the first one I'd done with Madison, and yet my head was a mess like it had been then. I wanted to give Abbie an orgasm, but I was far more excited about helping Madison do it. Why the fuck was that?

"Faster," I encouraged. "It's easier if your palm's up."

She followed my direction without hesitation, turning her hand over so her palm was facing the ceiling. It allowed her to drive her fingers deeper and faster, more likely to strike Abbie's G-spot.

I picked up my pace as well, aggressively rubbing the swollen clit beneath my fingers, and enjoyed the sound of Abbie's moans. They were building, racing toward the finish line.

"That's it," I said. "Is her tight little pussy clenching on your fingers?"

Madison's gaze snapped to mine. "Yes."

"She's almost there."

Maybe Abbie felt like she had to confirm it. Her words were as needy as her whimpers and moans. "I'm *so* close."

That helped Madison find another gear. She moved her fingers so hard and fast, I saw the flex of her bicep. The force of her thrusts made Abbie's hips shake. I leaned over her, swiping my tongue over her nipple, hoping to do whatever I could to push her over the edge, because I wasn't sure how long Madison could maintain such a demanding tempo.

Abbie's breathing grew more ragged until she let out a moan so loud, it stunned me for a single heartbeat. The muscles in the leg draped over me went tight, her toes pointed, and a shudder violently wracked her body.

"I'm coming," she groaned.

Madison and I both slowed, watching the pleasure roll through her.

The orgasm was short, but it sounded fucking *intense*, and as it subsided, Abbie's body went slack. My focus should have been on her, but I couldn't stop my eyes from turning Madison's direction. What did she think about this? It was the first time she'd brought another woman to orgasm. If she was anything like me, she should be fucking thrilled.

Wait, no. I didn't want her to be anything like me.

Her expression was—I don't know—fucking wonderment? She looked both proud and amazed, and whatever had been holding me back from taking what I wanted . . . fractured.

I leaned forward and trapped her face in my hands. Her eyes went impossibly wide as it became clear I was going to try to kiss her. If I wasn't a fucking moron, I would have realized she was frozen in panic, but I moved too quickly for it to register.

Just as my lips brushed hers in something too short to be called a kiss, she jerked out of my hold, backing away so abruptly she splashed in the water pooling around the drain.

"What the hell?" Nina's voice was full of irritation, and I was positive she was talking to me. Madison had set the boundary during our last scene, and it was on me for not asking if it was still in effect.

"I had the same rule as Madison," Scott's voice filled our earpieces, "when I first started out, and I stopped working with people who didn't respect it. You get it, Colin?"

"Sorry," I said genuinely to both the couple in my ear and the girl glaring up at me.

Abbie straightened and turned on the bench, nuzzling her lips into the crook of my neck. "Poor thing," she cooed in a patronizing tone. "Your stepsister doesn't want to kiss you." Her hand returned to my dick, squeezing just hard enough to make everything in me tighten with pleasure. "But I bet she wants to suck this cock."

I had to hand it to her.

Abbie knew exactly what to do to make sure our scene stayed on the rails. Her hand moved up and down in rhythmic strokes, and I pulsed under her grip.

As she pumped her fist, Abbie's focus swung to Madison. "Don't you?" she asked, although it sounded rhetorical. "Look at how hard and big he is. Don't you want to wrap your lips around this?"

I held my breath as Madison studied me critically. She was thinking about whether she could trust me, and I was pissed at myself for fucking that up. Of course, that self-directed anger died when she rose onto her knees, pinned her determined gaze on Abbie, and leaned in to steal a kiss from the other girl.

Watching their mouths move together and the sliver of tongue Madison delivered felt vindictive. She was flaunting what I couldn't have.

The thought made me burn hot.

I waited impatiently for them to finish, but as soon as it was over, it was like a switch had been flipped in her. She latched a hand around my dick, pushing Abbie's out of her way, and sank her mouth down around me. It happened so fast, air cut off in my lungs.

The heat of her mouth was scorching.

And awesome.

I sank back in my seat, letting my shoulder blades rest against the cold tile while her tongue cartwheeled over the head of my dick. Pleasure swam through my body, blurring my vision. Everything was fuzzy, and just as soft as her amazing tongue.

Abbie pressed her lips to mine, and I dug a hand in the hair at the back of her head to hold her at the angle I wanted to kiss her. It was weird, and new, to have my mouth on one girl while another had hers on my dick, but my stupid mind wouldn't be quiet.

All I could think about was how unfair Madison's no kissing rule was. She had no problem kissing Abbie, and no issue with where my dick was right now.

So why, exactly, couldn't I kiss her?

It made no sense, and I hated it, and I was beginning to hate it a lot more than I hated her.

Abbie's palm rested on the center of my chest with her fingers splayed out, and when her lips carved a line down my throat, her hand drifted down as well. It gripped me right at the base of my cock, holding me steady while Madison went down on me.

The slow, relentless slide of my dick into her mouth made my heart thump in my chest. Fuck, she looked so good when her soft pink lips pushed down as far as she could go, then steadily retreated. I watched her over the rapid rise and fall of my chest with heavy, lust-filled eyes.

I wanted to fuck her again.

Like, right now. Wanted to hear her gasp and moan, and feel her come on me while her whole body shook so hard, it seemed like she might rattle apart.

She bobbed faster, intensifying my pleasure. Instinctively, I reached out to put a hand on her head and guide her to take me deeper—but instead I dropped it onto my thigh and balled it into a tight fist.

I got a taste of what Abbie had gotten earlier, both of my partners focused solely on me, and it was fucking addictive.

When Madison lifted her mouth off me, it was hard to tell the reason why. Maybe her jaw was sore, or maybe she liked it too much, or most likely—she needed to pause to catch her breath. Her skin was dewy from the shower mist, and she pulled in ragged air through her parted, swollen lips.

"Stand up," Scott ordered. "Give them room so they can

both go down on you."

My legs were kind of woozy as I pushed off the bench, and I tottered to stand in the corner of the shower, wedging my back between the two walls for support. Abbie melted off the bench, sinking to her knees beside Madison.

Both girls looked up at me with their gorgeous eyes and glistening, naked bodies, and this was one of my fantasies come to life. I had to blink more than a few times just to make sure what I was seeing was real. Abbie smiled at me, running the tip of her tongue over her perfectly white teeth like she wanted to devour me. Shit, she was every bit the porn star I always wanted.

It was so sexy, but . . .

Fucking hell.

For some unknown reason, my gaze floated over to the good girl beside her. She wasn't a professional and didn't seem experienced when it came to sex, but that didn't matter to my body. I wanted her so badly, even though I'd already had her.

The girls shifted on their knees, moving closer to both me and each other, getting comfortable. Abbie was the first one to wrap her hand around me, and her long, tapered fingernails were painted a pale mint color. My skin was still wet from Madison's mouth, making Abbie's fist glide easily back and forth on my dick.

She gave me a few pumps before spreading her lips and easing her mouth around me. I let out a tight breath, watching my cock disappear inside her mouth, only for it to emerge a moment later, glossy with her saliva. She held me still with one hand and placed the other on Madison's shoulder, urging her to join in.

They ran their tongues across my throbbing erection, each girl taking one side. I pulsed, and a drop of cum beaded at the tip, but Abbie used her fist to stroke it away.

The mutual blowjob had started with her in charge, but as it went on, I subtly stole control away from her. It was so fucking amazing how her fingers squeezed me, holding me at the right angle so I could saw my dick from one girl's awaiting mouth into the other.

Back and forth I went, enjoying how they were perched at my feet and looked up at me like every turn they got was a motherfucking gift. It was so powerful, my knees went soft. Even the way the girls were with each other, how Abbie's free hand rested gently on the center of Madison's back, added to the experience.

They looked like friends who were happy to share me, and electricity traveled up my spine, radiating outward. The heat from it made my toes and fingertips tingle.

But I couldn't keep alternating between them forever because my body demanded *more*.

Faster, deeper.

When I had my dick as far back in Madison's mouth as it would go, Abbie abruptly pulled me out of her. It was as if she were too eager for her turn and took hers before the other girl's was over.

And Madison? She didn't like that.

The friendship between them cooled, and she gave Abbie a dose of her own medicine. She nudged Abbie out of the way and took over. I groaned through clenched teeth because warmth was spreading in my center. It was like they were fighting over me, and the darker part of my brain loved that.

I'd seen Madison competitive before. Was it possible she wanted to battle the other woman? Was she determined to win?

If so, the fight was short-lived. Abbie gave up, willing to play sidekick to the other girl, and her lips wandered down. She mouthed, and licked, and ran her fingernails softly across my balls. I couldn't stop the shudder of satisfaction that shook my shoulders. It was insane to have this much pleasure at once.

Madison sucked me deep, far deeper than she had before, and I let out an enormous moan. Everything was shrinking and focusing in, like a rope being twisted tighter and tighter, straining toward its breaking point.

I was going to come soon, and for the first time in forever, I wasn't sure I'd be able to control it. I barely had a hold of myself right now. My legs were both tight and wobbling as I stood with my back jammed in the corner of the shower, a hand on each girl's head. I'd done it to stay connected to both of them, but also because I hoped it looked sexy.

Except my body had its own agenda, and I was quickly becoming a slave to it. Without thinking, I found both my hands on Madison's face. She looked up at me with her bottomless eyes and my dick in her mouth, and I was filled with the urgent need to do more. To show her how much I wanted her.

I dragged my fingers up from the edge of her jaw, stroking her high, delicate cheekbone, and back into her hair so I could cup her head. I drove deep into her mouth and sighed appreciatively when her tongue caressed me. The other girl faded out, until it was only me and Madison.

Pinpricks of pleasure sped up my legs, accelerating like fire through gasoline.

The word was punched clean from me. *"Fuck."*

I was still lodged in her mouth as my orgasm descended on me, but warning sirens blared in my head, saving me from ruining the scene. I yanked myself out at the last second, grabbed my dick, and began to furiously jerk.

Abbie let out a sound of happy surprise. She cupped her tits and pressed herself to Madison, presenting me the perfect spot to finish. I continued to jerk off, painting several short ribbons of cum across their chests. Madison flinched as it hit her, but her expression was only surprise and not disgust.

I moaned as I came, and although my body was taut, I peered at the girls with unfocused eyes. Their pleased smiles kept the sensations going, and an aftershock of pleasure caused me to shudder. The running shower faded to silent. My mouth hung open while I tried to catch my breath, and the only thing I could hear was the rush of blood in my head.

Recovery was slow and languid.

As I loomed over them, Abbie got her hands wet in the shower, and then used them to wipe their bodies clean. It was sensual and erotic.

Madison must have thought so, too.

She leaned over and kissed Abbie. It was slow. Provocative.

I lifted my gaze away, staring off at nothing. I didn't care that Madison wouldn't kiss me, I reminded myself, because I hated her. She was the reason I got kicked out of my frat and wound up here.

A voice inside my head told me to take a fucking look around.

What about this was really so bad?

TWELVE

Colin

A bead of sweat trickled down the side of my face, and I used the back of my hand to wipe it away. It was hot outside, which meant it was a billion fucking degrees inside the pool house the Woodsons had turned into a gym.

The detached house was probably supposed to be for guests, but it wasn't finished inside. It had electricity and water, and there was drywall up on the walls, but the floors were bare concrete, and the ceiling was open. It didn't have air conditioning, but there were windows and a set of double doors at the back that could be opened for airflow, plus several rotating fans in the large room that held all the equipment.

Of which there was a lot. A treadmill, stationary bike, an all-in-one weight machine, and a rack of dumbbells. Yoga mats and exercise bands were rolled up and stored in a bin in the corner.

Other than the lack of AC, it was a nice space.

Last summer, I'd let my friend Troy talk me into working as a personal trainer at his gym. I'd considered doing it again this summer because of the free membership, but Troy wouldn't be there this time. His music career was taking off, and he was barely in town these days.

So, while this home gym didn't have endless rows of machines and free weights, it had everything I needed and was a hell of a lot closer. Not to mention, it was private. The first three days I'd come in here, I'd been alone. I didn't have to wear headphones while I lifted or worry about some bro silently judging me if I started too heavy and had to back down on the weight.

I streamed a mix of music that was rap and rock from my phone to keep myself pumped because today was a low repetition day, so I had to go hard and use the most weight I could. It meant easy things like putting on and taking off a shirt were going to suck for the next two days, because I'd be sore as fuck.

But it was worth it. I was in the best shape of my life, and it was important it stayed that way.

There were mirrors lining one of the walls, and I watched the flex of my bicep as I curled the dumbbell up to my shoulder. Five reps on each side, then I'd superset it with an overhead—

The door to the gym swung open, and I paused, turning over my shoulder to see who it was.

Great.

Madison stood in the doorway, looking at me like I'd ambushed her and not the other way around. Her gaze bounced from my sweaty, bare chest, to the t-shirt I'd tossed onto the weight bench nearby. It looked like she was thinking about turning around and bolting away, even though it was obvious she'd come here to work out. She had on a thin, white sports bra and black leggings, and a water bottle was clenched in one hand.

For a moment, she didn't know what to do. I could see the thoughts turning in her head. If she'd known I was out here, she wouldn't have come, but now if she backed out, she'd look weak.

She'd be letting me win—and Madison couldn't stand that.

Her chest lifted with a deep breath and her shoulders rose, like she was trying to look bigger and confident. Her face was a mask of indifference as she marched to the tread-mill and loudly slotted her water bottle into the cupholder.

I went back to curling the dumbbell. If she didn't care about sharing the space with me, then I didn't either.

The problem was the treadmill faced the mirror wall. So, if my gaze strayed at all from my form, it naturally went to the other person in the room. After her warmup of a few minutes of walking, she increased her pace to a jog. Her eyes were up and forward, probably purposefully not looking at me, and it was impossible not to notice how little help her sports bra was giving her.

Her tits bounced and swayed as she ran, and I pictured what she'd look like if it wasn't there, covering her. She had such an amazing body, especially her tits, with tight, pink nipples I wanted to suck and bite and pinch.

My dick stirred inside my gray athletic shorts, which would do fuck-all to hide a hard-on. And then awareness pricked down my back.

Not only had I stopped lifting to look at her, but Madison had glanced down to find me in the mirror, meaning she'd caught me staring. *Fuck.* I blinked, snapped my attention back to myself, and resumed what I was supposed to be doing.

I had no idea how many reps I'd done, so I set one of the weights down on the bench and hoisted the other over my head, holding it with both hands. When I slowly lowered it behind me, back to my shoulder blades, my muscles whined about fatigue, but I pushed through.

Instead, I focused on the song blasting from my phone. It was one of my current favorites by some obscure band Spotify had turned me on to last month. It had a driving rhythm and a rock anthem feel that was perfect for working out. If it annoyed Madison that my music was playing and I wasn't wearing headphones, well, too fucking bad.

I was here first.

Except when my gaze darted to her, I found her moving her lips along with the words. It wasn't the chorus either— she knew the song well enough she'd memorized all the lyrics.

Yet another thing to remind me I didn't have a clue who this girl really was.

I finished my set, and as I rested, I checked myself in the mirror. I wasn't the type of guy to take swole selfies, but if I was, now would have been the perfect time. My muscles were swollen and extra defined, and I was glossy with sweat from the warm room.

The same awareness I'd had earlier prickled across my skin.

I'd been caught staring earlier, but now it was Madison's turn. Her gaze was locked on my chest, and since didn't realize I was looking, I saw every inch of desire that filled her eyes.

When her gaze floated up to discover the smirk tilting my lips, her face went blank. *Like what you see, don't you?* I wordlessly asked. She scowled and dropped her attention to the control panel of the treadmill.

At least it was good to know I wasn't the only one battling the attraction between us.

We managed to successfully ignore each other for a while after that. She finished her short run, climbed off the treadmill, and went to the weight machine in the center of the room. It was a large tower with a weight stack, pulleys, and an inclined seat. There were different bar configurations and rope pulls stored on the side that could be clipped on in various places to work different sets of muscles.

She peered at it like the thing was intimidating, and she wasn't exactly wrong. No matter how good the design was, there was a learning curve. Even I'd had to watch a YouTube video my first day in here, just to make sure I was doing everything right.

She adjusted the pin on the weight stack, sat down on the seat, and tucked her ankles under the leg extension bar. Except she hadn't changed the cable over, so it wasn't set to pull weight. When she pushed her feet forward to straighten her legs, there was no tension, and the bar went up easily.

Because I disliked her, I should have been happy to watch her struggle, especially when it was something I could easily solve. She got up off the seat, put her hands on her hips, and examined the machine, before deciding to reset the pin in the weights—clueless that it wasn't the issue.

I should have enjoyed it, but instead it bothered me.

Keep your mouth shut. You don't owe her anything, and if the roles were reversed, she'd do the same to you.

The second time she sat and attempted to use the leg extension part of the machine, she got exactly the same results. Her face contorted with frustration.

So, I ignored the voice protesting in my head, put down my weights, and strode to the machine. Her suspicious gaze was laser focused on my reflection in the mirror as I approached, and she watched how I turned the knob to activate the pulley for the leg developer. I stood back, crossed my arms over my chest, and lifted an eyebrow.

There, my expression told her.

She swallowed a breath, pushed her feet forward, and this time it was what she wanted—it was a challenge to move the bar.

The word from her was quiet and begrudging. "Thanks."

I didn't acknowledge it, but not because I was being a dick. It was because I'd been the last one to use the machine and I was taller than she was, so she had the bar set too low. It had to be uncomfortable. She was putting all the strain on the tops of her feet, rather than the base of her shins.

Fuck it.

I'd already helped her. What difference did it make if I did some more? Plus, if she hurt herself, it might take her out of rotation as a scene partner . . . and I couldn't have that. I didn't like her, but the two hottest sexual experiences of my life had included her. I was more than a little curious to see if I could get that streak to continue.

She jolted to a stop, making the weights clank loudly when I leaned down in front of her and pulled out the adjustment handle, shortening the length of the center bar two notches. The handle locked back into place, and I straightened beside her, waiting for her to try the machine again and make sure it was right.

It was.

"Thanks," she muttered under her breath.

I didn't know what to say. I was uncomfortable with her in every way possible. She made me twitchy and feel things I didn't want to, so the word stumbled from my lips, making me sound like an asshole. "Whatever."

She sucked in a sharp breath at my shitty response, and inside I winced, but on the outside, I pretended not to care. I trudged back to the weights I'd abandoned and focused on finishing my set, trying to block her out.

It was so fucking hard not to think about Madison when she was right there. It'd been hot in this place before she'd shown up, and now it was an oven, slowly baking me to death.

I snatched up my water bottle and drank, but no amount of water seemed to quench my thirst.

"Do you know if this machine does any other leg exercises?" Her voice was careful, like she was sure she was going to regret asking me.

I lowered my bottle and considered how to answer. My workout was done. I could shrug, walk away, and leave her to figure it out. But she'd asked the question, even as she expected me to be a dick about it, so I wanted to prove her wrong.

"There are ankle cuffs if you want to work your calves, but if it's a leg day, I'd recommend squats." I scratched the back of my neck. "Or I'd have you pick up weights and do split lunges on the bench."

She stared at me like I was speaking gibberish, and then her expression and tone turned dark. "I'm sorry. Are you telling me what to do?"

I closed my eyes and pressed my fingers to the center of my forehead. "No, I didn't mean it like that. Habit." I opened my eyes and gave her a plain look. "I was a personal trainer last summer."

She stared at the ceiling for a moment. "Of course you were."

I shook my head and racked the dumbbells I'd been using. Who the hell was she to judge me? I grabbed my water bottle and shirt—

"Wait," she said, rising from the seat at the machine. She didn't offer an apology with words, but her embarrassed look was enough of one. "Split lunges. What do those look like?" Her voice lost some of its power. "I mean, if I wanted to do them?"

"Grab some weight and I'll show you."

I had no fucking clue why I said it. I should have been on my way back to the main house because I had a group meeting for a class project, and I really needed to take a shower. Instead, I took another sip from my water bottle and waited for her to move.

Madison eyed the rack of dumbbells. "How much weight?"

"Fives? Tens? It's whatever you want. All your body weight, plus the dumbbells, is going to be on a single leg, so maybe start light."

She grabbed a five-pound dumbbell for each hand, and then her hesitant gaze swung my direction, awaiting further instruction.

"Face me," I said. "Hold the weights at shoulder level and put your toe from one foot up behind you." I gestured to the bench.

She shot me a dubious look but followed my directions. One foot went up on the bench, so she was standing on one leg, and she brought the dumbbells up to her shoulders.

"Now, bend your knee like you're lunging."

She did one and blinked in surprise. "It's hard. And awkward."

A smile tugged at my lips, but I strangled it back. "Move that front foot out so you're farther away from the bench."

Because it'd take some of the strain off her knee. She repositioned herself, and this time when she lunged, her eyebrows pulled together. Her expression feigned outrage, and her tone was playfully exasperated. "But that makes it even harder and *more* awkward."

This time the smile came too quickly for me to stop, and it spread across my lips. And it must have been infectious because a soft smile brightened her face. It caused my heart to stumble out of rhythm.

She'd spent two years with Jack, but my eyeballs hadn't worked then, huh? In all that time, how the fuck had I never noticed how gorgeous she was?

Her smile abruptly froze at the exact moment mine did. We'd momentarily forgotten about all the shit between us, but it came roaring back then. I remembered the anger that had flashed in her eyes the second before she'd flung that fistful of mud, setting off a chain reaction that ended with us both kicked out of our chapters.

My tone went detached. "Five on each side and three sets, Mads."

"What did you just call me?" A storm brewed in her eyes, similar to the one that day.

"That's how I think of you," I said. "You're always angry. Mad Madison . . . Mads for short."

She stared at me like I was disgusting, which was bull-shit. I mean, I'd caught her eyeballing me earlier, and she definitely liked what she saw. But her voice was vaguely threatening. "Don't call me that."

I delivered a flat smile that told her I'd do whatev-er I wanted.

"And can you put on your shirt?" She sounded irritated, but I wasn't sure if I was the sole cause because she'd also resumed her lunges.

"Why?" I waved my hand dramatically over my toned chest and abs, like I was modeling them. "Do you find all *this* distracting?"

"Yes."

Her answer came so quickly, so honestly, it threw me off balance. "Yeah?" I fired back. "Your sports bra's just as bad."

Confused, she looked down at her chest like she had to make sure it was still there. "What's wrong with my sports bra?"

"I can basically see your tits, Mads."

She set down her weights on the bench, raised an eyebrow, and shot me a direct look. "So? You've already seen my tits."

Fucking hell. I tightened my jaw because while nothing in my statement had stunned her, her reply and the chal-lenge in her eyes had surprised me.

Jesus, it was exciting.

She was *exciting.*

"I want to kiss you." It came out so forcefully, I'd nearly demanded it.

Her mouth dropped open and her posture went stiff.

Horror filled her voice. "Now?"

Yes.

"No," I announced, frustrated with myself. Why did I say things without thinking whenever I was around her? "I meant during our next scene. What's the big deal, anyway? You kissed Abbie."

She balked. "I kissed Abbie because she's not . . . you." Her hands at her sides curled into fists. "She's not cruel."

What on Earth? I'd been accused of a lot of things, but this was a new one. "You think I'm *cruel?*"

"I know you are," she spat. "I mean, God. After the race, I'd already been humiliated when no one would believe me about Riley, but then you had to go and bring up how Jack cheated on me." Her anger flared like a match held to paper. "You threw it in my face, right in front of *everybody.*"

"What are you talking about? You're the one who cheated on—"

I stopped speaking so fast, my whole body jolted.

Oh, no.

Obviously, she wasn't the one who had her facts wrong. That person would be me.

"It was him?" I asked. "He . . . he told us it was you."

"Us," she repeated bitterly. The pain in her eyes was a knife in the center of my chest. She couldn't look at me any longer, and her gaze turned away. "No. It was him."

Thoughts battled for my attention. There was no doubt in my mind she was telling the truth. I was angry that Jack had lied to everyone, but I was even more pissed at what he'd done to her. How was this sexy, beautiful girl—who was way out of his league—not more than enough for him?

How dare he cheat on her?

The sweat on my body suddenly went icy cold. That day on the field, after I'd brought up the cheating and tried to shame her, Jack had just stood there. Hadn't said a goddamn word. No, that asshole was perfectly fine letting everyone think he was the victim and not her.

Fuck. No wonder Mads had lost her shit.

If I'd been a better guy and not goaded her on, would we have avoided the whole mess, and still be at our separate houses?

"I'm sorry," I said automatically, then frowned. I meant it genuinely and needed to clarify what I was apologizing for. "Especially about what I said. I didn't know, and I wasn't trying to hurt you."

An incredulous laugh burst from her lips, and she was right because what I'd just told her was ridiculous. Even without knowing the truth, my goal that day *had* been to embarrass her.

My mouth was sticky with regret, making me mumble. "I didn't mean to be cruel."

The room went impossibly still, and the heavy air between us glued me in place. But something in her seemed to snap, and it was clear Mads wanted to be anywhere but here.

"Whatever," she uttered.

She racked the dumbbells before stalking over to her water bottle and snatching it out of the cupholder. And she didn't glance back at me as she fled the gym, pulling the door closed behind her with a thud loud enough it made me flinch.

Well, fuck.

I was so early for our Monday scheduling meeting; I was the first one there. I slid into the same seat I'd taken last time and scrolled mindlessly on my phone, waiting for everyone to show up. Really, I was waiting for Mads to appear. I hadn't seen her the rest of the weekend, which wasn't surprising. Finals were coming up, so we were both busy, plus I was sure she was avoiding me.

Part of me had wanted to seek her out and attempt a better apology, but another part of me was afraid. Some dumb, thoughtless thing would fall out of my mouth the next time we were together, and I'd said enough already.

She thought I was cruel.

I'd had people call me an asshole or tell me I was being a dick, but it had never gotten under my skin before. I mean . . . sometimes they weren't wrong. But it bothered me that she thought I was heartless.

I wasn't mean. Hell, I wasn't a bad guy.

She'll come around. She can't avoid you forever.

Especially not since we lived in the same house and there was this weekly meeting we had to attend.

Naturally, she was the last one to show up. She ducked into her seat and did a great job of pretending I didn't exist. Everyone got to see her friendly smile except for me.

"Before we get to pitching," Nina said, "I wanted to let everyone know I've spoken with Madison and Colin about their test results. They've both been cleared and said they're willing to work without condoms."

"Yay," Abbie said with a giggle.

My gaze flicked to Mads, but she kept her focus glued to Nina. I sensed she knew I was looking at her, though. Her expression was fixed, like she was trying too hard to look natural.

Nina uncapped a dry erase marker and scribbled our names along the top of the board, then drew lines to separate them into columns. "Does anyone want to go first?" When no one spoke, she turned to face the table. "Okay, we'll start with the ladies. Madison, what have you got?"

Mads was the kid the teacher had just called on who hadn't done the assigned reading. Panic swarmed her eyes. "Uh . . ."

Always trying to be helpful, Abbie leaned over to the other girl. "I use whatever I've been fantasizing about recently. Like, a few weeks ago I was all hot about sleepy sex, where I wake up and some dude's fucking me. Remember that one, Jaquan?"

She gave him a sexy wink, and he chuckled. And judging by his face—yeah. He definitely remembered that scene.

She turned her attention back to Mads. "Don't worry about throwing out ideas. None of us are going to judge you, I promise, and honestly, whatever it is, I'll probably think it's super hot."

Abbie's encouragement must have disabled whatever was holding Mads back. "Working out with a personal trainer," she said abruptly. The room was silent, forcing her to elaborate. "Where he's telling me what to do, but then his instructions turn dirty."

Fuck me running.

Every muscle in me corded, making me rigid. This was her fantasy? Because it was exactly like mine, too. There was no way I hadn't inspired this idea. Had she spent the entire weekend thinking about it, just like I had?

Did she imagine me touching her body to correct her form? My hands would start off innocent, but then I'd slide them into a place that would draw out a startled moan. Her thin sports bra wouldn't stand a chance against me.

Beneath the table, my hand rested on my thigh, and I clenched it into a fist. My dick was growing hard, and I shifted in my seat, uncomfortable.

"I'll do it," I announced. Ideally, no one would notice how strangled and urgent my voice had become.

Everyone turned to look at me, including her. Dismay crossed her face, but something else darted through her eyes. It was as if she didn't like that I'd volunteered, but also . . . maybe she did? I saw an electric charge of excitement—and I hoped I wasn't imagining it.

"It's a good idea for a scene." Nina's expression said she was about to deliver bad news. "So good, in fact, Scott had the same idea a few months back, and we've already filmed it."

"Oh." Mads' gaze went to the whiteboard and the empty column under her name. Literally back to the drawing board.

"But we can rework the concept." Nina's brow furrowed as she thought about it. "Instructions that turn dirty," she repeated, mostly to herself.

"A tutor?" Jaquan offered.

Anxiety spiked inside me. I wanted to do another scene with Mads and could feel my chance slipping away.

A lightbulb went off in Nina's mind, and her smile was wide as she turned to her husband. "A *professor*."

Scott considered it and nodded. "Sure. We could use

the office."

The conversation was moving too fast. He was the logical choice and had just agreed to play the role, which meant he'd be Mads' scene partner—not me.

"What do you think, Madison?" Nina turned back to face the table. "You could be the cute co-ed willing to do anything to get a good grade."

"Me," she said slowly, "and Scott."

When her hesitant gaze flicked to me, my heart stopped. Was she nervous about performing alone with Nina's husband, or was this disappointment I wouldn't be her partner?

"It could be during the professor's office hours," I said abruptly, "and I wander in to catch them."

Nina tilted her head to the side as she thought about it, but her lips skewed. "It's okay, but it's kind of similar to your last scene. You don't want to be known as the guy who's always walking in on people."

"Okay." She made a good point, and my brain scrambled to come up with an alternative. "Then, let's say I have an appointment with the professor to discuss something. But Mads shows up before that because it's open office hours and ambushes him."

"Mads?" Abbie asked quietly.

Before I could say anything, Nina leaned forward and put her hands on the table. She'd latched on to the idea, and the scene was taking shape in her head. "What could the appointment be about?"

Mads abruptly came to life, and her lips twisted into an evil smile. "The professor caught him *cheating*."

She put extra emphasis on it, which wasn't necessary. I

understood the subtext. This was about her claiming the Sigs had cheated in the tournament.

"Does Colin join in on the fun," Nina asked, "or does he only get to watch as punishment?"

Maybe she'd only been thinking out loud, but once the question had been asked, it became obvious only one person could answer it.

I looked at Mads and swallowed thickly while everyone waited on her decision.

THIRTEEN

Madison

After I'd changed into the wardrobe I'd been provided, I let Abbie do my hair and makeup, and she assured me for the tenth time it was totally fine I was about to fuck a man in front of his wife.

"He's such a professional," she said as she applied blush to the apple of my cheeks.

The thing I struggled with the most, but couldn't bring myself to tell her because I couldn't put it into words, was *everything* about it turned me on. I was confident Nina had no issue with Scott performing with me, but it still felt . . . dangerous. Taboo. Which was thrilling.

Plus, while it wasn't the fantasy I'd pitched, the story we'd landed on was sexy. In my four years of college, I'd never been blessed with a young and attractive professor, but I understood the appeal and why it was a common trope. Scott was incredibly good looking, and it wouldn't be hard to pretend I was hot for teacher.

The thing that turned me on most of all, though, was Colin would be in the scene. He'd enjoyed watching me with Abbie, but how would he feel when my partner was another man? Would he get hard? Would he get jealous?

There was a throb low in my belly.

I'd barely made it through my two classes this morning.

Anticipation had me jittery and excited, and it was so fucking hard to think about anything else.

My wardrobe for the scene was a sleeveless black dress patterned with tiny white dots. The flared skirt was short, but not too short, and the cinched waist fit me perfectly. It was both innocent and flirty, especially because I had on black thigh-highs. Under the skirt, they just looked like leggings, but when I walked or if the skirt rode up at all, there was a flash of the sexy lace at the tops.

After Abbie finished spritzing me with makeup setting spray and declared she was done, I walked over to the full-length mirror hanging on her bathroom door and sucked in a breath.

My makeup was understated, and my light brown hair fell past my shoulders in soft waves. I looked good. Sexy. Hopefully every bit the part of a student ready to seduce her college professor.

"Thank you." My voice was full of appreciation. "You, uh, do nice work."

Abbie laughed and waved a hand as if to say, *it was nothing.* "Have fun!"

I simply nodded because I wasn't sure what to say.

Everyone in the house had spent the evening yesterday transforming the business office of Petal Productions to look like a professor's space.

There were built-in bookcases on the back wall, already decorated with books, but we removed the personal items from the shelves. The large wooden desk was pushed to the center of the room and cleared off. Diffused cling film went up on the windows to control the light. And the guys brought a small couch down from the storage room so we could stage it against the back wall.

When I came down the stairs and turned into the office, I found the 'professor' there. Scott had a costume for the scene as well, and his included a pair of glasses and a tweed blazer with honest-to-God patches on the elbows. His hair was styled conservatively, and—Jesus. He looked like the textbook definition of a hot professor.

"Hey, Madison." His eyes were warm behind his fake glasses. "You look nice."

"Thanks. You, too."

On top of my eagerness, I felt nervous. Nina's comment from the night we'd met flashed through my mind. She'd said lots of people would pay for the chance to sleep with Scott . . . and that's what I was about to do. I was anxious for the scene but was surprised I wasn't more excited.

Maybe it was because I was more concerned about pulling off my role. I'd never tried to seduce someone before.

"Can you grab one of the reflectors from the hallway?" he asked as he examined the camera angle on the tablet he held. "We need to bounce more light this direction." He gestured to the left side of the room.

"Sure." I turned to walk through the doorway and immediately ran into someone's hard chest.

Hands gently grasped my elbows, drawing my eyes up. Colin took in a long breath as he peered down at me, and it was like he needed to gather strength to endure the sight of me. To survive his hands resting against my skin.

Goosebumps lifted on my arms, and my stupid heart fluttered. I had absolutely no fucking clue how I felt about him now. It was why I'd been avoiding him as much as possible. Sure, our short conversation in the gym had taken some of the sting out of what he'd said, but . . .

I wasn't ready to move past it.

If there was one thing I was good at in this world, it was holding a grudge.

Just ask your parents.

"Sorry," I said automatically, stepped out of his hold, and tried to get by him to complete my task. But he'd heard Scott's request, too, and so he beat me to the large white shade that would help reflect light.

I ended up standing awkwardly by the door, watching my two scene partners finish preparing the room. Nina was already downstairs in the editing room, Scott told us. She'd been editing and uploading the previous week's videos, then scheduling their releases.

He had his monitor in his ear and passed ours along to us. After a sound check, we discussed the story beats and stepped through the blocking for the scene, making sure the lighting was right with Nina.

"Your wedding ring," I said abruptly.

Scott glanced down at his hand, then back to me. "We thought it would be hotter if I left it on." His tone turned playful. "You're seducing a married man, after all."

Whatever expression was on my face, it wiped away his amusement in an instant.

"I'll remove it," he said quickly. "I want you to be comfortable, Madison."

I shook my head, but it was more at myself. "No, sorry. It's fine. I just meant that your ring looks different."

I'd noticed the silver band on his ring finger, which had seemed out of place. Didn't he normally wear a black one?

"Oh, yeah." He relaxed his shoulders. "Nina thought I should wear my traditional band for the scene." With that settled, he glanced at Colin and then back to me. "Everyone ready?"

We were.

My pulse drummed in my neck as I waited in the hall. I closed my eyes, drew in a deep breath, and tried to get into character, shutting the rest of the world out.

But it was impossible with Colin standing nearby. Every inch of my body was aware of the cocky frat boy who lurked beside me. Fuck, he smelled good. He looked good too, wearing a pair of dark jeans and a fitted maroon t-shirt that tapered perfectly to his form.

In another life, I would have been all over him.

And in this life, you've already been all over him twice.

In the room next door, we heard the quiet squeak of the chair as Scott seated himself behind the desk. Any second now, he'd give a thumbs up to his wife, and Nina would start the cameras, and I'd have to—

"Can I kiss you?" Colin's low, urgent voice disrupted me, and my eyes flew open.

I turned to look at him with disbelief. He could not be serious. "Now?"

The word had tumbled out of my mouth before I realized it was a stupid question. Of course he didn't mean right now.

But his expression was cryptic. "During the scene."

I opened my mouth, but no sound came out. Letting him kiss me seemed like a really, *really* bad idea. It was so much easier when I hated him, but I didn't know how I felt about him anymore, and I worried that if he put his mouth on mine, it could be the key to unlock the answer.

It was safer this way because ignorance was bliss. I did not want to like Colin in any capacity.

"We're rolling," came Nina's voice in my ear. "Madison, whenever you're ready."

I lifted my hand to knock on the door.

"I need an answer, Mads." It was hard to hear how much desperation his hushed voice contained, but the amount was definitely more than zero.

I leveled a hard gaze at him, both intrigued and irritated at this nickname he'd given me. "No," I said. "You can't kiss me."

His shoulders stiffened. My answer pissed him off, and—shit—that was fucking fascinating. Was this a power thing? Maybe he didn't care about kissing at all, not until he discovered it wasn't allowed.

It didn't feel like that, though. I got the sense it was something else, but I was clueless as to what it could be. Why the hell did he want to kiss me so badly?

I didn't have time to think about it right now. Instead, I raised my hand and rapped my fist gently on the door in front of us that was ajar. "Professor?"

"Come in," Scott announced.

I swallowed a breath and marched through the door, shutting it behind me on an irritated Colin, who had to wait in the hallway.

As expected, Scott was seated behind the desk, holding a pen in one hand, and pretending to review the stack of papers in front of him. He pushed up his glasses on the bridge of his nose as his eyes focused on me. "What can I help you with?"

"I was hoping we could talk about," I sashayed up to the front of the desk, "my grade."

He glanced down at his watch. "It will need to be quick. I have an appointment with another student soon." The pen was set down on the papers. He leaned back in his chair, rested his elbows on the armrests, and laced his fingers together. "What did you want to discuss?"

The way he peered at me was aloof and discerning, and he was selling the shit out of his role. He was the condescending, elitist professor, and I knew I had to up my game as the sexy student.

I walked around to the side of the desk and put a hand on the desktop, leaning provocatively toward him. "I was wondering . . ." My voice went sultry. "Are there any ways I could bring my grade up?"

He appeared confused. "Like extra credit?"

"Sure." I grabbed the hem of my skirt and balled it in a fist, dragging the bunched fabric to hover over the center of my thighs. It made the side of my skirt lift just enough so he could see the lacy top of my stocking. "We can call it extra credit if you want."

He inhaled sharply and sat up straight in his seat, his expression going stern. "No. I don't know what's gotten into you, but I don't do that sort of thing. I'm married, and you're one of my students."

"Yeah?" I turned my lips up into an evil smile. "Does your wife know how you look at me during class?"

He scowled. "I don't know what you're talking about."

My smile widened into a full-out grin. One of the hardest things to do as an actor was to perform like you *were* acting, which Scott had just done masterfully. I nearly believed it, that he was the professor who lusted after his student while trying to pretend he didn't.

"Yes, you do." I moved to seat myself on top of the desk, facing him as he sat in his chair. My feet dangled over the side, and he risked a longing glance at my legs. "You look at me the same way you're looking at me right now."

His gaze snapped to mine, and his tone was full of irritation. As if he didn't have time for a silly girl like me. "And how is that?"

"Like you're wondering if I'm wearing any panties under this dress." I placed my hands behind me, leaned back on my arms, and arched my back seductively. Then, I began to inch my knees apart. "Don't you want to find out?"

"No," he said quickly, moving to wipe a hand over his mouth. His gaze darted side to side, as if he were checking to see if anyone was watching, even though we were alone in his office. "Look, you're a very pretty girl. If I looked at you inappropriately or if I made you feel uncomfortable, I'm sorry."

"Why? I'm not." I continued to part my legs. "I'll only be sorry if you don't put your hand up my skirt."

"Stop that." Only it came out strangled, like it was the last thing he wanted.

"Stop what?" I teased.

My knees were spread wide enough that my left leg was right in front of him, only a few inches from his hand that was now clenched tightly on the armrest. He looked up at me with a strained expression, full of desire he knew he shouldn't act on.

"I think you should go."

But his voice contained no power, and his gaze dropped again to my legs. The skirt was barely draped over my thighs, but I was still covered enough to leave him guessing.

"I think you want me to stay," I whispered.

I shifted my weight so I was leaning back on one arm, and then set the hand I'd freed up on my thigh. Up I dragged, drawing my skirt with it. I moved painfully slow, revealing more skin inch by inch. His gaze was glued to the glide of the fabric, watching it like a trainwreck he couldn't bear to look away from.

"Wait," he pleaded. Agony and anticipation twisted in his handsome face.

But I didn't wait. When I reached my hip, I curled my fingers around the skirt, pulling it up to show him I was totally bare underneath. When I'd been given the wardrobe yesterday, I'd asked Nina about the missing panties, and she told me to go without.

He sucked in a sharp breath and stared at my nakedness like a starving man who'd been shown a buffet and told he wasn't allowed to eat at it.

I wasn't shy, but never in a million years did I think I would be this confident. This bold. Scott had seen me naked more than once, but it had always been onscreen, so this felt like the first time. It was thrilling and empowering.

His breathing went shallow as he continued to stare at me. "This is *highly* inappropriate."

"I know," I cooed, "but don't you want to touch me? Because you can."

His gaze darkened and he turned bitter. "No, I can't." But, oh, how he wanted to. "I could be fired for this."

"I won't tell anyone," I said seductively, "if you don't."

He was torn. His mouth opened to say something, to protest, but no words came.

"How about, then . . ." I spoke slow and hypnotic. "You just watch?" I let go of the skirt, where one side was bunched at my waist, and my fingers crept down to touch myself. As he watched me rub my clit in tight circles, he once again pushed up his glasses on his nose.

Like he wanted to better examine what I was doing.

Heat pooled inside me, not just from my touch, but from the entire experience. I'd never masturbated in front of someone else—at least, not as a performance, and because of the scene we'd created, he was the professor, studying and grading me.

We'd been told that every orgasm needed to be real, but it was okay to embellish our performances if we wanted, and so I let out a soft moan. Touching myself felt good, but it didn't feel *that* good—at least, not enough to warrant the whimper of pleasure I gave.

But it had the desired effect. The professor neared his breaking point.

"Stop," he begged, reaching up to cover my hand with his and get me to cease moving. "We can't do this."

Except now his hand was between my legs, and he couldn't resist temptation any longer. As I slid my hand out from beneath his, his fingers remained, his palm falling against the band of lace at the top of my thigh-high.

His shoulders lifted with an enormous breath as he

stared at where his hand rested. He pretended this was a decision he struggled with, but instead of pulling away, his raised his index finger and tentatively brushed it over the most sensitive part of me.

"Fuck," I gasped.

He did it again, and with every gentle stroke of his fingertips through my slit, reluctance faded from his expression until it was completely wiped away. Once the hesitancy was gone, it unleashed all the desire he'd been holding back.

He straightened so he sat in the office chair with perfect posture, and it only added to his authority. He was touching me with his left hand, and his right one slipped beneath my skirt and held on to my bare hip. It was to keep me in place as he pushed a finger inside me.

My mouth rounded into a silent 'oh,' and I flung my free hand behind me, arching with pleasure.

"I shouldn't be doing this," he said. "This is so wrong."

But he didn't stop or even slow down. His grip on me tightened, his fingers biting into my skin, while he eased a second finger in to join the first. The stretch of his invasion was uncomfortable, but in a pleasurable way. This time when I moaned, it was completely real.

"Is this what you were hoping for?" he demanded.

"Yes," I gasped.

"Fuck." He stared at me like he was angry, but I couldn't tell at what. He acted like I'd forced him into this, given him no choice. But he also seemed pissed at himself for not being able to stop.

"Oh, my God," I gasped because it felt really good. He had me pinned to the desktop and two fingers deep inside me, pumping at a tempo that made the desk squeak quietly. I squirmed and rocked my hips, matching his pace.

He seemed content to listen to my gasps of satisfaction and work his slick fingers in and out of me for a long while, but time also seemed to slow down.

"You wanted to discuss a better grade," he reminded.

"Yeah." It was hard to think over the steam he'd filled my body with. "I'd . . . do *anything* for an A. Whatever you want to do to me. Doesn't that sound like a good deal?"

"Hmm. Why don't you let me think about it," his tone was authoritative, "while you suck my cock?"

"Yes, Professor." His fingers withdrew when I began to sit up, and I found his expression pleased.

There was a strange thrill coursing through me as I climbed down off the desk. I really enjoyed going down on another person, but this . . . wasn't that.

Well, shit.

I swallowed thickly as I realized the source of my excitement.

It meant Colin would be coming into the scene soon. I pushed the thought away, determined to focus on what I was supposed to do.

Scott swiveled his chair a little to the side, making just enough room for me to kneel between his legs. I coursed my hands up over his legs, not going too high up his thighs so I'd stay out of his way as he worked to undo his pants.

Like me, he wasn't wearing underwear, so as soon as his belt and zipper were undone, the pants were open enough that his impressive dick was revealed. My heart beat quicker as I watched him stroke himself, making him grow hard and bigger until his cock was impossibly stiff.

Fitting that inside any part of my body was going to be a challenge.

I'd been so awestruck, I'd stopped moving, but maybe this was a reaction Scott was used to. He grasped one of my hands and guided it to him, gently urging me to touch him.

Don't be afraid, his eyes seemed to say.

Which was sort of amusing to me. I wasn't scared. I'd committed myself to the experience, and I was happy to be 'all in.' I'd only been living at the house for a couple of weeks and had already fulfilled some of my wildest fantasies.

It was exciting to think about how far I could go, if I could satisfy every single craving I had and discover all sorts of new ones too.

When I tightened my fist and dragged it down his dick, Scott's lips parted to release a heavy breath. His fingers quickly went to the buttons of his shirt, undoing the bottom two so he could part the fabric out of my way.

The main camera was on a tripod in the corner of the room, angled so the viewer could see most of the backside of the desk. I swept my hair over my shoulder that was farther away from the lens, leaned forward, and ran the tip of my tongue in a line up the underside of his dick.

An appreciative sigh came from him, and his hands gripped the armrests of the chair so tightly, his knuckles went white. I licked my lips to moisten them, then opened my mouth and took him inside.

Goddamn, he was big.

I went as far down on him as I could, before slowly dragging my mouth back up to his tip.

"Yes," he breathed.

I pushed down on him again, and the head of his dick was at the back of my throat when his wife's voice filled my ear.

"Scott, can you angle another inch toward the camera? The armrest is blocking part of the shot."

I didn't have to do anything. He disguised the move by tangling a hand in my hair and pretending to control the speed of my blowjob. It was all for show; there was no tension in his hold as he shifted us subtly.

"Yes," Nina said. "Perfect."

It was wild to me she sounded so pleased when her husband's dick was lodged in someone else's mouth. But her voice was warm and happy.

I didn't know Scott and Nina that well yet, but I'd seen nothing but proof they loved each other. That they were *in love* with each other. His gaze followed her whenever she was in the room, and she almost always had her hand laced with his. I'd never seen an adult couple so enamored with each other like they were two teenagers.

I'd told Jack that people in love didn't sleep with other people, but maybe my mindset was too narrow. Just because I couldn't sleep with other people while I was in love didn't mean other people couldn't do it.

I closed my eyes and tried to imagine being that comfortable with someone else, that confident they could be intimate with someone else while staying committed to me. It was impossible. Promises were made to be broken.

And I knew I couldn't depend on anyone but myself.

Scott's hand let go of my head, and his arm dropped heavily onto the desk. I pictured us as the scene Nina was seeing through the different cameras. Her husband in his glasses and tweed jacket, with his pants and part of his shirt undone while he leaned back in his chair.

My head bobbed, and his glossy dick disappeared between my rose-colored lips. Since I was on my knees, my flirty dress was back in place.

Did she like what she saw? Was she all alone in the editing room and turned on so much, she'd put a hand down her shorts and touch herself? Fuck, the idea turned my blood to lava, and I slid my mouth even faster on him.

But my heart froze when there was a loud knock on the door. I'd gotten so lost in my fantasy, it hadn't registered when Nina called for Colin, and for a moment the scene became real. I was worried we were going to get caught.

I pulled my mouth away, letting his damp cock fall against his stomach, and even though I was hidden behind the desk, I turned my gaze in the direction of the door.

"Yes?" Scott asked loudly.

It wasn't an invitation, but it was interpreted as one. The door creaked open, and footsteps rang out as the person entered. Even though I couldn't see him, I sensed his presence. The air in the room changed, charging with static electricity.

Colin.

FOURTEEN

Madison

There was a camera near the door which gave a similar view to the one Colin was likely seeing. He'd walked in to discover his 'professor' seated behind his desk. Maybe he thought the way the man was angled was just a casual pose, and not that he was using the desk to try to hide how his pants were undone or that he wasn't alone.

I pretended to be shocked and kept quiet behind the desk.

Scott glanced at his watch, then leveled his gaze across the room. "Carter," he said, using Colin's stage name. "You're early." His tone was brusque. "Our appointment isn't for another ten minutes."

"I know," Colin sounded apologetic, "but I didn't know how long this meeting was going to be, and my next class is on the other side of campus." He paused expectantly, but when his professor didn't say anything, he continued. "What's this about? All your email said was you wanted to speak with me in private."

"Yes."

Scott acted like he was going to say more, but I interrupted his thoughts when my palms smoothed up his thighs. The character I was playing was the naughty girl, and she wanted to keep going, even with someone else in the room.

A panicked sound escaped the back of his throat when

I gripped his dick with both hands. He made a half-hearted attempt to push me away, but I was too insistent, too determined, plus he was doing his best to not make it obvious what was happening.

When I took him back in my mouth, he choked back a groan of satisfaction.

"Okay. So . . . what did you want to talk about?" Colin asked, pretending to be oblivious.

"You plagiarized your paper," Scott accused in a voice that was tight, clipped with agonizing pleasure.

"What?" Colin gasped. He attempted to sound flustered, but unlike Scott, he wasn't as good at acting like he was acting. It sounded forced. "No, I didn't."

Scott's breathing went shallow when I picked up my pace, but I had no idea if he was really struggling to hide the pleasure from his face, or if he were just pretending.

"Don't bother denying it," he said. He tilted his head up to the ceiling for a moment to regroup. "I've, uh, decided to let it slide this time, but don't . . ." He inhaled sharply as I made a production out of sucking hard, hollowing out my cheeks, and his statement came out in a rush. "Don't do it again."

For a moment, there was no sound.

Time hung awkwardly, and I pictured Colin standing there, wearing a bewildered expression. His professor had arranged this meeting to discuss his cheating, but rather than report or sanction, he was simply giving him a warning.

"That's it?" His tone was dubious.

"Yes," Scott said breathlessly, making it sound much more like it was meant for me than his other student. But then he must have realized how it sounded, because he cleared his throat. "You can go."

I let loose a deep moan.

"What was that?" Colin asked.

"Nothing." Scott waved his hand toward the exit. "Shut the door on your way out."

"Is there somebody back there?"

"No, of course not—"

But Colin's footsteps got louder, and then he was there, peering over the edge of the desk to see me with my lips wrapped around Scott's dick. I held my breath, unsure of how he would react.

I'd done two scenes with him already, but that didn't mean he had any claim over me. Still, I wondered—would he be jealous seeing me with another man? And did I *want* him to be jealous?

He wasn't. A shit-eating grin twisted on his lips. "What's going on here?"

"It's not what it looks like," Scott said.

I kept a hand wrapped around his dick as I lifted my mouth off him. "Oh, it's *exactly* what it looks like." I giggled. "I'm trying to get a better grade."

"Yeah?" Colin tilted his head. "My grade's looking better now, too."

When I tried to go down on Scott, he seized my shoulders. "Can you stop for a minute?" He sighed and turned his attention to Colin. "You didn't see anything, just like I didn't catch you cheating. Understood?"

"Gotcha. I definitely didn't see you getting blown just now by the hottest girl on campus."

My breath caught, and it wasn't an act. Most of the script

was improvised, but this line felt weirdly real. As if he hadn't thought about it and it'd just fallen out of his mouth.

"Yeah," Scott muttered. "Well, she hopped up on my desk and flashed her pussy at me, so I couldn't resist. Trust me, you wouldn't have been able to either."

He'd given me the perfect opening, and my pulse climbed. "Should we find out?"

"What?" both men said at the same time.

I got up off my knees, and as I sat on the top of the desk, I turned to beckon Colin closer, curling my finger back toward myself. Then I pinned my gaze on the other man. "Let's see if he finds this pussy as irresistible as you do, Professor."

His shoulders lifted as he drew in a breath. Deep in his eyes and behind the actor, I could see he was pleased with the transition.

Colin stalked to the desk and then around the side, coming to a stop near Scott's chair and facing me. His eyes were piercing as he stared at me, waiting for the show to begin.

It shouldn't have been hard. I'd had no problem doing this for Scott, and I wasn't revealing anything Colin hadn't seen before. And yet, that damn tremble in me began again. My breath went shallow and ragged as I inched up my skirt.

Blood rushed through my head, drowning out all sound but the pounding of my heart. Why was it so different this time? Was it because he looked at me like this was real for him? As if he couldn't *wait* to see what I was going to show him?

I peeled the fabric all the way to my waist, letting cool air waft over my newly exposed skin, and I opened my legs wider. I wanted it to sound confident and seductive, but I faltered, so my question was breathless and uneven. "What do you think?"

"Fuck." I felt Colin's gaze between my legs the same way as if he'd run a hand between them. "That pussy looks good enough to eat."

Jesus.

Scott was up out of his chair so fast, it rolled away on its wheels. "I agree."

He slid his hands under my thighs and jerked me at an angle to the edge of the desk, which made me collapse onto my back. And then his hot mouth was on my pussy, his tongue slicking over my clit.

The pleasure was white-hot.

"Oh," I gasped. "*Yes.*"

There was nowhere else I could look. My head lolled, turning to Colin, and fire seared across my cheeks in a blush. It was erotic having him watch as someone else was going down on me. I threaded my hands into my hair and bowed my back, trying not to fall off the side of the desk as I enjoyed the sensation of Scott's fluttering tongue.

My moans were loud, and deep, and real.

Scott knew what he was doing, but I sensed my response was more than just that. My whole body felt sensitized under the power of Colin's gaze. I watched him through hooded eyes, and . . . I wished he was the one with his head between my thighs. I wanted that to be his tongue that was massaging my clit and making moans pour from my lips.

The tremble in me—that was him. It only happened when he was with me. Touching me. *Looking* at me.

Did he know?

"Shh," Scott ordered. "Someone's going to hear."

Colin stepped up to the side of the desk, only inches away from my head. "Should I put something in her mouth to help her stay quiet?"

Shit, his question was loaded with sin, and I squirmed against the smooth, lacquered wood. "Oh, my God, yes."

I reached out, hooked my fingers under the waistband of his jeans, and jerked him even closer to me. He was already hard, tenting the front of his pants, and I was eager to have them gone. His hurried hands undid them, and the denim fell down his legs, revealing his strong thighs and rock-hard dick.

It was pointless to keep denying there was a connection between us, and my lungs let out the softest sigh of relief when I touched him. One single stroke of my hand down the length of him, and his expression shifted. He didn't have to act right now.

"Fuck," I cried.

Because as I prepared to take Colin in my mouth, Scott had pushed two fingers deep inside me. Pleasure surged through me. It sped up my spine and lit across every nerve ending in my body. I was so distracted by it, I didn't realize Colin had taken off his shirt until it was gone.

My gaze traced over the perfectly sculpted landscape of his chest. I'd watched him work out last week, and as much as I hadn't wanted to, I'd spent days afterward fantasizing about him. God, he looked so amazing.

He set one hand flat on the desk beside my head and used the other to scoop me up, holding on to the back of my neck as his hips pushed forward. I parted my lips, enjoying the sinful glide of his cock into my awaiting mouth.

We were a circuit connected, power flowing between me from one man to the other. Was Nina seeing that onscreen? I was sprawled out on the desk as a toy for them to use however they saw fit.

I was focused on keeping my head at the right angle so Colin could fuck my mouth, but bliss was building inside me from Scott's fingers and wicked tongue. It was getting harder and harder to stay still.

My moans where muffled by Colin's dick in my mouth, and it was so fucking sexy the way he moved. His whole body rocked and undulated, not just his hips as he thrust and retreated. I lifted a hand and flattened it on the center of his chest, desperate to have more of a connection to him.

The pace of the fingers moving inside me sped up, demanding they were all I think about. Scott's tongue was a flurry of pleasure, and I had to drag air in and out of my body through my nose because my mouth was occupied.

Everything narrowed in. Heat closed down around me.

I had to pull my head back just enough to break the connection so I could gasp, "I'm going to come."

No sooner were the words out before the orgasm descended on me. It erupted from my center and flooded outward in a blast of icy fire. My body stole control from my mind, making my muscles flinch and contract as each wave rolled through me.

Maybe he hoped to keep me quiet because Colin urged his dick back inside my mouth as I came, but I wondered if it were more than just that. Had he wanted to be a part of my pleasure, to be joined with me as the orgasm wracked my body?

Even with his wide cock at the back of my throat, I was still loud. My satisfied moan filled the room.

I hadn't finished recovering when Scott straightened. I caught glimpses of him as he shed his tweed jacket, tossed it onto the chair, and finished unbuttoning his shirt. It too was taken off and cast aside, then his pants, socks, and shoes were dealt with.

He had a nice body. Not quite as chiseled as Colin, but he was still in great shape and incredibly attractive.

My legs were boneless from my orgasm, but it didn't matter much.

Scott pulled me off the desk and supported my climax-weak body in his arms, before turning me around. Colin stepped in between me and the desk, and since my brain was in a bliss-filled fog, I must have missed the moment when he'd taken the rest of his clothes off.

As Colin leaned back against the edge of the desk, Scott pressed me forward. I had to put my hands out, causing them to squeal on the desktop as I was bent over and trapped Colin between my arms.

We'd choreographed this before filming, but it was so fucking different now. Everything inside me was tingling and sluggish. It made me grateful for my partners' hands to guide me exactly how I needed to be, especially when Nina made a comment about angles.

The back of my skirt was flipped up around my waist by the man behind me, but my attention was solely on the one in front of me. Colin had a hand pumping his dick and gripped the side of my face with his other. It forced my eyes to stay on him.

As if I could look anywhere else.

Scott's rough palm grasped my hip as he prepared to take me, and my heart skipped. There were three people in this room, but Nina and the cameras were watching, too, and I held my breath. Despite that, I was most interested in what Colin thought. Had he ever shared a girl with another guy before?

A part deep inside of me hoped he'd like it at least half as much as I'd liked sharing him with Abbie.

The head of Scott's cock nudged at my entrance, and I held my breath.

"Anything for an A," he said in a dark voice. "Right?"

"Yes," I breathed.

My unblinking gaze was fixed on Colin, and he watched my reaction intently as Scott began to slide inside. My eyes melted and my mouth dropped open, but no sound came out. Goddamn, he was huge.

I was worried this might have been a turn-off, but if anything, it had the opposite effect on Colin. Lust thickened in his eyes, and a smile ghosted across his lips. "That's it," he urged. "Take that big cock."

I gasped, and although Scott was the one claiming my body, I was sure Colin was claiming my mind.

"Fuck, Scott," Nina's tone was full of awe, "look at how you make her tremble."

My face contorted, and I blinked in confusion. My shaking wasn't because of Scott. The shudder that shook my shoulders and rattled my legs was all due to Colin, and I, for some reason, needed him to know that.

I took a hand off the desk and grabbed his shoulder,

steadying myself so I could lean in and set my lips against the side of his neck. I trailed my kiss up to the shell of his ear, the one that wasn't wearing the monitor.

"Not him," I whispered so no one else would hear. "You."

He jolted. Both of his hands closed around my shoulders and eased me back so he could stare at me in disbelief, like there was no way he'd heard me right. My heart tumbled through my body. Yes, it was true, but . . . *why the fuck* had I told him? His intense eyes announced he wanted to kiss me.

You cannot let that happen.

I didn't give him a chance to try. I slid my hand from his shoulder down to grip his cock and dipped my head. Just as Scott established his rhythm, I did the same with my mouth on Colin.

His groan was a mixture of frustration and satisfaction.

I couldn't focus on it because, within an instant, my body went on overload. Scott drove deep, and Colin's dick filled my mouth, and it was crazy that this was really happening. My list of fantasies was extensive, but this was one I'd never thought could become a reality.

Both men were naked, and it seemed strange to still have clothes on, but Colin's fingers discovered the zipper at the back of my dress. He inched it down while I swirled my tongue around his dick, going fast enough it made him pulse.

When the zipper was halfway down, Scott took over and tugged it the rest of the way. The dress split open, and the sides fell to catch on my elbows. It was awkward, so I quickly unlooped each arm and let the dress hang, bunched at my waist.

My wardrobe included a lacy black bra that matched the

stockings, but viewers wouldn't get a good look at it because Scott's fingers worked the clasp on my back. The tension went out of the band, and the straps slipped down my arms.

As it fell to the floor, Scott grabbed my waist. One of his hands fisted my dress, twisting it until it was a belt that he could use for leverage, and my breasts bounced with each of his thrusts. It took me several attempts to find the right rhythm as I rocked between the two guys, and although I had support from Scott's hold and one hand on the edge of the desk, it felt precarious.

I enjoyed what I was doing, but it also had me out of breath. My legs and arms shook because of Colin . . . and also with fatigue. There was so much to think about, I vaguely acknowledged the sounds of pleasure that came from the guys.

When I was barely able to stand any longer, Scott seemed to know.

"Let me have that mouth," he said, although I wasn't sure if he was speaking to me or Colin.

He jerked me upright and spun me around in his arms. My dress dropped to the floor, leaving me in only my thighhighs, and he picked me up and sat me down on the desktop just as soon as the other man moved out of the way.

I was a puppet, and they were pulling all my strings, positioning me how they wanted. I was more than fine with it. My overwhelmed mind no longer remembered the choreography of the scene. I flopped down on my back with my body draped over the corner of the desk, my head hanging over the edge.

It wasn't comfortable, but it gave Colin room to step in between my legs. The determined look on his face stole my breath. He hooked my trembling knees over his arms, and he didn't waste any time getting inside me. One quick shove, and he was buried all the way to the hilt.

His impatience was incredibly sexy. It made me feel like he'd been dying for this moment.

Had I been, too?

Because he made my body sing with satisfaction. I let out a loud moan, and then a hand was on my cheek, turning my head to the side. It was so I could give Scott what he wanted. I opened my mouth, letting him push his cock past my lips, and he held my head as he began to thrust. Thankfully, it took some of the strain off my neck.

Time began to blur.

I was sticky with sweat. As Colin slammed his body into me, beating his hips against mine, I inched dangerously closer to the edge of the desk. But he held my legs tightly and kept me from falling over the side.

God, I loved the feel of his hands against my skin—almost as much as the way he drove into me. My feelings toward him were . . . messy. It was hard to dislike someone who made you feel so incredibly good.

Scott held my head steady with one hand while he sawed his dick back and forth between my lips and used the other to squeeze one of my breasts. Maybe Colin didn't want to be outdone by the porn star, or perhaps he just wanted to touch me, too. He set his hand just above where we were joined and used his thumb to tease my clit.

It doused me in pure fire.

And it sent me racing toward another orgasm.

These two beautifully muscle-bound men not only took

pleasure from me, but they worked together as a team to deliver it right back. Everything was shaking, like my world was enduring a massive earthquake, and yet the guys were impervious.

Scott's pinch on my nipple struck a perfect balance of pleasure and pain, but Colin's thumb was diabolical. It stirred faster, making pressure build inside me, spiraling toward release.

I jerked my head away from Scott and bowed off the desktop, my hands clutching at the sides. "*Fuck.*"

This orgasm was different than the first. It was deeper, fuller. The pleasure was more of a band that wrapped around me and squeezed, rather than a sharp jolt of ecstasy. Its grip lasted longer, too.

I gulped down air, shutting my eyes, and savored the sensation, but Colin didn't give me much time to recover. His pace quickened, and the single arm that was supporting most of my lower body turned to stone.

"This pussy," he growled, "is gonna make me come."

My eyes opened quickly enough to see the men exchange a look. Maybe Colin was looking for confirmation that Scott was ready, too. The message was received because Scott clamped a hand around his cock and began to furiously stroke it.

Colin pumped into me with a few final thrusts, before pulling out to do the same.

My heart was still going a mile a minute after my orgasm, but if it hadn't been, I was sure it would have kicked even faster watching the show. Both men worked to bring themself to orgasm and finish as close together as possible.

Colin went first.

His ragged breathing cut off abruptly and his shoulders punched forward before he let out a loud grunt of pleasure. Then, his fist switched from sliding along in rapid, shallow strokes to slow, long ones. I flinched as the first wave of his cum splattered across my stomach, but then an enormous smile spread across my lips.

Shit, he looked sexy when he came. His jaw was tensed, and his gaze was focused on the ropes of cum he painted across my bare skin, all while heavy, labored breath came and went from his lungs.

When his post-orgasm eyes lifted to find me watching him, every muscle in my body tightened. *Jesus.* He stared back at me, and it was bottomless. I could get trapped inside his intense gaze if I wasn't careful, and he looked at me like that was exactly what he wanted.

A groan of pleasure snapped me out of my stupor.

Scott wasn't far behind Colin, and as he came, he was expressive. It was exciting to not just see, but also hear his enjoyment. I'd been studying up and watching porn every night since moving into the house, and the videos where the men were just as vocal as the women?

So hot.

We'd discussed beforehand that he'd come on my chest, but I wasn't prepared for how fucking sexy the final act would be. The warm, thick liquid shot across my breasts, dripping down the sides of my chest.

I wore the product of both of their orgasms on my skin, and unexpected warmth bloomed inside me. I liked how we'd all gotten off together. My gaze shifted from Scott to

Colin, and then back again as my body cooled and reality began to return.

"Madison, ask about your grade," Nina prompted.

Right.

I opened my mouth to say the line, but Colin's hands wrapped around my arm and helped pull me up, so I was sitting right at the edge of the desk. I did my best to keep my expression normal, because gravity was now in effect, and the sensation of cum trickling down my skin was awkward as hell.

Even more bizarre was the way he nuzzled into the side of my neck. This wasn't in the script, and his unexpected kiss just below my ear gave me a delicious shiver. Was he trying to get me to cave and turn into his kiss? I couldn't.

I locked my gaze on Scott while I endured Colin's persuasive mouth. My resolve not to kiss him was crumbling every second.

"So, Professor," I drawled, "do we both get an A?"

Scott's slow smile was sinful. Since Colin was already sucking on one side of my neck, he must have decided to bookend it, and leaned in. Without giving it any thought, I saw my opportunity and took it.

I couldn't kiss Colin if I was too busy kissing Scott.

Scott inhaled sharply when I put my hand on his shoulder, turned toward him, and planted my lips on his. My action had surprised him, but he seemed okay with it. His head tilted to a better angle, his soft lips parted, and his tongue filled my mouth.

It was . . . nice.

Pleasant.

But that was all it was. The earth didn't shake, and my heart didn't beat faster. At least, not until the mouth at the side of my neck paused. The warmth of Colin disappeared as he realized what was happening.

A chill swept over me as my kiss ended with Scott, who seemed oblivious to the frigid storm front moving in—the one originating from the other man.

"Yes," Scott said, finally answering my question. "You'll both get A's . . . as long as I see you again the same time next week."

He held his smile until his wife's voice came through our monitors.

"Got it," she said. "Nice job, everyone."

The scene was over, but now I had no idea what to do. Once again, he seemed to know. "Stay there," Scott said gently. "I'll grab everyone a towel."

As he stepped away, I sucked in a breath. I hadn't looked at Colin since I'd kissed Scott, because I didn't want to see how much I'd pissed him off. This frat boy was probably used to getting his way, and I expected him to pitch a fit.

Only, when I risked a glance, I didn't find anger in his expression. I saw something far worse—he looked hurt. Betrayed.

I felt like absolute shit. Last week, I'd accused him of being cruel, but the way he stared at me now? It left me wondering who between us was really the cruel one.

FIFTEEN

Madison

I'd trekked across the back yard to the gym every day this week, hoping to run into Colin so we could talk, but he was never there. I even mixed up my schedule to increase my chances, but no luck. He was either working out insanely early, not at all, or had figured out when I planned to head over and went at a different time.

Since his room was in the opposite wing of the house, the only place I'd encounter him was the common areas, but he must have eaten his meals in his room or on campus.

He was avoiding me.

For a half-second I'd considered knocking on his door to have a conversation, but what the fuck would I say?

I'm sorry I won't kiss you because I'm afraid of what will happen if I do.

He'd successfully dodged me through the weekend, but it was Monday afternoon now. In a few hours, he'd have to sit across from me at the house meeting, and there was no avoiding that.

I finished the last bite of my lunch and tossed my napkin on top of my plate. I usually brought my lunch, but I'd been so unmotivated to attend my psychology lecture this morning, I'd told myself if I went, I'd reward myself with a nice lunch after. I had a long break between classes, and there was a cozy bistro nearby.

Plus, I had money now—not a ton, but it was enough to give my bank account some breathing room if I wanted to splurge like this.

I had the money because I'd done my first solo video for Petal Productions the day after my group scene. We filmed it in the studio in the basement, and all I'd had to do was play with a vibrator while repeating the sexy dialogue Nina had fed me through an earpiece.

Easy.

Except during it, I'd wondered if I'd ever shoot a scene like this with Colin.

Which was ridiculous. There were four other people in the house, two of whom I'd yet to film with. Why was I so hung up on him?

It was frustrating, and I sighed before picking up my tray and carrying it over to the trash can. As I scraped my plate into the garbage, a familiar voice caught my attention.

How ironic.

Apparently, I could only run into Colin if I wasn't looking for him.

The garbage can was divided from the dining room by decorative lattice, but I could see through the empty spaces in the wood slats, and I spied him sitting at the booth just on the other side.

The man across the table from him was older, and judging by his resemblance, this guy was probably his father. The other thing that was a dead giveaway was Colin's posture. It was tense and unnatural for the frat boy who'd up until now always seemed so confident and relaxed. It reminded me of the way I was around my parents.

Did he not get along with his dad? There were plates on the table in front of both men, but Colin's lunch was only half-eaten. His father wore a suit and tie and appeared to be a more distinguished version of his son, and far more serious.

I knew I shouldn't eavesdrop, but I was too curious not to.

"I wish my client hadn't canceled," his father said, "but I'm glad we got to do this."

"Yeah. Me too." Except Colin's voice was flat.

"You don't have another class today, right?" His father gathered his things onto the tray. "I'll give you a lift back to the Sig house."

Alarm shot through Colin that he quickly tried to disguise. "Oh, no, you don't have to—"

"It's fine." His father waved a hand. "I've got some time to kill before my next appointment, and I wouldn't mind seeing the place again."

Oh, my God. He hadn't told his parents he'd been kicked out?

You didn't tell yours either.

My relationship with my parents was undoubtedly different, but I still felt a pang of understanding. The way I'd acted and the things I'd done that had ended my sorority life were embarrassing, plus it wasn't surprising he hadn't told his parents about his new living arrangement.

"Actually, I was planning to study at the library," Colin said. "You know, for finals."

His father had begun to slide out of his seat but stopped and peered at his son critically. "Really? You don't have your laptop with you." His expression turned plain. "Did you forget it back at the house?"

When Colin didn't have an answer, his father shook his head as if to say, *classic Colin*. He stood and reached for his tray. "C'mon. We'll put your bike in the back of my car."

Colin's expression was pained. He was trapped with no way out, and something inside me shifted.

I stacked my tray and rounded the corner, stepping into view. "Hey, Colin." I strode toward him, ignoring how his eyes went wide with shock, then narrow with distrust. He glared at me like his day had just gone from bad to worse.

"I'm sorry to interrupt," I flashed a shy smile at his dad before turning back to him, "but I'm so glad you're here. I need a really big favor." I took in a deep breath. "Can you—uh—walk with me to my next class?" I tucked a lock of hair behind my ear, trying to look nervous and sell the story. "There's this guy who's been hitting on me and will not take a hint. If he sees me with someone else, maybe he'll stop."

For a moment, he simply blinked.

Then, there was a spark of hope in his eyes before his gaze darted to his father and back to me. I was offering him a chance to escape, and Colin was happy to take it. "Yeah, of course."

"Aren't you going to introduce me?" His father's tone had an edge of irritation.

"Yeah. This is Mads." Colin made a face. "Madison Perry," he corrected. His posture straightened as his attention swung back to me. "This is my dad, Rob Novak."

Mr. Novak thrust out his hand, and I took it, finding his handshake oppressive.

"Nice to meet you, sir," I said.

"Same," he replied.

His gaze worked me over head to toe, probably evaluating my relationship with his son—but he wouldn't get it right with a million guesses. Hell, even I didn't know what Colin and I were to each other.

"How do you two know each other?" He'd attempted to sound casual but couldn't have been more obvious if he'd tried. Mr. Novak wanted to figure out if we were dating. Or maybe he knew his son's reputation and was wondering if we'd slept together.

"We're friends," Colin lied.

"At a Greek mixer," I said at the same time.

Our mismatched story hung for a moment, but Mr. Novak didn't seem to care. His gaze settled on his son. "How about you walk her to class, I'll take your bike back to Sigma Phi Alpha, and I'll meet you there when you're done."

Once again, worry swept through Colin. He peered at me with dread. This was my moment to land a critical blow and win the war between us, and he fully expected me to take it. To tell his father there was no reason to go to the Sig house because Colin was no longer a member.

But instead, I lifted a shoulder in a half-shrug.

"That's why I said it was a big favor." I gave a sheepish look. "My class is in Slater Hall."

It was total bullshit. My next class was only a few blocks away, but Slater Hall was on the other side of campus, and about as far away from the Sig house as you could get. It'd take us fifteen minutes to walk there, and at least as long to walk from it to the frat house.

"Oh," Mr. Novak said, understanding quickly. "Should I

give you both a lift there?"

"I don't want to inconvenience you," I started, but Colin cut me off.

"We won't all fit with my bike in the back seat." He did his best not to sound pleased. "Don't worry about it. I'll walk my bike over with her to her class, then ride it home after."

His father glanced at his watch and did the math in his head, perhaps determining his plan for seeing the frat house wouldn't work out. "All right. Next time, then." He picked up his tray and Colin's too. "I've got this. You better get going if you don't want to be late to class."

"Thanks." Relief poured through Colin's expression. "And thanks for lunch."

His dad nodded. "Nice meeting you, Madison. I hope Colin can help you."

I swallowed down the lump in my throat. As much as it pained me to admit it, his son had already helped me. "Thanks," I pushed out. "Nice meeting you, too."

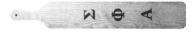

I followed Colin to the bike rack outside and said nothing as he unlocked it. We didn't speak as he grabbed the handlebars and began to pull the bike down the sidewalk. It was May now, and the afternoon sun was already hot as it blazed down on us, making me sweat.

The silence was awkward between us, but in a different way. Instead of animosity, we were tense with unspoken things we knew we should be talking about.

I waited until we'd crossed several streets because I

wanted to make sure his dad wouldn't see when we changed directions. "We don't have to go this way."

"It's the fastest way to Slater," he said.

"Except I don't have a class in Slater. I made the whole thing up."

He pulled to a stop. "What?" For a single heartbeat, he looked lost, but then suspicion clouded his eyes. "Why?"

"Because you needed an excuse not to go back to the Sig house."

We were in the middle of the sidewalk, so he lifted his bike and carried it a few steps onto the grassy lawn before parking it under the shade of a huge oak tree so we wouldn't be in anyone's way.

"You could have told him I got kicked out."

"Yeah," I said softly. "I could have."

He stared at me with disbelief. Like he expected me to rip off a mask and reveal a new person beneath at any moment. "Why didn't you?"

I drew in a breath. "Because it's not my business. I'm sure you have your reasons for not telling him."

He looked . . . confounded. "I do," he said quietly. "But why'd you help me?"

That was harder to answer. I dropped my gaze to the tree roots that poked up out of the ground at my feet. "I don't know." But I *did* know. "We're not friends, but we're"—I searched for the right word—"partners. I thought I should have your back."

It was such a strange explanation, and it made him take in a heavy breath. His voice was unsteady. "Okay. Well . . . thanks."

"Yeah, no problem."

Except it was a problem when I lifted my gaze up to meet his. He looked so good standing there with his strong hands gripping the bike's handlebars and seat, and dappled sunlight splashed across his fitted t-shirt. The wind ruffled the leaves overhead and played with his dark hair, making him look like an advertisement for picture-perfect college life.

And whatever I was feeling about us? He felt it, too.

His gaze deepened and intensified. "Mads, I—"

"I kissed Scott," I blurted, "and I didn't kiss you."

His expression hardened over. "Yeah, I noticed."

"Can I tell you why?" My heart climbed into my throat. "It's because I don't want to like you."

"Um, what?"

I set my hands on my hips. "Look, it's a bad idea. We live together and, uh, *work* together, and—what was it you said when we showed up for auditions?"

His eyebrows tugged together.

"You told me not to fuck this up for you," I continued, "and I'm trying not to. It's better for both of us if we don't like each other. It's easier. Safer."

The muscle running along his jaw ticked. "But you kiss other people you *work* with."

I pressed my lips together. "Well, I wish I could tell you it's not personal, but it is."

"Because I'm cruel," he guessed, sounding bitter.

"No, because I know how I feel about them. I don't with you. And I don't know what'll happen if we kiss, Colin." I leveled my hardest gaze at him. "I don't *want* to know."

His hand on the seat tightened instinctively, like my

statement had caused the urge for him to reach out but he'd had to strangle it back.

"So, I don't want to like you," I declared, "and I don't think you want to like me either. Right?"

It took him a long time to answer, and it made me nervous with how unconvinced he sounded. "Right."

"Good." I used my fingertips to scrub my forehead and glanced up at the clock tower. "Well, I actually do have a class soon, so I've got to go." I adjusted my bag on my shoulder and gave him an awkward wave goodbye before starting for the sidewalk.

"Mads."

I turned to glance at him. He hadn't moved from the shade. It was like the tree roots had grown up around his feet.

"Thanks for explaining it." This time he sounded more like himself. "And again, for helping with my dad."

"I'm sure you would have done the same," I said automatically, and as I turned back around, I grimaced. I didn't see a dubious expression on him, but I didn't need to.

I was smart enough to know there was no way it was true.

By the end of the week, I was mildly concerned I was developing a Colin problem. Outwardly, things between us were better since I'd confessed my reasoning for not kissing him, but inwardly, it was getting harder not to think about him.

When I went into the gym on Saturday afternoon, he was there, and without prompting, he showed me a few upper body exercises. I'd done my best to listen and absorb what he was saying, but he wasn't wearing a shirt again, and it was hotter than a sauna in the gym.

I was so fucking curious about him.

Why hadn't he told his father he wasn't a Sig anymore? What was causing the tension between them? And most importantly, how had Colin's first scene without me gone?

Monday night we'd pitched our ideas at the meeting and had been paired with new partners. Nina was to be the horny stepmother who'd seduce her eager stepson while her husband was out of town, and Jaquan would be my private masseuse whose wandering hands became irresistible.

I didn't feel jealousy over Colin or envy Nina. But I'd had a touch of disappointment that I wouldn't get to watch them together—I'd have to wait like everyone else for the video to be posted the following week.

It must have gone okay, though, because everyone acted the same afterward. One night when I'd been eating dinner alongside Abbie, she'd mentioned you could tell when someone had struggled through a scene or if it had gone off the rails. You could feel the tension in the air, she'd said, and it was a major buzzkill.

I watched Colin as he lay on the bench and did skull crushers with a set of dumbbells that were probably too heavy for me to even pick up. Did he wonder how my scene with Jaquan had gone?

After we'd spent an hour depersonalizing my bedroom, Nina had dressed the set to look as generic as possible, and then we'd filmed in there.

Jaquan had worn a white polo shirt and khaki pants, and he'd carried a collapsible massage table with him as I ushered him into the room. I'd asked politely if we could do the massage in here, and as he'd set up the table, I'd lit some candles. My wardrobe had been a string bikini beneath a robe, and I'd shed it as soon as he'd said he was ready.

After I'd gotten on the table, he'd draped towels over me, then filled his hands with massage oil while I undid the strings of my bikini.

I would have been a fool to not enjoy the scene, and I had. He was gorgeous and sexy, and—good God—his hands were divine. Like Scott, Jaquan was an experienced partner who made me feel safe and comfortable, and was skilled at leading me through my part.

But . . .

Maybe that was what I liked so much about performing with Colin. We were both new, and so he felt more like an equal than anyone else in the house. It was as if we were bonded by coming up at the same time.

My heart still raced when the towel slipped off, exposing my naked breasts to Jaquan, but it didn't race quite as fast as it had with Colin. I still got a thrill when Jaquan touched me, but it was slightly muted. When his hand delved between my thighs, it brought me pleasure—but not to orgasm.

Not until I closed my eyes and pretended it was Colin's hand.

That was my first inkling that I had a problem.

Despite that, I still really liked what I'd done with Jaquan. It was hot and his massage at the beginning was sensual. We'd discussed everything beforehand, and I'd told him I was fine with kissing on the lips—but when it happened, it was the same as it'd been with Scott and Abbie.

Fun.

Safe.

But definitely not amazing.

After he'd made me come, he'd turned me over onto my stomach, stripped off his clothes, and urged me to go down on him. Like everyone else in this house, he was toned and fit and well-endowed, and I loved listening to his quiet sounds of satisfaction as I traced the tip of my tongue along the length of his cock.

When he couldn't endure the blowjob any longer, Jaquan climbed up on the table and straddled my legs, taking me from behind. He felt so good, and when I clamped my hands around the edge of the padded table, he glided his fingertips sensually over my oil-glossed back.

My moans were real, but I also played them up for the cameras.

The experience was exciting and new, but I wondered if that was all it was. Once the newness wore off, would the excitement fade and this sex work would truly feel like work? I hoped not. Everyone else seemed to enjoy what they did.

After he came and the scene pulled to a close, Jaquan gave me a final, sweet kiss, and I couldn't help but grin. He was so fucking handsome and nice that for a long moment the Colin problem faded into the background.

But then Nina's voice came through the earpiece, and it reminded me of the last scene I'd done—and who I'd done it with.

At first, I thought finals week would save me. I'd be too busy studying and finishing up projects to give any of my thoughts to Colin, but the universe had other plans.

It was unseasonably hot and humid in Nashville for mid-May, and by Monday the temperature outside soared to almost ninety degrees. Scott claimed to have turned on the air conditioning . . . but it obviously wasn't working.

It was especially bad upstairs, where the worst of the heat collected. Only dry, warm air came out of the vents, and as the temperature outside climbed, so did the thermostat inside.

"I'm sweating my tits off," Abbie proclaimed at our house meeting.

"I know," Nina said, looking apologetic. "We called the HVAC place, but the earliest they can come out is tomorrow afternoon. We'll bring the fans over from the gym, and you can sleep in the living room or the studio downstairs tonight if you get too hot."

Abbie glanced across the table, and a smile slunk across her lips. Her tone was sultry. "Hey, Jaquan."

He laughed knowingly. "Hey, girl. I'm looking real good tonight, huh?"

"You sure are." She swooned dramatically. "What with your big muscles, and your beautiful smile . . . and all that sexy cold air in your room."

"Wait," I said. "The guys have AC?"

"That side of the house is on a different unit," Scott explained. "We've cranked it down and put a fan in the doorway to help push the air, but it's a smaller unit. It can't keep up."

My envious gaze flicked to Colin. He was looking at the table and seemed lost in thought. Maybe he was thinking about how he hadn't gotten such a bad deal after all with the smaller room.

Shit, it was so hot on the second floor. It wasn't as bad here in the dining room, but it was still uncomfortable, and we only began to pitch ideas before Nina lifted a hand.

"You know what? Let's postpone this to tomorrow night," she announced. "The heat's making me cranky, and everyone looks like they'd rather be somewhere else."

Which was true.

But I lingered at the table while everyone else got up and dispersed from the stifling room. I wasn't eager to deal with my options. I needed to study because my final tomorrow morning accounted for a fourth of my grade, and I needed to get some sleep because I couldn't be a zombie for the test either.

It was too late to think about getting a hotel room, and probably too expensive, plus I'd have to pay for a rideshare to get there and back.

"Mads."

Colin's voice startled me out of my thoughts, and I looked up at him. While everyone else had cleared out, he'd remained. He stood beside his chair, and a bead of sweat from his temple ran down his handsome face as he gazed at me with a cryptic expression.

"If you want," he said, "you could, uh, stay in my room tonight."

My heart skipped at his offer, but my brain issued a warning. I needed to focus right now, and that would be impossible if he was around. It wasn't *that* hot, I told myself. I'd take a cold shower before bed, sleep naked, and survive the night.

"Thanks," I said, "but I'll be fine."

He almost looked relieved that I'd turned him down. "If you change your mind, you know where I'll be."

I spent the rest of the evening studying at the kitchen table, and at ten-thirty, I went upstairs and took a shower that was reminiscent of the ones I'd had at the Lambda house. There was an oscillating fan at the top of the stairs that was pushing air down the hall toward my room, but it wasn't helping. The upstairs thermostat read eighty-five, and it was warmer than that outside, so opening the windows wouldn't do anything.

I stripped off my clothes and everything from my bed so it was just the sheets and climbed in. For once, I viewed my warm-natured body as a curse and not the blessing it usually was. Unlike my friends, I rarely got cold or needed to wrap myself in a blanket while hanging out around the house.

Ten minutes in, I was so sweaty, I felt like I needed another shower.

Thirty minutes in, I was doing the math in my head about the amount of sleep I'd get if I fell asleep in the next hour, and if it'd be enough.

After an hour, I was filled with dread about the rest of the night, and regret that I'd turned down Colin's offer. I turned onto my side and glanced at the clock, which made me scowl. It was late. Probably too late to show up and ask him if his offer was still good. He had finals tomorrow, too, and was probably fast asleep between his crisp, cool sheets.

Goddammit.

Lying here in indecision was dumb. If I was going to do this, there was no sense in waiting.

I needed to go now.

SIXTEEN

Colin

I should have been asleep, or—if I was going to be awake—I should have been studying. But what I should be doing versus what I actually did were rarely the same, which was why I was about to jerk off instead.

It was the third time I'd watched this video, which was ridiculous. I had free access to all of Petal Productions content, including the stuff from long before I'd started here, and yet I'd barely touched their library.

Every night I came back to the same video.

It was Mads on the bed in the studio, staring into the camera as she held a black vibrator to her clit and said she wanted us to come together. Of course, the *us* she meant was her and the viewer, but I liked to pretend she actually meant me.

Last week, I'd tried to jerk off to our audition video, but it didn't work for me at all. No matter how hot she looked, my focus inevitably shifted to myself, and I found a million things to criticize. I disliked the way my voice sounded, or whatever dumb thing I said made me cringe, or my pale ass looked stupid.

Mads' solo video eliminated all that. I could just focus on her.

Even with the lights off, it never got that dark in my room

because the blinds didn't close all the way, and the exterior lights shining on the house stayed on all night, but I'd gotten used to it over the last month. I adjusted my headphones, got comfortable on my bed, and held my phone in one hand while I jammed the other inside my underwear.

I wrapped my fist around my semi-hard dick, but I only made it a single stroke before freezing.

Was . . . someone knocking on my door?

I paused the video, pulled off my headphones, and listened—but there was nothing. The silence stretched and all I heard was my own breathing.

Maybe I'd imagined it.

I went to put my headphones back on, only to hear quiet footsteps outside my door slowly walking away. Shit. I hurried up off the bed and yanked my door open, startling Mads, who was in the dark hallway, carrying a pillow and a thick comforter.

She turned, and her eyes widened until they seemed to be all white. I was only wearing a pair of short boxer briefs, and her gaze dragged over every inch of my body, which I enjoyed. She'd seen me naked three times already, but she still acted like she was seeing something that was forbidden.

"I'm sorry," she whispered. "I didn't mean to wake you."

"I wasn't asleep," I said. "What are you doing here?"

She shifted the bedding in her arms. "Trying not to have an orgasm."

My pulse kicked. "What?"

"It's too fucking hot in my room." She leaned against the wall and gave me a desperate look. "It feels so good down here."

"Changed your mind, huh?"

She nodded slowly. "Is that okay? I would have texted, but . . ."

We didn't have each other's number. I pushed my door open wider and gestured for her to follow me. "Yeah, it's fine. Come on in."

She walked to the edge of my room but hovered at the threshold, like she was unsure if she could make herself cross it.

The lights were off in my room, but there was still some low light, and my eyes were adjusted. Was her hair darker than normal? Wait, no. It was wet. She'd pulled it up into a messy bun on the top of her head and didn't seem to be wearing any makeup. She had on a white tank top and a pair of barely-there shorts that showed off her toned legs.

Fuck me—she was just as hot as she'd been in the video I'd started watching.

She scanned my room, and she seemed more curious than critical, but what was with her hesitation? I lifted my eyebrows to wordlessly ask, *are you coming?* She swallowed a breath and stepped into the room, moving out of the way so I could shut the door.

"What's the story on the comforter?" I motioned to the folded blue quilt she was holding.

"I don't have a sleeping bag." Her gaze was pinned to my chest, and her shoulders were tight. It was strange how she looked more nervous now than she'd been during our audition.

It took me a second to get why she'd want a sleeping bag—she thought I'd make her sleep on the floor.

I set my hands on my waist. "You can sleep in the bed."

"What about you?" Her gaze snapped up to finally meet mine. "Where are you going to be?"

"Uh . . ."

I scratched an itch behind my ear. Up until a second ago, I'd assumed I'd be in the bed with her. It was *my* bed, after all, and a voice inside me protested loudly that she'd been partly responsible for getting me kicked out of my frat. It'd be a bit much to let her kick me out of my own bed too.

"There's room," I said. "I guess I was thinking we'd share."

She turned to look at the rumpled sheets on the queen-sized bed, and her expression was full of trepidation. Like it might burst into flames at any second.

"Hey, it's okay." I tried to sound reassuring. "It's just sleep. I'll stay in my lane, and because I'm such a nice guy, I'll even let you pick which side gets to be yours." Still, she looked unconvinced. I held in the sigh I wanted to make. "There's not a lot of room, but if you don't feel comfortable sharing, I can take the floor."

"No." She drew in a deep breath and pushed it out. "It's fine. I'm comfortable with you." The second her statement was out, she looked like she wanted it back. "I mean, I'm comfortable with sharing. We've shared plenty of other things, right?"

I lifted a corner of my mouth. "Yeah, we have."

Her focus shifted back to the bed. It was obvious which side I preferred, and I was relieved when she claimed hers by tossing her pillow onto the other one, which was wedged in the corner.

The comforter wasn't needed, so she dropped it beside

my dresser, and it was strange watching her climb into my bed. I'd had plenty of girls sleep over when I lived at the Sig house, but it'd always been after we'd had sex. They'd stayed out of exhaustion or obligation, or maybe holding out hope that I'd wake up in the morning and proclaim they were now my girlfriend.

I'd never invited a girl into my bed to just sleep.

As Mads crawled toward her pillow, her hand brushed something and gave her pause. It was my phone that I'd discarded to answer the door, and I lurched forward to grab it, but it was too late. When she bumped the phone, the lock screen lit up, revealing the title of the video that was paused.

Annika Adore Orgasm Countdown.

Her little gasp was quiet yet deafening. "Were you watching one of my videos?"

I gathered up my phone and headphones and set them on the nightstand as I considered not answering her. But there was no point in lying. She'd seen that I had been.

"Yeah."

"Why?" She went breathless, either excited or horrified to hear my answer.

I crossed my arms over my chest and leaned back against the wall. "I was curious."

That wasn't a lie—I *had* watched it the first time because I'd wanted to know how her solo video had turned out. She didn't need to know I'd seen it more than once, or my reasons.

She folded her legs beside her as she sat on the mattress as far across from me as possible. Her chest rose and fell quickly, her lips pressed into a line, and it looked like she was considering something.

"I watched yours, too." Her statement was quiet and rushed.

I straightened abruptly from the wall. "Yeah?"

Like her, I'd done my first solo video two weeks ago. It'd been . . . fine. Sort of awkward. I jerked off regularly, but this? It was very different. I'd never made such a production out of it before. I'd had to be vocal and descriptive and rub my hands over my chest like that did something for me when it totally didn't.

It was a performance, and when it was over, I wondered aloud who'd want to watch it.

"Mostly dudes," Scott had replied.

That was surprising, but it didn't bother me. I was straight, but if some guy wanted to watch me stroke my dick and it made him hard, well . . . that was kind of flattering, I guessed.

Interest pumped through me, knowing Mads had watched my solo.

"Why?" I asked.

"I was curious."

She took the easy way out by feeding my answer back to me, and it set thoughts firing off in my mind. Had it turned her on? Had she played with herself while watching? Had she been like me and viewed the video multiple times?

But I couldn't ask her any of that without risking having to answer those questions myself, and that was way too dangerous. It'd probably make her flee my room, and I didn't want that.

I kind of liked seeing her sitting there, looking like she was waiting for me to join her in my bed.

"Do you have to be up early?" I asked. "Should I set an alarm?"

She shook her head and pulled her phone out from where she'd tucked it into the waistband of her shorts. "I've set mine for seven-thirty. What about you? Do you have a final in the morning?"

"I've got one for my advance media strategies class at eleven."

I plugged my phone in to charge, then navigated to the playlist I always listened to when I went to sleep, starting the first song and adjusting the volume so it wasn't too loud. Then I grabbed a fistful of sheet and slid into bed, lying on my side to look at her.

Mads tilted her head in question.

"What?" I mashed the pillow beneath my head. "I listen to music when I sleep." If she had a problem with it, too bad. I figured it was my room, so my rules.

She got under the covers, lying on her side so she could look at me from the other side of the bed. "I wouldn't have guessed you listened to emo music."

Because the music was soft and stripped down, just piano, or acoustic guitar. "Yeah, well, we don't really know each other, do we?"

Why did something like sadness flicker through her eyes? It was gone a heartbeat later. "No. We don't."

"That reminds me. Give me your phone."

Her expression turned suspicious. "Why?"

"I'll give you my number."

She unlocked her phone and reluctantly handed it over. I opened a new text message, put in my number, and typed out a message. As soon as I hit 'send,' my phone's screen brightened with the incoming message, momentarily lighting the room.

When I passed her phone back to her, she read what I'd sent and gave me a plain look.

Madison: Hi Colin, it's Mads. You've got a big dick.

I flattened my palm to my chest, acting pleasantly surprised. "Why, thank you."

She didn't want to be amused, but she did a terrible job of hiding her smile. The bed shifted as she got comfortable, pulling the sheet up over her shoulder. If she was sending a message she wanted to sleep, I didn't get it. Her eyes were alert as she peered at me. If she didn't want to talk, I would have expected her to roll away from me.

"Are you going to the ABC party on Friday?" I asked.

"At the Sig house?" She looked at me like I'd lost my mind. "Um, no."

Every year at the end of finals, the Sigs always hosted the biggest party of the semester. This one was going to be an 'Anything But Clothes' party, where people showed up wearing all sorts of crazy things like shopping bags or beer boxes duct taped together.

"Why not?" I asked. "We got kicked out, but we're not banned. The party's open. Anyone can go."

"Oh, gee, I don't know." Her tone dripped with sarcasm. "Maybe because I'm public enemy number one over there?"

"You're not. The Fidelity Cup shit went down a month ago. That's like a lifetime to us frat guys, plus—"

"Jack will be there."

My heart thudded slower. "You're still hung up on him?"

"What? No." She made a face. "But you said he told everyone I cheated on him."

I didn't understand why I cared about her going, but I pressed on anyway. "Then go to set the record straight."

Her laugh was empty. "Right. Because they all *totally* believed me when I said Riley cheated."

She had a point. Her focus drifted away, moving down to look at my hand that rested on the mattress between us. She seemed to trace each of my fingers with her gaze, and the room went quiet, other than the gentle music streaming from my phone.

"Can I ask you something?" Her voice was hushed. "Another favor."

"Sure."

She seemed to struggle with how to put it into words. "I know it's stupid, and it doesn't matter anymore, at least not to anyone else, but Riley cheated, Colin." She swallowed a breath and her gaze slid back to mine. "Even if no one else believes me, it'd mean a lot . . . if you did."

Tightness squeezed my lungs, making it hard to breathe.

There was no reason for her to lie about this, not a month later, and if she were telling the truth, she wouldn't really gain anything except my support. She'd lost her friends and her house, and she stared at me like if she'd known that was going to happen—she *still* would have told the truth.

"I believe you," I said.

She sighed as if she'd been holding it in for the last month, and her body softened with relief. It was such a big response for a simple, small thing.

"Thank you," she said genuinely. "You probably think it's

strange I wanted that, but I went through some stuff a while ago with my parents, and since then, I've been," she searched for the right word, "sensitive."

It felt like it was okay to ask. "What happened?"

She took so long to speak I wasn't sure she was going to answer, but then she shifted subtly closer to me. "My dad's a compulsive gambler." She let that statement sink in before continuing. "He hid it really well, too, but by my senior year of high school I started to suspect. Stuff would go missing—like, the expensive stuff—and he had these wild mood swings. Some days he'd come home from work elated, and other times he was so angry you could barely talk to him."

There wasn't much emotion in her voice, but I wondered if she was working hard to keep it that way.

"When he lost his job," she said, "he told us he couldn't find a new one. My mom believed him, but I wasn't as sure, so I decided one day to skip school and follow him to one of his *interviews*."

"Where'd he go? The racetrack?" I guessed.

She shook her head. "The casino. When I told my parents, my dad said it was a one-time thing. Plus, he'd won that day, so he was riding a high. My mom wanted to believe him so badly, she wouldn't listen to me. Ignored all the evidence I gave her."

My heart beat faster with secondhand anger on her behalf.

Her bottom lip quivered, but otherwise she didn't break. "He needed help, but no one would believe me. I tried to tell my aunts and uncles, but my mom said I was exaggerating. It wasn't until she caught him sneaking a bracelet out of her jewelry box—a gift he gave her for their twentieth anniversary, by the way—that she finally acknowledged he had a problem."

There was a shift as bitterness swept through her.

"But by then," she announced, "it was too late. He'd cleaned out my family's savings, every account, including all the money I'd saved up for college. More than twelve thousand dollars I'd accumulated over my life, most of it from jobs I'd worked. It was all gone."

"Oh, shit." I didn't know what else to say. Her mother hadn't believed her, and her father . . . He'd *stolen* from her.

She reached up and tugged at the loops of her hair, adjusting her damp, messy bun, but I got the sense she'd done it to occupy herself rather than have to look at me and see pity.

"I know he couldn't help it, his addiction." Her voice was detached. "I know I should forgive them, and I think someday I will, but I'm not there yet." She gave me a flat smile. "So, like you, I didn't tell my parents that I got kicked out of my house, but," she lifted a shoulder up to her ear, "we don't exactly talk these days."

Her story weighed heavily on me, and I had to battle back the strong urge to do something. I wanted to—I didn't know—hold her? Offer some kind of comfort? But surely I was one of the last people she'd want that from.

"That's . . . understandable," I said quietly. "But what about the summer? The holidays? Do you go home?"

"Only when I have nowhere else to go, but I always take classes during the summer semester. It's why I'm graduating this fall, ahead of schedule."

"I'm taking a few classes this summer, too." I grimaced. "My parents told me I needed to lighten my load for my senior year."

"You don't get along with them? It's none of my business, but things seemed tense with you and your dad."

"Yeah, tense is one word for it," I started, not sure if I wanted to get into the whole thing.

But she'd told me something personal, and it seemed only fair to reciprocate. I raked a hand through my hair as I considered where to start.

"My parents are strict," I said finally. "It's very much 'my way or the highway' with them, which I was okay with until I got to high school. Sophomore year, I had a girl over, and she shut my bedroom door. The door *had* to stay open, according to my parents. Like, it was rule number one."

And open didn't mean cracked or six inches of gap. They wanted it *all the way* open.

"After that incident, which was a big fucking deal," I continued, "I could forget having girls over. I got a bullshit curfew and wasn't allowed to stay overnight at friends' houses anymore." I sighed. "It fucking sucked."

It was clear she was trying to reconcile this information with the guy I was today and struggled do it.

"I don't think they realized that the harder they tightened their grip, the more I pushed back. I found ways around a lot of their rules," I said. "Maybe my friend has car problems, or the boss wants me to stay late at work. They always bought whatever I came up with, so for my senior prom I decided to go *really* big."

"What'd you do?"

My smile was evil. "I told them I didn't have a date, so I wasn't going."

I'd built up interest in her, and she waited expectantly

for more, but nothing came. Her expression changed, looking like I'd stranded her on the edge of a cliff. "That's it?"

"My cousin's wedding was in Kentucky that same weekend. I told them to go without me." I affected a pathetic voice. "I was too sad about my lack of a prom date to go."

She saw where the story was going. "You threw a party."

"Hell, yeah, I did. It was supposed to be just a few couples, but a lot more people showed up, and there were so many cars in front of the house, one of the neighbors called my parents. They left the wedding and drove straight home."

She bit down on her bottom lip, and if I wasn't so wrapped up in the memory, I probably would have found it sexy. "How pissed were they when they got home?"

"About the party? That was really bad, but when they walked in to find me fucking Gretchen Fuller in their bed— well, that was *unforgivable*."

"Oh, no." She put her hand over her mouth and spoke through her fingers. "In your parents' bed?"

"Not my best idea, but space was limited, and I'd already let my friends Preston and Cassidy use my room."

It wasn't done out of kindness. My bed was just a twin, and he was so wasted, I figured nothing was going to happen— and I'd been right. I found out later that Cassidy had driven Preston's drunk ass home only a few minutes before my parents arrived, so they'd narrowly avoided getting caught.

"I'm not kidding," I said, "when I tell you my parents felt so disrespected, they tried to disown me. I bounced around that summer between friends' houses until my sister talked to my parents. She convinced them to let me come home," I lifted my hands to make air quotes, "on a *trial basis*." My mouth filled with a sour taste at the memory. "Which I've been on ever since, the last three years. I have to do exactly what they say. Any kind of fuck-up, and they'll pull me from school."

"That's why you didn't tell them about getting kicked out."

I nodded. "I had to beg them to let me join Sigma Phi Alpha. The only reason they did was because it wasn't a party house back when my dad pledged. They have no idea how much it has changed since."

She hesitated. "Do you have a plan for telling them you're not a Sig anymore?"

"Not a good one, but it's worked so far. If I can survive the summer semester, I'll tell my parents I want to move out and live off campus my final year. I think the hard part's over. They don't check on me as much in the summer." I let my expression turn serious. "I almost didn't make it, though, with that surprise lunch. He caught me totally off guard, which was stupid. I was overdue for a check-in."

"A check-in?" She looked confused.

"My dad told me he was on this side of town and his client canceled, but I doubt it. It was most likely an excuse so he could make sure I was going to class."

She frowned at the idea, and—yeah. It sucked. I'd spent three years being perfect to try to rebuild their trust, but I hadn't made any progress at all. It was why I'd decided to give up, say *fuck it,* and take the job with Petal Productions.

I pretended to resettle myself on the bed, using it to move subtly closer to her.

"Do you have any idea how much you saved my ass?" I asked. "Seriously. Thank you."

"You're welcome." She shifted, trying to get comfortable, and it brought her near. "Thanks for letting me crash in your bed."

"Anytime."

I'd said it as a joke, but it didn't come out that way, and the scary thing was I might have meant it. It clung in the air like a fog enveloping us, urging us forward, so I inched closer. Whatever wall was between us, it was crumbling fast.

"Hey, listen," I said, hushed. "About the tournament? I'm sorry about everything." Surprise blinked through her face, but I kept going. "I'm sorry that Riley cheated, and no one believed you, and for the stupid thing I said."

Her mouth opened, just wide enough to let out a breath. Then, she leaned forward, like she wanted less space between us. "And I'm sorry for the stupid thing I did. If I hadn't lost my temper, we wouldn't be here."

"Being here . . . isn't so bad." I'd put weight behind the statement, wanting her to know I wasn't just talking about the house.

The music I'd put on wasn't just sleepy—it was romantic. The atmosphere in the room filled with gravity, pulling us toward each other.

I felt *close* to her. Not just physically or intimately, but like the bond between us had strengthened. She was the only person who understood everything I'd been through. Was I now the same for her?

I knew it wasn't allowed, that she was going to shoot me down, but I told her anyway. "I want to kiss you."

She swallowed so hard, I heard the click of her throat. "Now?"

"Yes, Mads," I said. "Right now."

Time slowed, and she did with it. I waited for her to remind me of why we shouldn't, but she seemed frozen. Had I broken her?

Finally, she pulled in a shaky breath, and it came from her in barely a whisper.

"Okay."

SEVENTEEN

Colin

Mads looked legit terrified as I lifted my hand and traced my fingertips over her cheekbone. I sensed I was only going to get one chance at this, and I did not want to fuck it up.

She held her breath when my hand came to rest on her cheek, and I leaned in, closing whatever space was left between us. I didn't kiss her, though. Not yet. I wasn't trying to tease her, but I'd wanted this moment for weeks. Now that it was here, I didn't want it to be over too quickly.

I hovered my lips just outside of hers, letting her feel their warmth and the threat of my kiss. If she took a breath, we'd share the same air, but she didn't seem to be breathing.

A tremble worked its way up her body, making her shoulders shake. Fuck, I loved it. She'd confirmed I—and I *alone*—was the cause of it during our last scene together.

You, she'd whispered.

I didn't tremble on the outside like she did, but inside? She made me feel the same way. Unsteady. Nervous. Excited.

The moment suspended, and everything else ceased to exist.

It was just me and her.

"Colin."

My whispered name came from her in a mix of desperation and frustration. She didn't want to wait any longer.

I went in gentle, brushing my lips against hers to test the waters. One soft kiss to get an invitation for more, and she gave it to me when she let out the tiniest of sighs.

This time, I went all in.

I cupped her cheek, brushing my thumb over her cheekbone as I sealed my mouth over hers. Her soft lips gave way as I slipped my tongue into her mouth, sliding against hers. This kiss was lush and thorough.

It made satisfaction pour through my body.

We'd been lying on our sides facing each other, but I moved in, urging her to roll onto her back so I could deepen the kiss. I rose onto my arm and eased my knee between her legs, pressing my body to hers while my mouth moved against her mouth, my tongue tangled with hers.

There weren't cameras around to capture what we were doing. There was no script or promise of money, no one in our ear telling us what to do. Mads let me kiss her because she wanted to. This chemistry between us? It wasn't just explosive.

It was real.

Her hand threaded through my hair, clutching a fistful, and in response, I shifted my knee. I used the top of my thigh to press against the center of her legs and was rewarded with a quiet, pleasurable moan. The sound of it shot straight to my dick. Could she feel how fucking hard she made me? How badly I wanted her?

I grasped her hip, pinning her to the mattress for a second, only for my hand to start sliding up, carrying the bottom of her tank top up with it. Things began to spiral, and so when she flattened her palm in the center of my chest, it took me a long moment to read the signal.

She was pushing me back.

I broke the kiss and stared down, worry tensing my muscles. "What's wrong?"

Her gaze darted away, and again she swallowed so hard, it was audible. "It's late, and my final's in the morning, and I . . ."

She came to my room to try to get some sleep.

Not to have deep conversation, or share a mind-blowing kiss, or let it lead to anything more.

The idiot voice inside my brain said I could help her fall asleep faster if I gave her an orgasm, but I was smart enough not to listen to it. Instead, I slowly withdrew and shifted back to my side of the bed. Every inch of me wanted to keep kissing her, though, and sleep was the farthest thing from my mind.

"Right," I said.

I settled next to her, maybe encroaching on her side a little, but I couldn't help it. I wanted to be near in case she changed her mind, or to have an excuse to accidentally brush against her if we got too close. To remind her I was there, right beside her.

She stared up at the ceiling, and I imagined the same thought running through my head was running through hers. *What happens now?*

"Okay, well . . ." she whispered. "Goodnight."

She abruptly rolled away and slid across the sheets, scooting into the corner and as far away from me as she could get.

What the *hell?*

I didn't like how she'd run away from me after everything

we'd just shared. I hadn't done anything to make her feel un-safe. Why was she acting like she was afraid of me?

For a long beat, I simply stared at her while the slow, sleepy music from my phone filled the awkward space between us.

Really?

The springs in the mattress made a quiet squeak as I rolled away from her, and my voice was gruff. "Yeah. Goodnight."

I sat on the bench outside the science building, watching the door. I'd finished my final ten minutes ago, but Elijah was still in there, and I wanted to catch him before he left. It meant I couldn't look at my phone or I might miss him, and that left me with nothing to do but think about last night.

Mads was gone when I woke up, which wasn't surpris-ing. I was a heavy sleeper and didn't get up before ten unless I had to. I imagined her alarm going off and her sneaking out of my bed, trying not to wake me.

Had she lingered at all, watching me sleep? Or had she bolted out the door, wanting to get away as fast as possible and pretend the whole thing never happened?

I frowned at that idea.

Maybe she was confused about her feelings for me, but . . . I wasn't. Yeah, it'd be easier and safer—as she'd said—if we didn't like each other, but that ship had fucking sailed. I didn't want to any more than she did, and I got that it was messy, that it made things more complicated than they already were, but denying it wasn't going to magically stop it from being true.

I liked Mads.

And I liked her a lot more than I'd liked anyone else in a long time.

My thoughts were interrupted when one of the doors in the large set at the front of the building swung open and Elijah stepped out. He made it to the bottom of the steps before I caught up to him.

"Elijah," I said.

His expression brightened when he recognized me. "Hey, Colin. How'd you do?"

He was asking about the media strategies final we'd just finished. "Crushed it. You?"

"Yeah, same." Except his answer came slower and less sure than mine.

That was Elijah in a nutshell. He was such a follower and people pleaser, I'd sort of worried he'd never fully developed his own personality. I'd met him last year when he'd been my randomly assigned partner in our psychology class, and we'd hung out a few times. He'd wanted to rush Sigma Phi Alpha, and although he was nice enough, he wasn't Sig material. He was never going to get a bid, so I'd encouraged him to rush TKE instead.

No good deed went unpunished, and from then on, he seemed to think we were closer friends than we were.

"That's good," I said. "Hey, man, I've got to ask you something." My tone turned serious. "Why'd you let Riley cheat in the Fidelity Cup finals?"

His smile froze. "What?" And then his gaze darted away.

"I didn't."

I'd meant what I'd said when I told Mads I believed her, so I was both relieved and pissed off to have the truth confirmed. Elijah couldn't have looked more guilty if he'd tried.

I jammed my hands into my pockets to keep myself from balling them into fists. "Tell me why," I demanded.

Finally, he looked at me, and there was so much regret in his eyes, for a split second I was concerned he might get emotional. But he sucked in a breath and let it fill his chest.

"I screwed up." It poured from him in a rush. "When he threw her baton, I was so surprised, I just . . . I don't know. I kind of froze." He scrubbed his fingertips over his forehead. "I should have blown the whistle, but I didn't, and as soon as she was gone, Riley was all up in my face, telling me I was his hero. Saying how awesome I was for helping out the Sigs and keeping the cup from going to the Lambdas."

Son of a bitch. The muscles in my arms went taut. "*That's* why you defended Riley when Mads said he cheated?"

Confusion pulled his eyebrows together. "Who?"

"Madison Perry," I growled. "The girl you fucked over." Wait, that wasn't accurate. "The Lambda we all fucked over."

"I panicked, man. You beat her to the finish line, and all the Sigs were celebrating. I hadn't done what I was supposed to, and, shit, how was I going to explain it? If I'd said, 'yeah, he cheated,' then I was going to be taking that win away from all of you." He had the audacity to look at me like I was being unreasonable. "You're my friend, you know. Plus, we'd both rather have Sigma Phi Alpha win over those"—he said it with pure disgust—"Lambdas."

Oh, fucking shit.

Hadn't he told me something earlier this year about a Lambda he'd tried to ask out? I vaguely recalled the conversation. He'd been at a tailgating thing and tried to get a Lambda girl's number. Instead of giving it, she'd laughed at him in front of her sisters.

"But they would have won if Riley hadn't cheated." I'd barely beaten Mads to the finish line, and there was no telling how far ahead of me she would have finished if it had been a fair contest. "They *did* win, and you helped take that away from her. From them."

He didn't like hearing that. His shoulders snapped back. "Yeah, well, it's over." He lifted his chin, trying to look confident. "Nothing's going to change it now."

"Oh, no," I patronized. "See, you're going to come clean to the council and tell them the truth."

He blinked. "Um, why would I do that? No one even cares anymore."

My expression turned to steel. "*I* care. You called Mads a liar in front of everyone when she was telling the truth."

His false bravado crumbled, and it was like I'd landed a blow in his stomach. He looked stricken. "I know, but do you realize what would happen if I came forward? They could kick me out of Tau Kappa Epsilon for violating the code of ethics." Seriousness grew in his expression until it turned to fear. "What do you think they'd do to Riley if they knew? And who do you think he'd blame for it?" He shook his head. "Look, I'm sorry for what I did, but there's no upside to telling anyone what happened." Once again, he made an attempt to look strong. "I'm not saying shit."

Well, I'd been wrong. He *did* have a personality after all.

"You're an asshole," I snarled. He'd hurt Mads, forcing her to relive a painful situation where no one believed her, and it was so unfair, acid rose in my throat. Something inside me snapped. "I hope you fucking failed that final in there."

He recoiled in shock before his eyes turned dark. "Yeah, whatever, man," he said. "I'll see you around."

Anger kept me locked in place as he scrambled away. I didn't have a way to force him to tell the truth, but . . . he wasn't the only person I needed to confront. Much more of the blame lay with someone else.

Look out, Riley. I'm coming for you.

I packed my costume for the ABC party into my bag and carried it out into the garage, slapping a hand on the button to open the garage door. As it rolled up, I got my bike down from the hook and then paused. Should I text Preston to see if he was home? I hadn't seen my friend since spring break. Vanderbilt finished school a few days earlier than Davidson did, and I'd be riding right by his dad's place on my way to the Sig house.

I pulled out my phone.

Colin: Are you home at your dad's?

Preston: No. Why?

Colin: My new place is close. Was going to stop by and say hi.

Preston: My mom's in town. Next week?

I sent back the thumbs up emoji, put my phone in my backpack, and slung it over my shoulders. The pedals clicked quietly as I walked my bike out of the garage, and when I reached the keypad on the side of the door, I began to type in the code to close it. But movement caught my eye.

There was someone in the side yard.

"Can I help you?" I asked.

The woman yelped and straightened. I hadn't meant to startle her, but at the same time, I didn't feel bad about it either. Something about her was off, like she'd been sneaking around out here, not expecting anyone to notice her or the measuring tape she held.

She looked to be around my mom's age, late forties, or early fifties. She was skinny, with short, blonde hair, and as she turned to look at me, I saw her full-on resting bitch face.

The tape measure and phone she'd been using to take pictures were quickly pocketed in her shorts.

"Hello," she said. "Are Mr. or Mrs. Woodson home?"

They weren't. Scott was out of town filming, and Nina was at a conference. I wasn't about to tell that to a strange woman lurking on their property, though. Alarm bells rung in my head. Scott was a big star, and Abbie was coming up, too. What if this woman was a crazed fan or a stalker?

"You're welcome to use the doorbell," I said, "like a normal person, and find out." The security system was sophisticated. The doorbell had a camera and microphone and was linked to Scott's and Nina's phones.

The woman made a face to tell me I was being rude. "I'm not trying to sell them something." She put a hand on her hip and gazed at me like I was beneath her. "I'm Judy Malinger, the president of the homeowners' association. I need to talk to them about the new unit they had installed."

She wasn't a stalker—she was something way worse.

Fuck, I should have recognized her. A while ago, this woman had a major hard-on for Preston's dad. But he wasn't interested, and she hadn't handled the rejection well. She'd been extra pissed off when she'd found out he was dating a woman half his age. It wasn't her fucking business, but she didn't approve of their relationship, and so she'd used every opportunity since to make Dr. Lowe's life difficult.

Scott and Nina were trying to stay off her radar. I had to tread lightly.

My whole demeanor changed, and I put on my most charming smile. "Oh, hi, Ms. Maligner. Nice to meet you." I glanced up at the house. "They're out right now, but I'd be happy to pass along a message."

Judy's eyes narrowed. She appreciated how my attitude had changed when she'd dropped that she was the HOA president, but she was still suspicious. "Have we met before? You look familiar."

I tightened my smile. I looked familiar because I'd been Preston's friend through high school and spent every summer hanging out in his dad's pool—not to mention Dr. Lowe had been nice enough to let me crash there for a few weeks after the prom debacle. Judy was fucking nosy and watched her neighbors' houses like she had nothing better to do, so she'd seen me plenty of times.

But we'd never been introduced. "No," I said, "I don't think so."

It was clear she didn't believe me, but she couldn't place

me either. She gestured to the side of the house. "Please tell them they will be fined if their units don't match."

My gaze went to the three AC units that sat in a row on concrete pads beside the house. One of them was brand new, installed this morning, and had been pumping out icy cold air upstairs ever since. The large box was shielded in a gleaming dark metal, when the other two were smaller and a dull gray, probably original to the house.

"They're different brands," I pointed out. "I was around when the service guy was here. Sticking with the same brand was going to cost fourteen hundred more, and the output isn't as good as this one."

She wasn't deterred. "They need to match."

My brain was slower than my mouth, and it just slipped out. "They're air conditioning units on the side of the house. Who gives a fuck?"

Judy gasped like I'd just spat at her. "They're *unsightly.*"

What she was asking was insane. To get them to match, they'd have to rip out the new unit and replace it with an inferior one . . . or upgrade the other two units *that worked perfectly fine.* I knew I should stop digging, but I couldn't. "But you can't even see them from the road."

That didn't matter to her one bit. "The HOA rules are clear. Tell them to expect fines until they have this corrected."

I clenched my jaw so hard it was a miracle I didn't break any teeth. "All right." If I could have told her to get fucking lost, I would have. Instead, I let ice creep into my voice. "Thanks for stopping by."

Thankfully, she understood it was time for her to go. She flashed a vindictive smile, telling me she'd won this battle, before turning and starting her long walk down the hilly driveway.

My irritation rose when I got to the Sig house and discovered Riley wasn't there. It was early, though. The party didn't start until ten, and it wouldn't really get going until eleven, so I had a few hours to kill. I spent my time hanging out with Jorge and a few other guys, helping them finish their 'not-clothes' for the evening.

It was weird to be back in my frat, and I nearly went upstairs to my old room to change before remembering I didn't live there anymore. But there were things that never bothered me before jumping out at me now.

Like, how a house full of college dudes was fucking gross—especially the bathrooms. In the short month I'd been with Petal Productions, I'd already become accustomed to the weekly housekeeper service they used. I only had to share a bathroom with Jaquan instead of five other guys, so it was always decent.

The one I currently stood in was filthy, and who knew what decade it had been the last time someone cleaned it.

I stripped down to my underwear and pulled on the half apron, using clear packing tape to seal the waistband closed around my hips. It was gladiator style, with pleat things dangling down to create a skirt and hide my junk, but it also kind of looked like a tutu. That was because it was made from glossy, pink striped paper, and the *Victoria's Secret* logo was branded right across the front of the waistband.

One of my sister's friends worked at the lingerie store and had the hookup over spring break, giving me as many extra bags as I wanted to create my costume. I completed the look with a matching paper bowtie and checked myself out in the mirror.

I looked awesome.

And hilarious. My cut chest and abs were the perfect contrast to the girlie pink skirt.

"Shit, bro," Jorge said, eyeing me with jealousy when I came out of the bathroom. "Do you even work out?"

His costume consisted of three small donut-shaped pool floats stacked around his hips and thighs, each float a different color. He'd developed a bit of a beer gut this last semester, and his belly rested on the top float like he'd had to squeeze himself into it.

He should have gone with the bedsheet toga we'd tried to talk him into, but he was committed to the pool floats.

I followed him down the stairs to the basement, where the party had already begun. Music blasted from the speakers behind the ping pong table, where beer pong had been set up, but no one was playing yet.

The first group of girls had arrived, and people were gathered in groups, talking loudly and laughing over the music while they drank from their red cups. I made my way to the keg and surveyed the outfits—or lack of them—while the freshman assigned to work the tap poured me a drink.

There were girls wrapped in dresses of yellow caution tape, or halter tops and skirts made from metallic fringe decorations. So much skin was showing, and the chance of a wardrobe malfunction was very high, and yet . . . I wasn't as interested as I should have been.

I could get laid tonight. It wasn't much of a challenge, normally, but tonight with my shirt off? It'd be so easy. Whatever girl I picked out wouldn't stand a chance. She'd find some excuse to put a hand on my bare chest, and that'd be it. I'd have to go back to using condoms in my scenes until I got tested again, but having a partner outside the house wasn't, like, illegal.

But as I stared at the sea of hot girls in front of me, my mind wandered elsewhere. I knew what I wanted.

And she isn't here.

So, I stood to the side and drank my beer, irritated at my situation. Tonight was supposed to be fun. I'd finished my last final, was ready to get wild, and I'd been looking forward to this party for forever. It sucked that I was spending it bored in the corner, wishing I was somewhere else.

More people streamed down the stairs, filling up the poorly lit and not-at-all-ventilated basement, and as it got crowded, the temperature rose. The people in plastic wrap and foil began to sweat, and I was glad I hadn't gone that route.

I snickered at the guy dressed as a giant box of wine with the dispensing nozzle placed right in front of his dick. The thing actually worked, too—a girl had gotten down on her knees and drank from the nozzle while the guy made a face like she was blowing him.

I scanned the packed crowd and faked interest when a girl wearing a bunch of balloons asked about my costume. She clearly misunderstood the assignment—the point was to get as naked as possible.

I was about ready to give up and head home when I finally

spotted Riley back by the water heater, talking to some poor girl he'd obviously trapped there. He wore an honest-to-God barrel, held up by red suspenders that were draped over his gangly shoulders.

"What's up, Victoria?" he asked when I approached.

"I'm gonna get another drink," the girl said. She'd seen her opening for escape and took it, hurrying away.

Riley was displeased that I'd run her off and gave me an irritated look as he took a sip of his beer. His tone was pure sarcasm. "Nice costume."

"It takes a real man to wear pink," I said. "Hey, listen. We need to talk about the Fidelity Cup tournament, and how you cheated."

I'd expected him to act confused or deny it, but instead his tone was disinterested. "Did your new girlfriend tell you that?"

My what? "No. Elijah did."

Finally, there was a reaction. A flicker of surprise went through his eyes, but then it died. "And?"

His cavalier question corded my muscles. "And," I continued for him, "you're going to tell the Sigs what you did. You should have been disqualified, and if you hadn't cheated, Mads—Madison," I quickly corrected, "would have beaten me. Either way, the Lambdas won."

Riley wrapped his free hand around one of his suspenders and adjusted it to sit better on his shoulder. The barrel looked heavy, but I suddenly worried that the uncomfortable look on his face was solely from his costume and not what I'd said.

Why was he staring at me like he held the upper hand?

"Look, I get it," he said. "She's hot, and I know she's sucking your dick on the regular now, but this cheating thing . . . You should tell her to let it go."

A chill glanced down my spine. "What the fuck are you talking about?"

"She put you up to this, right?"

My heart beat too fast for my body, and although I was standing still, it felt like I was running. "Who?"

"Madison." An evil smile peeled back his lips. "Or is it Annika Adore?"

Oh, fuck.

EIGHTEEN

Colin

I fixed my expression and steeled my body, trying to keep myself under control. This information hadn't come from me because I hadn't told a soul, and I highly doubted Mads had shared it with anyone either. "How the fuck do you know that name?"

Riley took another sip of his beer, dragging the reveal out, and I considered how hard I'd have to punch if I wanted to break through the barrel and hit him right in the stomach the same way he'd done to me by uttering Mads' stage name.

"If you asked me to make a list of my top five favorite porn stars, I'd probably give you Lexi Grey's name five times." His gaze drifted off as he thought about Abbie. "She's so fucking hot."

I was grateful for the barrel now. Twenty bucks said he was sporting a boner under it.

His focus snapped back to me. "I watch anything of her I can find." His smug smile made my stomach turn. "I wish you could have seen my face when I recognized it was Madison in the shower with Lexie, and then you—you fucking legend—walked in."

Well . . . this was a *goddamn disaster*.

My mind raced into damage control, and I struggled to catch my breath. "Who else have you told?"

I wasn't embarrassed that he knew I was working in adult film, but it did make me uncomfortable to think he'd watched any of my scenes. Strangers enjoying my work was kind of hot, but someone I knew? Definitely not hot.

And he was the absolute worst person to have this information about Mads.

"No one," he said. "Yet."

His threat caused so much anger to flare inside me, it burned away the last of my self-control. I wrapped my hand around his neck and shoved him back against the water heater. His eyes went wide, nearly bugging out of his face, and his beer sloshed over the side of his cup, dripping down over his hand.

"What the fuck—?" he gasped.

I relaxed my grip so there wasn't pressure in my fingers, but I held him pinned in place like that, letting him see how deadly serious I was. "No one," I snarled. "You tell no one. Understand?"

"Dude, chill. I know you've got a good thing going on. I'm not going to fuck it up for you."

We couldn't stay like this. My aggression hadn't gone unnoticed by some of the guys nearby, and I felt their gazes drilling into me. They sensed the threat of a fight, causing them to go on alert, readying to break it up.

So, I released Riley with a final shove and stood back, glaring at him as he straightened and rubbed his neck.

"Tell me how you did it," he said.

"No."

He wasn't even listening. "How'd you get the job?"

"Drop it, Riley."

"I will, but you gotta give me something, man. I'd kill to get into the business." The sad thing was he looked serious. "Was there an open casting call?"

"No."

"Then, how?"

It was clear he wasn't going to let it go until I gave him some sort of an answer. I didn't trust him at all, but throwing him a crumb felt safe, and it might help him keep his mouth shut about Mads. "I answered an ad."

"Online? Which site?"

I instantly regretted saying anything. He wasn't going to be satisfied until he had everything he wanted, and that was never going to happen. "This conversation is over, and we're not having it ever again. Got it?"

He opened his mouth to argue, but I stepped forward, dominating his space.

"You utter a word, and I'll have Elijah tell everyone you cheated. Half the frat wants you gone, and this is just the excuse they need to send you packing."

He scowled in disbelief, and I saw his thoughts play out on his face. *That can't be true. I'm awesome. Everyone loves me.*

Jesus, he was delusional.

"So, we both keep our mouths shut," I said. "Tell me you get it."

His eyes were dark and grudging. "I got it."

"Great. Enjoy your summer, Riley." I turned and walked away before he could say anything else.

The basement was fucking packed, and I wove my way through the crowd, ignoring the drunk people who bumped into me as I went. I'd come to the party to confront Riley, and now that it was done, I wanted to get the fuck out of—

"Colin!" A hand grabbed my shoulder, getting me to turn around.

Fuck my life. I stared at Jack, who wore a white bath towel around his waist, held closed by binder clips. His eyes were glazed. He was either high or drunk or both, and his idiotic smile did nothing to calm me down after my conversation with Riley.

"Glad you made it," he said, slurring his words. "Such a shitty situation what happened. We've missed you around here."

If I'd never gotten to know Mads, maybe I would have been pleased to hear him say this, but all it did was make me rage-y. Jack's lie had powered my cruel statement, which sparked the mudslinging, so I was pissed about that. But I was even angrier about him running around on Mads.

"What the hell, man?" I yelled over the music. "You told us she cheated on you, but it was the other way around, wasn't it?"

His smile hung. "What?"

"Madison." I glared at him. "I don't know how you landed a girl like that, but then you go and cheat on her? What the fuck is wrong with you?"

He didn't bother denying it. Instead, he flattened a hand to his chest like I'd mortally wounded him. "I made a mistake. I was lonely and homesick, and she was five thousand miles away."

I sneered. "Not an excuse."

"Don't tell the guys. I'm not proud of what I did." The thought finally occurred to him. "How'd you find out?"

"She told me."

He swayed and peered at me with a dubious expression. "And you believed her?"

I'd been holding myself together since talking to Riley, but my restraint threatened to snap. "What kind of fucking question was that? Of course, I believed her." I sucked down a breath to keep myself in check. "A girl like Mads . . . you didn't deserve her."

His expression soured. "What the hell do you know?"

"That she's too hot, too smart, and too fucking fearless for someone like you. If she was mine, she'd be more than enough for me."

"But she'll never be yours," he said. "She's too much of a good girl to go for someone like you."

"Colin," came from a voice to my right. I turned, and my brain emptied of thought.

Mads stood in front of us, looking like she'd heard everything. Her expression was intense and focused on us, like she was unaware of the party going on.

She'd understood the assignment, because her dress was cut low in the front, and the skirt barely covered her ass, showing off her legs. The dress was made of something white and frilly. Coffee filters? She'd folded some into half circles and they covered her boobs but revealed tons of cleavage. The waist of the dress was banded in silver duct tape, before bursting out into a fluffy skirt.

She was so sexy, so beautiful, I had to look away.

"I want to kiss you," she announced loudly.

I blinked, stunned. My gaze swept over Jack and the crowded room before returning to her. "Now?"

She nodded quickly.

"Then," I said, "get the fuck over here and do it."

She stepped forward as I leaned down, making it easier for her to reach up and thread her hands through my hair. Her fingers laced together at the back of my neck, and she pulled my mouth to hers.

Our kiss was *fire*.

Unlike anything I'd had before.

It was much too passionate for me to think this was all for show, that she was just doing it to make her ex jealous. She was kissing me now because she wanted to.

I put my hands on her back to draw her closer, only to stop immediately. Her costume looked delicate, and she'd obviously put a lot of work into it, so I didn't want to rip it.

Her tongue filled my mouth, and it set my body buzzing. Fuck, how I wanted her, even after I'd already had her. It was a scary, new experience. She had me fucking addicted, and I wasn't even mad about it.

I pictured us as Jack saw us. Me bare chested in a pink kilt and her wearing a ruffly white dress, kissing each other like it was the only thing we'd been put on the Earth to do.

But he'd vanished when we finally came up for air.

"What are you doing here?" I whispered, still shell-shocked from her kiss.

She acted like it was a strange question. "Didn't you tell me to come?"

The memory of her lingered on my lips as she stepped back, putting some space between us, and it helped clear some of the fog from my head.

Mads raked a hand through her long hair, shaking out a

tangle. "My friend Jenn said she wanted to go, so I came with her." Her gaze wandered appreciatively over my chest, and amusement lit her eyes. "Nice outfit."

"Yeah, same," I mumbled, suddenly aware of things outside of the Mads bubble I'd gotten sucked into. I surveyed the sea of partygoers until I spied Riley. "We need to leave."

"What?" She bristled. "I just got here."

I grabbed her hand and squeezed, so I'd have her full attention. "Mads, trust me. We gotta go."

Whatever face I was making, she could tell I was serious. "Okay."

I held on to her as we shouldered our way through the crowd, heading toward the stairs and ignoring the strange looks we got. Last time these people had seen us together, we'd been throwing mud and fighting over the Fidelity Cup.

Now we looked like a couple.

I . . . didn't hate that idea.

But she probably would, and it couldn't happen, anyway. How did you date someone when both of your jobs required you to fuck other people—sometimes in front of each other?

And even on the off chance she did go for it, what happened when the relationship inevitably fell apart, like every one of mine had in my past? It'd be too messy or hard to keep working together.

Nina and Scott made it work.

But they had to be the exception, plus they were fifteen years older than Mads and I. They knew who they were and where they were in their life.

Mads and me? We were still figuring it out.

Once we made it upstairs, I led her down the hall and

ducked into Jorge's room where I'd stashed my backpack and clothes.

She waited until I shut the door. "What's happened?"

I didn't want to tell her. I shoved one leg into my shorts, then the other, and pulled them up under my pink skirt, making the paper crinkle.

Her tone was sharp. "Colin."

I tore the skirt free, balled it up and tossed it in the overflowing garbage can beside Jorge's desk. "Riley knows."

"Riley knows . . . what?"

I snapped off the bowtie and tossed it on the pile. "He knows you're Annika Adore."

She recoiled so hard, it flung her back, and betrayal flooded her eyes. "You *told* him?"

"What? No." I scowled. "I'd never." I jammed my head through the neck hole of my shirt and jerked it on. "Apparently, he's one of Lexi Grey's super fans."

Her voice turned small. "Oh." Then her shoulders slumped as she continued to absorb what this could mean. "Who else knows?"

"No one, or so he says."

"You believe him?"

I lifted one shoulder. "Honestly? I'm not sure. But we did come to an understanding about him not telling anyone else."

Her shoulders pulled back. "How's that?"

"I told him to keep his mouth shut about you, and I'd keep mine shut about him cheating."

"And that worked? I thought you were on the course when it happened and didn't see."

"I didn't, but I talked to Elijah. He's the guy who was the—"

"I know who he is," she snipped. "And so, he confirmed it?" Her tone turned bitter. "Told you that I wasn't lying after all?"

I was slow to understand why her attitude had changed so abruptly, but then it hit me. Even though I'd told her I believed her—she thought I hadn't meant it.

"You've got it wrong. I confronted Elijah *because* I believed you," I said. "I didn't go to him for confirmation."

She pulled in a deep breath. She wanted what I'd said to be true, but she was hesitant. "Then why'd you confront him?"

"I needed to know why he'd lied about it."

"Did he tell you?"

I relayed the same story he'd given me, how he had frozen in the moment and then been persuaded by Riley to back him up. That he was biased against the Lambdas because one of her sisters had rejected him.

"I don't know if I can force him to come forward," I said, "but I made Riley think I could, so hopefully it's enough to keep him quiet."

Her gaze drifted down as she thought about something, and then worry etched her face. "If he knows about me performing with Abbie, then he knows about you too."

"Yeah."

Her worry turned to confusion. "But you're only concerned that he knows about me. Why?"

"Because he's not going to do anything to me. He thinks I'm a god, living the dream." I sighed. "I don't like him having that kind of leverage on you. It feels dangerous, and I fucking hate the idea that he's . . . seen you. That he can watch you whenever he wants."

This jealousy made no sense. I'd been with her when she'd performed with Scott, and I'd watched her scene with Jaquan once it had gone live on the site. I hadn't felt an ounce of possessiveness then.

All it'd done was get me hard as a rock.

But Riley caused a different kind of response. The desire I felt now was to shield and protect her.

Not that she needed my help. She lifted her chin, striving to look strong. "I know, but we can't control that." Her voice softened. "But thanks for trying, Colin."

I nodded.

The mood in the room shifted, and I didn't miss the way her gaze darted to Jorge's bed. I was sure she was wondering if my friend would be upset if we used it.

My heart thudded painfully. I knew what I needed to do, but still I fought against it.

"I don't have a final tomorrow," she said. Her voice was uneven, but her expression was sure. "In case you wanted to finish what you started the other night."

"Fuck, I do, but . . ." It killed me to say it. "We can't."

Surprise flitted through her. "Why not?"

"You didn't want to kiss me because you said you didn't want to know how you feel about me. Well, now you do— and guess what?" I gave her a determined look. "I feel the same way."

She inhaled a tight gasp and stared at me with beautiful, unblinking eyes.

"But you're right," I continued. "Us liking each other is a bad idea. We work together."

Her breathing went shallow and nervous, like she knew

something she wanted was about to be taken away. "We don't have to let feelings get involved."

I stepped closer until we were chest to chest, and she peered up at me with so much longing it nearly broke me. But it was further proof I was doing the right thing.

"All right," I whispered. "Tell me every time you kiss me it doesn't mean anything. That every time you tremble for me you don't feel a thing." My gaze slipped over her face, tracing every inch. "I'll believe almost anything you say, Mads. But I won't believe that."

I lifted a hand to cup her cheek and hold her still as I delivered the final blow.

"Maybe I'm wrong," I whispered, "and you can keep your feelings to yourself, but I know I won't be able to."

Instead of lowering my mouth to hers, I did the same thing I'd done the night of our audition when she hadn't allowed my kiss. I pressed my lips to her forehead. It wasn't the connection either of us wanted, but it was the best option.

When I pulled back, she was left speechless. Her body was so tense, it was like she worried she'd come apart if she moved. She knew everything I'd said was true, but she didn't like it any more than I did.

"Hey," I said softly. "We should go. I'll walk you home."

She swallowed thickly and slowly returned to life, but she was cold and detached. Her single word was curt. "Fine."

NINTEEN

Madison

It was ridiculous that I'd gone from hating Colin, to hating that I couldn't be with him—at least not the way I wanted. We'd never been alone. Even during our audition, there'd been cameras in the room and voices in our ears.

It wasn't that I didn't enjoy seeing him with other people, because I did. Oh, my God, I did. But I wanted him all to myself, just once, where I knew everything was real. I'd gotten a taste of it in his bed, but it'd ended up being a wicked tease.

I sat on the lounger beside the pool, baking in the early June sun, and ignoring the reading for my fraud and ethics class that I was supposed to be doing. Watching Colin as he lay on a foam mat and floated in the pool was far more interesting. As he drifted around the deep end, he didn't move a single one of his delicious muscles, and he was so relaxed and wearing sunglasses, I began to wonder if he'd fallen asleep.

I gazed at him with longing. I understood why it was better if we remained coworkers and nothing more, but it didn't make it any easier.

"You can join me, you know," he said abruptly.

Because he'd noticed me staring at him. I sat up straighter, shifting the laptop in my lap. "I think dinner's going to be ready soon."

Scott, who manned the grill nearby, was putting slices of

cheese on the burgers.

The house didn't eat together much as a group, but Nina had announced they planned to barbeque this evening and took everyone's order for the grill. It was a totally different dynamic at the Petal Productions house, and the structure was looser, but it was vaguely like the sorority I'd lost.

We were a family.

Well, sort of.

Because I'd slept with everyone. So, maybe not a family, but just a tightly knit group.

We'd all gone to Jaquan's graduation and then out to the bars afterward to celebrate. Abbie helped me with poses and backgrounds for a set of nudes I'd shot for Petal Productions' website. Nina drove Colin to his farthest class, so he didn't have to ride his bike when it reached triple digits outside.

We were all close. We had fun and enjoyed working together. But the way I felt about him? It wasn't the same. And it seemed to grow stronger every week.

I told myself it was just an absence thing. We hadn't worked together since our scene with Scott. I'd done one with Abbie, and one with Jaquan, and last week a super hot scene with Nina and Scott where I played a naïve babysitter who they seduced together.

But the Colin hiatus was ending tomorrow, and I couldn't fucking wait.

It was his pitch we were going to film. A couples' swap, where I was playing Jaquan's girlfriend, and Abbie was Colin's. It was hard to tell which part excited me the most. I'd never been with three other people before, and I hadn't had a scene where I'd fully shared Colin with another woman yet.

And there was the little thing that kissing was no longer off limits. At least, it wasn't for me. We hadn't discussed it, but it'd been three weeks since we'd kissed in the basement of the Sig house, and I was dying for the excuse to do it again.

I peered over at him, glistening with droplets of water as he stared at his phone and used his thumbs to type on the screen. He was so good looking, it was annoying.

My phone vibrated with a text message.

Colin: Don't look at me like that.

A smile quirked on his lips, but I lifted a disapproving eyebrow and typed out my response.

Madison: I'll look at you however I want.

He snickered.

Colin: What are you thinking about?

Madison: Our scene tomorrow.

I debated saying anything else and decided to pull the trigger.

Madison: I'm looking forward to performing with you again.

I was curious if it'd cause a reaction in him when he read it, and he didn't disappoint. He lifted his head to look directly at me, and although his eyes were hidden behind his sunglasses, I felt his intense gaze.

He trapped me with it for a long moment, before returning his attention to his phone.

Colin: Same.

The next morning, Colin was the first to show up at my bedroom door, ready to help me with setup. Once again, we were using my room for a scene, but there was a lot more to do to transform the space this time.

We were swapping out my headboard and moving furniture around, so the bed was the main focus of the room.

I helped him move my dresser into the closet, which was so big and cumbersome, we were too busy struggling with it to notice the corner had snagged on the plastic bag covering my formal dress. It wasn't until we heard plastic tearing that we both froze.

"What was that?" Colin asked, setting the dresser down.

I hurried to the white bag that hung from the rack and was stretched awkwardly across the corner of the dresser, grabbing the hanger to pull it down. I peeled up the plastic, revealing the dress so I could examine it for damage.

The golden sequins twinkled at me as the fabric moved. Thankfully, everything looked okay.

"Fancy," he said, eyeing the dress and the tag still attached. "What's it for?"

"Nothing now. I bought it a while ago for the Lambda Theta Chi formal." I tugged the plastic back in place. "But obviously, I didn't get to wear it."

I hung the dress back up lovingly, and it didn't go unnoticed by him.

"Do you miss it?" His voice was quiet. "Being a Lambda?"

I considered my answer. "Sometimes. I let it take over my life, and it got to the point where it was part of my identity, you know? So, it was hard when that was suddenly gone."

He nodded like he understood and that maybe it had been the same for him. He'd been a frat boy, and it seemed like he'd completely embraced that identity.

"How about you?" I asked. "Do you miss it?"

"Parts of it, yeah." He extended his arm across his chest and grabbed his bicep with his other hand, stretching out a tight muscle from all the heavy lifting. "But other parts, not at all." He let go, his arms dropped to his sides, and he moved, closing the distance between us until his shadow fell on me. "Plus, it's pretty great here."

There was hardly any space between us to breathe, and the gravity in his eyes sucked me in. It hinted that I was a big reason why he liked being at the house so much. My heart fell out of rhythm and then resumed faster. God, it was amazing how he could make such an impact on me with a single look.

I opened my mouth to declare I wanted to kiss him, but footsteps approached.

"Madison?" Abbie asked.

"In here."

She rounded the corner and stepped into view, pulling up short when she discovered I wasn't alone. Her curious gaze noted how close Colin and I were, and she must have sensed the tension between the two of us. She crossed her arms and leaned against the doorframe, wearing a knowing smile.

"What's going on in here?" she teased.

"Nothing." Colin's tone was flat, perhaps overcompensating, as he shuffled away from me. "Just moving furniture."

He'd made an effort to sound disinterested, but it was wasted. The glimmer of awareness in her eyes said she didn't believe a word of it.

I didn't get a chance to talk about kissing with Colin after that. Scott showed up soon after Abbie did, and then we were busy placing lights, cameras, and sound equipment.

Once Jaquan and Nina arrived, we moved on to the choreography, finding the best way to make transitions happen fast while still feeling natural. With four people, there were a lot of moving parts, so we had to practice and figure out our marks to make sure we were framed right.

And when all that was done, we moved downstairs to the living room that Nina and Jaquan had set up for filming—and repeated the whole process. At least it went faster down here. The story didn't plan on us spending much time on the couch before moving the scene upstairs.

Then we parted to go get prepared. Abbie and I did our hair and makeup together before getting dressed in the wardrobe we'd picked out for the scene. We were both in cocktail dresses. Our characters had decided to dress up because we were 'getting drinks with the other couple,' according to the storyline.

My excitement about the scene climbed higher when everyone except for Nina gathered in the living room. She would stay downstairs in the edit bay the entire time, watching the shots and providing direction to both us actors and Scott, who'd serve as a cameraman.

My gaze flicked to Colin, taking in his black button-down shirt and dark gray slacks. He looked older and sexy in a whole new way when he wasn't dressed in a t-shirt and jeans. The frat boy faded, and a composed man emerged in his place.

He was breathtaking.

Jaquan stepped up beside me, giving me a smile and a nudge with his elbow. He wore a fitted white shirt, with the top few buttons undone, over navy slacks with a brown belt. The silver watch on his wrist gleamed, and he appeared confident and wealthy.

He looked pretty damn amazing, and I couldn't have been more pleased to have him as a fake boyfriend. I wove my hand through his arm, linking us together, and gave him a friendly smile.

Abbie saw this and did the same, curling herself around Colin's arm. It didn't bother me to see it—they were just preparing for the scene like I'd done.

It wasn't real.

"Everyone ready?" Nina asked in our earpieces, and when we confirmed we were, she called for us to start. "Action."

Scott held the camera and backed up as we strolled forward, going to sit on the couch, each couple on one side with the girls closest to each other. There was a bottle of wine that had been opened, and re-stopped with the cork, chilling in an ice bucket on the table beside the couch, along with four glasses.

As Jaquan grabbed the bottle and began to pour wine into the glasses, Abbie and I made small talk. She complimented my dress and told me how great I looked. I thanked her, drank a sip of the wine, and pretended to be shy.

"My girlfriend and I," Colin said in a voice full of seduction, "were wondering if you two have ever swapped before?"

"No," Jaquan said. "Have you?"

Abbie nodded enthusiastically and matched Colin's seductive tone. "Is that something you'd be interested in?"

Jaquan stretched an arm over the back of the couch and pulled me closer, nuzzling into the side of my neck. "I don't know." His breath was hot right beside my ear. "What do you think?" He mouthed kisses against my neck like I needed to be persuaded. "Do you want to?"

I didn't have to fake being breathless. "How would it work?"

She leaned over and coursed a hand provocatively up my leg, drawing patterns on the top of my thigh with the tip of a finger. "Well, you and I could start while the guys watch."

It was intoxicating having Jaquan's lips on my sensitive skin and Abbie's finger teasing me, all while Colin watched from the other end of the couch. His eyes were heavy with lust, and a satisfied smile lurked at the edges of his mouth.

He liked seeing me like this as I struggled not to drown in desire.

It got harder when Abbie hooked a finger around the strap of my dress and peeled it oh-so-slowly down. The fabric clung to my skin and caught on my pebbled nipple for a moment until it finally fell free.

The air in the room heated and thickened, making time slow.

Her mouth was on my breast and her hand worked its way up my skirt, while Jaquan eased the other strap down, trapping my arms at my sides. When her fingers found my clit, I moaned. The sound of it made Colin shift on the couch.

So he could touch her.

While he watched me.

Jaquan picked up my leg and draped it over his, opening me more to Abbie's touch. Her eager fingers slid inside me, making me gasp with pleasure. She nipped at my breasts while she fucked me with her fingers, and Jaquan's hand smoothed up and down my leg, stroking me sensually.

But my gaze was locked on the one person who wasn't touching me—the one I most wanted to. My focus bounced between Colin's handsome face and the movement of his hands as he inched Abbie's skirt up, revealing her teal-colored panties.

My chest rose and fell heavily with my ragged breath.

He reached around her body to slide his hand down the front of her underwear, causing her to let out an appreciative sigh. He was touching her, but he was watching me, and just the connection of our gazes was more powerful than any other contact.

Jaquan drew slow circles on my breast with the pad of a finger while his mouth sought mine. I turned into his kiss out of obligation, wishing I hadn't needed to because I wasn't ready to be done looking at Colin.

The kiss was nice, but I was just going through the motions. This was a performance, an act, and I hoped Colin understood. There was a camera directly across from us, documenting it all. Jaquan's mouth moved from mine, drawing a line of kisses down my throat, and my gaze found Colin's immediately.

He licked his lips. It was like he wanted to be the one kissing me and was preparing to do it.

I hadn't realized how obvious my staring had become until Jaquan's warm, rich voice rang in my ear. "You want to fuck him, don't you?" He already knew the answer. "What do you think? Do you want to watch your boyfriend fuck someone else?"

I exhaled loudly, wanting to dispel some of the heat that was accumulating in my body. I was already on fire, and we'd only just started.

"I think," I whispered between two enormous breaths, "we should go upstairs."

Abbie giggled like it was the best idea she'd ever heard. She sat up, leaning back into Colin as he continued to move his hand beneath the lace of her panties, making her eyes hood.

As Jaquan stood from the couch, I pulled my dress straps up to cover myself, and then took his offered hand. He pulled me to my feet, wrapped an arm around me, and squeezed a handful of my ass. Like I was a good girlfriend, and he was so pleased with me.

His kiss was full of sex and sin. And when it was over, he cast his gaze on the other couple. "Are you coming?"

Nina waited a beat before speaking.

"Cut," she said. "That looked great, but let's move fast to the next location. I don't want to lose momentum."

Scott led the way up the stairs, turning on the lights and the other cameras in my bedroom while we waited in the hall, before telling Nina he was good to go.

"Action," she said.

Jaquan and I led the other couple in, and as soon as we were through the door, Abbie was on me. Her mouth crushed to mine, and her greedy hands clutched at my dress, tugging it up. We were a blur of kisses and desperate hands as we stripped each other out of our clothes, leaving us clad in only our lacy thongs.

I was vaguely aware the men were shedding their clothes, too, but Abbie demanded all my attention. She stroked and caressed and kissed me like this would be her only chance to in the scene.

Jaquan's bare chest flattened to my back, and his hands settled on my hips, pulling me tight to him. It was as if I was leaning against stone covered in soft, warm skin. Like me and Abbie, he was naked except for his underwear, and I sighed contently when his strong hands moved up to cup my breasts from behind. I lifted my hand and curled it behind me, holding on to the back of his neck while he kissed the place where my neck met my body.

But where was the partner I craved the most?

My eyes were hazy with desire as I searched for Colin. He hadn't gotten his clothes off as quickly as the other man had, and he hurried to catch up. When it was done, he did the same as the other man, moving in to stand behind his 'girlfriend' and wrap his arms around her.

She arched back into his touch as his hands gripped her breasts, making the piercings in her nipples glint in the light. But as he touched her, his gaze was fixed on me, and I didn't dare look away.

He looked powerful and sexy, but there was a hunger lurking in his eyes. It told me the gorgeous girl in his arms wasn't what he really wanted. She stretched and reveled in his touch the same way I did Jaquan's hands, enjoying the sensations, but I craved another man.

It was wild. Erotic. Hedonistic.

Anticipation twisted tighter in me when Abbie stepped out of his arms, shifting her sultry gaze up to Jaquan. She trailed her fingers over one of his hands, gently peeling his hold away from me, and then she tugged him toward the bed. As she backed up to it, pulling him along, she had a sexy smile and crooked a finger at him with her free hand.

Come join me, she said.

With Abbie and Jaquan partnered off, it brought me to the moment I'd been waiting for. Three long weeks since we'd last kissed, and I didn't want to wait any longer. Colin didn't either because he launched at me. Two swift foot-steps and then his hands were on me, his mouth crashing down on mine.

Fire ravaged my body, searing across every inch of my skin.

Yes, I unleashed in my head.

"Oh, so we're kissing now?" I could hear the smile in Nina's voice.

Beneath his lips, I wanted to grin, but I was much too busy being swept away. God, his kiss. It was deep, and thor-ough, and . . . *possessive.* Like he wanted to kiss me in a way no other person could.

But we were on the clock and had a job to do.

I sucked in a breath when he scooped me up, urging me to wrap my legs around his waist. But as I was carried the few steps to the bed, I kissed him again. It was probably distract-ing and made it more difficult on him, but I couldn't help myself. His mouth was addictive.

It was a short fall as he laid me down on my back on the bed, dropping me beside Abbie. They were farther ahead of us because Jaquan's head was between her legs. Seeing it turned me on even more. It was so fucking hot, watching his tongue stroke over her sensitive skin and how it made her contract with pleasure. His dark hand snaked up her body, grabbing one of her breasts, and her hands held his head to her.

"Fuck, that's it," she said. "Lick that pussy."

A sharp pang of heat ricocheted through me.

Colin's mouth crawled down my body in a trail of hot, damp kisses, and when he reached the lace of my panties, they were jerked down my legs. He tossed them away, shoved my legs apart, and descended on me like he was ravenous.

"Oh, my God." I arched up, bowing off the mattress when his mouth made contact. The pleasure of it was an acute shock, a jolt of bliss.

As my moans mingled with Abbie's, so did our hands and lips. We kissed and caressed each other while the men feasted on us, and behind them, Scott watched through the viewscreen of his camera.

His expression was serious and focused, more con-cerned with capturing the action than anything else. And why wouldn't he be? As a professional, he'd seen and done it all. This might even be tame or routine to him. But to me?

It was scorching hot.

Sweat beaded on my skin, and the air I dragged into my lungs felt thick and humid. It grew stronger when Abbie crawled backward on the bed, moving up until she lay across it at an angle, her head by the pillows. It allowed Jaquan to stand and walk to the side of the bed. He pushed down his underwear until it stretched across his powerful thighs, exposing his impressive dick, and inviting her to use her mouth on him.

Time had slowed when we were on the couch, but in the bedroom, it moved at light speed.

As soon as she had her lips wrapped around Jaquan's cock, Colin seized my waist and turned me over onto my stomach. I shifted on the bed, matching her angle as I settled between her legs. She was all bare and pink, and her skin glistened with either her arousal, or Jaquan's work, or a combination of the two.

I rested on my bent elbows, pushed my hair out of my way, and lowered my mouth to her soft skin.

Her moan was deep and grateful, muffled by the cock filling her mouth. As I spun circles on her clit with my tongue, her toes went into points and the muscles of her legs tightened. I loved how responsive she was. I'd gone down on her three times now, but it still felt new and thrilling, and I was beginning to wonder if that would ever fade away.

I hoped not.

The bed shifted as Colin climbed on, his warm, bare legs straddling mine. His underwear was gone, and the heavy weight of his hard cock fell across my ass. My heart lurched forward.

Had it been a decade since we'd last been together? Because it felt that way. Everything in me clamored for him.

I ceased moving my tongue on Abbie when I felt his hand go to his cock and his tip brushed at the seam of my legs. He nudged forward, inching inside, and I gasped. It made my warm breath bounce off her skin, and my hand on the inside of her thigh instinctively clenched.

Fuck—that stretch of my body around him.

It flooded me with bottomless pleasure, going on and on

as he continued to advance. To take and fill. To possess.

"Yes," I gasped, embracing the shudders he caused. Always with him, it was his tremble now.

He planted a hand on the bed beside me and used the other to sweep my hair back over my shoulder, giving him full access to do as he pleased with my exposed skin. He leaned in, setting his mouth on my shoulder as his hips began to move in a languid thrust.

It felt so fucking good, my eyes fell closed.

His lips glanced across my skin, working their way up the side of my neck and causing goosebumps to burst across my arms. I tried not to lose focus and needed to return to Abbie to play my role in the scene. So, I moved in. My tongue flicked and cartwheeled, drawing out more sighs and whimpers of satisfaction from the girl.

It was so fucking hard to go down on her while Colin was inside me. Not physically, though. It was that the undulation of his body was sinful, and the flex of his hips made it impossible to think about anything else. His chest was pressed to my back, and I could feel him everywhere, including his pounding heart.

And since his mouth was so close, I abandoned my task, turned my head, and captured his lips with mine.

Inside me, he pulsed, and his deep, slow thrusts abruptly stopped.

Had kissing me catapulted him right to the edge of orgasm? He held perfectly still, enduring my mouth on his, before slowly, *finally* resuming. When the kiss ended, he leaned forward and closed the gap over my shoulder, dropping his mouth to Abbie's slit.

An excited gasp filled my lungs.

It was in the script, but nothing could have prepared me for how erotic it was. I got to watch up close as his tongue slicked over her clit, teasing her, all while he moved inside me. *Jesus.*

I fucking loved it.

Our bodies rocked together, and we took turns sharing her intimately, sometimes breaking it up to exchange short, gasping kisses with each other. My body trembled harder than it ever had, making it hard to support myself on my shaking elbows, but he'd already proven that if I fell, he'd catch me.

That was the thought that sent me spiraling upward.

When the pitch and frequency of my moans swelled, everyone was excited about it.

"Yeah," Jaquan said. "Make her come on that dick."

"Give it to him," Abbie ordered, before resuming the blow job she'd been giving.

Everyone wanted it, but no one as much as Colin. His uneven breath rasped in my ear, mixed with his moans that could have doubled as pleas. There was urgency in the way he fucked me, steady and relentless.

I climbed, racing toward my release, and yet it still caught me by surprise when it happened. The orgasm made me shudder inside and out.

"Oh, fuck, yes," he gasped. "I can *feel* you coming."

Sound faded and was replaced with buzzing while ecstasy rocketed through my body. I dropped my head forward, laying my cheek on Abbie's thigh, surviving the orgasm whose grip was like a vise.

The sensations diminished until I could breathe and

think over them, and Jaquan must have decided that was a good place to transition because he pushed his underwear the rest of the way down his legs and started to climb onto the bed. Abbie slid back and sat up, moving to make way for him.

It caused us to move, too. Colin rolled us so we were both on our sides and faced the other couple. The change in position made him fall out of me, but the connection was only broken for a moment, and I sighed with satisfaction as he reclaimed my body.

Jaquan had barely finished lying down before Abbie grabbed his dick, threw a leg over his waist, and slid all the way down on him. They didn't start slow. He clamped his hands on her hips, urging her to ride him hard, and she looked thrilled to do it.

Shit, it was sexy the way her breasts bounced, and her blonde hair swung as her body slammed down on his. But it was even sexier the way Colin's hand smoothed up over my breasts, coming to a stop so his thumb and forefinger were just under my chin. He used them to hold my head steady, commanding me to look at the other people while he fucked me.

"Look at them. Do you like that?" His voice was wicked and hypnotic. "Watching your boyfriend fuck someone else?"

"Yes."

I didn't hesitate because I didn't have to act. I found this incredibly hot.

I knew I wasn't supposed to, but it no longer mattered. I'd spent my life believing in monogamy, but there'd been a seismic shift in me since stepping into this world, and I had no desire to go back.

I wanted his question to be real, that Colin was asking Mads, and not Annika, if I'd like watching my boyfriend with other people. And I wanted him to be asking because *he* wanted to be that boyfriend.

"Yes," I repeated.

TWENTY

Madison

The rest of the scene was a blur of sex and pleasure.

Jaquan brought Abbie to orgasm, and then I was kneeling over Jaquan's face, letting him fuck me with his mouth while Colin knelt on the bed beside us. It allowed Abbie and me to kiss each other and take turns sucking his cock.

His face twisted with satisfaction and his intense gaze burned with heat, and I loved the way it always seemed to find me. There were two other people in the scene, but they only seemed to exist in the background. Secondary characters, while he treated me like I was the main one.

Even as the scene drew to a close, and Abbie and I were on our knees in front of the men preparing to finish, he barely glanced at her. Once he started to come? Well, then he didn't look at her at all.

He stared at me with eyes full of things he wanted to say, but then the orgasm was too powerful for him to keep them open any longer. God, he was beautiful.

When it was over, I was supposed to kiss Abbie, but it was cut short. His hands went under my arms, and I was pulled up to stand so he could seal his mouth over mine.

The kiss was blistering and made me go weightless. I might have swayed, but his arms locked around me, holding me up. He kissed me, knowing that time was running out, and when the scene was over, we'd have to go back to the safety of whatever we'd been the last three weeks.

Coworkers?

Friends?

I hated that and didn't want the kiss to end, and he didn't either.

But Scott cleared his throat in the attention-getting way.

"I guess they didn't hear Nina say cut," Jaquan teased, although it was true. Everything stopped when Colin's mouth was mine.

"Aw, leave them alone." Abbie's tone was warm and sweet. "They're so cute."

All the blood in my body rushed to my face, heating it until it was as hot as the surface of the sun. Colin and I separated, both making an attempt to not look embarrassed, although I was sure he was more successful than I was.

Shit.

If this was what every scene was going to be like with him from now on, I was in big trouble.

Colin and I didn't see each other until a few days later. I wasn't avoiding him, but I'd been busy with classes, and only able to work out in the mornings, when he seemed to prefer the afternoons.

I was in the kitchen, prepping my meals for the rest of the week, when he strolled in. His footsteps slowed as he made his way to the fridge, caught off guard at seeing me unexpectedly.

"Hey," he said.

My body was taut, acutely aware of him. "Hi."

He pulled a sports drink from the fridge, unscrewed the cap, and drank as he watched me mince garlic. "What are you making?"

"Honey sriracha meatballs and rice."

"Nice."

He lingered like he didn't want to leave, but also had no fucking clue what else to say. Things between us had changed, and he felt it too, but neither of us knew where to go from here.

But before we could figure out anything to say, the door to the garage opened and shut, and Scott appeared in the doorway from the mud room. He held a stack of mail, but one letter had been opened and read already, judging by the way he clutched the unfolded paper in his hand.

The pissed off expression on his face was another clue.

"Fucking HOA," he groaned to no one in particular.

It was a sore subject around here these days. The Woodsons had fought the association about their mismatched AC units . . . and they'd lost. It was stated in the by-laws that all exterior equipment visible from the homeowner's driveway had to match.

Scott offered to put up a fence, but naturally the HOA declined them a permit.

Then they suggested landscaping to hide it, but the plans couldn't get approval.

After paying the outrageous fines for three weeks, Scott and Nina had caved. They'd decided it was better to cut their losses and get back in Judy Malinger's good graces, so they'd upgraded the other two units to match. It had cost a lot of unnecessary money, but then it was over and done, and Judy stopped making impromptu visits to check on the mismatched equipment.

"What's going on now?" I asked.

Scott tossed the crumpled letter down on the counter. "They're raising the monthly association fee. I don't fucking get it. With all the ridiculous fines they collect for every goddamn thing, how do they not have enough money already?" He dropped the rest of the mail and leafed through it, but his irritation didn't dissipate. "I swear, if we'd known, we never would have moved in."

"Can't something be done?" I asked. "Like, a group complaint or a—"

"Several of us homeowners tried to recall her in February," his expression turned bitter, "but she got wind of it, and the board—who all fucking love her for some reason—voted to change the rules. We couldn't reach the new quorum of eighty-five percent, so the effort failed."

"How much is the increase?" Colin asked.

"Twenty percent, and keep in mind, it was already outrageously high. I don't know what it's paying for. The common areas look like shit. The grass in the front of the subdivision hasn't been mowed in weeks and is starting to seed."

He placed his hands on the counter and hung his head, looking momentarily defeated, before blowing out a long breath and readjusting.

"These are the joys of home ownership," a sarcastic smile tweaked his lips, "that make me long for the awesome condo Nina and I had back in Chicago." He straightened and scooped up the letters and junk mail, then seemed to force himself to be positive. "I don't miss the taxes, though."

He strode across the kitchen and sorted the mail into different boxes above the built-in desk, which was our own little mailroom. I rarely got much, but a few times a month, there'd be something from school or a bank statement in the box labeled with my name.

There was nothing for me today, though.

Scott finished his task and turned to leave, but Colin suddenly stood tall, straightening away from the counter he'd been leaning against. "Hey, Scott. Do you have a minute to talk?"

"Sure." The older man nodded and waved a hand to encourage Colin to follow him into the living room.

Colin's gaze darted to me, and I didn't understand his expression. It was like he faced some sort of decision and still hadn't made up his mind. But then he broke the connection of our gazes and followed Scott out the door.

That was . . . weird.

Was it self-centered to think their discussion was going to involve me?

I'd spent much of the weekend brainstorming what kind of scene I would pitch on Monday night, and how it needed to be something that would pair me with Colin—and no one else.

We hadn't done that since our audition, and I wasn't the only one who wanted it.

Petal Productions allowed moderated comments under

their videos, and if I ever needed an ego boost, all I had to do was read them.

Annika is FUCKING HOT. But I need more
Carter & Annika please.

Yes! They must be together IRL. The chemistry
is too good.

The comments gave me an unexpected thrill, and I was glad to know that what I felt with him was coming through onscreen.

On Monday evening, I was still considering a few different storylines for my pitch when my phone's screen lit up with a text message. Had he known what I was thinking about?

Colin: Do you have time to talk before the meeting?

Madison: Sure.

Colin: Want to meet now? I'm in the dining room.

Madison: Heading down to you.

He was sitting in his usual spot, and it was wild to me how quickly my pulse rushed at the sight of him and his warm smile.

"Hey," he said as I dropped down into my seat across from him. "I pitched my scene to Nina already, and she's cool with it, but I need your approval."

My breath caught. He'd likely need my approval because he wanted me in his scene, and hopefully he couldn't hear how much I liked that idea. "What's the pitch?"

"Okay, so . . . you're a virgin."

A needle dragged across a record inside my brain. He was well aware I was *not* a virgin. "Uh, what?"

He made a face, annoyed with himself, but then pushed ahead. "For the story. You're a virgin, it's prom night, and I'm your date." There was a sudden weight to his voice. "It'll be our first time together."

I swallowed a breath against the hard clench of my body. His expression hinted at the meaning he buried in his words. Since we'd gotten to know each other, he'd become a different person to me, and kissing had only added to the newness.

The people we were now had never been together.

We needed a new first time.

He rested his arms on the table and leaned over like he wanted to be closer to me. "I figured you could wear that pink dress in your closet, and since we'd be going to all the trouble of getting dressed up," he shrugged, "we should do something before."

Awareness washed down through me. "Like what?"

"I dunno." But he clearly did. "Have dinner."

"That sounds like a date."

He let the comment glance off him like he hadn't heard it. "I didn't go to my prom, and you didn't get to go to your sorority formal." His smile was playful. "Maybe this will help us get into character."

He knew his argument was a stretch, but I wasn't going to call him on it. If he wanted to play dress up and have dinner with me? Yes, please. I was all in on that.

But I sat back in my chair and crossed my arms, trying to be cool and pretend like I was considering it. "You'd be my boyfriend in this scenario?"

His shoulders lifted with a deep breath, and his intense gaze trapped mine. "Sure. If that's what you want."

"And you think people would buy that?" I teased.

He smirked. "I do."

"All right. Let's do it."

His pleased smile? It was sexy as hell.

I'd gone to my senior prom, but I hadn't felt a fraction of the excitement then that I did tonight. Abbie, with all her years of beauty pageant experience, was a master at curling and pinning my hair into an elegant updo. I'd done my make-up, cut the tags off my dress, and put it on.

When I found him waiting in the living room, he wasn't alone—but he might as well have been. I couldn't see anyone but him, and the elegant black suit and tie he wore. Had he gotten a haircut this morning? His hair was neat and styled, giving him a polished look.

God, he was devastatingly handsome.

How was I supposed to function when he looked like that? All I could think about was telling him how badly I wanted to kiss him.

But that would be a bad idea. First off, I might die if he said no. And second, what would Nina and Scott think? They stood nearby and had been chatting with Colin until I appeared in the doorway.

At my entrance, all conversation ceased.

This was all pretend, but good lord, did it feel it real. Like he was my date, and Nina and Scott were my surrogate parents. They gazed at me with admiration, but it was the way Colin looked at me with stunned eyes that caused the strongest flush. It heated my body and sucked all the air from the room.

His gaze started at the bottom of my dress and swept upward, gliding over my curves and the delicate, sparkling sequins, moving up until he reached my face. He didn't have to say a word because I felt it in my bones. He wanted to kiss me just as much as I did him.

"You look beautiful," Nina said.

"Yes," Colin agreed.

My voice was as unsteady as I felt. "Thank you."

Nina was unaware of the force swirling between me and this frat boy who no longer looked like one. She lifted her phone, angling the camera toward him. "Let me take some pictures of the two of you."

My heart beat wildly as I strolled over to stand beside Colin. When he put his arm around me and his hand came to rest on my hip, I drew in a deep, sharp breath. My response didn't go unnoticed by him; he pulled me tighter, closer.

We smiled as she took the pictures, and when she lowered her phone, her expression was playful and devious, her question for her husband. "Should we make them do the prom pose where he's standing behind her?"

"Please don't," Colin said, sounding like he was only half serious. But since I was pressed against him, I could feel the tension in his body. He didn't want to have to put his arms around me right now—not when we both knew we couldn't do anything more. They were our bosses, and surely they didn't want us messing up the dynamic in the house.

Scott dug a hand in the pocket of his shorts, produced a set of keys, and handed them over to Colin. "You kids have fun tonight," he joked, then sobered. "But not in my BMW."

Colin chuckled then played the part of the son getting to drive daddy's expensive car for the first time. "No, sir," he quipped.

"Right," Nina said. Her tone turned overly dramatic. "Make good choices."

She'd lobbed it at us like she was kidding, and yet . . . her sparkling gaze lingered on mine. Even the way Scott looked at us was off.

Like everyone was in on the joke but me.

I waited until I was seated in the passenger seat of Scott's car before mentioning it to Colin. "Was it just me, or were they acting weird?"

"Who?" Colin slid into the driver's seat and buckled his seat belt.

What did he mean, *who?* "Nina and Scott."

He shrugged, pushed the button to start the engine, and then his fingers wrapped around the gearshift. "They seemed fine to me."

The restaurant was downtown, and during the drive, we talked about school. I was curious how he'd picked his major of public relations, and then regretted asking because he said his parents 'had strongly influenced his decision.' It was a nice way of saying he'd just been following orders. They were paying for it, he'd said, but were *considerate* enough to let him choose . . . as long as it was within the school of business.

He'd been on such a short leash with his folks, had joining the frat been the first time he'd really tasted freedom?

After he'd parked the car in a parking garage, we took the elevator down to the ground and walked one block to the hotel that also contained an upscale restaurant. We were young and overdressed, and I could see confusion in other people's expressions as we were led to our table.

They were wondering what event we were dressed for. Maybe they thought we were music or Hollywood stars, since Nashville had become a trendy place to retreat to.

The waiter glanced at my dress as he filled my water goblet. "Are we on a schedule this evening? In case I need to alert the chef, so we stay on your timetable."

"No," Colin said. "No schedule."

The waiter gave me a pleasant, curious smile. "Then, are we celebrating something?"

We're pretending it's prom, wasn't going to work, but I drew a blank on how to answer.

"It's our first date," Colin announced, pulling his lips into a grin. "Go big, or go home, right?"

I laughed softly—only to realize he wasn't joking.

My heart did a cartwheel inside my chest.

If the waiter thought this was ridiculous and we were just two kids playing dress-up, not an ounce of it showed on his face. He moved on to filling Colin's water. "Wonderful. Shall I tell you this evening's specials?"

After our drinks were delivered and our orders were placed, Colin lifted his gaze from his bourbon and Coke and fixed it on me.

"I made a mistake."

His tone was serious, causing concern to skyrocket inside me. "What'd you do?"

"I told you we shouldn't be anything more than coworkers."

I hesitated, letting his meaning sink in before every muscle in me went tense. My throat tightened, making it impossible to speak, but it was all right because he wasn't finished.

"So, I'm taking it back." His eyes became magnets, pulling me in. "I didn't think I wanted you that night we auditioned together, but I was wrong. *So,* fucking, wrong. And after that scene? The way I wanted you . . . it just got stronger." He said it as if he'd been trying to resist something unstoppable. Something inevitable. "I want you all the damn time."

My lungs refused to work. If I took a breath, it might break the spell between us, and I didn't want that.

His head tilted a fraction of a degree. "It's the same for you, isn't it?"

How could I not answer him? It was just a ghost of a word. "Yes."

Jesus. He looked relieved to hear he wasn't alone in this crushing desire. "Aren't you tired of fighting it?"

"Yes, but . . ."

My gaze fell to the tabletop, and yet I felt his on me, holding me in place. It was so hard to organize my thoughts. There were reasons we shouldn't get involved, but what were they again?

People in love don't sleep with other people.

We weren't in love, but wasn't that the goal if we started dating?

I frowned, glanced around to make sure no one was listening, and then lowered my voice. "Our job is to sleep with other people."

"And?" He was so casual about it.

"That doesn't bother you, seeing me with other people?"

Oh, he was prepared for this, and his eyes glinted with sin. "Fuck, no." He leaned forward, matching my low voice. "It turns me on. Watching you with Abbie or Jaquan? Or Scott and Nina? You have no idea how much I like it."

I wanted to believe him, but it was hard to accept. "Really?"

He picked up his drink and tilted it, slowly rolling the ice around inside the glass. "It surprised me, too. But seeing you enjoying yourself, even if it's with someone else?" He shrugged. "It's fucking hot. Sure, I like it better when I get to be a part of it, but no, Madison. It doesn't bother me, seeing you with someone else."

I blinked, utterly stunned.

With everything he'd just admitted, it was his use of my full name that shocked me the most. I hadn't heard him say it in months, and—holy shit—I didn't like it nearly as much as the nickname he'd given me. He was the only one who used it, and I liked how—just like the tremble he caused in me—it was only for us.

Once upon a time, I would have hated his smug smile, but tonight? It was doing things to me. "Tell me it's not the same for you." His demand was rhetorical. He knew I wouldn't say it because it'd be a lie. "Tell me you don't like watching me with other people. *Sharing* me with other people."

My mind instantly went to the moment we'd taken turns going down on Abbie, and Colin didn't miss the shudder of pleasure that glanced through my shoulders at the memory. Victory lit up his expression.

"I do," I confessed, except where did we go from here?

"But what are you suggesting?"

"Everyone already knows we like each other. Even before our last scene, Scott said it was the worst kept secret in the house."

"That's what your talk with Scott was about?"

"Kind of." He took a sip of his drink. "I asked him how he made things work with Nina when they started dating."

Oh, my God. He'd gone to Scott for relationship advice. I worried I was going to melt into a puddle and ruin the nice chair I was sitting on. "What did he say?"

"I asked him if he worried about what would happen if they broke up. Wouldn't it be too hard to keep working together?"

I swallowed a breath. This was one of the biggest things holding me back. What if we were foolish enough to try a relationship, and when it crashed, it burned up everything with it? I enjoyed performing, but I doubted I'd ever want to make a career out of it.

I didn't know if the same was true for him. Men typically had a longer shelf life than women in the industry. What if Colin wanted to do this long term? I didn't want to jeopardize any of his opportunities.

"What was his answer?"

"He told me that he didn't have that concern with Nina."

I pressed my lips into a flat line. "Because he knew they'd get married?"

"No, because she didn't do much acting. She went to work at some private sex club pretty soon after they met." He massaged the back of his neck and looked contemplative. "Which, honestly? I don't think I'd be into that, the 'not knowing.' And I'd definitely not be into the 'not seeing' part."

"Yeah," I said, understanding.

I wasn't always in the room when Colin performed, but I could log in to Petal Productions website right now on my phone and watch any of his scenes. The door was never closed between us. But I deflated when I realized Scott didn't have any experience or guidance for our situation.

Colin adjusted the knot of his tie, so it sat loose around his neck. "He reminded me we're actors. He doesn't have feelings for his scene partners, and he knew it was the same for Nina when she saw clients. And then he told me before Nina, he had a girlfriend who was also in the business. Their breakup went okay. Hell, they even did a few scenes afterward. They figured out how to keep it professional."

My lips parted with surprise. "That's good, but once doesn't mean that's always going to be the case."

"Okay. How many times does it need to be?"

"What?"

He laid his phone on the table, tapped the screen to unlock it, and then pulled open his Notes app. There were pairs of names listed in a block of text that extended down to the bottom of the screen.

"These are all the real couples that Scott's worked with or knows about. Not all of them are together anymore, but they're all still performing."

"You, like, collected data?"

He smirked. "I figured you'd like that."

Fuck. He'd done homework to help convince me, and I was glad he hadn't put it in an Excel spreadsheet. I would have been a goner.

Seriousness crept back into him. "Look, I'm not saying it'll be easy. If we do this, it might change the dynamic in the house, but we can talk about it. Like, if you only want to do scenes with each other, or if you want to be on set when I'm with someone else, that's fine. I'm willing to give that a try if you think we need it to make this work."

I stared at him with disbelief. The suit hadn't just transformed him physically, it must have done something to him emotionally too. Because he'd put in a lot of thought and effort to this conversation, and his words made me so weightless, I struggled not to float away.

"I love performing with you," I said softly, "but I don't think I'd need exclusivity for it to work."

I didn't know how to put what I wanted to say into words, but his smile was warm. "Hey, I get it. I don't want you to feel limited."

Yes, that was exactly it. I nodded. "Plus, I don't think Nina would be thrilled if we said we'd only perform with each other."

"Well, she told me there's a strong demand for real-life couples."

"Of course you already talked to her about it." *That* was why she and Scott had been acting so strange earlier. They knew all about Colin's plans.

"I came prepared tonight, Madison."

"Stop calling me that," I blurted.

Oh, he fucking *loved* my reaction to him not using my nickname. I might as well have told him he'd won every battle we'd ever fought. His grin was wide and triumphant. "Okay, Mads." His eyes glimmered with persuasion.

"I mean, viewers already think we're together. Why not make it official?"

"You sure you're not a marketing major?" My tone was begrudging because it was irritating how good he was at this.

"I'm not, and you didn't answer my question."

I wanted to tell him what he wanted to hear, but I was nervous. My last relationship had ended specifically because he'd slept with someone else.

But that was different. You'd be going in with eyes wide open.

"If this has any chance of working, we have to be honest with each other, so I can honestly tell you—I'm scared."

His expression softened. "I know. I'm . . . well, yeah. It's new for me, too. Maybe we'll get to a point where we want to go throw mud at each other again, but I think we could be worth the risk."

I drew in an enormous breath and then lifted my hands in surrender. "Fine."

He blinked. "Fine?"

"You wore me down." I'd tried to sound annoyed, but shit, I failed miserably. My voice was a little too excited. "I'll be your girlfriend. Happy?"

He raised an eyebrow, and then a slow smile crawled along his lips. "Yes."

My heart drummed in my chest, heating me all over as I stared at my new boyfriend. It was wild and exhilarating.

After our entrees arrived, he straightened in his seat and took a preparing breath. "About tonight," he said. "There are two options."

"Oh?"

"The first is after we're done with dinner, we'll go upstairs to the room Petal Productions has booked for us, which has the lights and cameras ready to go, and we shoot the prom night scene."

This sounded great to me, but . . . "What's the other option?"

"After dinner, we go upstairs, but we don't turn the cameras on."

I hesitated. "Why wouldn't we do that?"

"Because we could be ourselves. Maybe we need one night where there's no script and no one watching." His eyes were dark, inky pools. "Something that's only for us."

Holy shit. I'd never wanted something so badly in all my life as I wanted this.

But there was no way Petal Productions would pay for a room if they weren't going to get content out of it. He'd been so prepared, surely he'd asked about it and had a plan. "Nina would be okay with that?"

"Yeah. As long as we film something later or, you know, in the morning."

In the morning. I didn't even need to think about it. "We're doing the second option."

Fuck, his laugh was sexy.

TWENTY-ONE

Colin

I hadn't paid much attention to the hotel room earlier this afternoon when I'd been in here with Scott setting up the equipment. I'd been too busy running through the points I wanted to make to Mads over dinner. I wasn't sure how much convincing she'd need. It was obvious she liked me, but would that be enough to overcome all the other shit?

It was, thank fuck.

After we'd finished our dinner and split the check—since she refused to let me pay for her—I'd led my brand-new girlfriend up to the room, which was masculine and sexy. It was decorated in charcoal gray and brass, with a huge textured wall behind the bed, and long mirrors stretched to the ceiling over each nightstand.

The sun was setting outside, painting the tall buildings with orange and pink hues. It reminded me of her dress, which clung to her body in all the right ways. I liked the subtle hint of glitter it gave as she strolled to the window and looked at the view of downtown.

When I joined her, she didn't say anything. She flashed a nervous smile, and it made me wonder if, without a script, she wasn't sure what to do.

But I was.

I took my phone out of my pocket, opened my music app,

and pressed play on the song I had ready to go. When the opening strains of the music started, I set the phone down on the windowsill, and her surprised gaze darted up to mine.

Her eyes grew even wider when I took her hand and wrapped my arm around her, resting my palm on the small of her back. She sucked in a sharp breath as I urged her to move with me.

To dance with me.

Maybe it was a little over the top—but fuck it. It felt right because we were dressed up, and it gave me an excuse to get her in my arms.

Once she recovered from her shock and began to follow my lead, I expected her dubious expression to fade, but it didn't.

"*You* like Troy Osbourne?"

I nearly laughed. There was a threshold of mainstream that, once an artist crossed it, guys my age deemed them no longer cool. Had Troy gotten to that point? Mads had recognized his voice immediately and assumed I wouldn't listen to him.

"Yeah, I like Troy," I said. "Full disclosure, we're friends. We went to high school together."

There'd been a time when I would have said he and Preston were my best friends, but Troy had gone out of state for college. We'd stayed as close as we could, but once his music career took off, it'd been a lot harder to find time to hang out.

Didn't mean I wasn't fucking thrilled for him.

"Oh," she said softly.

Conversation lulled as we turned in a slow circle, moving

to the rhythm of my friend's guitar while he sang about falling for a girl who didn't know he existed. The ballad, paired with the sunset and our slow dance, was romantic and seductive.

My plan had been to make it through the song, but I'd had this fucking desire for her burning in me for what felt like a century. I couldn't wait any longer.

"I'm going to kiss you," I said.

She nodded. It had always been a question before, but tonight was different.

"Now," she pleaded.

I lowered my head and brought our mouths together in a kiss slow enough to match the sway of our bodies. The idea was to make it last. Tonight would be *real*—just us, and I wanted to savor it.

But it made no difference how slow and measured I moved. Once we started kissing, it lit the fuse. The dance was forgotten because we had more important things to do.

She clasped her hands on my face as I latched mine on her waist, using my grip to press our bodies together, crushing her dress to my suit and tie. Her mouth was so soft. So warm and inviting, and the little sigh of pleasure she gave when my tongue brushed against hers heated me up.

Her hands bristled over my jaw when I adjusted the angle of the kiss, deepening it. My pulse had been steadily building, just like the urgency inside me. Our kiss had started slow, but it grew needy and desperate.

Our hands couldn't stay still either.

I wanted to be touching her everywhere, and it must have been the same for her. I grabbed fistfuls of her skirt, jerking it up so I could get at her legs, while she tried to peel me out of my suit coat. It meant I had to momentarily abandon my goal so I could let her get the coat off, but did she know this wasn't a victory for her? I'd only let her win because the coat was halfway off, caught around my arms, restricting me.

It fell to the floor, and then I went right back to my task, finally getting a hand on her bare leg beneath all the fabric of her dress. Up it traveled, carrying her skirt until it was bunched over my forearm and my fingertips discovered lace and satin.

"I was wondering if you were naked under here," I said.

Her fingers were working lose the knot of my tie, but they paused, and she gave me a pointed look. "I was supposed to be a virgin."

Oh, yeah.

I smiled. "I'm glad you're not tonight."

"Me too." Her hand trailed down the line of buttons on my shirt, over my belt, and landed on the bulge swelling beneath my fly. "This is a lot to take for a first time."

Satisfaction over her touch and her words competed in my head, short circuiting my thoughts. "Is it? You took me like a champ our first time."

"Oh, did I?" Heat seared up my spine when she squeezed and rubbed me through my pants. Her tone was dark and patronizing, but still sexy. "You were pleased with my performance, Colin?"

"It was just the hottest sex of my life."

She froze. We'd been teasing each other, but whatever expression I was making, she could see I wasn't kidding about this.

"It was for me, too," she whispered. "I didn't want it to

be, though."

"I know. I was pissed when you wouldn't let me kiss you."

Her expression was resigned. "Because I didn't want to like you."

I slipped my hand between her legs, caressing her through the thin satin, and watched her eyes hood with pleasure. "But you like me now."

As I touched her clit, she grabbed my biceps and her head fell forward, planting her forehead on my shoulder. It was mumbled against my dress shirt. "God, I do."

There it was. That fucking tremble of hers I loved so much.

She began to quiver as I pushed her panties to the side and touched her with nothing between us, finding her wet. Her hands tightened on my arms. Was she already having a hard time standing?

"You know, I'm torn," I said, rubbing her fast enough it pulled a moan from her lips.

She was already breathing hard. "Between what?"

"Getting you naked or fucking you under this dress."

Her only answer was another moan, and her body undulated, riding my hand. It was so hot. Of course, everything she did these days was sexy to me. I eased a finger inside her, enjoying the heat of her body and the gasp of satisfaction she gave.

"Do you have an opinion on that?" My tone was forced indifference, teasing her like this was a simple conversation and I wasn't finger fucking her.

"Colin," she whined.

Hearing my name on her breathless lips brought everything into focus. It sharpened the need inside me until it was white-hot, the only thing I could think about, and my body took control.

I withdrew my hand, letting her dress fall back into place, and like I'd done when we auditioned, I scooped her up into my arms. She squeaked with surprise, but I didn't let it slow me down as I strode toward the end of the bed, and then set her down there.

Her yelp of surprise was louder when I gave her shoulders a gentle but urgent shove, forcing her down onto her back. I was impatient, and my knees hit the carpet in a loud thud.

"You want some honesty?" I asked as I pushed the layers of fabric back, billowing the skirt of her dress around her waist. "I got jealous watching your scene with Scott and Nina."

She lifted her head to peer down at me, kneeling between her legs, and her mouth dropped open. "You did?"

I curled my fingers around the sides of her panties, which were sexy but had to go. "You came when she went down on you." She lifted her hips, making it easier for me to tug her underwear down her legs. "That means I'm the only person in the house who hasn't done that yet, made you come with their mouth." I tossed them aside and delivered a determined look. "But I'm about to."

She swallowed hard, making her throat bob, and then uttered the same thing she'd said during our audition, the phrase that had driven me wild. Except this time, it wasn't a challenge.

"Then fucking do it already," she whispered.

Shit, she created a fire inside me, and sweat slicked my skin, making my shirt cling to my back. I smoothed my hands up her legs until I got to her knees and then pushed them back to her shoulders, opening her to me.

Her pussy was all wet and perfect, and I dove in.

My tongue barely made contact with her clit before the tremble in her ratcheted up. Her legs shook, vibrating under my palms, and while I sighed with enjoyment, she sighed with exasperation.

She put her hands on the insides of her thighs like she could stop it or hold them still.

I paused and trailed my fingertips over one of her hands. "Does it hurt? The trembling?"

"No. It's just annoying."

"I fucking love it." I smiled before bringing my mouth back to her. She didn't like the tremble, just like she hadn't wanted to be attracted to me, but her body had other ideas.

I spun the tip of my tongue across her clit, fluttering it back and forth, and as I worked, her little gasps and moans grew louder and more intense. Her body arched and bowed and writhed, while her hands alternated between clutching at the sheets, or gripping a handful of my hair.

Her skin was so soft and . . . sensitive. For a second, I considered slowing my tongue and backing her down from the orgasm that seemed to be building inside her, but—

No, that was a terrible idea.

I'd wanted this since our audition, and I wasn't going to wait any longer. I was pretty sure I would have gotten her over the edge with just my mouth that night if she hadn't distracted me with the blowjob.

I listened to the pace of her breathing. The whimpers that seeped from her lips. How she stretched and contracted with pleasure, watching for any dramatic change to signal she was getting close.

And she didn't make me wait long.

"Oh, *yes*," she said urgently. "Like that."

I moved my tongue in a flurry, lashing at her damp, lush skin. One of her hands speared into my hair while the other reached out to ball the sheet in her fist.

"I'm coming," she cried, but I would have known even if she hadn't said a word. I'd watched her videos so many times, my ear was tuned to the sound.

Her orgasm was short but powerful, judging by how hard she shuddered and the gasp it punched from her lungs. I slowed my tongue, giving her long, languid strokes while she came down, and I didn't stop until her hand on my head urged me back.

Her voice was quiet and appreciative. "Fuck."

Hmm, yes. It was exactly what I wanted to do.

I planted a kiss on the inside of her quaking thigh before rising to my feet. My shadow fell on her as she stared up at me, looking blissfully happy . . . but still hungry. Her orgasm was just the appetizer, and I was ready for the main course.

She studied me with eyes that were heavy with lust as I jerked off my tie, hurled it to the floor, and got to work on the buttons of my shirt.

"I want to see your tits," I demanded, yanking off my shirt. "Can you pull your dress down, or do I need to take it off?"

She grabbed one of the straps and peeled it down to her elbow, then did the same with the other side, giving me everything I wanted. Jesus, her tits were my favorite part of her body, and I stared at her tight nipples while I undid my pants.

As I finished getting naked, she didn't just lie there, waiting patiently. She reached a hand between her legs and moved her fingers back and forth over her clit. Slow. Enjoyable. Teasing.

My gaze drifted from her hand up to her eyes, and I saw the provocative gleam in them. She was showing me how she touched herself because she knew how much I liked to watch.

When I climbed onto the bed, I kissed her and urged her to scoot back. It was awesome not to have to worry about if this transition looked awkward, or if I was blocking the shot, or if someone was going to make a comment in my ear that our kiss ran a little long. Don't get me wrong—I enjoyed per-forming—like, a *lot*.

But I didn't know just how good it was going to be to have Mads all to myself.

As our mouths melded, our hands explored. I cupped her breasts as she wrapped her fingers around my dick and began to stroke me. Pleasure seared up my body, intensifying my need to get inside her.

She was on her back with the dress trapped around her waist, and I was naked, over her with my knees between her legs. I rubbed my bare dick against her pussy, and it felt so good, my heart went into overdrive. She'd come to the house to experience new things, and so had I.

She was the first girl I'd ever had without a condom, and I'd struggled in that scene with her not to come too quickly. Because she felt so fucking good.

I reached between our bodies and grabbed myself, brushing the head of my dick teasingly over her clit, but she shifted under me. It felt good, but it wasn't what she wanted.

It wasn't enough. So, I lined up our bodies and sank into her.

Our moans synced up, both sounding like relief. Maybe she'd wanted this as much as I had, but was that even possible? The tight fit of my cock inside her was insane. I had barely moved, and every inch of me was burning with pleasure. Once I was buried as deep as I could go, I found her hands and laced our fingers together, pressing them to the mattress beside her head.

It forced her eyes to flutter open.

She was so beautiful it made breath halt in my lungs. Why the fuck had we waited so long and fought so hard against this? I leaned down and kissed her the way I wanted. Hard. Passionate. Unlike the way I'd kissed anyone else.

I brought out a tremble in her, but she unlocked this part of me. This desire to connect in a way more than just mutual pleasure.

The movement of my hips started slow. It was deep and sensual. It wasn't fucking, it was . . . something else. New. Different. Kind of intimidating, but in a thrilling way.

The walls of her body surrounded me, gripping me with scorching heat, and even though I wasn't moving fast, I was out of breath and my heart pounded in my chest.

But Mads was struggling to catch her breath too, and she broke the kiss to swallow gulps of air. I shifted, inching my mouth across her cheek and down to the place where her neck met her body, nipping gently and kissing the sensitive skin there.

Her legs wrapped tighter around my hips, begging me to move faster—so I did. It caused her hands tangled with mine to squeeze hard and whimpers of enjoyment to roll from her mouth.

"It feels so good," she gasped.

I couldn't agree more, and I loved that it was real. She wasn't saying this for the camera's benefit or because Nina was in her ear monitor instructing her to say it. Mads was saying it because it was true.

But as I moved faster, the urgency in her labored breathing and moans intensified. Was she getting close again?

It came from her abruptly. "Let me be on top."

Well, how could I say no to that? I rolled off her and onto my back, helping her hold her dress out of the way as she moved to straddle me. As soon as I was lodged inside her again, she sat upright and began to ride me at the pace she wanted.

When I'd pinned her hands by her head, it had lifted the straps of her dress, and one of them was back in place on her shoulder while the other hung down over her arm. I put my hand on her exposed breast, massaging and playing with her hardened nipple.

It made her rock faster and grind harder. I'd told her during our audition she'd get her chance to fuck me, and I had a large amount of regret that it'd taken me this long to deliver on my promise. Because this? It was seriously hot.

A few strands of her hair had escaped from the pins holding them up, and they curled softly at her neck. Her skin was dewy with sweat and her chest heaved as she panted for air. I had one hand gripping her waist, helping her keep up with the demanding tempo she seemed to crave, and my other hand drifted down the slope of her body.

I wedged my fingertips between us, touching her as I

fucked her from beneath. In response, she arched and leaned back, making it easier for my thumb to press and massage her clit. The pitch of her moans rose, as did the quivering in her legs on either side of me.

The view was so sexy, but . . . there was a downside.

I didn't like how far away this position put her from me.

When we'd auditioned, I'd pushed her hand out of the way and told her I was the one making her come, and I didn't want it like that tonight. We were a partnership. The thought made me move. I took my hand off her waist and planted it beside me on the bed as I sat up. I hooked my other hand behind her neck, giving her support as I thrust from below.

"Touch yourself," I urged. "Help me get you off."

She watched me as she did it; our gazes were locked on to each other. There wasn't anywhere else to look or any-where else to be but with her. Her parted lips trembled right alongside the rest of her body as her orgasm seemed to ap-proach. Whatever she was feeling, all that pleasure . . . I felt it ten times over. Deep in my core, my body begged for release, but I had to hold back.

"Oh, my God," she gasped, and her eyes slammed shut.

I felt her violent shudders inside and out as she came, and it sent ecstasy crashing into me so hard, there wasn't a thing I could do to stop it. She launched forward, maybe wanting the connection of our mouths as we were connected in pleasure, and I was greedy for that, too.

My heart bounced out of tempo, and each pulse of my orgasm was matched by the grip of her body, prolonging and intensifying the sensation. It felt so fucking amazing, it was as if all the air had been sucked out of the room. So, our kiss wasn't one long one, but a series of desperately short kisses while we struggled to catch our breath.

I wrapped my arms around her and pulled her down with me as I collapsed onto my back. As we recovered, our kisses grew longer and deeper, and since I held her so tightly, I could feel her heartbeat slowing to a measured pace.

Our bodies cooled, but it did nothing to calm the fire I still had for her. The guy I'd been before Mads would have been looking for an exit strategy now that the sex was over. But the idea of either of us getting out of this bed? That was the last thing I wanted. It blew my mind how I was looking forward to what came next.

Would we talk? Cuddle?

Either option was good with me. Just as long as we got to stay together and be who we wanted with each other.

Eventually, she slid off me and wriggled out of her dress before curling up at my side. Her hand rested on the center of my chest, and her face was buried in the crook of my neck. Her lips moved, tickling me as she whispered the word. "Wow."

"Wow is right," I said.

Her fingers drummed mindlessly on my skin, right over my heart. "Is it going to be like that every time?"

"No idea." I had my arm around her and used it to pull her tighter to me. "But I'm looking forward to finding out."

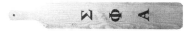

Preston stared at me like I'd just told him I was going to become a monk. He'd been lying on his back on a float in the deep end of his pool, but when I'd mentioned I had a girl-friend now, he sat upright. It caused the float to fold under him, making my friend sink chest-deep into the water.

"Are you serious?" Annoyance ripped through his expression. "First Troy and now you. How am I the only one who's single?"

Leave it to Preston to somehow make my news about himself. "Whatever, dude." I laughed to mask my irritation. "You were with Cassidy for years while Troy and I were single."

"Yeah, but that was a long time ago."

I didn't miss the way his gaze flicked up to the house. Was he thinking about who his ex-girlfriend was with now?

His attention returned to me, and he flashed a lazy smile. "She must be a *special* lady. Never thought you'd commit to one pussy."

I snorted, and for a single heartbeat, I considered telling him what we did in the house up on the hill, but—no. As much as I trusted my friend, it was bigger than just me. Preston could keep a secret, but I couldn't risk him slipping up.

I could tell him Mads and I were in an open relationship of sorts, but what if he judged us?

"She is special," I said.

"How'd you meet?"

"She's in the house," I said. "The same mentorship program as me." I'd felt bad about lying and feeding him the same story Scott had given me, that the Woodsons were mentoring us, but Preston lived next door to Judy Malinger. It felt safer keeping things consistent.

"You live with her?" His smile was incredulous. "Your parents must love that."

"Yeah, I haven't mentioned it to them yet." My tone was dry.

I wondered how long I could keep up the lie with my parents. They were pissed when I told them I'd left the Sig house and moved into the "program" without consulting them first, but they were pleased I didn't need money for housing.

They had questions, though. They wanted to know how and why I'd applied, and more importantly, where the house was, no doubt so they could keep tabs. It felt like eventually I'd have to ask Nina and Scott for help, either to play pretend for a day and meet my parents, or . . .

I'd need to ask them for a loan.

I only had one year of school left, so it wouldn't be for an outrageous amount, but doing that was risky. What if it made things weird, or put me under a contract I wasn't sure I could fulfill?

There was movement behind the window upstairs that caught my eye and disrupted my thoughts. Cassidy was in the living room, talking on her phone as she peered out at the pool, and when she saw me, she gave a friendly wave.

I waved back, somewhat confused. I hadn't seen Dr. Lowe's car in the garage when I'd gone out there to grab another round of beers.

"Your dad's home?" I asked.

"Nope."

That made no sense. If her boyfriend wasn't home, but her ex *was*, why was she here? "Cassidy's just, what? Hanging out at your house now?"

"Kind of." His voice was flat. "She moved in at the start of the summer."

Oh, shit. I swallowed a breath. Cassidy had been with his dad for a while now, so my friend had suspected this was coming, but it still had to be rough.

It'd been hard for me to wrap my head around it when the whole thing went down. I liked Cassidy as a friend, but my loyalty was to Preston, and when she'd started dating his dad, I'd been so pissed. It was fucking messy, and I didn't know how it could work out, but somehow they'd all learned to deal with it.

"How's that going?" I asked.

He stared at the ripples in the water and gave an unconvincing shrug. "It's not bad. I mean, it's been two years, and he did ask me if it was okay."

It'd always be awkward, but time had smoothed things over, and once Preston moved out, that would be a huge help.

I was eager to take his mind off it, and I glanced across the lawn, up to the house next door where Troy's music manager and girlfriend Erika lived. It was where he spent the majority of his time when he was in town, and his tour had just ended.

"Have you seen Troy since he got back?" I asked.

He shook his head. "Not yet, but the three of us need to get together soon. I can't wait to see his reaction when he finds out hell's frozen over."

"What?"

He laid back on his float and got comfortable. "Colin Novak is no longer single."

After we got out of the pool, Preston and I played Call of Duty for a while, and when I realized what time it was, I said goodbye and headed out the back door. Mads and I had a date in the gym, and I needed to hustle if I wasn't going to be late.

Today we'd be working on our cores, and afterward I'd try to talk her into showering together. The gym had a box AC unit, but it couldn't compete with the mid-summer heat. All it did was keep the temperature bearable in the room, so we'd both be sweaty after the workout I had planned.

It was great living close enough to Preston's that I could walk home, but it sucked I'd have to go by Judy Malinger's house to do it. She was his neighbor on the other side, and as I came out the gate on the far end of the house, I peered across the lawn to Judy's place.

There was an older model Ford Fiesta parked on the street in front of her house, with faded paint, a big dent in the bumper, and a Davidson University sticker in the back window. It seemed like the kind of car Judy would despise and find a way to fine for marring her perfect neighborhood— and yet it was parked in front of her fucking house.

Her front door swung open abruptly, two people came out onto her front porch, and since one of them was Judy, I ducked behind an evergreen bush in the front yard of the Lowe house.

I wasn't so much trying to spy on her as I was hoping to avoid being seen. Our last interaction hadn't gone so well, and I was sure I'd run my mouth if we spoke again. Plus, she hadn't made the connection I was one of Preston's friends, and I wanted to keep it that way. If she put it together, she'd find new ways to take it out on the Woodsons.

The man she'd come outside with didn't look any older than I was. He was broad shouldered, with big biceps and a shirt so tight it was almost laughable. He was a total bro, and I wasn't basing that just on his appearance.

I recognized the guy.

He'd been in one of my advertising classes last semester. What was his name? Parker? I couldn't remember, but I was sure he belonged to Pi Kappa Alpha.

"Pleasure doing business with you," he lobbed toward Judy as he strolled toward his car. He paired it with a huge grin, causing Judy to scowl and glance around to check if anyone had heard him.

What the hell?

She stood on her porch watching him as he got into his car and pulled away, and the way she looked at him as he drove off . . . it seemed like she was missing him already.

Holy shit.

Was she fucking this guy? Because if so, that would be really fucking rich. Parker was half her age. She'd gone after Dr. Lowe, telling him his relationship with Cassidy was inappropriate because she was too young for him. She'd given her neighbor Erika a hard time for dating Troy because of the age gap between them, but if Judy was getting it on with Parker . . .

What a fucking hypocrite.

TWENTY-TWO

Madison

Once Colin and I started dating, the summer seemed to move at light speed. It was like it had barely started, and it was already coming to an end. There were three weeks left before the fall semester would start, and then fifteen credit hours were all that stood between me and graduation.

I finished dividing up all the chicken I'd roasted in the oven, filling the containers laid out in front of me on the kitchen counter. Colin's meal prep containers were plastic, and it was hard to get the lids to snap into place. That was the only thing I didn't like about the arrangement.

I enjoyed cooking, and since I was doing meal prep anyway, it wasn't hard to make extra for him. He paid for his share and was super grateful, and in exchange, he was training me. This helped me stick to a schedule, and I didn't struggle with motivation when I knew I was going to see my boyfriend shirtless every day.

It was a total win-win. I enjoyed planning our menus as much as he did planning our workouts, and we both loved getting to spend time together.

It was funny that I'd been so nervous to date him. Everything was clicking for us these days. We didn't always film together, but most of our scenes were with each other. If one of us had a different partner, as soon as the scene was over, we'd race to tell the other about it, or go down to the editing bay to watch the footage.

Fuck, it was so hot.

We'd shot a scene earlier this week that played off it. I'd fucked Jaquan in front of Colin after he'd encouraged it on screen. As he watched, he jerked off, enjoying being a cuckold.

Just the memory of it made me shiver.

I had to push down the lust swelling inside me and focused on sealing the last of the containers. Colin would be here any minute, and then we'd walk across the back yard to the pool house and begin our workout. He wouldn't let me distract him, either.

I knew because I'd tried multiple times.

But my boyfriend's self-control was rock solid in that department. He'd only let me get naked after his training sessions were over, and then he'd reward me for being a good girl, or he'd show me just how much he appreciated what I did for him.

We'd banked quite a few extra videos for Petal Productions too.

The door to the garage slammed shut, hurried footsteps rang out, and a very sweaty Colin appeared, wearing regular clothes and carrying his backpack. "Hey. My class ran long."

He wiped a hand over his forehead, stopping the sweat from running into his eyes. Walking up the Woodsons' steep driveway was hard; I could only imagine what biking up it was like, especially today since it was triple digits.

"No problem," I said. "I'm just finishing up." I stacked the containers on top of each other, picked them up, and as I moved toward the fridge, he came over and pulled the door open for me. "Any sign of Parker when you went by Judy's?"

"Nope. I asked Preston about it the other day. He hasn't seen him either."

So, if she was having a tryst with a younger man, she was doing a good job of hiding it—but the whole thing seemed unlikely. From everything I'd heard, she didn't strike me as the type. Plus, she sounded too uptight to have had sex anytime recently.

I put away the meals, shut the fridge, and set my gaze on Colin, noting his street clothes. My tone was dubious. "You ready?"

"Let me drop off my bag and change," he said, "and then I'm all yours."

He probably hadn't meant anything deeper, but a thrill shot through me. *Yes*, I thought. *You are mine.*

Before he turned to leave, a chime rang out from the speaker on the desk, followed by an electronic voice. "Unfamiliar person at the front door," the system said.

We paused, unsure what to do. The security system was linked to Nina's and Scott's phones, not ours, and we'd been instructed not to answer the door. But last time the doorbell went off, it'd been Judy, and she'd been pissed she'd had to wait for Scott to open the door.

Swift footsteps grew louder as someone moved through the living room, but rather than go toward the entryway, the person headed toward the kitchen.

It was Nina, and she pulled to a stop when she discovered us standing there. Her attention swung from me to latch on to Colin.

"This guy is at the front door asking for you." Was she

irritated? "Do you know him?"

She thrust her phone forward, and I couldn't help but look at the screen too.

Holy shit.

"Is that Riley?" I asked.

I turned to stare at Colin with disbelief. We weren't supposed to tell anyone where we lived, and he'd told mother-fucking *Riley* of all people?

"Yeah, I know him," he said quickly, "but I don't have a fucking clue how he knows I'm here. I haven't told anyone, I promise." He scowled as he stared at the live image of Riley waiting impatiently on the front porch. "I'll take care of it."

He didn't wait for a response from either of us, and as he stalked toward the entryway, I followed. Maybe he'd been too focused on Riley to realize I was behind him, because when he went out the door, he nearly closed it on me.

"Mads, no," he uttered under his breath, but it was too late.

Surprise hit the other guy as I stepped out onto the porch, pulled the door closed, and stood next to a disgruntled Colin. He'd wanted to deal with his former frat brother himself, but that wasn't going to work for me. We were partners.

Tension held Colin's shoulders tight as he glared at Riley. "What the fuck are you doing here?"

He tried not to look intimidated, even though Colin was taller and stronger. "I was leaving my sociology class and I saw you on your bike." He rested his hands on his waist, maybe to look bigger. "I've been trying to talk to you, but you won't answer any of my text messages. So, I followed you."

It was then I noticed his Lexus parked in the driveway. Colin's expression darkened and he took a step forward, causing Riley to retreat down the porch steps and put up his hands.

"Look, man, I just wanted to talk about getting an audition for Petal Productions," he said. "When I saw you, I thought maybe you were heading to work, and I could talk to the director myself." He tried to peer around us and through the windows beside the front door. "Is that why she's here? Are you getting ready to film right now?"

"Leave." Colin's voice was frosty. "And don't come back here. You feel me?"

Riley's face contorted, and I could practically hear the thought in his head. He didn't follow Colin all the way over here just to give up. "Okay, I will, but you need to do me a solid. If I send you something, will you pass it on to the director or your—I don't know—manager?"

"Not a chance."

He frowned like this was unreasonable. "Why not?"

"A bunch of reasons," Colin snapped, "but mostly because of what you did to Mads." His posture straightened abruptly as the thought occurred to him. "Maybe if you apologize to her right now, I might reconsider."

Riley laughed, thinking it was a joke, and his amused look soured when he realized it wasn't. "What do I have to apologize for?"

Oh, my God. Was he serious? "You cheated, and then you lied to everyone about it."

He rolled his eyes and crossed his arms over his chest. "So, I got in your way a little bit, but we were just having some fun."

My mouth dropped open. "*Fun*?"

318 | NIKKI SLOANE

He smirked. "I mean, you looked hilarious when you were chasing after the baton, but then you had to go and make a big deal out of nothing."

I balled my hands into fists and prepared to breathe fire on him, but Colin spoke before I could.

"You should have been disqualified," he said. "Do you get that? It *is* a big deal because it means the Lambdas actually won."

Riley's focus swung to the other man, and his eyes narrowed. "You're taking her side, after what I was trying to do? Some brother you are." He shook his head. "Yeah, I cheated, but it was for a good cause. I wanted us to win so we could help Grady, but then she started that fight, which cost us the prize money—all because she couldn't handle losing." He gave me the full power of his sneer. "As far as I'm concerned, you stole that money away from Grady's sick mom. If anyone should apologize, it's you."

I sucked in a breath.

I knew Grady from my time with Jack, and I'd liked him more than most of the other guys at the house. But I hadn't known his mom was sick, or that the Sigs had planned to give their prize money to him. It only made me angrier. If any of the Sigs had told us Lambdas, it was possible we would have voted to give the prize money to Grady.

A new water heater seemed stupid in comparison.

But the idea that I owed Riley an apology—that was ludicrous. Laughable.

"That's never going to happen." My smile contained no warmth as I peered down at him at the base of the porch steps. "And since we're talking about things that'll never happen, just know that as long as I'm here in this house? You're *never* getting in."

I didn't understand why Colin stiffened suddenly. It wasn't until Riley pulled his chin back and a line creased between his eyebrows that I realized my mistake.

"Wait. Y'all live here?" He took a step back and stared up at the house with new eyes.

Oh, God. A lump grew in my throat, clogging my ability to speak.

He hadn't known we lived and worked here . . . but he did now. Despite the heat outside, a cold chill washed down my back.

Colin stepped in front of me, like he could somehow shield me from what I'd done. His tone turned absolute. "Remember our deal. You keep your mouth shut about this, and I won't tell anyone about your cheating in the tournament."

"What happened to you, man?" Riley's voice was full of disappointment. "You used to put your frat brothers first. Now you're pussy whipped. She's got you wrapped around her little finger."

"Fuck off," Colin snarled, "and don't come back."

Whatever expression was on his face, paired with his confrontational posture, was strong enough to knock some sense into Riley. He blew out a frustrated breath, turned, and stormed back to his car.

Colin and I didn't move or speak as he got in, started the engine, and then sped off down the hill.

I was sick to my stomach. Not only did Riley know about our stage names and what we did, now he knew where we did it too. Colin turned, and I expected to see disappointment in his eyes, but it wasn't there. Only concern.

"I fucked up," I whispered.

He didn't deny it. Instead, he folded me into his arms. "It's going to be okay," he said. "Eventually, he'll lose interest and give up."

It was a nice idea, but I was sure he didn't believe it any more than I did.

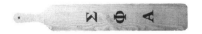

I sat on my bed and peered at the screen of my laptop, scanning the HOA's website. I was on their covenants, conditions, and restrictions page, which listed every rule the homeowners agreed to abide by as long as they lived in this neighborhood.

The page was daunting.

And endless.

But I wasn't going to be defeated. The Woodsons had received a new fine in the mail today, stating their mailbox was suddenly out of code. The letter told them they needed to purchase the same exact style of mailbox that the rest of the subdivision had.

Scott lost his mind when he saw it was five hundred dollars.

For a fucking *mailbox*.

The letter threatened if they didn't fix it in the next thirty days, they'd be fined another hundred dollars, and it'd continue every month until they complied.

I was mad on principle, and eager to do something to

help since I'd let it slip that Petal Productions operated out of this house. It was a long shot, but maybe if I read the rules, I could find a loophole. Something to exploit or use in defense against Judy's tyranny.

I read every line, making notes on my phone about questions or possible vagueness in the rules, but . . . nothing immediately leapt out at me. When I finished, I clicked the link to the board's meeting minutes.

That seemed to be a non-starter as well. They had held a vote about the mailbox rule, and since no homeowner raised an objection at the meeting, it had passed unanimously. I scowled. Had they even given notice of a meeting? It wouldn't surprise me if the answer was no.

At the end of the minutes, there was a brief report from the treasurer, and a link to the quarterly financial statement. Like the nerd I was, my heart beat faster and I sat upright.

"Come to mama, you sexy spreadsheet," I murmured as I clicked to download the Excel file.

It wasn't a complicated spreadsheet. Just a few rows and columns, and for a moment, I was bummed at the paltry amount of data I could sift through. But as I stared at one figure in particular, awareness pricked at the back of my neck.

That couldn't be right.

The number in the 'fines collected' column was too low. It was barely three digits for all of April through June, which had to be wrong. The Woodsons had racked up over three hundred in fees in June alone when their AC units didn't match. Plus, there was no way Nina and Scott's house was the only one in the entire subdivision—for three whole months—who'd been fined.

Was it a typo?

I dug back through the posts until I found the previous quarter's statement, and when I saw the figure for collected fees, I tilted my head. I'd moved into the house in April, so I didn't have firsthand knowledge, but this sum also *felt* low. There were forty-five houses in this subdivision, and since I'd read the entire rulebook, I now knew how expensive most of the fines were.

This figure accounted for one or two houses at most.

So, I went back farther, looking at the previous year, and discovered more of the same.

The HOA had gotten out of control over the last two years, Scott had said. Fining the homeowners for every little thing, and it had grown bad enough that some of the owners tried to recall the board.

But these figures didn't reflect that.

It looked a hell of a lot like there was some creative accounting going on. Maybe a second set of books? I was so busy considering that, I almost ignored the voice in my head telling me to keep looking. My subconscious had recognized a pattern and wanted me to take note.

One of the line items was for legal services, and the numbers from each statement gradually increased in perfect increments. It meant the monthly retainer they were paying now was more than double what it'd been two years ago, and still seemed to be trending up. How did that make any sense?

The overall fund seemed low, and Scott's gripe from two months ago echoed in my head. *With all the ridiculous fines they collect, how do they not have enough money already?*

I thumbed out a text to Scott.

Madison: Weird question for you. When the home-owners tried to recall Judy, did someone put together a list of fines the HOA had imposed?

Scott: Yeah.

Madison: Could you get me a copy?

Scott: I think so. Why?

Madison: I want to check something.

I had a hunch money was missing, but I wasn't going to say anything until I had more data, or even better . . .
Proof.

The union was one of the only places open for lunch during the summer semester, and Jenn sat across from me as we ate. Every so often, the conversation would lapse, and her skeptical gaze would drift over to Colin, who sat beside me. She was still trying to come to terms with him being my boyfriend, which I understood.

Four months ago, if you'd told me I'd be here, I never would have believed it. He wasn't known for being with the same girl twice, and after the tournament he was one of the last people I would want to date.

Of course, I wouldn't have believed I'd be a growing adult film star either.

She dipped her carrot in her hummus and was about to take a bite when she abruptly froze. Her eyes widened and she melted down into her seat, clearly trying not to be seen.

"What's happening?" I asked.

She was halfway under the table. "I had too many White Claws at a house party a few weeks ago, and in a moment of weakness, I went home with that guy. It was supposed to be a 'one night only' engagement, but he's been blowing up my phone ever since." Her tone was dry. "This is what I get for being so good at sex."

Colin nodded in understanding. "It's a curse."

I pressed my lips together to hold in my laugh. "Who is it?"

"The Pike." She subtly pointed him out.

I nonchalantly glanced over my shoulder to take a look. There were several guys in the area she'd pointed to, but only one who I recognized from Pi Kappa Alpha. He was kind of cute.

But Colin's tone turned serious. "You mean Parker?"

I turned back around and exchanged a knowing look with my boyfriend. This was the guy he'd seen leaving Judy's house.

"Don't judge me." She was almost completely under the table now. "It was the White Claws, and sometimes I like my guys big and stupid."

"He fits the bill," Colin said. "Pretty sure he failed the class I had with him last year, and it was a fucking cake walk."

"It wasn't even worth it," Jenn whined. "He sucked so hard on my boob it left a bruise."

I snorted. "I believe when that happens it's called a hickey."

She ignored me. "After it was over? Oh, my God. He would *not* shut up about how much money he'd just won from some bet he'd made. Thousands of dollars off a stupid baseball game."

Her statement hit me hard, knocking all the amusement clean from my body, and an eerie sensation replaced it. When my father had gotten banned from the casino, he'd searched for other ways to get his fix. Betting on sports had been his main focus until my family finally convinced him to get help.

"When was this?" I asked.

"Three weeks ago? A Friday."

Hadn't it been a Saturday three weeks ago when Colin had seen Parker at Judy's house?

Alarm bells clanged in my head.

TWENTY-THREE

Colin

Mads shifted on the bed, rolling into me, and made a cute noise in her sleep. It was weird I was awake before her, but she'd had more to drink last night than I had. I glanced at the empty glass on her nightstand. I'd filled it with water and gotten her to drink it before we'd collapsed into her bed and gone to sleep.

I doubted she'd get a hangover anyway, but I was glad the water was gone just in case.

Last night, I'd introduced her to my friends. We'd gone out to the bars with Preston, Troy, and his girlfriend Erika, and because of her connections and his rising fame, we'd been ushered into the VIP area of the club. Preston and I were happy for Troy, but Preston was a little more excited than I was, because he'd taken full advantage of our friend's celebrity status to lure women over to our table.

I glanced at Mads asleep beside me and grinned. My friends didn't know it, but we had celebrity status, too, except ours was as Annika and Carter. Nina had created a section of Petal's website that was for our exclusive content, and it currently had the most followers.

Which reminded me—it'd be a good idea to shoot something else soon. We had a few videos banked, but the fall semester was starting soon, and I wanted to keep the buffer in case either of us got hit with a hard class.

Maybe when she woke up, we could shoot it on my phone, passing it back and forth as we took turns going down on each other. Our followers really liked the authentic stuff we'd been putting out recently.

But would I have enough battery? Since we'd crashed in Mads' room, I hadn't plugged my phone in last night. I pulled it off the side table to check and saw the notification for a text message that had come in after we'd fallen asleep. I tapped the icon.

Shit. It was from Riley.

I knew I should block him, but not knowing what he was up to made me uneasy. It was better to just deal with the sporadic messages he sent. They'd been all over the place, though. Some were apologetic and others whiney, but they all had the same goal. The guy was fucking delusional if he thought I'd help him break into the business.

This message wasn't text. It was a video, and I didn't understand what the thumbnail was showing me. I was too curious not to click play—even as I sensed I'd regret it.

Oh, fucking, shit.

It was shot selfie style. The camera had been up close, and as the video started to roll, it pushed out to reveal Riley sitting in a chair.

He was naked.

And while he held his phone in one hand, he used the other to stroke his stubby dick.

"Yeah." His over-the-top sexual voice had me cringing. "You like that?"

I was frozen in place with horror. Was . . . was this the

thing he'd wanted me to pass along to Petal? I'd already told him no, so why the fuck did he think sending me this was okay?

"I'm going to use all of this big dick to fuck you," he said.

Mads stirred when I jolted, and her voice was sleepy. "What are you watching?"

I scrambled to stop the video and lock my screen before she saw it. The image was unfortunately seared in my brain now, but I could spare her from it.

"Just a stupid video," I whispered. "Sorry, I thought I had it muted."

She flopped over, turning away from me, desperate to go back to sleep. I held perfectly still, waiting until the cadence of her breathing slowed, before unlocking the screen again.

Beneath the video, there was a message telling me to send it to Petal Productions. He wasn't even asking—this was a demand. It felt like there was an implied threat too. Send it to Petal Productions *or else.*

It made my blood boil, raising the anger inside me past my breaking point. I'd tried everything else with him and it hadn't worked. It was time I got direct.

> **Colin:** Don't send me shit like that. Give it up. You don't have the looks or the equipment to work for Petal.

It was harsh, but honest, and hopefully it'd break through to him.

The 'read' label appeared below my message, and then the three dots blinked, signaling he was typing his reply.

But then the dots disappeared.

I waited, but there was no response, and I wasn't sure if that was good or bad. My gut said it was bad, and that I was stupid to believe this would work. I wasn't comfortable that he knew where we lived, but it wasn't something I could control, and besides . . . Riley was an asshole, I told myself, but he wasn't evil.

Right?

I needed this to be the end of it.

Fuck, please let him move on.

The second to last day of the summer semester, my dad texted me he was free for lunch, was on this side of town, and would pick me up after class. I tried to get out of it altogether, but he was persistent, and I had to settle for meeting him at the deli.

At least he wouldn't have my bike in the back of his car, so he couldn't use that as an easy excuse to drive me to the Woodsons' house. My parents were hungry for more about this mentor program I'd been accepted into, yet all I'd given them was crumbs.

As we ate, I did my best to distract.

"A girlfriend?" My dad's expression filled with surprise. "When did this happen?"

"A few weeks ago."

Now he looked displeased. "Okay. When do we get to meet her?"

"You already did," I said. "Mads is the girl who asked me to walk her to class."

He considered something, and then a tight smile twisted on his lips. "Did she make up that story so she could talk to you?"

No, she did it to save me from you.

"No," I said, which wasn't a lie. Mads *hadn't* made up the story because she wanted to talk to me—we weren't even friends back then.

"Oh." My dad's gaze dropped to the sandwich resting on his plate. "Well, tell me about her. What's her major?"

"Accounting. She's graduating early, too. This fall semester will be her last one."

He brightened. "Sounds like she's pretty smart."

"Can't be that smart," I deadpanned. "She's dating me, after all."

My dad's smile was pained, and it made me want to laugh. He'd never gotten my sense of humor, probably because he'd been born without one. My parents were so fucking uptight. Honestly, it was a miracle my sister and I had been born, because I was convinced they were terrified of sex.

My phone vibrated in my pocket, only it wasn't a text message. My phone was ringing, and when I saw Mads' name on the screen, a cold chill slide down my spine. Up until now, we'd always texted. She wouldn't call unless it was something important.

I was instantly on edge but tried to play it cool as I motioned to my phone. "Hold on. She's calling me." I tapped the button to accept the call. "Hello?"

"Hey. Where are you?" There was urgency in Mads' voice, or maybe panic.

My gaze was fixed on my father, who studied me right back. "I'm having lunch with my dad. What's up?"

"A little while ago, someone tried to post our real names

in a comment under one of our videos."

My heart began to pound. I forced myself to sound unconcerned. "Riley."

"The comment got caught in moderation, so it never went live."

I relaxed my shoulders, but my relief was short lived because she wasn't done. The panic in her words grew more intense as she spoke.

"When that didn't work, he posted it to social media instead. It's on Instagram and Facebook, with a bunch of screencaps from our videos, and it's all our information. Our stage names, and our real ones, and the *fucking address of the house.*"

I went numb, freezing into place. For a moment, my brain went blank, unable to process what I was feeling because there were too many things at once.

"Colin," her tone shifted, filling with dread, "he tagged you in the posts."

I sucked in a sharp breath and if my unnatural posture wasn't a dead giveaway to my dad that something was wrong—this did it.

His head tilted. "Everything okay?"

I blinked, unable to answer because Mads was still going.

"I reported the posts, but they're in review and—oh, God—everything I'm reading says it could be more than a day before they come down." She took a breath, regrouping. "You need to get on your socials and un-tag yourself right now. Call me back when it's done."

"Okay," I said quietly. "Will do."

After I hung up, concern filled my dad's face. "Colin,

what's wrong?"

I was disoriented as I rose from the booth. "It's nothing," I lied and gestured toward the restroom. "I'll be right back."

That did nothing to convince him, and he frowned as I walked away from the table on unsteady legs. I had to focus on my actions, because if I thought about anything else, it became overwhelming.

Go to the bathroom.

Get into a stall.

Look at your phone.

Once I got those tasks accomplished, I could think about the next steps.

My heart dropped into my stomach as I saw the notifications popping up on my phone. I went to Instagram first and found the post Riley had tagged me in. He'd been smart enough with the screencaps to not post outright nudity, but it was heavily implied with me bare chested and Mads' naked back. The Petal Productions logo sat in the corner.

Sure enough, everything was spelled out in the caption.

I removed the tag, reported the post, and then blocked his account. I went as fast as I could, because every second that slipped by before it was done made me feel worse. I was sweaty and jittery as I opened the Facebook app. I hadn't used it in ages, and it made me update and log in, which sent my frustration through the roof.

Finally, I got it open and repeated the process. The post was less than thirty minutes old, but already had a few 'wow' face emoji comments, some left by my former frat brothers.

And when it was done, I angrily thumbed out a text message to Riley. It took every ounce of restraint I had to compose it, because unleashing my full fury wasn't going to help.

As much as I hated it, I needed action from him.

Colin: Take down the posts.

There was no response. Only the checkmark that it had been sent.

Colin: This isn't a joke, it's fucking dangerous. Posting the address threatens our safety.

Still nothing, so I had to move on. I punched the button to call Mads, who answered right away.

"Have you told Nina and Scott yet?" I asked.

"Yeah. When she came to me about the moderated comment, that's when he made the post to Instagram."

"At least he didn't tag Petal Productions." I clenched my teeth. "How pissed is she?"

"She's upset, but I think it's more with worry for us."

Even though she couldn't see, I nodded. "Pack a bag. I'll text Preston and see if we can crash at his place until the address is down."

I didn't say *until it's safe* because I didn't know if that'd ever be true. It was possible Nina and Scott would tell us we couldn't come back.

"Okay," she said. "Are you coming home soon?"

There was a desperation in her voice I hadn't heard before, and it nearly broke me. She was scared and wanted to be with me.

"Yeah, I'll be there as soon as I can."

We said goodbye, and after I hung up, I got so angry, I started to shake. I'd thought Riley wasn't evil, but I'd been so, so wrong. He was trying to ruin our lives, and for what? All because I wouldn't help him get into the business?

You also said he didn't have a big enough dick.

Oh, fuck. My heart thudded to a stop.

Was this my fault?

I didn't think I could possibly feel worse until that thought hit me. But I'd been gone from the table too long. I needed to get back there, find a quick exit, and do it without raising my dad's suspicion any more than I'd already done.

I slid into my seat, only so I could grab my backpack. "Hey, so, Mads isn't feeling well and needs my help—"

Something was wrong. My dad was sitting so still, he'd become a statue, and the air coming off him was icy cold. It was ironic because fire burned in his eyes. He looked so upset, he could barely speak.

And he didn't need to. He set his phone down in front of me, displaying Riley's Facebook post on screen. I wasn't tagged in it any longer, but it didn't matter. The damage was done. I didn't use Facebook anymore, but a lot of my friends and family did.

I swallowed hard as I stared at the image of me and Mads, and the caption that congratulated us on our new careers as porn stars.

"Your mother sent me this," he said, "after your aunt Diane asked her about it. Is this true?" His face twisted with equal parts of disgust and horror. "You've been in a porno?"

I could lie.

I'd gotten so good at it with them over the years, but it was unlikely they'd buy it with the photographic proof and how cagey I'd been about the mentorship. Plus, I was so goddamn tired. My parents treated me like a child, but one who wasn't allowed to make any mistakes.

The second chance they'd given me after the prom incident? It hadn't really been a chance at all. Ever since they'd caught me in their bed, they'd been waiting for this. They'd known without a shadow of a doubt I'd disappoint them again.

Happy to fulfill the prophecy, I though bitterly.

He'd asked if I'd been in a porno, and I lifted my defiant gaze up to meet him. "Several."

The muscle running along his jaw flexed. He hated my answer, but he hated how unapologetic I'd said it even more. His infuriated eyes demanded an explanation, but I wasn't going to give one.

"After that night," he said finally, "I didn't think I could be more ashamed of you . . . but I was wrong."

It was like a kick to the chest. My pulse raced and blood rushed loudly through my head, but I didn't show him the impact of his words. I pretended they bounced harmlessly off me.

"Get your things," he snarled. "I'm taking you home, and the first thing we're going to do is pull you from school."

"No."

My dad had already begun to stand and froze halfway out of the booth. "No?" he repeated with disbelief.

"I'm twenty-three years old. I don't have to do what you tell me."

He sat back down and stared at me like I'd just spat in his face. "You will if you want to have a roof over your head."

Up until today, I could have told him I already had a place to live, but thanks to Riley, things were less stable now. But still . . .

"What's the point?" I sighed. "If I come home, it's just going to be more of the same, where you're waiting around for me to disappoint you again. I'm *never* going to be good enough." The last three years, I'd done everything to get back in their good graces, and it hadn't made one iota of a difference. "I tried so fucking hard, and for what? God, I wish I'd stopped trying a long time ago."

He recoiled, unsure of how to respond, but he didn't deny it. He let the statement lie between us that I wasn't good enough, and every second it remained unchallenged, the chasm between us grew larger.

Finally, his face hardened. "This is it, Colin." He sounded grave. "You've pushed us to our breaking point. Come home now, or . . . I don't think you'll be allowed to come home again."

We were really doing this, then. If I didn't accept their complete control, they'd cut me from their lives.

As I stared at him, I felt nothing but emptiness.

I didn't have much money, and things were falling apart, so I should have been scared shitless—but I wasn't. Mads had done this. She'd walked away from her parents and survived without their help.

She could show me how to do it.

I swallowed hard, hooked my hand through a strap to my backpack, and pulled it on. "Okay," I said. "Tell Mom I said goodbye."

Maybe he'd been bluffing, because his mouth dropped open, but I didn't let it stop me. I had to get out of here. I slid out of my seat, not even giving him a final look before I turned and walked out of the restaurant and out of my parents' lives.

TWENTY-FOUR

Colin

Before I went to the Woodsons' house, I rode my bike to my old frat, pounded on the door, and scared the crap out of the guy who answered it when I demanded to talk to Riley.

Except I was told he wasn't there, and since his car wasn't in the back parking lot, I climbed back on my bike, rode home, and went straight to Mads' room. I found her sitting on her bed, her chin resting on her knees as she peered at the screen of her phone like it was a ticking time bomb.

She looked exactly like I felt. Exposed. Raw. Drained.

But when she saw me, her expression lifted. She dropped her phone and bounded off the bed straight into my arms.

"Hey," she said, greedy to have her arms around me.

It made my heart flip upside down. I was just as glad to see her as she was me and squeezed her tightly. "My parents saw the post."

I felt the jolt go through her body, and concern flooded her eyes as she stared up at me.

"It's okay," I said.

"It is?" She couldn't have looked more dubious if she'd tried.

"I mean, no, it's not. My dad told me to come home with right then, or don't come home at all." I raked a hand through my hair before returning it to rest on the small of her back.

"But *I'm* okay."

"I'm so sorry, Colin."

"Is it weird that part of me is—I don't know—relieved? At least it's done and out there. No more lying or hiding."

"It's not weird," she said softly.

"How about you? How are you doing?"

"I was feeling powerless earlier, but Nina talked to her attorney. They're creating a cease-and-desist letter for Riley, and then they'll send a copy to Instagram and Facebook. She's told that makes the companies respond faster." She sighed. "I just want the posts down."

"Me too." I nodded toward the small suitcase sitting beside her bed. "Are you all packed?"

She was, so I grabbed her bag and carried it downstairs. She hung out in my room while I pulled my shit together and texted Preston.

> **Colin:** Need a big favor. Can Mads and I crash at your place tonight?

> **Preston:** I'm sure my dad will be cool with it. I'm here whenever you want to come over.

> **Colin:** Thanks.

Once that was done, I put my phone on 'do not disturb.' The notifications and texts from people were coming now in a steady stream, but there was nothing left I could do to get the posts down, so I didn't need the constant fucking reminder.

As we got ready to leave, Scott was waiting in the hallway. Shame instantly slammed into me. The Woodsons hadn't asked for any of this, and it was their address posted.

Even though Petal Productions wasn't tagged, their logo was in the bottom corner of the screenshots Riley had posted.

"I'm sorry," I said. "I had no idea he'd do something like this."

That surprised him. "You think we blame you?" His expression softened. "You're not responsible for his actions. Do I wish he hadn't posted our address? Yeah, absolutely. But Madison told us what happened, and it sounds like he put you in a tough spot. So, don't think Nina and I blame you—because we don't."

I hadn't realized how much I needed to hear it until it'd been said. It took a small amount of weight off my shoulders that had been dragging me down.

"Thanks, Scott."

He nodded, and his gaze went to the bags in my hands, then Madison at my side. "Where are you staying? I'll drive you."

"My friend's place. You don't have to drive us; it's just down the road."

He waved my comment off. "It's faster this way. Plus, if Judy catches you walking down the street with suitcases, she's going to have questions."

It was a good point, so we loaded into his BMW and let him drive us down to the Lowe house, where we found Preston outside mowing the lawn. When we pulled into the driveway, he stopped the riding mower and jogged over to meet us.

"Hey," he said as I pulled the bags one at a time from the trunk. His gaze slid over the BMW and on to the driver, and his head tilted in confusion. "Do I know you?"

Scott's window was down, and a shadow of a smile crossed his lips. "I live up the street."

That seemed to satisfy Preston, and when I shut the trunk, I was surprised to see my friend pick up Mads' suitcase and carry it toward the house.

"All right, you two," Scott said. "If you need anything, you know where we are. Let us know if anything changes, okay?" He was only fifteen years older than we were, but he nailed the fatherly concern. "Stay safe."

Mads nodded. "Thanks, Scott."

Out of the corner of my eye, I saw Preston's posture straighten abruptly.

We followed him through the open garage and up the two steps into the kitchen, where Cassidy was baking cookies. When she saw us, her expression hung.

"Hi, Colin." Her voice was overly cheery, like she was trying too hard to sound casual.

"Hey, Cassidy." I motioned to Mads. "This is my girlfriend, Mads."

"Madison," Preston corrected before I could, amused. "Only he gets to call her that."

Because I'd informed him the nickname was mine alone when I'd introduced her to everyone the night we'd gone out to the club.

"Nice to meet you," Cassidy said.

Mads smiled. "Yeah, you too."

Now that the introduction was out of the way, Preston zeroed in on me. "Scott Westwood, huh? I can't believe you didn't tell me." But then a shit-eating grin spread across his face. "Mentor program. If you're going to learn, learn from the best, am I right?"

Cassidy used a spatula to transfer the cookies from the baking sheet to a wire rack. "What are we talking about?"

"Nothing," I said.

Preston ignored that. "Colin and Madison just got dropped off by Scott Westwood. He lives up the street. Fucking wild." He paused. "Do you know who that is?"

"Yeah," she answered quickly, focusing all her attention on her cookies.

"Oh, really?" Preston either couldn't leave it alone or didn't believe her. "You're familiar with his *large* body of work?"

She set down her spatula and leveled a gaze at him. "I was more familiar with it when we were together. I don't need to watch it these days when I want to get off."

Holy shit, Cassidy.

Mads sucked in a sharp breath, and the air in the kitchen crackled with tension. I expected my friend to lose his mind, but instead he laughed, snatched up one of Cassidy's cooling cookies, and raised it at her. Almost as if saying, *sick burn and I respect it.* He took a bite of the cookie, which was too hot because he left his mouth open.

Cassidy turned her attention back to me and her voice was hesitant. "How are you doing?"

I sighed. "You saw the post."

"Not to be a dick," Preston said, "but everyone's seen it, dude."

"Your dad?"

He swallowed his bite. "I doubt it. He doesn't really do social media."

"Plus, he's been in surgery all afternoon," Cassidy added.

"Any idea how he's going to react when he finds out?" Because there was no way Dr. Lowe would stay in the dark about this. Our suburb of Nashville was like any other small town. Everyone was in each other's business.

"You worried he's going to say you can't stay here?" Preston's tone was skeptical.

Maybe it was a stupid question. Dr. Lowe had let me stay here after the prom debacle, and he'd always been a 'cool' dad. Part of it was because he was young, and the other part was he wanted desperately to repair his relationship with his son.

I'd been so envious of Preston. He'd gotten away with murder, while my parents had kept me under lock and key.

"Even if he said you couldn't stay here—which he wouldn't—it wouldn't matter. Cassidy and I already talked about it, and we overrule him, two votes to one."

I blinked in surprise, looking at Cassidy for confirmation, and saw her nod. It kind of floored me. "Thanks."

Preston shoved the rest of the cookie in his mouth, garbling his words. "Just don't film anything here, okay?"

"We'll try to refrain," I said dryly.

For once, sex was the last thing on my mind.

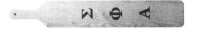

Preston led us upstairs to the guest bedroom, gave us the Wi-Fi password, and left us to finish mowing the yard. Later that night, we ate pizza with him and Cassidy, which gave me weird flashbacks to high school. They'd been best friends once, but it felt like a lifetime ago. So much had changed, but I was glad to see they were repairing the friendship.

Mads and I both had a hard time falling asleep that night.

We spent a lot of it on our phones, fielding questions from people who'd reached out to ask if we'd seen the pictures. Plus, we were constantly checking to see if the posts had gotten removed. It was draining, but I was so fucking grateful I wasn't going through it alone.

I lay in the guest bed with her snuggled up against me, both of us trying to fall asleep, but I was sure her mind was as noisy as mine. Everything had been going so great, and then it changed in the blink of an eye.

A little after midnight, the mechanical whine of the garage door ground out below us, signaling Dr. Lowe was home.

"It's late," she said quietly.

"Yeah. He usually isn't here whenever I come over. He's always working or on call."

"That must be hard for Cassidy. Was it for Preston when you guys were younger? Not having his dad around?"

It had been awesome as far as Troy and I were concerned. It was total freedom at the Lowe house. "I don't know. It might have been better his dad was so busy. Things weren't great with them even before Cassidy entered the picture."

"But they're doing good now?" She shifted on my arm, getting comfortable. "I mean, they're all living together."

"Which is fucking crazy to me. She's Preston's ex, and now she's with his dad."

Maybe my tone had been too harsh because Mads seemed surprised. "Are you mad at her?"

Was I? I frowned. "No, it's just—the situation sucks for my friend."

"I'm sure it's not easy for her either, but you can't blame

344 | NIKKI SLOANE

people for who they fall in love with." Her voice lost some of its power. "Sometimes it happens, no matter how much that person might not want it to."

I went still.

She wasn't talking about Cassidy anymore, and I held my breath, waiting for her to say something else. For her to tell me she'd tried so hard not to fall for me, but it had happened anyway.

Part of me was scared, but a much larger part of me wanted to hear it.

And if she said it, well . . . I'd tell her it had been the same for me.

But the screen of her phone lit up with a notification, casting a pale, eerie light in the room and made her roll away from me. She glanced at her phone, then snatched it off the nightstand and bolted upright.

"Nina said the posts are down."

I picked up my phone. Not only was the Instagram post gone, but the entire profile no longer existed. "Did they take down his whole account?"

"It's gone?" she asked. "Which one?"

"Instagram."

She scrolled through her search results. "I think his Facebook account vanished too. It's not coming up when I search."

We both switched apps and confirmed we couldn't find his accounts. Had he gotten suspended, or was this a permanent ban? I was relieved the posts were gone, but it didn't solve all our problems. This couldn't be undone, and I worried he'd see his accounts going down as our fault and retaliate some other way.

I still had my phone in 'do not disturb' mode, which meant I hadn't gotten the text message notification from a few minutes ago.

> **Riley:** I'm sorry. I fucked up. I was hammered and meant it as a joke. Wasn't thinking.

Fire poured through my muscles, tensing them to the point of pain, and I angrily thumbed out a response.

> **Colin:** Are you fucking kidding me? You tried to ruin our lives.

> **Riley:** I was so smashed I don't even remember posting. Been passed out & just woke up to a shitstorm.

> **Riley:** Saw your texts & deactivated my accounts.

If his story were true, that meant he'd gotten wasted before noon—but that was believable. He was totally that kind of guy, known for having a morning beer in the shower as he got ready for the day.

Usually, it was to delay his hangover.

If he'd deactivated his accounts, I was sure he hadn't done it as a gesture for us. He'd done it to get the posts down before he lost his accounts for doxing.

> **Colin:** Do you know what you've done, asshole? My parents said I'm dead to them.

> **Riley:** I'm sorry. I didn't mean for that to happen.

> **Colin:** You can fuck all the way off. Stay the hell

away from the house, and me and Mads, or I swear to god, I'll make you regret it.

Riley: Gimme some credit. I'm trying to own my mistake here.

Mads had been reading over my shoulder, and she made a sound of disgust as she saw his response. The guy was un-fucking-real. He'd forever changed my life, and he barely acknowledged it. He didn't care. Instead, he was whining that I was pissed at him for fucking everything up.

He'd made a mistake—but I had, too.

I should have gone no-contact with him the second he'd figured out Mads and I were working for Petal Productions. At least this was a mistake I could correct right away.

I brought up his contact information, scrolled down, and tapped the option to block him. The action gave me some feeling of control.

When I set my phone face down on the nightstand, Mads did the same with hers, and then put her arms around my shoulders. She rested her head against mine as I blew out a breath.

"At least the posts are down," she said.

"Yeah. Except the damage is done."

"We'll figure it out." She squeezed my shoulder. "You believe me, right?"

I turned to peer into her eyes, which were deep and beautiful. My voice was soft but sure. "Of course I do."

TWENTY-FIVE

Madison

My heart was racing as I sat in the back seat of Nina's Porsche and stared at the entrance to the clubhouse. It wasn't an intimidating building to look at. Just big enough to house a meeting space, some storage, and a set of locker rooms for the community pool that was behind the clubhouse.

I was nervous because Judy and the rest of the HOA board were inside, and I assumed they were gearing up to come after Petal Productions.

We didn't know for certain what this emergency hearing was about because the letter that arrived from the HOA yesterday was light on details. It only said that attendance was mandatory for everyone living at the Woodsons' house and that they needed to discuss an urgent matter.

But it had been a week since Riley's posts, and two days ago Colin and I had returned to the house. The timing of the meeting was suspect.

It hadn't taken much to convince us to move back in.

"No one's come by the house," Nina had said.

"Our security system is top of the line," Scott added. "One of us can drive you to and from classes when school starts next week."

He wasn't just talking about me, either. After we'd spent the night at Preston's place, Colin had gone straight to the bursar's office to figure out a plan. Since his parents had prepaid for the fall semester and he wanted to stay enrolled, the school denied his parents' request for a refund.

They were incensed, but it forced them to talk to their son, even if it was only long enough for him to say he'd pay them back after he graduated. I felt awful for him, especially since I knew exactly what it was like to have your plan for the future evaporate in an instant.

Since I wasn't friends with Riley, I hadn't been tagged in either of his posts. Anyone in Greek life on campus knew I was acting in adult films now, but that was it. My circle of friends wasn't big, and my family wasn't in my life.

Colin had taken a much bigger hit than I had. *Everyone* knew.

And yet, he was handling it so well. He refused to be shamed or embarrassed, and it was so fucking impressive, I was in awe.

After the dust had settled, it was hard not to go after Riley, but we'd made the difficult decision to let it be. Retaliation had gotten us expelled from our houses, so Colin said he'd try to be the bigger man and learn from his mistakes.

But we spent plenty of nights indulging in fantasies of Riley getting what he deserved. Hopefully, time would dull our anger toward him, and we could move on. Plus, we had more immediate things to focus on.

"It looks like everyone's here," Nina said from the driver's seat. And she didn't just mean everyone from our house, either. Most of the homeowners we'd spoken to were gathering in the parking lot.

"You ready?" There wasn't an ounce of anxiety in Colin,

but maybe a hint of excitement.

I felt that a little, too, but my nerves were much louder. If things didn't go well, Colin and I wouldn't be the only ones ending up homeless tonight. I swallowed thickly and pushed open my door. "Let's do this."

The meeting space was a multipurpose room, available to homeowners to rent out for parties, so it was bland and generic inside. There was a long table set up at one end, facing a single row of folding chairs.

When we came in, the five board members were seated behind the table and chatting with each other, but all conversation stopped as the room began to fill with other homeowners behind us.

Erika, who I'd met with Colin's friends, surveyed the room, and her gaze zeroed in on the cart of folding chairs in the back corner. "We're going to need more seats."

Judy's scowl was epic as she rose to her feet. "Excuse me. This hearing is private."

Everyone who wasn't part of the Woodson house ignored her and went to the cart, noisily pulling out chairs.

"We waive our right to privacy," Nina said.

Judy didn't like that at all. "Well, the board doesn't." She turned her attention to the folks who were busy setting up chairs behind the row that was meant for us. "Y'all need to leave."

All the nerves I had leading up to this evaporated. "If this board intends to vote on anything tonight, the rules stipulate the meeting must be open to homeowners."

Her narrow gaze settled on me, and it was clear she expected me to wither under it, but I saw right through her. She thought she was untouchable, all powerful, but then how had I trapped her?

This hearing was a sham, and if she sent the homeowners away, she wouldn't be able to push through whatever vote I suspected was coming—the one she'd hoped to do without the rest of the neighborhood knowing.

I feigned innocence. "Is there a motion on the agenda?"

The smile she delivered was ice cold. "You're right. My mistake. We do have a motion to debate." Her gaze dropped to the papers on the table in front of her, and she did a terrible job of hiding her thoughts. She wasn't pleased with this setback but was confident in the end it wouldn't matter. She'd still get what she wanted. "Once everyone's settled, I'll call the meeting to order."

There weren't enough chairs, and when people filed in to stand at the back, the board members seated on either side of Judy looked uneasy. It was kind of hilarious. Didn't they know this wasn't even everyone in the subdivision? We'd gotten all we could with short notice.

The number of people in the room irritated Judy, and her voice was clipped. "Let's get started. I call this meeting to order." Her posture straightened, like she wanted to look down on everyone. "It's come to the board's attention that the Woodsons misrepresented themselves. When they moved in, we were told they were running a program to help underprivileged college students . . . which was a lie. The truth is they've been exploiting these poor kids, using them in their pornographic films."

She paused for dramatic effect, or perhaps to allow the audience to gasp—except it didn't happen. No one reacted the way she expected them to, and she glanced around with disbelief.

But Judy took in a breath and regrouped.

"I'm sure we all feel the same way about this," she continued, "and don't want people producing that kind of *filth* in our neighborhood."

"I don't mind," came from someone seated behind me.

I glanced back to see it was Lilith, who was grinning ear to ear. I'd met her, along with her boyfriends and neighbors Clay and Travis, when I'd stepped up my investigation effort last week. They sat on either side of her now, one looking amused and the other serious.

She wasn't much older than I was, and I'd liked her right away.

"You're not a homeowner," Judy snapped.

Lilith's grin continued. "I'm my parents' proxy."

"Fine." The older woman waved this off, not wanting the distraction. She picked up her papers and tapped them into a neat stack as she refocused on her goal. "This association doesn't have the power to evict a homeowner, but what we can do is revoke the agreement we made with the Woodsons, which allows them to collect rent and have tenants."

She looked so fucking smug about evicting Abbie, Jaquan, Colin, and me. My jaw hurt from how hard I clenched it, holding back what I wanted to say.

"Therefore, I move we rescind the agreement we have with the Woodsons. Their tenants will need to move out, and the Woodsons can expect to be fined for noncompliance until that happens." She was almost giddy as she asked it of the board. "Who would like to second the motion?"

"I will," said the elderly woman sitting beside Judy, who was likely the vice president.

"Great." Judy glanced to her left and then right, checking in with the rest of the board. "Are we ready for the vote? All those in favor of the motion—"

"Wait a minute," I said. "You didn't open the floor for discussion or debate."

Her attention snapped to me as if I were a bug she'd like to squash. "I don't see a need for discussion."

Was she serious? "If you don't open the floor, the vote won't count."

She sighed, crossed her arms over her chest, and sat back in her chair, making a whole meal out of her frustration. "All right. The floor is open for discussion. Who would like to go first?"

"I would," I said.

"What a surprise." Her tone was flat. "What specifically in this motion do you want to discuss?"

"The fines."

That made Judy hesitate. "What about them?"

"I'd like to know if they will go into the HOA's fund," my pulse climbed, "or directly into your pocket."

The other four members on the board looked confused, but not Judy. She stayed absolutely still, and her expression was vacant, but I didn't miss the fire burning behind her eyes.

Her voice was a warning. "Excuse me?"

I stood from my chair and lifted the folder I'd brought with me. "This is a list of nearly every fine the HOA has levied over the last two years. It's not all of them, because some people have moved out, plus I wasn't able to talk to everyone.

But this data in here? It doesn't match the quarterly state-ments this board has put out—not by a long shot."

The vice president looked lost as she turned to Judy. "What is she talking about?"

"I have no idea." There was the tiniest crack in Judy's front, and I wasn't the only one who saw it.

"You're lying," Nina said.

The man at the end of the board table lifted a hand to get everyone's attention. "You're saying there's a discrepancy?"

"Yes. Only a fraction of what was collected is reflected in the statements."

Maybe this president had everyone snowed except for this guy because something flitted through his expression. He worried I might be telling the truth. "How much?"

I'd gone over the numbers three times to be sure. "Over twenty-five thousand."

One of the board members gasped, and every pair of eyes in the room turned to Judy. She sat in her chair like it was a throne and glared at me as a peasant who'd dare to question the queen. She didn't slump her shoulders or break down or even look nervous.

Jesus, it was uncanny how much she reminded me of my father when I'd confronted him. She hardened and dug into her anger to protect herself.

"Where's the money, Judy?" I demanded.

"This is ridiculous." She arched an eyebrow and sneered. "You barge in here, waving around a folder like it's supposed to mean something when I'm sure it's either empty or full of lies, and I won't have it. This is simply a desperate attempt to distract us from our vote."

I opened the folder and jerked out the papers inside. "It's not fucking empty, and numbers—unlike you—*don't lie*."

She stiffened as if I'd slapped her, bristling at the profanity and my accusation. Then, her expression turned so dark, she became ugly. "The only one lying is the girl in front of us who sleeps with people for money. The Bible has a word for what you are."

Both Colin and Nina launched to their feet, maybe in an effort to protect me, and his single word was a stark warning to Judy. "Don't."

"Do you seriously expect this board," her tone was patronizing, "to believe you, over me?"

For a split second, I was right back in the living room at my parents' house, staring at my mom in shock as she asked me why I was making up stories about my father. I'd wanted that day to be an intervention for him, and he'd spun his lies so successfully, it had become one for me instead.

No one had listened to a word I'd said.

But I wasn't in my parents' living room now, and the boy standing beside me, the one curling his hand around mine? *He* believed me, and even if no one else did—

That was enough.

I tossed the five sets of stapled papers down on the table in front of Judy, and the stack spun across the flat surface until she put a hand down on top to stop it.

"They can see for themselves," I said. "I made copies."

Time hung in a long, drawn-out moment as our gazes locked on each other. It was clear she was evaluating her next step, trying to find a new angle to attack me from, but it would be wasted. She wasn't aware she'd already lost the battle, and I hadn't even brought out the big guns yet.

The guy at the end of the table reached a hand out, motioning for her to pass a copy to him, but instead of doing that, she wrapped her hands around the stack and scrunched the papers beneath her death grip.

Like she was a child not wanting to give back the toy she'd just stolen from another kid.

And that action? It said it all.

"Judy," the woman next to her whispered, stunned.

"There's more," I said. "What legal services are Walters Law Offices providing to the board?"

The crack in Judy's armor widened and she let out the tiniest sound of dismay.

"Judy could answer that better than the rest of us," the guy said, "but we were told they review the language if there are by-law changes or new rules we're voting on."

I gave him a plain look. "Then, you'll be interested to know that when I asked Walters if they'd have a conflict of interest in bringing a suit against this board, they said no. They haven't done any work for this HOA before."

"What?" one of the board members asked.

"That can't be right," another said. "They've been on retainer for years." The woman turned to stare at Judy, whose gaze was glued to the tabletop. "Ever since you brought them on."

"Who's been doing it, then?" the vice president asked.

"My guess?" I said. "No one."

Alarm seized the guy at the end of the table. "How much have we paid out for legal services?" When no one on the board immediately answered, he glared at the woman beside him. "Vicky? You're the treasurer."

Vicky clearly had no idea, and her embarrassed gaze shifted my way.

"At least twelve thousand," I said, "but probably a lot more. That's why the fund has hardly any money in it."

The board degraded into shouting angry questions at each other. Some wanted to know how this had happened, and others looked to shift the blame.

"I never wanted to be the treasurer!" Vicky cried. "I told Judy I didn't have the time, but she said it'd be easy. She did the budget and the reports, and all I had to do was sign off on them."

That must have been the moment when Judy realized she'd lost control and there was no coming back. No lie she could tell or story to spin would let her walk away from this. Her face crumbled, she gave a painful wail, and tears spilled down her cheeks.

But even as she buried her face in her hands and her shoulders shook with sobs, I struggled to believe her. Her emotions were too forced, and I couldn't help but think these insincere tears were a tool to help so she wouldn't have to face consequences.

The guy was having none of it. "Stop that. You don't get to play the victim when you stole—" His gaze darted to me.

"Thirty-eight thousand."

"Thirty-eight thousand dollars from us," he finished. "Christ."

"We've already discussed the situation with some of the homeowners," Nina said. "We think we can get everyone to agree not to press charges if Judy resigns and pays everything back."

This made Judy cry harder. "I don't," she choked out between sobs, "have it."

"Because you gambled it away," I said.

Her tears suddenly ceased, her shocked gaze snapped to mine, and the thought in her mind was loud on her face. *How the hell do you know that?* When I didn't give her an answer, she sniffled and wiped her nose, striving for a reassuring tone. "I can get it back."

"Yes," came from a chair a few rows back. It was Dr. Lowe. "You can sell, or the HOA will foreclose on your house to recoup what you stole. I'm sure I'm not alone when I say I'll be thrilled to watch you move out."

Her mouth dropped open, but before she could put together a response, a new voice spoke up. It was Lilith's serious-looking boyfriend Clay, the one who wore glasses and had been reserved when I'd met him.

"Put the Judy situation to the side for minute," he said, "because there's a motion on the table that needs to be addressed first. This board made an agreement with the Woodsons, and I feel strongly you should continue to honor it. These 'kids' Judy claims are being exploited? Just look at them." He tossed a hand at us. "They're *adults*, and what consenting adults do in the privacy of their own home is no one's business." Frustration seeped into his voice, sounding like this was deeply personal to him. "We've had enough judgment out of this board to last a lifetime, and if it wasn't for this girl, who knows how long that was going to continue? This is the least y'all can do."

Colin squeezed my hand, and breath was held tightly in

my lungs as the board exchanged looks.

Judy gaped at the board. "You're actually considering it?"

The vice president shifted uncomfortably, visibly nervous. "I'd, uh, like to withdraw my second on the motion."

It was quiet as everyone considered what that meant.

"*What?*" Judy shrieked, realizing that while she was about to get kicked out, potentially no one else would be.

"I think we have to vote on accepting her withdrawal," Vicky said. "All in favor?"

"Aye," the four of them said.

"Opposed?"

"Nay," Judy hissed, knowing it was futile. She'd lost, and as she scanned the room, she must not have found a single sympathetic face because her expression filled with bitterness. "I don't know what is wrong with you people. You're all a bunch of perverts and sexual deviants."

Gasps and sounds of disapproval filled the room.

"Sure we are," Erika said sarcastically, before turning utterly serious. "And we're not going anywhere. So, why don't you take your five-hundred-dollar mailbox and get the fuck out of our neighborhood?"

The room erupted in applause.

On the first day of the fall semester, I spotted a 'for sale' sign on Judy Malinger's lawn as Nina drove me to class.

I was glad I'd been able to help the Woodsons and the rest of the neighborhood. We even had a little party over at Dr. Lowe's house afterward to celebrate toppling Judy's regime, and everyone expressed their gratitude for my investigation.

It'd been nice getting to know Colin's friends better, especially Lilith.

Our situations weren't the same, but we were both in non-traditional relationships, and I found her poly one with Clay and Travis fascinating. It was something I wasn't sure I would have understood five months ago because I'd had such a narrow view of love. Now that my eyes were open, it made total sense.

The three of them fit together perfectly, complimenting one another, and it gave me hope for me and Colin long-term.

After the first week of school, I told Nina I no longer needed rides to class. I felt safe and everything was going great . . . which meant I should have known better. The universe had a habit of striking precisely when I let my guard down.

I'd just come out of my corporate finance class and was halfway across the green when a figure stepped out from beneath the shade of a tree and blocked my path. I jolted and my heart stopped.

Riley.

He looked . . . weird. Nervous. His gaze darted around the quad, maybe checking to see if Colin was nearby.

"Madison, hey. Can we talk?"

"No." I tried to get around him, but he side-stepped to stay in front of me.

"Please? I wanted to tell you I'm sorry."

I narrowed my eyes as I scrutinized him, my body filling with distrust. "Sorry for what?"

He shoved a hand through his hair, visibly uncomfortable. He was a guy who never did anything wrong, so he never needed to apologize, and now he struggled with how to do it. "Everything."

Seriously? "That's it? I don't have time for this." Once more I tried to get by him, and he moved to block me.

"Wait. Fuck." He sighed. "I'm sorry I got in your way at the tournament, but I wanted to win." When he realized how that sounded, his eyes widened. "For Grady," he amended. "I wanted to win for Grady."

I wasn't sure if I believed him, but what did it matter now? I'd moved past it. Plus, he'd done something much worse that he needed to apologize for.

So, I simply stared at him, saying nothing as I waited.

"I don't know if Colin told you," he finally continued, "I was fucking wasted when I made those posts. Like, blackout drunk. When I came to later and saw what I'd done, I took them down as fast as fucking possible." He set his hands on his waist and his shoulders slumped. "I was pissed at Colin for what he'd said and how he wouldn't help me. I mean, come on. I wasn't asking for much." He frowned at himself for straying off topic. "Look, I don't know why I did it because I don't even remember making the posts, and obviously I wasn't thinking about the aftermath."

"That's not an apology," I said. "It's an excuse. Do you know what it did to us? To Colin?"

He winced like I was causing him pain. "I know, and I'm sorry. I wish I could take it back."

But he couldn't. There was no un-ringing that bell, as Nina had said.

Riley's guilty gaze drifted away from mine. "Will you tell Colin for me? I think he blocked my number."

My pulse sped up. His apology seemed genuine, but there was likely a motive driving it. "This isn't going to do anything to get you in with Petal Productions. You know that, right?"

He'd burned that bridge until it was nothing but ash.

"Yeah." He shifted on his feet. "It's just—I hate feeling like I fucked everything up."

I stared at him. "But that's exactly what you did."

He didn't like what I'd said, but he seemed to know better than to argue. "Look, I can't undo what I did, but I was thinking—maybe I can make it right."

"How?" I couldn't have sounded more skeptical if I'd tried.

"The Sigs are having a party on Friday."

"Pregame Rush Week," I said. There was no alcohol allowed at social events during Rush Week, so every year they had hosted a party the weekend before. It was an unofficial recruitment event for the fraternity.

Riley nodded. "All the seniors will be making two-minute presentations on why the Sig house is the best on campus." He gave a lopsided smile. "It sounds dumb, but it's actually hilarious."

Surely my expression screamed at him to get to the point.

"I was thinking I could use my two minutes to tell everyone I cheated and apologize to you and Colin."

My breath caught. I thought I'd moved past it, but what he was offering was appealing. It was the public vindication I'd craved since that day in the mud, and I had to sink my teeth into my bottom lip to stay quiet.

"But I'd need you guys to be there," he said.

"Why?"

Confusion made him look at me like I was missing something obvious. "Because I can't say I'm sorry if you don't come?"

"No," I said, needing to clarify. "Why would you do that? What's in it for you?"

He sighed, and then shrugged as a surrender. "Like I said, I feel like I fucked everything up, and I don't want to feel that way anymore."

It was difficult to believe he felt guilty enough to make him want to do this, so the needle on my suspicion meter jumped all the way into the red. It got worse when he took a step forward, closing the space between us. There was a determination in his eyes that caused me alarm.

"What do you say? Will you come?"

Riley had proven he didn't give up easily when he wanted something, and the way he peered down at me now, I doubted he'd accept it if I told him no.

"I don't know." I swallowed thickly. "Let me think about it?"

It wasn't the answer he wanted, and for a single breath he considered pushing it, but must have decided it'd be better not to. His expression was fixed. "Okay. Talk to Colin and have him let me know what you decide."

I nodded, and relief coasted through my body as he finally let me by.

Had there been a slight smile ghosting his lips as I went, or had I just imagined it? God, I needed Colin, because that conversation . . .

It left me with a terrible feeling of dread.

TWENTY-SIX

Colin

I made it a solid month of working out with Mads before she got me to crack. She hated working on her core, especially her lower abdominals, and so when I'd told her we were doing leg circles, she'd told me she could think of a million other fun things to do—for example, sucking my dick.

"Nice try," I said from the mat beside hers. "We're doing three sets of ten in each direction."

She blew her breath out in a huff, lay down on her back, and lifted her feet a few inches off the ground. I did the same, and as we stared up at the unfinished ceiling of the gym, we began to rotate our feet in clockwise circles.

"I have an idea to pitch for our next scene." Her voice was strained with effort.

"Yeah? What is it?"

"I'm your girlfriend. Nina is your stepmom." She finished going clockwise and began to swing her feet in the other direction. "She sees us messing around and," she had to stop talking for a moment because it was so challenging, "then she joins in to, like, tutor us."

I finished the set and dropped my feet to the ground at the same time she did, considering her pitch as we rested. I rolled my head toward her and flashed a teasing smile. "You think we need a tutor?"

She let out a short laugh. "No, but I'm sure she could teach us a thing or two." Her head lolled toward me, making it so I could see the desire in her eyes. "I was thinking about it because I haven't seen you two together yet. Not in person." Her voice turned throaty. "I haven't gotten to watch you fuck her."

My blood heated as lust grew inside me. "And you want to?"

She pressed her lips together and nodded enthusiastically.

I rolled onto my side, bringing us closer together, and asked it even though I already knew her answer. "Is that your fantasy? Watching your boyfriend fuck someone else?"

She didn't have to think about it. "It's one of them." She chased her breath. "One of many."

A pleased chuckle rumbled out of me, and I had to adjust myself in my shorts because all the heat in my body surged to my dick. "Fuck, Mads. You're getting me hard."

"Am I?" She blinked innocently before reaching over to put a hand on my swelling erection. "I can help you take care of that."

Yes, my dick chanted.

Wait a minute. I seized her hand and held her still as she cupped me through my shorts. "You're just trying to distract me so you can get out of leg circles."

"Who, me?" She acted offended, but her hand moved beneath mine, stroking me with just the right amount of pressure that it sent pleasure roaring up my spine. "I would *never*."

I shoved her hand away, but rather than lie back down on my mat, I climbed on top of her. She was surprised and thrilled with this development. Even though we still had our clothes on, I nudged my hips between her legs and thrust slowly, letting her feel how successfully her ploy had worked, and enjoyed the moan she gave.

"We're finishing the sets," I instructed, "after we're done here."

She gave me a patronizing smile to tell me that was bullshit. "Sure, we are."

I lowered my mouth to hers, letting her win, because it was a win for both of us.

Her kiss was just as amazing as it had been every other time. It drew me in and felt like a secret. As if she had a special kiss and I was the only person in the world she could give it to. Plus, I'd watched her kiss other people, so I knew what we had wasn't the same as what she gave everyone else.

And that's how sex was for us too. Nothing was as deep or as scorching hot as when it was us together. No other connection compared.

My tongue was in her mouth and my hand was wedged inside her sports bra when her phone chimed with a text message. I kissed her harder, trying to convince her to ignore it, but when it chimed a second time, she groaned and extracted her phone from her pocket.

As she read the message, her body tensed.

"What's wrong?"

She hesitated. "It's Jack."

"Your ex? What does he want?"

"To get coffee together."

A foreign, possessive feeling sliced through my chest. She'd just talked about watching me with another woman, and now here I was, upset over the idea of her having coffee with someone else. I shouldn't be jealous.

It's not the same, and you know it.

Because while I didn't have feelings for Nina, Mads had been in love with Jack, and that asshole had broken her heart.

"Why does he want to get coffee?" I forced myself to sound casual. "You don't even drink it."

"He says he has something important to tell me."

Like he wants her back, a voice warned in my head.

"Something he can't say in a text?" I asked.

I was propped up on my arms, trapping her beneath me as she lay on the mat, her wavy brown hair poured around her. God, she looked so beautiful, even when surprise lit up her eyes.

She lifted a hand to touch my cheek. "What's going on? Are you jealous?"

"What? No." I clenched my jaw, which she had to feel. Fuck it. "I don't know. Maybe." I sat back on my heels, and before my brain could stop me, the words spilled out. "Sometimes I feel like I might not be good enough for you. You're too sexy, and too smart, and too," I searched for the right word, "perfect."

She rose to sit and face me. "Um, I am *far* from perfect."

"Perfect for me," I said. "But I don't have a fucking clue where I'm going, especially now that the safety net of my parents is gone." I motioned to her phone on the mat beside her. "A guy like Jack has it all figured out, and there's history between you two I can't compete with."

"Compete?" She looked lost. "Colin, what the hell are you talking about?"

I scrubbed a hand over my jaw. "I'm saying that if this

is an attempt to win you back, it makes me . . . I don't know."
But I did know. "Nervous."

She blinked like she was stupefied, and then a laugh
fell out of her mouth. "If he's trying to win me back, it'll
never work." Her gaze captured mine, and the gravity of it
wouldn't let go, not that I wanted it to. "I'm already in love
with someone else."

Holy shit.

My heart crashed against the side of my chest, beating
wildly, but I did my best to keep my cool. "Is that so?"

She nodded. "And the guy I love? I don't care if he doesn't
have it all figured out because I don't either, and I thought,"
she shrugged, "maybe we could figure it out together."

"Yes," I said.

Her head tilted, and her smile was shy. She was pretty
sure I felt the same way she did, but it was still a big deal to
say it, and it took her a moment to work up the courage.

"I love you, Colin."

I launched forward, sliding my hands into her hair and
whispered it just before I crushed my lips to hers. "God. I
love you, too."

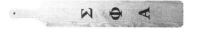

When we met Jack at the coffee place in the union, he
was sitting at a table meant for two. His eyes brightened
when he saw Mads, but he looked less happy to discover me
alongside her. It was like I'd disrupted his plans.

Good.

I grabbed an empty chair from a nearby table and

dragged it over, making the legs scrape loudly across the floor.

"Sorry." Jack's tone was insincere as he looked up at her. "Didn't realize you weren't coming alone."

As she dropped down into the chair across from him and I took my seat beside her, all I could think about was the last time I'd seen him. He'd told me she'd never be mine, that she wouldn't go for a guy like me.

I grinned at him. *How you like me now?*

He barely glanced my way. All his focus was on her. "Thanks for meeting me."

She nodded but didn't say anything. This was hard for her. It was the first time they'd talked since the break-up more than a year ago. When she'd asked me to come with her, at first I'd thought she done it to make me feel better, but I realized it was the other way around.

She wanted me there with her for support.

Jack's gaze dropped to the cardboard cup on the table in front of him, and whatever he wanted to say, he was reluctant. My impatience got the best of me, and I cleared my throat, ordering him to get on with it.

"I'm sorry about Germany," he said. "I shouldn't have left you."

Oh, wow. Ballsy of him to do this right in front of me.

Mads didn't react. "I think what you meant to say is, I'm sorry I cheated on you."

"Yes," he said quietly.

"And I'm sorry I lied about it to my frat brothers and told them it was you."

His Adam's apple bobbed with a hard swallow. "Yes."

"Okay," she said simply. "Thanks." Her voice was flat.

"Did we need to get together for this?"

His gaze flicked to me, and I saw it all. None of this was going the way he'd wanted it to. I wasn't supposed to be here, and he had hoped his apology would have made a bigger impact. One that might have created an opening he could use to wedge his way back into her life.

He frowned. "There's something else I need to tell you." He set his arms on the table and leaned forward. "The Sig seniors are doing these presentations at the pregame party on Friday. If you made a PowerPoint, they told us we could upload our files to the frat's Dropbox, and when I went to add mine . . . I accidentally clicked on Riley's."

The tension in his voice dropped a stone in my stomach.

"He doesn't know I've seen it," Jack continued. "We're not supposed to because it's a competition over who has the best one." His gaze moved from her, to me, and back again. "There's a video of the two of you in there. Where you're"—he struggled to find the right word—"together."

Horror filled her face. "He's planning to show one of our videos to the entire frat?"

Thanks to Riley's posts, everyone we were friends with knew we were putting out adult content, but most of them had only seen a tame screenshot. This was way worse.

"That motherfucker," I growled. "That's why he invited us." Because she'd told me about how he'd cornered her earlier this week and tried to convince her to come to the party. "He wants us there so he can see our faces when he plays it."

"Obviously, I'm not going to let that happen," Jack said. "My first thought was to delete it, but then I realized—this idiot uploaded porn to a school server. Once I report it, they'll have no choice. They'll have to kick him out of the house, and I'm sure the school will discipline him too."

"What the fuck is his deal?" She crossed her arms over her chest like she felt vulnerable, and I put my hand on her leg, wanting a connection to her. "He made those posts, tried to ruin our lives, and we didn't even retaliate. We did *nothing* to him."

Jack sat back and ringed a hand around his cup of coffee. "Look, everyone knows what he did was not cool. He's been getting a ton of shit around the house ever since we got back. There was even some discussion the first week about kicking him out for doxing you guys, but Colin's not a Sig anymore, and social media is a gray area."

"Jesus," I groaned. "That's why he's doing this. He thinks it's somehow our fault he almost got kicked out."

"There's no escaping it this time," Jack said. "Once I report him, he's gone." He peered at Mads. "I just wanted to talk to you first, and make sure you're okay with me showing it to the dean."

"No," I said.

They both turned to look at me with surprise, but an idea was taking shape in my mind, and my pulse picked up as I fit the pieces together.

"Jack," I said, "I'm going to need you to send me the link to his presentation."

Suspicion clouded his eyes. "Why?"

A slow grin spread across my lips. "Because we're going to give Riley exactly what he wants."

The line to check IDs was backed up nearly to the sidewalk out in front of the Sigma Phi Alpha house, and it was fucking weird not to bypass the wide-eyed freshmen and walk right in.

I stood beside Mads as we inched our way closer to the door. The sun had set an hour ago, and it'd cooled off enough that it was nice outside tonight. I wasn't looking forward to going down into the basement, where it would be hot as fuck, but at the same time, I was confident it'd be worth it.

The guy manning the door was surprised to see us but waved me and Mads through without glancing at our IDs. She stuck close to me as we went down the stairs into the basement that the Sigs typically used only for parties. Did she feel like we were descending into a pit?

The space was dark, crowded, and loud.

When we reached the bottom of the stairs, our gazes were drawn across the room. A large screen had been set up, and a slideshow with pictures from last year flashed across it.

I was in several of them, along with my brothers.

Tailgating before a home football game.

The Halloween party.

And then there was me covered in mud and grinning as I crossed the finish line at the tournament. The white ribbon was stretched across my chest the second before it broke, and Mads was just behind me, looking heartbroken at losing.

Right on fucking cue, Riley materialized from the crowd. "What's up, man? I was starting to think you weren't gonna come."

He looked both relieved and thrilled we had, and he held out his hand, wanting me to grab it and pull him into a half-hug, but—

Fuck that.

Instead, I stood as a statue, ignoring the gesture.

He dropped his hand, glanced at Mads, and gave her an acknowledging nod, before squeezing out a quick smile. "Y'all should get your drinks before we start. I think I'm up second, so you won't have to wait long."

Truer words had never been spoken by me. "Looking forward to it."

"Yeah. Me too."

He didn't need to tell us because his eyes buzzed with chaotic energy. At least he did a decent job of hiding his evil smile before disappearing into the crowd, heading toward the roped off area where the laptop running the slideshow was stationed.

Mads and I made the rounds, ignoring the way some people stared at us. We'd talked about it beforehand and decided this was the best way to handle our situation. If we didn't make a big deal out of everyone knowing, maybe they wouldn't either. And people needed to see us, to know we were here.

I didn't miss the envious way some guys looked at me as I stood next to Mads. She was hot as sin, a genuine porn star, and I was very aware of how lucky I was to be with her.

We got some drinks, hooked up with Jorge, and found a spot near the back of the room to watch the show.

The first presentation was by Mike, who used his two minutes to discuss the alcohol served at parties around campus. He wore shorts and a t-shirt, and put on a tie around his bare neck for his segment, pretending to take the whole thing seriously.

He had charts and figures showing which drinks tasted the best versus which tasted the best on the return trip when you'd had too much, and I heard Mads snicker at the tiny asterisk noting all his data was made-up bullshit.

He finished it off by showing a graph proving the Sigs served the winning drinks in both categories, based on his empirical evidence. The presentation ended, and people clapped and cheered when he chugged his beer, whipped off his tie, and dropped the mic.

My heart beat faster as Riley bent and scooped it up off the floor, and I put my arm around Mads, pulling her closer. I glanced down to see the anxiety I felt mirrored on her face.

This was it. No going back now.

Riley had returned to the laptop and started his PowerPoint, and a simple title filled the frame. *Great Men of Sigma Phi Alpha*. It was underwhelming, especially in comparison to the one we'd just seen. Mike had put in a lot of effort into the whole performance, but it seemed like Riley was going to rely on his content to carry him through.

He lifted the mic to his mouth. "Why should you rush Sigma Phi Alpha? Because being a Sig prepares you to do great things. For example," he tapped a key on the keyboard, "you could go on to become a congressman."

The screen changed, filling with a picture of one of our state's congressmen, including his name and the year he'd been elected.

"An astronaut."

The image morphed to an old one from the eighties, showing a guy in a NASA suit holding his helmet.

"An Olympian."

This picture was of a swimmer in a pool, mid butter-fly stroke.

"Even a porn star." A shit-eating grin grew on Riley's face as he advanced to the next slide, which was a video marked with a large play arrow in the center. He tapped a key on keyboard, and his gaze focused in on Mads and me at the back of the room.

It was a clip from the beginning of our audition, where we stood apart and faced each other. On screen, I pulled off my shirt, tossed it aside, and glared defiantly at Mads.

"Your turn," I told her.

The crowd in the room had only been half paying attention to the presentation, but once the video started, people got quiet fast.

"Hello there," a girl up front said to the shirtless version of me on screen, and a few people snickered at her exaggerated lust.

In the video, Mads grabbed the sides of her sweater and pulled it off, revealing her gray bra as her hair cascaded down over her shoulders. Fuck, she looked amazing, and I wasn't the only one who thought so. There were whistles from some guys in the audience.

We'd made it known we were here tonight for this moment. A lot of heads turned and strained to look at us at the back of the room and see what we thought about the video rolling up on the screen.

It was so easy to look shocked. I dropped my mouth open and blinked as if I were too stunned to do anything else, and I felt her stiffening beside me—even though I knew she was okay with this.

"It's not any different than people seeing me in a bikini top," she'd assured me.

We played our roles of unsuspecting victims so well, Riley bought it hook, line, and sinker. He crossed his arms over his chest as he stared at us on the other side of the room. He thought he owned us.

On screen, Mads twisted her arms behind herself and reached for the clasp of her bra. The crowd stirred. Some were excited, and others seemed hesitant that she was about to be topless.

Riley was too busy watching us and gloating, he didn't realize the video had cut to a new scene right as her bra started to come off.

This new camera angle was fisheye and placed at waist level, distorting the three figures who stood on a stone front porch.

"You cheated, and then you lied to everyone about it," Mads said on the video.

On screen, Riley looked annoyed. "So, I got in your way a little bit, but we were just having some fun."

What was fun was watching the live version of Riley now. His arrogant expression froze, and then was replaced by confusion as he turned to look up at the doorbell camera footage Scott had spliced into the presentation.

"I mean, you looked hilarious," Riley blabbed on screen, "when you were chasing after the baton, but then you had to go and make a big deal out of nothing."

I was at an angle to the camera so viewers could only see the side of my face as I spoke. "You should have been disqualified. Do you get that? It *is* a big deal because it means the Lambdas actually won."

While he whined on screen about how I'd taken her side, the live Riley at the front of the room finally figured out where the video had come from. His attention snapped to me, and rage seared across his face.

"Yeah, I cheated, but it was for a good cause." His voice rang through the speakers as he reached out to close the laptop. "I wanted us to win so we could help Grady—"

The video changed again before he could do it, and as the new image filled the screen, he went wooden. He recognized himself sitting shirtless in a chair, talking to the camera.

"Yeah. You like that?" he cooed to the viewer.

It was the video Riley had texted me. Scott had edited it with the rest of the clips, zooming in and moving the frame up so Riley's dick wasn't visible, but the rest of him was in the shot. Because his chest was bare and the way his arm moved, it was obvious he was jerking off.

"I'm going to use all of this big dick to fuck you," he told the audience.

"What the fuck?" some dude groaned beside me.

"Boo," a girl jeered.

"Gross," someone else whined.

Riley slammed the laptop closed, making the screen behind him go black, and his nervous gaze darted around the room. Judging by his expression, he wasn't seeing any faces of people who'd enjoyed what they'd just seen.

His eyes went darker than the screen as he found me. If he had any sense left in his brain, it seemed to abandon him now. Riley took off, storming toward me and Mads as his chest puffed up and hands balled into fists, readying to fight.

I was prepared for this and urged her to get behind me and Jorge.

"You fucking asshole," he roared, pushing his way through the people.

I wasn't scared. I was bigger, faster, stronger. "What are you talking about? I gave your video to Scott *just like you asked me to.*"

He'd nearly reached us when several of my former frat brothers intervened. The last thing they wanted was a fight breaking out, and they tangled together, holding him back as I stood my ground.

"You brought this on yourself," I said. "You could have left us alone, but no. You had to keep pushing. You wanted to humiliate us, and instead you got a taste of it instead. How does it fucking feel?"

Riley squirmed against the arms locked around him. "Get off me."

"Right now, you should be asking yourself, was that *all* the video you sent me?" I gave him the most serious look I had as a warning. "What if the full thing got posted somewhere, where everyone could see? How do you think your friends and family would like that?"

Well, that got his attention. Riley abruptly stopped struggling with his brothers and his face went blank. "You wouldn't."

I arched an eyebrow. "Don't *make* us."

"Come on, Riley," said one of the brothers who'd been holding him back. "Let's take a walk."

Because the Sigs needed to defuse the situation. If they

could get him out of the house, or at least out of the basement, and calm him down—it'd be better for everyone. Up
front, the screen lit back up with the image of a desktop, and
a Sig picked up the mic, declaring they were moving on to the
next presentation.

Anything to get people's attention away from us
in the back.

I didn't know what the plan had been for Riley, or why
he'd thought showing the video of me and Mads together
was a good idea. Jack had told us his brothers weren't happy
about him doxing us. Did he think forcing the video on them
was going to somehow change their minds and he'd come out
looking like a hero?

Maybe it was the other way around and he felt he had
nothing left to lose.

He was realizing now that wasn't true. He still had a lot
to lose. Everyone had heard him confess to cheating, his solo
performance hadn't been well received, and any loyalty the
Sigs had toward him?

It was gone now.

He stood rooted to the ground, tension holding him in a
tight, unnatural pose, and stared at me, considering his options. If he broke free and tried to fight me, I'd win. I had the
physicality and the support of the guys around us, and when
that was done, I had the threat of posting his unedited video.

Riley shook off the guys' hold, and his face twisted with
a mixture of anger and fear, and for the first time ever . . . he
seemed to acknowledge he was beaten. His chest heaved with
his uneven breath, and then he abruptly turned. He stormed
off for the stairs, going so fast and determined, he didn't slow

down when his shoulder collided with another guy's and sent him reeling.

I blew out a long, calming breath as he plodded up the steps with two Sigs following close behind him, making sure he was going. Mads' hand found mine, linking us together, and I gazed at her with relief.

"That went better than I thought it would," I said.

"Yeah." Her shoulders relaxed. "Same."

Adrenaline had pumped through my body, preparing me for battle, and now that the threat was gone, I was riding a high. But we barely got a moment to ourselves before Charlie, the Sigs' president, appeared.

"Colin, hey." Even in the low light of the basement, I could see just how embarrassed he was. "I'm sorry about Riley, and what he tried to do."

"Just so you know, Mads and I will be filing a complaint against him with the ethics board."

He nodded. "That's understandable, but maybe I can save you the trouble. I'll be calling a house vote tomorrow morning about Riley losing his Sig membership." He had a cup of beer in one hand and used the other to massage the back of his neck. "Given all the shit he's pulled, I expect it'll pass unanimously." Charlie's gaze slid from me to the girl at my side. "He cheated at the tournament?"

"Yup," she said.

"So, the Lambdas won?" It was more of a statement than a question.

Her tone was pointed. "Yup."

He sighed. "What a fucking mess." His gaze drifted off as he considered something. "All right. I'll report it to the council and see what they want to do." He took a sip of his beer and focused in on her. "I'm sorry. For what it's worth, none of us knew."

"I know," she said. "Colin told me."

He studied our hands laced together. "Last time I saw you two, it looked like you wanted to kill each other."

She shrugged. "Things change."

I laughed because she was absolutely right.

Look how much you've changed.

I was out from under my parents' control. I had a job that could turn into a career if I wanted it to, according to Scott and Nina. And I didn't just have a girlfriend . . . I'd fucking fallen in love.

As I grinned at Mads, and she smiled back at me, I wondered what came next for us. God, I couldn't fucking wait to find out.

EPILOGUE

Madison

I'd watched the YouTube video twice and followed the recipe exactly, but the pecan pie in the fridge looked weird and soupy, and I was seriously considering tossing it out and buying a new one before we headed over to Scott and Nina's house.

I sighed and closed the fridge, leaving the pie inside. I was a decent cook, and I'd baked things before that had turned out fine. Why, today of all days, had I failed? I'd need to check and see which stores were open on Thanksgiving before committing to plan B. I didn't want us to show up for dinner empty-handed.

I padded on my bare feet from the kitchen, through our bedroom, and into the bathroom where Colin was brushing his teeth at the sink, wearing only a pair of underwear.

His words were garbled by the toothbrush, but I understood him well enough. "What's the verdict?"

"Pie still looks weird." I leaned back against the counter and crossed my arms over my chest. "Maybe we need to stop and buy something to take instead."

He nodded, spat out a mouthful of toothpaste, and rinsed his brush.

I hesitated to ask it but couldn't put it off any longer. "Any word from your folks?"

He wiped his mouth with a towel. "Nope."

"You okay with that?"

Because this was his first holiday since they'd fallen out. He'd talked to them once since they'd come to an agreement about school. Colin had needed them to write a letter stating they weren't giving him any financial support so he could apply for a grant and student loan, and they'd done that.

But they'd gone radio silent when they found out Colin and I had moved in together.

It'd been dumb luck we'd found the one-bedroom apartment close to campus and still available. We felt confident no one was going to come knocking on the Woodsons' door looking for us, but this was for the best.

Riley had been voted out of Sigma Phi Alpha the morning after the party, and when Jack provided the dean with proof that Riley had uploaded porn to the school's server— he'd been put on academic suspension.

It seemed unlikely he'd retaliate against us. We had the video as a deterrent, plus it had been three months since the Rush Week party, and we hadn't seen or heard a word from him.

But still—moving to a new place was the safest option.

I'd asked Colin if he was okay with not hearing from his parents, and he shot me a lopsided smile. "It's fine."

I was sad for him, but I fully understood. Life was too short to spend it with toxic people.

He strutted to the shower, slid open the glass door, and started the water, then hooked his fingers in his boxer briefs and tugged them down. "You joining me?"

Fuck, it was a tempting offer, but I shook my head. "I

won't be able to keep my hands off you."

We had a scene coming up, and although his recovery time was good, I didn't want to cause any issues with his performance. The first thing we were scheduled to do when we arrived at the house was a big group scene. All six of us, playing and swapping with different partners in the same room.

There was no story line for this one, but it didn't need it. Shit, it'd be hot enough on its own. And after the scene was over, we'd have Thanksgiving dinner together. They weren't the family we'd been born into, but the one we'd found, and I was so grateful for them.

After we'd moved out, we continued to work for Petal Productions. Occasionally, we went over there for scenes, and sometimes we met them on location. Most of the time, Colin and I performed as a couple or shot solo scenes at our apartment and turned the footage in to Scott and Nina.

We'd even started doing some live shows, which was a different animal all together, but a lot of fun, not to mention—lucrative. We'd saved enough to buy a used car, which I'd need soon. I was only a month away from graduation, and then I'd start the job I'd lined up as a budget analyst for a firm downtown.

Colin frowned at how I'd turned down his offer of joining him. "I don't mind if you can't keep your hands off me."

I pointed to the shower. "You're wasting hot water."

He stepped in and pulled the glass door closed. I lingered, leaning against the sink as I watched the water sluice down his perfect body. That hadn't changed since I'd met him on that muddy field seven months ago, but practically everything else had. He wasn't a frat boy anymore, even though a small part of me would probably always think of him that way.

I'd changed, too, and it was all for the better. My narrow view of love had broadened into something deeper. More amazing, and exciting, and fulfilling. Just thinking about it started a fire in my heart, and a need that was suddenly too powerful to resist.

I whipped off my tank top and hurried out of my shorts, getting naked as fast as possible. Then I launched forward, pulling open the shower door and startling the shit out of him.

"I want to kiss you," I said.

He was covered in shampoo and wiped the sudsy foam from his eyes, staring at me in disbelief. "Now?"

"Yes, now," I said breathlessly. "Always."

MORE BY NIKKI SLOANE

THE BLINDFOLD CLUB SERIES
Three Simple Rules

Three Hard Lessons

Three Little Mistakes

Three Dirty Secrets

Three Sweet Nothings

Three Guilty Pleasures

THE SORDID SERIES
Sordid

Torrid

Destroy

SPORTS ROMANCE
The Rivalry

THE NASHVILLE NEIGHBORHOOD
The Doctor

The Pool Boy

The Architect

The Frat Boy

FILTHY RICH AMERICANS
The Initiation | The Obsession | The Deception

The Redemption

The Temptation

THANK YOU

As always, no book I write could happen without my incredible husband. I decided to try to write Colin and Madison's story in two months—while also training for my first marathon—and his support and encouragement made that crazy idea possible. Thank you, Nick!

Thanks to my editor Lori Whitwam. I tried so hard to get you a completed draft on time. One of these days it will happen!

And to you, dear reader—thank you so much for all the love you've shown the Nashville Neighborhood series. I love writing these stories and I'm so glad folks like reading them.

ABOUT THE AUTHOR

USA Today bestselling author Nikki Sloane landed in graphic design after her careers as a waitress, a screenwriter, and a ballroom dance instructor fell through. Now she writes full-time and lives in Kentucky with her husband, two sons, and a pair of super destructive cats.

She is a four-time Romance Writers of America RITA® & Vivian® Finalist, a Passionate Plume & HOLT Medallion winner, a Goodreads Choice Awards semifinalist, and couldn't be any happier that people enjoy reading her sexy words.

www.NikkiSloane.com

www.twitter.com/AuthorNSloane

www.facebook.com/NikkiSloaneAuthor

www.instagram.com/nikkisloane

Printed in Great Britain
by Amazon

23264881R00223